ARKLIGHT
RECONDITE

Also by G. B. Holley

From the ARKLIGHT Ancient Alien Series

ARKLIGHT Revelations

ARKLIGHT

RECONDITE

An Ancient Alien Adventure

G. B. HOLLEY

Arklight Recondite
An Ancient Alien Adventure

Copyright © 2017 by G. B. Holley

Spirit Owl Books, LLC
P.O. Box 3547
Seminole, Fl 33772

First Edition: September 2018
Library of Congress Control Number: 2018950266

ISBN: 978-1-7320128-3-7 (e-book)
ISBN: 978-1-7320128-4-4 (paperback)
ISBN: 978-1-7320128-5-1 (hardback)

Printed in the United States of America

Book Cover, Interior Design, and Formatting by: Jera Publishing, Roswell, Ga.
Petroglyph artwork by: Laurie Allen Klein

This novel is dedicated to all first responders, military personnel, and their families. Your courage and the sacrifices you make every day to serve and protect others are gratefully appreciated.

"A human being is part of the whole, called by us 'the universe.' Our task must be to widen our circle of compassion to embrace all living creatures and the whole of nature in its beauty."

ALBERT EINSTEIN

PROLOGUE

Ninurtu looked out at the thousands of small gray bodies scattered across the field of battle, some already partially buried by shifting desert sand. Lying among them were the remains of the brave human and Igigi warriors who had crushed the Etu Inu Idimmu in a final decisive battle. Few of the Etu Inu Idimmu, the name given to the Dark-Eyed Demons by the Sumerian people, had survived the savageness of their assault. The smell of death filled the air in the hot, late afternoon.

The Idimmu had walked into Ninurtu's elaborate trap. Feigning the weakness of his forces, he knew the Etu Inu Idimmu would try to destroy what they believed were the last vestiges of human resistance. The Idimmu had targeted several population centers around the world, but they had committed the bulk of their forces to the cradle of what would become the heart of humanity and the greatest civilization.

For two days humans and Igigi had battled against the Etu Inu Idimmu. The human forces had suffered great losses as they slowly retreated, allowing the Idimmu to advance between two phalanxes of hidden reserves. Ninurtu had finally ordered the human warriors, all hungry for revenge, to close the trap and they slaughtered the Idimmu in close-quarters battle. A small number of Idimmu had found a break in the lines and had managed to retreat toward their ships.

Ninurtu looked to the west and saw the small dust clouds created by the thrusters of the Etu Inu Idimmu landing craft as they lifted off, turning the distant horizon a brownish-red hue. The Idimmu had begun their conquest after landing in this desert years ago. It was only fitting that their greatest defeat was here. Ninurtu's victory, and the others he'd coordinated around the world over the last two days, assured that humanity would not perish.

"Ninurtu, they're leaving," said the man standing next to him, speaking in an ancient language.

"They are, indeed," Ninurtu replied.

"Is it over?" the man asked.

"Yes. By all reports, the Idimmu are leaving. They no longer have the ability to continue their conquest. You have defeated them. You are safe." Ninurtu once again gazed at the dead in the desert.

The man stood straighter, but he was still more than a foot shorter than Ninurtu. "You said that once they had been vanquished that you and your kind would leave us. My people ask that you stay."

"That isn't possible."

"Look!" the man shouted, pointing up at a ship.

Ninurtu lifted his emerald eyes from the carnage and saw the last of the Etu Inu Idimmu ships scream directly over them, heading toward the vacuum of space. It was their last great act of defiance as they fled back to their home world. He knew that none of the Igigi spacecraft in orbit would attack them. He watched the triangular-shaped-craft until they were but black specks in the sky. Then he dusted the sand from his crimson robe, the front of which bore the crest of the Regulus Clan and the black blood of the Idimmu he'd killed.

Ninurtu had led the Regulus Clan and the human warriors in all of the battles they'd fought against the Etu Inu Idimmu. He was tired, and his arms and legs ached from exertion, but he was also proud of what they had accomplished, even if their actions defied the wishes of some of the other Igigi clans.

"Ninurtu, we will not forget what you have taught us," the man said.

"And we will never forget you, my friend."

He could see the human warriors in the distance returning from the west. He motioned for the others of his clan to gather around him. He reached back and freed his braided, white, shoulder-length hair and shook it loose. His skin was no longer pale like that of the other Igigi clans. His skin, and those of his clan, was brown from years of living among the people in the desert. All Igigi were tall, like Ninurtu, each over seven feet. Those of Regulus were more muscular and hardened from the battles they'd fought and the work they'd done in the fields teaching the people how to cultivate the land.

Ninurtu addressed the others of his clan, speaking quickly in the chirps and clicks of his native tongue. "We have succeeded in saving the people of this world. I am proud of all of you."

"Ninurtu, I've just received word that the Etu Inu Idimmu are already leaving orbit and are headed for deep space," Alulim shouted. His Igigi robes were also covered with the dried, black blood of the enemy.

Human cheers arose as the message was translated, drowning out the sound of the celebratory clicks of the Igigi.

Ninurtu nodded and then raised his battle staff. It was something he had never done before. The roar grew in intensity from the emotional release of thousands. After so many years of slavery and the threat of genocide, humans could once again move forward as a species.

He turned to Alulim and said, "It's time to face the council. This will not end well for us."

"We knew that when we started," Alulim replied. "Intelligent life is sacred, especially these people. We could not allow them to perish."

"I know, but the council will not agree with our actions."

"Then we will leave it to history to be our judge," Alulim replied.

Ninurtu stared at the desert and said, "Bury our dead and burn the bodies of the Etu Inu Idimmu. Leave no trace of their existence. If any of their ships remain, they must be destroyed."

Alulim nodded and issued the order.

Ninurtu turned and faced the other Igigi, then opened a communication channel to the others of the Regulus Clan scattered across the planet and said, "When we stand before the council, no matter the outcome, know that I will not forget your sacrifice. We have saved the human species from extinction. In time, the people of this world will forget what we have done.

You must take to heart that our efforts have not been in vain. These people will flourish because of what all of you have accomplished. You have my gratitude and that of the human race."

The other Igigi standing near him bowed as a sign of respect for their leader.

"Behind us," the man standing next to Ninurtu shouted, pointing at the horizon. "They're returning!"

Ninurtu and the other Igigi spun around. When he saw the Igigi interstellar ship low in the sky, he knew that the council wasn't wasting any time coming to him. It wasn't a coincidence that they were arriving while the battlefield was still littered with the dead. The council had watched for years as they'd taught the people to fight as one unified force. They had never come to a battlefield before. Now that the war was over, he knew the leaders of the other clans needed to see the carnage firsthand in order to validate their decision.

To watch war from a distance was one thing, but to smell the stench of the dead and taste the bitter, bloodstained sand that blew across the land was quite another. He hoped it would haunt the cowards' dreams.

"That is one of our ships," Ninurtu said, reassuring the man. "There is no danger."

As the massive ship touched down, the humans knelt, covering their eyes so as not to offend the gods from heaven. Ninurtu walked slowly toward the ship. Alulim followed one step behind him.

A hatch beneath the ship opened, and a ramp descended and touched the desert floor. Ninurtu and Alulim stopped at the base of the ramp as twelve members of the Igigi council walked down it in single file. Each wore a different-colored robe designating their clan affiliation. Their clan crest adorned their chests. The last Igigi to walk out onto the desert wore a forest-green robe. It was Nergal, the leader of the Guiding Clan.

Ninurtu waited as the group surveyed the battlefield, and then he bowed toward them when they turned to address him. He was the thirteenth member of the combined Igigi contingent, but his actions had removed him from the council long ago. He raised his head and looked at the other members. He knew what was to come. Their scowls told him his destiny. They would afford him a chance to defend his actions for the record, but he knew the ruling would not change.

"Ninurtu, what do you offer in defense of the actions and deaths you and the rest of the Regulus Clan have caused?" Nergal asked, motioning toward the bodies.

Ninurtu bowed his head slightly, then stood proudly and said, "As you know, for over six thousand years we have watched and nurtured these people. We brought them from their land when the sea washed away their great city and covered ours. We moved groups of people that we had developed to the other lands around this world. The people have worked hard and thrived under our guidance.

"When the Etu Inu Idimmu first arrived, we chose to do nothing. Nergal, I told you how I felt about letting these creatures destroy intelligent life. However, I obeyed the council's edict, stood idly by, and only observed as we allowed many thousands of people to die. For too long, we didn't respond. All of you know they would have perished if not for the actions my clan took. I ask you now, as I asked once before, are we not duty-bound to protect intelligent life?"

Ninurtu received nods from some of the members of the council, then continued, "It is my belief that I adhered to our doctrine, which dictates that we are responsible for protecting intelligent life. This is why I chose to disobey your wishes and fought alongside these most amazing people. My only regret is not having done it sooner. Some of you define the Etu Inu Idimmu as an intelligent species. I believe them to be predatory creatures that possess swarm intelligence. They do not act of their own freewill. A queen directs them, and they mindlessly follow.

"Can we define an aggressive, mindless creature that carries out the orders of one intelligent master as an intelligent, sentient being? I don't believe so. We were right to take the lives of the beasts that preyed upon these gentle people. These intelligent, freethinking people needed us to save them from extinction."

Only the sound of the wind blowing through the landing struts of the ship broke the silence. Ninurtu walked the length of the row of leaders, locking his gaze with each of them in turn. When he reached Nergal, he said, "We fought only with the weapons of the people of this land. We used none of our resources or any of our special abilities to defeat the Etu Inu Idimmu. The secret of the light is safe. Look out on the desert and you will see the bodies of brave, intelligent men and women lying there. These people died fighting for their very survival. Intervention was required or our mission to cultivate them would have ended in failure. Instead, we can continue our work and watch them blossom like the flowers of this world.

"Nergal, you are the bringer of the House of the Shimati, the place where life begins anew. You, among all of us, know what we did was righteous. You once told me that we should act to protect these people, but you did nothing to help, claiming you could not kill intelligent life even in the defense of other intelligent beings. I disagree with your position. We enforced a sacred doctrine to preserve an intelligent species, and now you stand here with those that accuse us of violating that same sacred oath."

Ninurtu took a step back and looked at each of the Igigi leaders again, and then he looked up into the sky and said, "We all know intelligent life is precious. We are all responsible for protecting it, especially when that life is one that we have helped to develop. I killed many of the Etu Inu Idimmu creatures, all of them animals by my definition, and I ordered others of my clan to do the same. If you choose to impose punishment, then punish me, and me alone, for it was my action and decisions that dictated the path of my clan."

Alulim stepped forward. "Leaders of the Igigi, I stand with Ninurtu, as do the rest of our clan. We killed only demons."

Ninurtu looked at Alulim. He was grateful for the support, but knew it would only condemn them all to the punishment the council was sure to inflict.

Nergal stepped forward. "Ninurtu, I see that Igigi lie among the dead. Are you not responsible for their deaths?"

He felt Nergal's words pierce his soul. "I am."

"Please wait with the rest of your clan while we conclave."

Ninurtu and Alulim walked back to the others as the leaders of the clans spoke quietly. Although Ninurtu could not hear their words, he knew some supported his argument. He did not expect that they would discuss his actions for very long, and they didn't. Nergal motioned for him to rejoin the council. He saw by the looks on their faces as he approached that they remained divided in their beliefs. His argument had struck a chord with some, but perhaps not enough to change the outcome.

"Ninurtu, leader of the Regulus Clan, the council has listened to your impassioned argument. We have watched and weighed your actions and understand your position. But your means of saving these people from extinction does not justify the taking of a single Etu Inu Idimmu life or the loss of any Igigi life. By your own admission, you are responsible."

Nergal sighed and looked out on the battlefield. "You and your clan are too attached to these people, and that has clouded your judgment." He turned back to face Ninurtu. "It is the consensus of this council that you and your clan are to be disavowed. You will not participate in the rituals of the House of Shimati, the Gisnu, and the Rites of the Dogita. That is our edict. The Regulus House of your home world will receive notification of our decision. If they so choose, they may send new emissaries to join us. If they do, none of your clan may speak with them."

Ninurtu nodded as Nergal stepped closer and said softly, "This was not an easy decision, and it is one that pains me. I will miss you, but I hope that you will continue your efforts to advance the people of this world. I will watch you until your passing."

Nergal stepped back.

Ninurtu said, "I wish to poll the members of the council."

Nergal nodded and said, "That is your right. All those in favor of sanctions imposed, speak now."

Seven of the clan leaders announced their agreement with the punishment. Nergal and four others voiced their opposition.

"The council has spoken," Nergal said.

"So shall it be," the other clan leaders answered in unison.

Anger raged within Ninurtu, and he knew Nergal could see it.

"The council has also decided that your clan will remain on Earth," Nergal said. "Ninurtu, you will not be allowed to remain in Sumer. Your future lies in the northernmost lands of this world. Those that live there must never know of the actions you have taken in this land. Each member of your clan will find a new group of people to join. You are forbidden from contacting your other clan members."

Nergal gazed at the members of the Regulus Clan. "All of you have proven your loyalty to your leader. Your intentions were noble. From this day forward, you all will be responsible for the protection of these people.

The damage you wrought cannot be undone, but we can prevent you from taking similar actions on other worlds."

Nergal paused, then added, "Educate the people. Teach them how to build cities and cultivate the lands as you have done here. Support them and provide them with laws."

Nergal turned to Alulim and said, "You and the remainder of this group will remain here in Sumer and see to it that the land is cleansed. You will erase all record of the Etu Inu Idimmu's presence here."

Alulim and the others bowed to Nergal.

The leader of the Guiding Clan closed his emerald eyes, then said, "It is with great sorrow that I have learned that some of the other clans have decided to return to our home worlds. They believe our mission has been tainted by your actions and want no part of what will become of humanity."

"What about your clan?" Ninurtu asked brazenly, knowing Nergal had not yet finished. He saw the flash of anger in his eyes before he answered.

"We will stay and watch to ensure that you and the others do not further corrupt these people. Ninurtu, we will send another ship to take you to your new home. We will never speak to you again. Farewell."

The leaders of the clans turned their back to Ninurtu and Alulim, then walked single file up the ramp into the ship. After the ship departed, the people rose.

Ninurtu walked over to the man who had fought beside him during the battle and put his hand on his shoulder. He knew the man didn't understand the language of the Igigi, so he wouldn't know what had been said. "This land is yours," Ninurtu said in the people's native tongue loud enough for all of them to hear. "Nurture it and each other. The killing of your enemy is finished. Follow Alulim's guidance, and you will prosper."

The man looked up at Ninurtu. "Where will you go?"

"To a new place far from here," Ninurtu replied.

There was nothing more to say. He patted the man on the shoulder, then walked into the desert to await the ship that would take him to his new home.

PART ONE

"Something mysteriously formed,

Born before Heaven and Earth.

In the silence and the void,

Standing alone and unchanging,

Ever present and in motion."

SUZUKI ROSHI

CHAPTER ONE

Aboard the largest interstellar Igigi vessel left on Earth, buried deep in the ice, Manatu stood facing the holographic symbols and images as periodic pulses of light danced across his pale face. He studied Tegan Leigh Strong-Locke's bioscan taken by the drone ship last night while she was aboard the *Whispering Winds* while docked at Scotland Cay. His long, white hair hung to his waist. It stood out in stark contrast against the forest-green robe he was wearing. The crest of his station and that of the Guiding Clan adorned the front panel of his robe. He was their leader, and he had served in that role for more than a thousand years.

It was clear that Tegan was a descendant of Ninurtu. Like her ancestor, she had a warrior's spirit. Manatu understood her essence, her very being, better than she knew herself. He also recognized what she was capable of becoming. Manatu accessed the detailed historical file on Ninurtu and began his review.

While in exile, Ninurtu had taken a Nordic human female, Oda, as his mate. The only biological information available on Oda revealed that she was fair-skinned with golden hair and blue eyes. Ninurtu had believed that adding Igigi traits to the human genome would strengthen humanity. The historical record wasn't complete, but Manatu discovered Oda had given birth to twin girls. Their firstborn twin daughter, Trudor, had looked very much like her mother, except for the color of her eyes. The child's eyes were a brilliant emerald like her father's. The other twin, Moyfrid, had her mother's blue eyes. They were the only recorded offspring from the pairing.

The twins were nearly identical, but they were far from being the same in their demeanor. Trudor had taken the first son of Alulim, Kuri, as her husband. She'd not been forbidden to travel to Sumer as her father had been, and no one had objected to their pairing. Ninurtu and Oda moved to the British Isles. After their joining, Trudor and Kuri traveled to the British Isles, where Trudor gave birth to twin girls. Tragedy struck shortly afterward. Both Ninurtu and Oda died during an ambush by an invading hoard from the north. Kuri had been forced to assume the leadership role of the remnants of the clan.

Kuri and Trudor, not bound by the covenant to remain silent about their father's heroic actions, passed down stories about them in oral renditions. They also created a written language based on the Igigi's old one to save as a record for all to witness. In time, that was lost. All that now remained was the symbolic language of the Celtic runes.

Moyfrid had a wandering spirit. She fell in love with a human and traveled south into France. Together, they created a dynasty that reigned for hundreds of years, extending to the Mediterranean Sea and east to the Ural Mountains.

After the last of the pure Regulus bloodline transitioned from this world, the Guiding Clan stopped keeping records. Folklore and mythical tales were all that remained of the Regulus Igigi accomplishments. Ninurtu's clan had passed down the knowledge of constructing the greatest structures still found on Earth, but the source of that knowledge was forgotten. Today, many people believe the great structures are the result of people having received help from beings from the stars. They would not be wrong.

As time passed, Manatu's clan had watched as the human shamans of the tribes corrupted their teachings in order to serve their own interests. Wearing robes imitating the dress of the Igigi, tribal leaders created ritualistic practices to subjugate and control their own people. Human civilization developed a culture of perpetual violence and greed. People turned against people, and millions had died over the millennia in the pursuit of power and wealth. Some Igigi believed this was Ninurtu's legacy.

Manatu thought otherwise. He saw the wisdom in Ninurtu's actions just as his great-grandfather, Nergal, had once seen. Ninurtu had succeeded in making humanity a stronger species, a race that wouldn't allow anyone to conquer them without a fight. Manatu also believed humans had the right to survive.

Manatu brought up another file and confirmed that Alulim, Ninurtu's second in command during the war, had lived out his life in Sumer and fulfilled his obligation. The Shin'ar provided the knowledge of farming, mathematics, and languages and established governing principles and laws. They built schools and studied the stars. The people learned and learned well. Alulim's influence was never recognized, but that had been by design.

Now, Tegan had somehow found the gatekeeper, a marker that had rested undisturbed for millennia. It had been infused with the power of the light twelve thousand years ago when the Earth was a much colder place and ice covered much of the planet. When the gatekeeper was put in place, the Little Bahamas Bank was a large landmass with fertile soil and a temperate climate. The Igigi built their massive city beneath the surrounding area. The land around their city was an ideal sanctuary for the indigenous people living there. Isolated from the rest of humanity, living a primitive existence, they had been the perfect specimens for study. When the sea level rose, the Igigi decided to seal their city and move the human inhabitants from the Bahamas.

Manatu opened another file and reviewed Tegan's thoughts concerning the Antediluvians and their genetically altered humans she called the Awakened. He knew by the description of them that she was referring to the Etu Inu Idimmu. The positions the Awakened held in the various governments around the world was disturbing. The Etu Inu Idimmu were a parasitic species and, unfortunately, they were still considered intelligent. Their gray skin, large head, and black, oval eyes made them appear like the evil ones they were. Their world, KTAR, once had an atmosphere similar to that of Earth, which is why they sought it as a substitute for their dead planet. However, they came to take the world as their own and destroy all that the Igigi had established, until Ninurtu had intervened.

Tegan's bioscan revealed both an intriguing and a disturbing possibility for the future of the world, and for the Igigi, if she survived. Manatu felt a pang of excitement. He felt a sense of a renewed purpose. His clan had stayed behind after all the other clans had left Earth. What was to come couldn't be predicted, but from the findings in Tegan's bioscan, he knew a new world would soon dawn. Manatu combined the relevant information into a single file and forwarded it to the other Guiding Clan Igigi aboard. He requested a conclave in thirty minutes.

$$\infty$$

In the council chamber, thirteen Igigi, all wearing forest-green robes, stood in a circle, facing one another. There were no tables or chairs in the room. Igigi law prohibited any kind of barrier between them while in dialogue. Holographic displays were illuminated around the room and displayed the technical data of Tegan's genetic composition. Her essence and all of her memories were there for them to review if needed.

Manatu began the discussion, saying, "As you can see, Tegan's touch has awakened a gatekeeper at an entrance to our once great city. She is the only one of our bloodline to come upon it, and it was quite by accident. The gatekeeper asks permission to allow access to the portal and the city beyond. Only those of true blood may pass through the outer barrier, and her genetic structure is as close to ours as we have ever seen in any human."

Takatu took a half step forward and said, "I see from the information you've provided it appears that you wish to discuss more than just Tegan Strong-Locke being granted access to the outpost. The data packet is replete with arcane historical references. I cannot help but wonder why you wish us to review Ninurtu's actions."

"You are correct, Takatu. Ninurtu made a difficult decision with limited information. Whether it was right or wrong at the time, it is not my place to say. We know the Etu Inu Idimmu scout ships still appear from time to time. None of their ships stay in the atmosphere for very long. The frequency of their exploratory visits has increased over the past few centuries, but nothing we felt was alarming. I believe that has changed, and it is the reason I have asked you all here. We may be faced with making the same decision Ninurtu did long ago."

There was a chorus of chirps of disbelief from the others.

Manatu raised his hand. "You can see from Tegan's bioscan that the Etu Inu Idimmu, those she calls Antediluvians, have genetically altered a select group of people. These Awakened could be a great threat to humanity's survival. They are in positions to prevent a military response to an invasion until it is too late. They won't be able to stop the Etu Inu Idimmu from doing what they attempted once before. If the entire Etu Inu Idimmu population arrives, as I suspect will happen, without our assistance they will carve a path of destruction, and humanity will perish."

"Are you seriously asking us to decide whether to intervene to stop the Etu Inu Idimmu?" Takatu shouted.

"I am not," Manatu replied. "But I do believe we should protect as many people as possible by hiding them. If we don't, the Etu Inu Idimmu will destroy them all. What I seek is confirmation that concealing them will not violate doctrine. If you all agree, I request that Tegan be one of those hidden."

"You wish to study her?" Takatu asked.

"Yes. My analysis of Tegan's genetic signature is conclusive. Wouldn't you agree, Takatu?"

Takatu was a biotechnical engineer and the one with the most knowledge of human genetics. He looked at Manatu and nodded. "I agree with your findings. I don't know how it is possible, but the analysis is not challengeable."

Manatu said, "I believe she holds the key to the future of humanity. Regardless of the outcome of the invasion, she must survive. To ensure her survival, we may need to take Tegan off-world."

"We have never taken a specimen from the host world before for any reason," Makita said.

Manatu nodded at his life mate. "I know. That is why I have asked you to review my findings. Do all of you concur with my assessment?"

After a lengthy discussion, everyone concurred that providing concealment for the humans did not violate doctrine. They all agreed that protecting Tegan for further study, even if it required taking her away, was acceptable.

"I thank you for your opinions and support. I will grant Tegan access."

CHAPTER TWO

Dr. Tegan Strong-Locke sat meditating on the trampoline netting at the bow of the *Whispering Winds*, a customized forty-four-foot Lagoon catamaran that was her home. Before she and her husband, Calvin "Cal" Locke, ran charters in the Abacos, Tegan had unknowingly worked for a secret group within the government known to a select few as Dark Moon.

General Cecil Westfield, her old boss, had recruited her under the guise of doing advanced research in virology for the CDC. After three years, she had been successful in creating the ultimate programmable synthetic virus medium, code-named Deep Sky, which was designed to test antiviral vaccines against all known viruses. When she learned that Westfield planned to turn it into a bioweapon, she left the agency and became a target for assassination.

She thought about all the things that had happened since then. Westfield's first attempt to kill her ended with the death of her family and closest friend, Alessia Stryker. Because she looked so much like Alessia, she was able to assume her identity and flee to the Abacos almost five months ago. She met Cal, fell in love, but hadn't told him who she really was until four days ago, just before her past caught up with her. Since then, her new friends, Alexandra Hutchins-Winslow and her husband, Nate, along with

Garth and Maggie Aldeberie and their children, Jessica and Edward, had found themselves drawn into the dangerous vortex of her life.

Tegan was supposed to be dead, but Westfield recognized her from an intercepted video call Alex had placed to Dr. Brian Lee about their incredible discovery, an ancient marker covered with unknown symbols. Cal and Alex had found the marker buried behind rock and coral thirty feet beneath the Atlantic Ocean on the east side of Great Guana Cay. By their best estimates, it had been there for thousands of years. It would still be hidden if a section of the coral hadn't broken away, exposing it.

Alex was a professor of archeology at Arizona State University, and Professor Brian Lee specialized in linguistics at the same college. Brian was a savant when it came to deciphering ancient languages, so they had asked for his help in determining the marker's origin. Alex and Nate had come to the Bahamas to witness Cal and Tegan get married. Alex was one of Cal's oldest friends. They'd grown up together in Florida.

Then the day before the wedding, three days prior, Westfield had sent two assassins to Man-O-War Cay to kill Tegan. During a fight with them, Tegan managed to kill one of the assailants, Marine Master Gunnery Sergeant John Grant, the same man that had killed her family and friend. Cal had subdued his accomplice, Navy Commander Robert Knolls, and had prevented Tegan from killing him. To stop Westfield from taking any further action against them, they took Knolls as their hostage.

The day after the wedding, Edward Aldeberie had contacted her and reported that Casey Lane, a former Navy infiltrator working for Westfield, needed to make contact. She told them that a special operations team sent to the islands by the President of the United States, Thomas Collingsworth, had killed Westfield in Hope Town earlier that day. Casey also said that the president was an Awakened and that there were many Awakened trying to help an alien species, the Antediluvians, invade Earth. The Awakened were genetically altered human beings controlled by the Antediluvians. According to Casey, upon Westfield's death, Knolls became the leader of Dark Moon.

They had been forced to form an alliance with Knolls. He was the only one who could organize any resistance against the Antediluvian threat, and he wanted her to prepare Deep Sky for war. *Didn't they say things always happened for a reason?* Tegan thought. She wondered if the reason she had felt the need to come to Man-O-War Cay was fate. That same feeling was telling her that all the answers were here. She believed the marker was the key and that they would be safe if she could unlock the meaning of the symbols.

The chilling event that had unfolded just hours earlier was still fresh in her mind. An alien drone ship had tracked her to Scotland Cay, scanned her body, and then tore off into the heavens. Now images of alien beings and symbols from a strange land permeated her mind. From the impressions left behind in her psyche, she knew the alien encounter last night was with the same alien beings that had left the marker and that it wasn't the Antediluvians who'd made contact. She needed to return to the alien marker. She felt as if it was summoning her, but in reality she understood it was because the drone's sender had told her to return to the marker.

She uncoiled from her lotus position, stood up on the trampoline, took in a deep breath, and stretched to her full five-foot-nine height. Her long, blond hair fell down over her tan shoulders as she turned and faced the sun. The early rays intensified the radiance of her emerald eyes. She looked out over the calm water and listened to the seagulls squawking above her. They would find the answers today.

Scotland Cay – 0730 hours

Cal was talking to Garth on the dock when he noticed the rest of the group approaching. Alex, Nate, and Jessica shuffled along the sandy path to the dock from the house they were renting on Scotland Cay. They'd named it Base Camp Alpha. Knolls and Casey chatted quietly as they walked behind the rest of the group. No one had slept well following the events of last night, and it showed on their faces. Maggie, Edward, and Sara Pinder, Edwards's fiancé, were still back at the house. They wouldn't be going on this trip to the site of the marker.

Cal looked at Garth and said, "I'm wondering if you shouldn't run Edward back to Man-O-War later today on the *Blue Angel* and pick up a few more scuba tanks and supplies from the shop."

"That's a good idea," Garth said. "While I'm there I'll check and see if there's any new information about the investigation into Westfield's shooting in Hope Town. Westfield and Casey killing the six-member team the president sent will be all anyone in the islands will be able to talk about today."

Cal noticed that Knolls was looking intently at him. He wondered what was bugging him this morning. Maybe Knolls wasn't a morning person. Knolls stood six-feet, four inches shorter than Cal, but his muscular physique made him appear larger. His short, dark-brown, military-style haircut, combined with his dark-brown eyes and youthful, lean face, gave him an All-American appearance. He was someone Cal thought he would've liked to have served with in the Coast Guard. They were about the same age, and had circumstances been different, they may have ended up working together in the intelligence community.

"If we alternate our scuba tank refilling locations and use different boats when we go into port, it will reduce the amount of attention we draw," Garth said. "I'll see if I can get additional burner phones and some more batteries for the short-range radios while I'm on the island."

"You may want to grab a few more batteries and chargers for the electronics," Cal said. "The diver communication units on the full-face masks and the transducer for the surface unit will need them. It wouldn't hurt to stock up on canned goods." He saw the look in Garth's eyes. It was the look only good friends could understand. The gravity and uncertainty of the future was all too clear.

"After what I saw last night," Garth said, "I agree. I'm not a doomsday fanatic, but if this invasion actually occurs, we may need to stay hidden for a very long time."

Cal nodded in agreement. "We have plenty of room to store supplies as long as we have use of the house." He looked at the entrance to the harbor. "While you're at the shop, pick up some more fishing rods and tackle, spear guns, dive bags, and any medical supplies you can get your hands on. We can live off the sea if it comes to that, and Tegan can patch up any injuries if she has the supplies. I've got a few dollars tucked away down below which will help with the cost."

Garth smiled. "Don't worry about the money. It may be worthless soon anyway. I've planned for many a hurricane, but never for an alien invasion, so I'm not sure exactly what we may need. You always forget something and don't realize you need it until it's not there. I'll bring everything I can without creating suspicion. Eventually, we'll need to inform people in the islands about what's going to happen."

Cal nodded. "We need to tell the whole world, but I have a feeling no one will believe us until it's too late. We have to plan for the worst possible scenario and hope for the best."

"I know. It's bloody maddening."

Cal could hear the frustration in his friend's voice. Garth and Maggie were born on Man-O-War Cay. Garth's ancestors had lived in the Abacos since the American Revolution, descending from Loyalists. Maggie's family arrived in the mid-1800s. Cal knew it would be hard for them not to stand and fight to defend those they loved and their island home.

"I'm afraid hard times are coming, my friend," Cal said. "We can't start a panic without proof, and disclosing what we know will only give the president a better idea of where and how to strike us. We need to trust Tegan's instincts and let her figure out what the marker represents. We can only hope it gives us something of value to show the world we aren't a bunch of dystopian fruitcakes. I want everyone alerted so we can respond as a unified front when the beasts arrive."

Cal noticed that Knolls was still eyeing him. "I really don't like that guy," Cal said, sounding annoyed.

Garth glanced at Knolls. "I don't either, but I guess we're stuck with him for now. If this alien apocalypse comes to fruition, he may actually turn out to be good to have around, since he's the leader of Dark Moon now."

"I still think he knows more than he's telling us, and he sure seemed rattled after Tegan's alien encounter last night. He strikes me as being more of the pedantic type. I'm sensing he's having confidence issues about how best to handle the situation."

"I agree with you. But, remember, he's now in command of an organization he only joined a few months ago. Knolls isn't going to have the depth of knowledge he needs to fight a battle effectively for a while. If I were in his shoes, I'd be pissed off all the time, too."

Cal knew that Garth's assessment was accurate, so he decided to cut Knolls some slack.

Garth chuckled. "He sure is giving you the evil eye."

"Maybe I should ask him what he thinks he's doing," Cal said. He felt like punching Knolls again. In their first fight, Knolls had nearly gotten the better of him. It was Knolls's hesitation to finish him off that allowed Cal to subdue him. Cal had wanted to help Tegan, but by the time he got to her, she'd already plunged a diver's knife into her would-be assassin's skull. It had been a gory scene, but she'd killed John Grant and had no remorse. He'd thought that with her being a doctor, she might feel a sense of guilt, but she was obviously glad the man was dead.

Garth said, "We have more important issues to tend to now. Best to let it go."

"I'm not sure I can. I know Tegan has a role to play in what's coming. Maybe a role she doesn't even understand herself. Being dependent on Knolls for our survival doesn't sit well with me." Cal had spent years assigned to a special joint operations unit. He had led intelligence missions into hostile foreign lands, seen combat, and had killed the enemy. He wasn't a novice when it came to intelligence and covert operations. He could tell Knolls was still struggling to grasp that fact.

"I'm sure Knolls has some good characteristics," Garth said.

Cal grinned at Garth's ability to say that with a straight face. "I hope you're right." Cal sighed. "Ever since last night, Tegan has seemed distant, as if the weight of the world is on her shoulders. Her mood swings over the last few days have me concerned, too. One minute she's her same old-self, and the next she's acting as if she's prepared for battle."

Garth squared off in front of Cal, took him by the shoulders, and said, "Cal, listen to me. She's feeling guilty about dragging all of us into this, and last night she had an encounter with an alien..." Garth paused, looking for the right word. "...craft, or whatever it was. It reached out and physically examined her. In addition, let us not forget she found time to marry you. I'd say the life-changing events of the last few days give her the right to be a bit moody."

Cal looked at the water. "I hear ya. I think that's why I'm so concerned. I couldn't stop what was happening to her last night. I just have a feeling I won't be able to protect her from what's coming either, and I don't much care for it."

"I understand. But, I think she can take care of herself."

"Agreed," said Cal as the group walked up to them. "Commander Knolls, is there a reason you're so interested in me this morning? You haven't taken your eyes off me."

Garth shook his head and Casey tensed. Even though she was shorter than Cal by a foot, she was solid muscle and would be a formidable opponent. She'd been able to eliminate part of a six-man team the president had sent to the island, so Cal knew she was a capable operator. He found he was more concerned about being able to win a fight with Casey than with Knolls. She'd been in combat and had killed people. He wasn't sure Knolls had killed anyone in his life.

Knolls stopped in front of him. "Actually, there are several reasons." Knolls appeared anxious but not aggressive. "I need to be able to trust you. I don't want to have to worry about watching my back all the time. I can tell you don't trust me completely, and with good reason." Knolls looked at Garth and then back to Cal. "As you know, I have limited assets to utilize, and I'm wondering if you would be willing to help fill the gap when the time comes. As odd as this may sound, I need to know I can trust you with my life."

His directness was something Cal didn't expect. "Trust is a two-way street. You didn't exactly come to us with open arms," Cal said, rubbing his side where Knolls had hit him. "As to whether you can count on me when the time comes, you can." After a short pause, Cal added, "Providing I trust your judgment and you don't put any of us in harm's way."

"That's the problem. If this mission pans out as I think it's going to, I'll need you to act without questioning my intentions or analyzing why I've asked you to do something. I'll need everyone to follow my directions. Cal, your friends and wife are already in harm's way. We need to minimize our exposure to the president and warn the world. We are going to have to trust one another to survive."

Cal took a step toward Knolls. "Rob, you'll have to impress the hell out of me and try very hard to earn my respect, because without it, your guidance and direction won't mean shit. I will not endanger the lives of my wife or my friends because you think they're expendable or you haven't taken the time to explore all other options. We aren't *your* soldiers. We're just people who have found ourselves in a unique and difficult situation. As far as military tactics, I think you'll find my résumé is a lot stronger than yours is when it comes to tactical operations. Are we clear?"

"You've made yourself very clear." Knolls said, softening his tone. "I'll draw upon your expertise, and I'll provide you with the reasoning behind my actions, if there's time. I will do my best to earn your respect."

Cal realized Knolls actually had genuine leadership traits. "Rob, wars have a way of making odd pairings. I'll give you the opportunity to prove yourself. I can't speak for the others."

"I guess that's a start," Knolls said, then extended his hand.

Cal shook it.

"Now that you boys have reached an understanding, let's get a move on," Garth said. "You need to show Knolls the marker, and after our dive I need to pick up Edward and get over to MOW before it gets too late."

Great Guana — July 28 — 0750 hours

The *Whispering Winds* and the *Deep Current* sailed toward the dive site. The *Deep Current* was a fifty-foot, custom Sea Spirit motor yacht that could make thirty knots. For this trip, Garth kept her at nine knots to match the *Whispering Winds*.

Tegan sat by herself, her legs dangling off the leading edge of the trampoline aboard the *Whispering Winds*, the saltwater spray splashing up as the twin hulls of the catamaran plowed through the gentle swells. Images of a wizard standing on a beach and of other strange places still danced through her mind. The high-pitched clicking sounds the wizard made reminded her of the sounds dolphins make when communicating. They were the same sounds she had heard briefly after the drone encounter. Were the images and sounds memories or something else?

Tegan stood as the *Whispering Winds* reached the mooring buoy near the site of the marker. After securing the line to the buoy, she walked back to the cockpit and prepared her dive gear without saying a word. She watched as the *Deep Current* tied up next to them and everyone climbed aboard.

"On this dive I'll buddy with Tegan and Alex," Cal said. "Rob, you're with Garth. Nate, Jessica, and Casey, you will be responsible for surface communications and safety. I'll wear one of the full-face masks, and I want Alex and Garth to use the other two FFMs. Any questions?"

No one had any.

Tegan dropped her BCD into the water and stepped off the dive platform. The warm Bahamian water caressed her as she watched the others follow her into the ocean. She put her mask on, cleared it, and dove with Cal at her side.

The site looked the same as when they had discovered it. The marker shimmered in the light. This was the first time Garth and Knolls had seen it. They ran their hands over the metal, appearing mesmerized as they traced the lines of the intricate symbols.

"This is incredible," Garth said.

Alex said, "It really is something to behold."

"You haven't seen the best part yet," Cal said. "Just wait until Tegan touches it."

The marker was four feet wide by three feet high and shaped like a squashed globe. Jessica had pointed out that if the symbols were removed, it would look like the image of the universe's cosmic microwave background radiation—the CMBR—she'd seen in one of her textbooks. The marker had six dark-colored patches, varying in size and shape, but the pattern and color changes in the metal appeared to have been made by design rather than from age. Three large symbols were spaced at equal distances apart across the bottom center, and two large symbols were on each side of the equatorial centerline. The largest symbol was near the top center, beneath the dark patch that capped the edge of the marker. The oddly shaped oval center didn't look like the other symbols. Dark, raised lines that tapered down to points on both sides surrounded it. Knolls touched each of the smaller, uniformly spaced, intricate symbols. The smaller symbols aligned vertically, and if traced horizontally from end to end, formed nine different planes across the sphere. Each symbol was different in complexity of design. Tegan could tell that both he and Garth were awestruck.

Tegan removed her mask, handed it to Cal, and then shouldered Garth and Knolls aside. She placed her forehead on the center symbol and felt the connection instantly. The blue light glowed around her and penetrated her eyes. She opened her mind instinctually to the source. A tidal wave of new images overwhelmed her. She could tell that the marker was trying to connect with her. Her head began to pound as a clicking noise reverberated within her skull. She wanted to stop, but knew that she was close to a breakthrough.

Suddenly, the intensity of the energy flow subsided, the blue light pulsed, and the clicking noise stopped. *What are you?* Tegan asked silently. A chill ran through her when the marker sent a short pulse of energy into her. It was responding.

Cal touched her arm. She wanted to continue, but Cal's tugs became more insistent. She wished he would stop. Suddenly, he did.

The energy field she had experienced days earlier returned and pushed Cal away from her. The marker had responded to her wish. She exhaled a stream of bubbles and slowed her breathing through her regulator. Then she projected a thought of Cal and her swimming hand in hand into a dark cave, the one she thought might exist under the island.

When Tegan conveyed her love for Cal, a new image of a strange place appeared in her mind, then faded the same way as the bright, blue-white light had blazed into her eyes earlier. She floated free, feeling a sense of disappointment. When she turned to face Cal, she caught the reflection of her enlarged emerald eyes glowing in the faceplate of his mask.

The marker had shut down. It had never done that before. *Was it because it couldn't understand how to respond to emotion?*

Tegan returned to the marker, reached out to it, and felt the connection again. She visualized stars and thought about how the marker looked like the CMBR, and then asked about the place where the people who had left the marker came from. It responded with an intense vibration and a shudder in the water. Tegan stayed focused and asked the question again.

The intensity of the vibration increased until it was a rumble. She broke contact and swam away from the marker. The coral and rock in front of her shook violently, creating a large silt cloud. Then came a strange crunching noise followed by pieces of coral, sponges, and sea fans suddenly drifting in the current. Fish bolted away from the silt cloud and into clearer water. Then all went quiet.

The sound of her air bubbles and the crackling of the coral were gone. She felt as if she had stepped into the vacuum of space. She grabbed her mask from Cal, put it on, and cleared it. A moment later, her hearing returned. As the large silt cloud dispersed, Tegan could hardly believe what she was seeing. In front of her appeared a shimmering wall of blue light that covered what they had thought was an entryway. The large, eighty-foot-wide illuminated barrier was outlined by a three-foot-wide, black border—made of the same substance that held the marker in place.

As Tegan gazed at the portal, a platform suddenly materialized, nearly hitting her shoulder. She moved away. Directly beneath the marker was a black, six-foot-square platform, and below the platform, a switchback staircase extended fifty feet down to the ledge. The surface of the shimmering wall that now spanned the opening reminded her of the surface of a pool on a sunny day. A bluish-colored energy field held back the seawater. She swam closer to the energy field, then stopped suddenly when she saw what lay beyond. Tegan clutched Cal's hand, squeezed it reassuringly, and looked into his deep blue eyes.

"Jessica, can you read me?" Cal asked. His voice sounded slightly distorted in the FFM.

"I can hear you, but you're breaking up."

"We've had an event. We're all okay. Did you feel the shudder on the surface?"

"Yes. It felt like an earthquake up here. What was it?"

"We'll tell you when we surface," Cal replied. "Garth, I see you had the presence of mind to keep recording."

"I did. Some of it may be a bit shaky, but I'm still recording."

"Alex, are you doing alright?" Cal asked.

"I most certainly am," Alex replied. "I hate to be the bearer of bad news, but I'm running low on air."

"Okay. Garth, grab Knolls and follow Alex up. We'll be right behind you. Jessica, we're coming up."

"Copy," Jessica replied.

When the others started toward the surface, Tegan checked her air gauge. She had a few more minutes of bottom time, and she wanted to stay, but Cal dragged her toward the surface.

"Is everyone alright?" Nate yelled as they broke the surface.

"We're all good," Cal shouted back.

"You won't believe what just happened," Alex said when they reached the stern of the *Whispering Winds*. "Tegan somehow opened a huge entrance into the island. There's an energy field keeping the water out."

Casey asked, "How big is the opening?"

"It has to be eighty feet wide and at least fifty feet high," Alex replied.

"That's a big hole!" Nate said. "What kind of an energy field?"

"The same kind of blue energy that Tegan had dancing under her hands on the marker."

Tegan knew that Alex was going to be a pioneer in a new field of archeology. Perhaps Dr. Lee's expertise in languages would be of help.

"There's a glow coming from behind the field," Alex added.

"Let me grab a tank. I want to see it," Nate said.

"Me, too," Jessica shouted.

"I'm not going to be the only one left behind," Casey said. "I'll come with you guys."

Tegan removed her BCD and handed it up to Casey. "I think before anyone goes back down there we should review what Garth recorded, and I'll tell you what I saw on the other side of the energy field."

"I think Tegan has a point," Cal said. "We know its alien. What we don't know is if that energy field is giving off radiation or something else that's harmful to us." He pulled himself up onto the dive platform.

"I don't believe it's harmful," Tegan said. "What we need to do is put a plan together to see if I can breach the field and get inside. I could see a massive cavern on the other side of the field and what looked like a ramp connected to the new platform. I'll take the lead until we determine what we're dealing with. I don't think everyone going down and poking at it is a good idea."

"I agree," Knolls said. "From what you've told us, and from what I've seen, the aliens that created that marker, and whatever is under the island, have an interest in *you*. I think you should be the one to decide who gets to go through the energy field."

"I'm happy to hear you agree," Tegan said. "Cal and I will be the first to try and go through. But first, I want to review what Garth recorded."

Palmer Land, Antarctica

Manatu received the signal saying the gatekeeper had granted access and the outpost portal was open and stable. He relayed the information to the others. He found it interesting that Tegan hadn't penetrated the barrier yet. Perhaps she was being cautious. He knew other humans were with her. He could block their access, but he felt that Tegan would be more comfortable if her companions joined her.

Manatu and the others had been attempting to find the Etu Inu Idimmu fleet. So far, there had been no evidence they were approaching. Perhaps the Etu Inu Idimmu had found a way to conceal themselves. He relayed his thoughts to the others and asked for further investigation.

From Tegan's scan, he knew that President Collingsworth could be a threat. From his research, he was nearly certain the president was under Etu Inu Idimmu control. Which meant the president was in a position to stop a military response to an invasion.

CHAPTER THREE

Washington, D.C. — July 28 — 0800 hours

President Thomas Baines Collingsworth—TC to those who knew him well—sat on a yoga mat in the basement gym of the White House. He was the leader of the Awakened. Although he no longer needed the Orb to communicate with his Antediluvian contact, Trakar, he had it floating in front of him anyway. The Orb had once been his only means of connecting to Trakar and to the other Awakened. It provided a conduit to receive and send information. At least it had until he had developed a direct neural pathway to mentally connect with them. Now he used it only to receive large volumes of information or to communicate with large numbers of Awakened at the same time. He'd been the first to make the direct mental connection with an Antediluvian, which wasn't supposed to have been possible.

The Orb glowed a brilliant yellow, then pulsed rapidly. Trakar had just told him the great news, making a chill walk up his spine. The first of the Antediluvian ships would arrive in a few days. He and Vice President Stacy Preston, another Awakened, had much to do to prepare for their arrival. Once he'd received his instructions, TC informed Trakar of his decision to focus on their arrival instead of tracking down the alien artifact in the Bahamas. A moment later, a sharp pain resonated through TC's body like an electrical shock. It was unlike anything he'd felt before. It was followed by an intense pain in his head. He had been informed that he'd made the wrong decision. He understood his priorities now. Finding the alien site was imperative. It represented a serious danger to them. He had to find it at any cost before they arrived.

The Orb went dark. TC stood and plucked the Orb from the air. He looked at his image in the floor-to-ceiling mirrors along one wall of the gym. He was thinner than he remembered. At five foot eight, he wasn't an impressive physical specimen, but his muscles were toned. He patted the wisps of his gray hair, which still stood on end from his punishment.

TC could hardly remember a time when he felt like himself. For twenty years he'd been a professor of physics at the California Technical Institute. He had joined the Progressive Reformist Movement as President Jackson's vice presidential running mate, and he had then been awakened. Vague memories of his deceased wife, Sandra, and his children sometimes invaded his thoughts. He'd had to kill Sandra after her rebellious reaction to being told what he was and what was going to happen to humanity. She hadn't been able to accept the inevitable. His sons, Thomas and Colin, had flown to D.C. for the funeral, but were now back in California. He hadn't contacted them since then. They were no longer of any importance in his life. He didn't even know why he was thinking about them.

TC was the final product of many generations of genetic alterations, and he was now the best of all the Awakened. His leadership was essential to allowing the Antediluvians access to this world and he would not fail them. He mentally connected with Stacy.

Stacy responded immediately to TC's mental touch. She was in her residence at the U.S. Naval Observatory preparing to leave for her office in the West Wing. The connection to him was so strong, it was as if TC were standing next to her and she straightened her suit.

Over the last few months, TC and Stacy had spent more time together than should have been necessary for their normal duties. Many of Washington's inner circle speculated they were romantically involved. Only a select few knew the real reason for their close relationship.

After her awakening, TC had appointed her to the office he'd vacated to become president. Her twelve years of representing the citizens of Maine as their congressional representative were over. No one ever questioned Stacy's appointment. She had impeccable credentials for holding the office. She'd been elected to her first term in Congress at the age of thirty-six. She had been more attractive back then. Now she kept her weight concealed under dark, custom-made business suits and dresses. Her gray eyes gave her an intense, almost predatory appearance.

She received TC's message about the change in plans. She was to send more teams to the Abacos to search for the alien artifact. When the connection ended, she picked up the phone and called the man who would get the job done.

$$\infty$$

U.S. Army Major General Clint Stewart was entering the Pentagon when his cell phone rang. He knew who it was. He'd felt her presence just before the phone rang. Newly awakened, and not nearly as adept in the use of his new powers, he still relied on the human mode to communicate.

"Yes, Madam Vice President," he answered.

"I need your services again. I need additional covert Delta teams deployed to the Abacos. Their primary mission is to locate the submerged alien artifact that your previous team failed to find."

"I understand. But they were successful in eliminating General Westfield, which was one of their objectives."

"They were also killed publicly. Their actions created a mess for me to handle, which I am still trying to put to rest."

"Sometimes opportunity knocks, and in my opinion, the team did its job."

"Not entirely or I wouldn't be calling you. The president wants that artifact found, quietly."

"If the artifact is being guarded, what are your instructions?"

"Find it, and then we'll decide what to do. I'm forwarding additional information that we have on those who are involved. Included in the file will be the intelligence on the professor they contacted in Arizona. One of them should be able to lead you to the artifact. Let's make sure there are no embarrassing issues this time."

"I'll see to it. I have several teams trained for this type of work. I'll just have to make sure they tone it down a bit."

"Thank you. I want briefings every six hours. More frequently if warranted. You have two days to locate the artifact. I suggest you have your teams in the Abacos by noon."

"It will be done." Stewart felt her disconnect before the line went dead. He hurried to his office.

Great Guana Cay — 0900 hours

Tegan and Alex stood on the trampoline netting on the bow of the *Whispering Winds*.

"Alex, why don't you call Brian," Tegan said. "I think we need his assistance after all. You said he'd discovered something significant in the photos of the symbols we sent him. See if he's still willing to come here, but make sure he understands the risk. It might be prudent to hear what he has to say about the symbols before Cal and I try to go through the barrier."

"He may not take my call. I was pretty rude to him when I cut him off the last time." Alex picked up the burner cell phone and dialed his cell number.

On the third ring, a woman answered. "Hello?"

"Crystal, is that you?" Alex asked. She wondered why Brian's wife answered his cell phone. Then she heard kids screaming in the background. Panic set in. "Where are you?"

"Hi, Alex," Crystal replied. "We're in Florida at Disney World. Katie and I are on Main Street. Brian dropped us off on his way to see you. Is everything okay?"

Alex relaxed, but couldn't believe Brian was coming to see them even after she warned him off. "Yes, everything's fine. Where exactly is Brian landing and when?"

"He wouldn't say. You sound like you didn't know he was coming in today."

"I didn't, but I'm glad he is."

"He told me about your great discovery and said you needed his help."

"That's true. We have found something very special, but I can't go into any details. Why do you have his cell?" Alex asked.

"He wanted me to keep it. He said not to use it unless it was an emergency and to wait for you to call me. He's been quite secretive. We drove almost nonstop for two days to get to Disney."

"You didn't fly?"

"No. Brian said we needed to stay off the grid. He even disabled the GPS chips in our cells. We used cash along the way and only used the credit card for the hotel room when we got here. Brian wanted us to stay elsewhere, somewhere that didn't require a credit card, but the places we stopped at were a little seedy. So we opted to stay in the park for Katie to get the full experience. What are you working on that's got him so paranoid?"

"All I can tell you is that bad people want to find our discovery and they may be listening to our conversation."

"Why?"

"Because they can."

"I understand. Brian said it might involve people with a 'long reach,' but he didn't say who they were. He said he'd fill me in when he could."

"When did Brian leave?" Alex asked.

"A few hours ago. He said he would call you when he got to wherever it is he's going in the Bahamas, then he'd need you to pick him up. To tell you the truth, this whole thing is spooking me. Why would anyone be so interested in an archeological site?"

"It's a long story, and the less you know the better. I wanted to brief Brian before he became too deeply involved. I guess that point's moot now. I'll have Brian call you when he arrives. If he decides to stay, I'll caution him about telling you any more than you already know. In the meantime, stay in public places."

"Now I'm really getting scared. Are we in danger?"

"I won't lie to you. There is an element of risk involved. Please, be cautious. The people interested in what we have found are not going to be interested in anyone who doesn't know where the site is or what it represents. You and Katie should be safe as long as you stay at Disney."

"Alex, have Brian call me as soon as he can."

"I will. I promise." Alex disconnected.

Alex gave Tegan a look that said everything. "Well, you're getting your wish. Brian has decided to play secret agent. He doesn't have a clue about what he's really getting himself into, and as you heard, he's on his way here."

"I guess we'll need to wait to take our next dive until we can pick him up. When did he leave?"

"Crystal said a few hours ago. How long does it take to get here from Orlando?" Alex asked.

"It all depends on whether he's flying commercial or private charter. His only landing choices are Treasure Cay or Marsh Harbour."

Alex rubbed her forehead. "I guess we'll just have to wait for him to call. This is becoming more complex by the hour."

"I think it will be good to have Brian here," Tegan said.

Treasure Cay Airport — 1000 hours

Dr. Brian Lee climbed out of the Cessna 182 he had chartered from the Kissimmee airport. The flight over was much faster than he had expected. He'd chosen Treasure Cay because it was the shortest flight and closer to Man-O-War Cay. He wasn't sure if his logic was sound, but it would get him close enough for Alex to find him. He entered the small terminal, and after clearing customs, found a quiet corner and called Alex.

"Hello, Brian," Alex answered, seeing the blocked number.

"How'd you know it was me?" Brian asked.

"I spoke to Crystal a little while ago, and she told me what you'd done. I think it was a reckless move, considering you don't really know what you're getting into."

"Crystal has wanted to take Katie to Disney for some time now, and this gave us the excuse. I think what you've found is worth the risk."

"You may not think that after we tell you what's happened. Where are you?"

"I'm at the Treasure Cay airport. How do I get to you?"

"You don't. We'll come to you. Just stay there. It shouldn't be very long."

"I'll be waiting."

Treasure Cay — 1100 hours

Cal stood by the railing watching the banks of the protected narrow channel looking for anything suspicious as the *Deep Current* motored to the Treasure Cay Marina. So far, they hadn't encountered anything or anyone that seemed interested in them. Cal hadn't been thrilled at the idea of being boxed in on the approach to the marina. He figured there wouldn't have been time for the president to have a new team in place, even if they had intercepted Alex's and Brian's latest call and were nearby.

Harbor Master Howard Finley waved at them as Garth maneuvered the boat into the slip. The fenders squeaked against the dock as they touched it. Finley walked over and took a stern line from Alex. Cal jumped off the bow and secured the forward line, then checked for anyone who looked out of place.

"Hey, Garth, what brings you over here?" Finley asked.

"I'm just exercising the yacht for the owners. My friends need to pick someone up at the airport."

Cal walked up to Finley. "Hey, Howie, haven't seen you for at least a month."

"Yeah, it's been a while. I guess your business is good."

"Business has been great. We've been spending more time around Marsh Harbour, Hope Town, and MOW. This is my friend, Alex. Is it okay to leave the boat here for a little while?"

"No problem at all."

"Thanks," Cal said, knowing if anyone unusual was hanging around, Finley would have mentioned it.

"Garth, you plan on staying here?" Finley asked. "We can do some catching up while your friends are gone. They can take the crew car." Finley pointed at the gray Chevy sedan parked next to the office. "The keys are in it."

"That would be great," Garth said. "Come aboard."

Cal and Alex pulled out of the parking lot and onto Treasure Cay Road. They drove north until they got to Bootle Highway. The paved, two-lane highway was the main road that connected Marsh Harbour to Fox Town at the north end of Great Abaco Island. If anyone decided to follow them, they would know it. The six-mile drive from Treasure Cay to the airport was a desolate stretch of road bracketed by scrub brush and pineyards. An occasional side road angled off the highway, and a few small businesses and homes dotted the landscape. Cal checked the rearview mirror each time he passed a side road. He didn't see any sign they were being followed. Only one car passed them headed south, and Cal could tell the occupants were locals.

They pulled into the nearly deserted airport parking lot. The small, modern terminal building stood in contrast to a rusting hangar next to it. Cal parked in a space nearest the terminal, and then he and Alex sat in the car for a few minutes. When Cal was satisfied they hadn't been followed, he and Alex got out and walked the short distance to the terminal.

Cal recognized Brian, who stood just inside the doorway. He was shorter than Cal remembered from the video call. He judged Brian to be five-feet-five and about 160 pounds. His Chinese ancestry was evident. He had dark brown hair and brown eyes, and his facial features made him look a little like Bruce Lee, but he wasn't as well built. "I'll wait here while you fetch him," he told Alex.

Cal felt as if they were sitting ducks. He glanced up at the lone exterior terminal camera and scanned the area. Except for some seagulls, nothing else was moving. It seemed too quiet. Dr. Lee and Alex walked out of the terminal a few moments later. Just then a small pickup truck pulled into the parking lot and stopped near the airport exit.

Cal felt an adrenaline rush. He tried to see who was in the truck, but the sunlight reflecting off the windshield blocked his view. It would be a good tactical move for them to block the exit. It was their only way out.

When Brian and Alex walked up to him, he grabbed Brian's suitcase and said, "Time to go." He nodded at the truck and scanned the area as they hurried toward their car. The passenger door on the truck opened, and a woman with a small child got out. The woman walked to one of the three cars parked on the lot, and then the truck pulled away. Cal allowed himself a moment to relax.

"Are things really so dangerous?" Brian asked.

"Yes," Cal answered. "Now, if you don't mind, I'd like to get back to the boat and off the island as soon as possible. I'm sure they know you're here."

"Who are *they*?" Brain asked.

"Let's get going," Alex said. "Brian, I'll explain on the way to the boat."

Brian got into the backseat of the Chevy while Alex jumped into the front seat. Cal checked his watch. He hoped Finley wouldn't still be talking with Garth. He wanted to get Dr. Lee aboard the *Deep Current* and get back to sea without any discussion.

Cal pulled out of the parking lot and checked the rearview mirror as they headed south. No one was behind them.

"Must we hurry like this?" Brian asked when Cal punched it.

Cal knew that Brian was growing more uncomfortable.

"Brian, we have some explaining to do," Alex said. "You're going to have to get used to our way of doing things if you plan on staying."

Cal watched Brian's reaction in the rearview mirror as Alex gave him the thumbnail version of what had transpired over the last few days and the people and aliens who were involved. From the look on Brian's face, Cal expected to hear him say he wanted to go back to the airport. "Do we need to turn around?"

"No. I'm just a little stunned," Brian said, looking paler.

Alex said, "Crystal wants you to call her. I suggest you do it soon. Don't tell her anything about our boat or where we're going."

When they got back to the marina, Cal could see Garth was alone. Cal threw ten dollars onto the dashboard of the Chevy for gas and left the keys in the ignition where he'd found them.

"It looks like the coast is clear," Cal said. "I'll grab the suitcase. Alex, get Brian aboard. The sooner we're away from here, the better I'll feel." The *Deep Current's* engines rumbled to life.

They moved quickly to the boat and jumped aboard.

"We're clear forward," Cal yelled.

"Clear aft," Alex said.

"Let's get out of here." Cal said.

Garth shoved the throttles forward, and the boat responded enthusiastically, its engines quickly spooling up to a loud roar. "Any problems at the airport?" Garth asked Cal.

"No, it went very smooth," Cal replied.

"Would now be a good time to call Crystal?" Brian asked.

Cal nodded, then said, "I think we can use the call to do a little misdirection." He smiled. "Whoever's listening already knows we're operating out of Marsh and MOW, so what I have in mind wouldn't sound unreasonable."

"I gather Marsh is Marsh Harbour, but what's MOW?" Brian asked.

"MOW is short for Man-O-War Cay," Alex answered. "Cal, what are you thinking?"

"Brian, tell Crystal we're driving south to a place called Hole-in-the-Wall on the south end of Great Abaco Island and that you just found out that you'll be at sea for a few days and won't be able to call her," Cal said.

"Okay, but she isn't going to be happy about it," Brian said.

"It'll be safer for her."

Brian frowned.

"I'll raise my voice and tell you not to say anything else about our destination. Whoever is listening will think you just gave up the general area of where we'll be working. I'm sure they'll recover the security footage at the airport. With luck, the security camera will show us leaving and headed south."

"Not a bad plan, Cal," Alex said. "Brian, can you do that?"

"I can do that. Are Crystal and Katie in danger?"

Cal stared at Brian and said, "I don't think anyone will harm them, but it wouldn't hurt to move them. They don't know anything, do they?"

"No."

"Alex said you used a credit card at Disney."

"We did."

"And Crystal used your cell phone when she spoke to Alex, so the people looking for us will eventually know where they are."

"I better have them pack and move now."

"Have Crystal disable the GPS on the cell phone and stop using credit cards," Cal said. "Is there a way you can tell her to head to the Florida east coast without mentioning a specific location?"

"Yes. We honeymooned near Cape Canaveral. I think that's enough." Brian made the call.

Cal could tell by Brian's reaction that Crystal was furious, especially after Brian explained they would be at sea and out of cell phone range for a few days. Brian reassured her that if he thought the situation was becoming too dangerous, he would leave immediately.

Ten minutes later, the *Deep Current* was clear of the channel and back into open water, picking up speed.

CHAPTER FOUR

General Clint Stewart was in his office at the Pentagon listening to the man on the other end of the line with growing annoyance. He scratched his crewcut gray hair and took a deep breath. "You mean to tell me you can't task a surveillance satellite for our target area?"

"That's correct, General Stewart," the man answered. "Everything we have is already deemed critically tasked. It will be at least three days, probably a week, until we can get one moved into position over the Bahamas."

"We won't need your satellite by then," Stewart barked, and hung up.

Stewart wondered if he should call the VP and get it done sooner. He decided to wait. One of his teams would be landing at Marsh Harbor in a few minutes. The other team had left an hour behind the first and would be soon landing at Treasure Cay. Each team consisted of twelve men. For the recon, each team would divide into two, six-man elements. The Marsh Harbour team would scout the Hub of Abaco, which included Marsh Harbour, Hopetown, and Man-O-War Cay. The other team would scout Treasure Cay, Green Turtle Cay, and Great Guana. If they couldn't locate Dr. Tegan or the others in those locations, the search area would be widened. A two-man element from each team would rent a boat and search for the *Whispering Winds*. He had faith they would find the catamaran by tomorrow. His teams were very good at what they did.

Vice President Preston had advised the Bahamian government that his teams were U.S. federal agents there to help in investigating the shootings. He still could not believe he had lost six good men to one old general and an unknown woman. There had to be more to what had transpired.

He could ask the Navy for a drone, but they would ask too many questions. He'd just have to rely on his ground troops. His phone rang. It was his contact at the NSA.

"General Stewart, we intercepted a cell phone call from one of the numbers you provided. I can email the transcript to you if you want it."

"Why wouldn't I want it?"

"I understand. It's on its way to you."

Stewart hung up. He opened his email and found the transcript. The conversation between Dr. Lee's wife, Crystal, and Dr. Hutchins-Winslow revealed little new information. Dr. Lee was flying to the Bahamas, and it was clear Dr. Hutchins-Winslow didn't know he was coming. It was also apparent Dr. Lee's wife knew nothing about the discovery. If only he'd been brought into this "Charlie Foxtrot" sooner, he could have grabbed Dr. Lee before he'd left Arizona. Dr. Lee's wife was of little value to him, but he decided to send two men to Disney anyway to keep tabs on her.

Base Camp Alpha – Scotland Cay – 1400 hours

Dr. Brian Lee had never heard of Scotland Cay, but that was where he was going.

Maggie, Edward, and Sara were waiting on the dock when the *Deep Current* arrived. Garth maneuvered the boat into a slip adjacent to the *Whispering Winds*. The *Blue Angel*, a fifty-year-old, twenty-eight-foot, wooden-hulled Chris Craft was tied to the dock next to *Little Breeze*. The *Little Breeze* was Cal's and Tegan's fourteen-foot, rigid-hull, inflatable dinghy they used to ferry clients to shallow-water beaches.

Tegan and Jessica came out of the *Whispering Winds* salon and joined the group. After introductions were made, Brian couldn't wait to give them the results of what he'd been working on. They walked to the house and found seats in the living room. He began his dissertation with a lengthy explanation of the methodology and interpretations he used for his comparative analysis of the symbols. Realizing he'd lost most of his audience with his explanation, he tried a different approach.

"Let me simplify," Brian said. "What you have found, I believe, is the foundation for all written forms of communication. It is the root of all languages found in the ancient world. The symbols on the marker are not phonetic in nature, but rather a combination of enhanced logograms and an advanced usage of ideograms. It could even be a context completely unknown, but I'm convinced fragments of the symbols appear in other written languages around the world. Since you said this was alien in origin, I think it could even be a construct-form language. I've been researching Xenolinguistics and Lincos to see if they would help, but so far nothing."

"What languages?" Cal asked.

"Xenolinguistics and Lincos are language approaches that take the position that any alien communication would have to be conveyed in a constructed language. I think mathematical models would be the most common ground on which to convey a message between two alien species. In this case, the symbols are what we have to work with, and I know they represent more than just words."

"I'm glad he simplified it," Jessica said with a note of sarcasm in her tone as she tucked strands of her strawberry-blond hair behind her ear.

"You're not the only one thinking that," Nate whispered.

"What's a logogram or ideogram?" Jessica asked.

"A logogram is a visual symbol representing words, but they aren't linked to phonograms, which represent phonemes, or speech. The symbols don't appear to represent letters that are pronounced. A single logogram can be used in many languages. They can represent many different words or have a similar meaning and are pronounced and sound different in whatever language is used. An ideogram is a symbol that represents an idea rather than words or sentences."

"I got some of that," Jessica said. "So basically, what you're saying is that the symbols aren't letters you put together to spell words that create sentences."

"Correct. In this case, I believe each symbol represents more than just a letter, word, or even a sentence. They are unlike any ancient hieroglyph or any other language I understand. Originally, I thought they might be related to Sumerian, Vinca, or even Sitovo. Now I think it's the other way around. Someone shared these symbols with people across the world a long time ago. This is *the* root language.

"Each civilization took bits and pieces from the language, then adapted and incorporated them into their own language," Brian said. "All of the symbols are unique and quite detailed. They represent a language that will take me more time to decipher than I thought. These symbols are far more advanced than anything I've ever seen, which is why I'm so excited and the reason I had to come."

"You don't know what the symbols on the marker mean, do you?" Tegan asked.

"No, I don't. I'm sorry. But what I do know is that emerging cultures had little if any contact with one another during the era when written languages were developed, yet somehow all of them contain distinct similarities to the symbols you found. The origins of written script, whether painted, chiseled, or scratched onto cave walls, stone pillars, papyrus, or animal skin, all appeared during a very short period in human history. Somehow, the emerging civilizations of China, Sumer, Egypt, Europe, and the Americas all drew bits and pieces from the symbols you found here in the Bahamas. They used the symbols to incorporate context into their first attempts at writing. These symbols and human development have to be connected somehow, which is why I don't think the site you found is the only one. There have to be others yet undiscovered. Perhaps there's a marker inside the Sphinx or maybe beneath the pyramids of Egypt or hidden in the jungles of Mexico."

"I can understand you're certain that early writing evolved from this symbolic language, but I don't see how you can be sure there are other markers hidden out there," Alex said.

"I can't say for certain. However, it would be logical. If there was direct interaction with the beings who created the marker, then there should be more similarity in languages scattered around the world. I don't think our ancestors were tutored. I believe they saw what the symbols represented and modified them to work for their culture. The symbols took on meaning that made sense to them.

"The symbols on the marker represent a highly advanced form of communication that uses a more efficient way of conveying meaning. I believe each symbol represents a complete message, or possibly even a story. It could represent the history of the world as they knew it when the marker was made."

"How can you be so sure the symbols convey any message at all?" Cal asked. "You said you couldn't read it. It could just be equations."

"I can't read or understand the meaning of the symbols, but I can interpret their linguistically engineered formatting. They could have mathematical formulas embedded in them, but I've made some assumptions based on what we talked about, and I can say without hesitation that these symbols are from a civilization that existed long before modern man ever thought about writing things down. Whoever these creatures are … well, they are very, and I mean *very*, advanced."

"They're alien. Of course they're going to be advanced," said Alex.

"Can you tell me more about the aliens that left the symbols?" Brian asked.

"All we know is that the marker only reacts to Tegan's touch," Alex replied. "Just before we came to get you, Tegan's interaction with the marker opened a portal to a cavern. And their drone contacted and interacted with her last night," Alex replied.

Tegan added, "The probe that scanned me displayed multicolored lights before the encounter. It tracked me like a bloodhound from where we'd anchored earlier to where we met Casey and then back to here. It lifted me off the deck of the *Whispering Winds* during the scan. It made no sound, and it seemed to be propelled by some type of antigravity system. After the drone left, I kept hearing clicking noises, as if that was their means of communication. It reminded me of the sound dolphins make."

"Fascinating," Brian said. "What about the marker? Alex said it reacted to your touch."

"It does. The marker produces some type of blue energy field whenever I touch it. The largest field it produced surrounded my body, and at one time it prevented people from touching me through it. It seems to understand me."

"No one told me you've been communicating with the marker," Brian said, frowning. "How could you've not mentioned that until now?"

"We wanted to hear what you'd learned before we tainted your theory," Alex replied.

"Tegan, why do you think the marker only reacts to your touch?"

"I think it has to do with my DNA. The marker reacts like a biometric system. Once it identified who I was, I think it sent a signal to wherever the aliens are, and they sent the drone to confirm. It was my last contact with the marker that resulted in the opening of a portal. I haven't touched it since the portal opened. I'm afraid it might close it if I do. We were hoping you could provide us with more information before Cal and I breach the barrier. Garth, please show him the video of the barrier."

"Give me a second," Garth said. He retrieved the laptop computer and set it on the kitchen table.

Maggie, Edward, and Sara gathered around him. They hadn't seen the recording yet. Brian found a place close to the screen. While Garth cued up the video, Brian noticed that Maggie seemed reserved. "Maggie, how do you feel about all of this?"

"I was a bit intimidated and scared after I heard about the gun battle in Hope Town," Maggie replied. "But I'm adjusting."

Maggie was Garth's age, fifty-two, although he looked older. She had short, light-brown hair, and she was the finest day-bread baker in the Bahamas, but her slender build didn't fit the stereotypical image of a baker.

"Alex said there'd been a shooting. What exactly happened?" Brian asked.

"Casey can tell it better. She was there," answered Maggie.

Casey Lane pointed to the bandage on her leg. "I'll give you the short version. A special ops team ambushed my boss and me. He died, and I was wounded during the firefight. We eliminated the six-man team the president sent."

Brian nodded. "That was short and to the point. Who was your boss?"

"General Cecil Westfield, the former commander of Dark Moon. Commander Knolls is in charge now."

"Dark Moon? What's that?" Brian asked, looking at Knolls.

Knolls said, "A secret organization President Truman created. Our mission was to covertly assess any alien encounters, determine the threat level, and respond accordingly. It was created after alien remains were found in Kawich, Nevada."

"Brian, the aliens that are a threat to us are called Antediluvians," Tegan said. "They aren't the same ones who left the marker."

"So there are *two* alien species," Brian said.

"Yes," Tegan replied. "And the Antediluvians are the ones that control the president and others like him. They're called the Awakened."

Brian gawked at her. "Are you serious?"

"Yes. One of the reasons we need you here is to help us communicate with the alien species that left the marker. I'm hoping they may give us some insight into what we're facing with the Antediluvians, in case the bioweapon I created doesn't stop them."

"Bioweapon!" Brian cried. "No one mentioned a bioweapon."

"I guess I left that part out," Alex said. "Did I tell you Tegan is a medical doctor?"

"No. Let's get back to the bioweapon. I feel like I've only seen the tip of the iceberg. Tell me the whole story."

"I think that's only fair," Tegan said. "Brian, I went to John Hopkins and specialized in molecular medicine, specifically virology and genetics. I have a Ph.D. in microbiology from the University of Washington. Until a few months ago, I thought I worked for the CDC. Then I learned I was actually doing work for the NSA, which turned out to be a front for Dark Moon.

"I created a programmable viral medium using nanotechnology that offered a means to synthesize and test vaccines against any virus on the planet. I designed it to function at the molecular level. It was code-named Deep Sky. That's what was turned into an alien bioweapon. I stopped work on Deep Sky and left because I thought they planned to use it on people."

"Wow," Brian said. "General Westfield was your boss?"

"Yes. He's also the man responsible for having my family and best friend killed."

Cal said, "Tegan killed the operator that killed them a few days ago."

He was trying to imagine this woman killing anyone. "You killed someone?"

"Yes, Brian. I killed the animal that murdered my loved ones."

Brian noted the cold edge to her voice. "May I ask how?"

"I slit his throat and drove a dive knife into the top of his skull," she answered.

Brian sat quietly staring at her for a moment. He looked around the room at all the solemn faces. All except Knolls. He looked at Tegan with a hint of anger on his face.

Knolls said, "To clarify, the animal was my partner and a good Marine."

"He was a killer," Cal shot back.

The atmosphere in the room grew tense.

Brian looked at Knolls. "So you and Casey were a part of Westfield's team?"

"Correct," replied Knolls.

"He was actually our hostage for a few days," Jessica said.

"Yes, I heard about that."

Tegan said, "Brian, I believe you have a right to know everything. Rob came here as our enemy. Now, both he and Casey are our allies. If there is anything else you want to know, please ask."

"I don't know what to ask."

"This is your new reality, Brian," Tegan said. "You'll need to get used to it. Now I think you understand why Alex didn't want to get you involved without knowing what was going on. Until we can go public and tell the world what we have discovered, we're sitting ducks. An alien-controlled president will be hunting us. The only thing that can change our fate is finding a way to decipher the symbols. We have to figure out what's on the other side of the barrier and find a way to stop the Antediluvian invasion. Do you understand what that means?"

Brian's thoughts went to his family. "Yes, I understand." The utter realization struck him like a freight train. He hadn't considered all the ramifications of his actions. He'd been drawn to the flame by his excitement and blind desire to see the artifact and help Alex make history.

Brian looked at Edward and Sara. He noted that Sara was holding Edward's hand. "How do you two fit in?"

He knew Edward was Maggie's and Garth's oldest child. Edward was the same height as his father, about five foot ten, but he was at least thirty pounds lighter. Sara had a pretty face, with freckles dotting her nose, blue eyes, and short, blond hair that hung to her collar. He figured she was around twenty-three, about the same age as Edward.

Edward said, "We just happened to be in the right place at the time and helped Tegan out. I run a ferry service in the Abacos with my boat, the *Alde I*. It's a thirty-eight-foot, twelve-passenger ferry. I took care of my father's businesses while they were trying to sort this out. Then Casey arrived, and Sara and I got more deeply involved. I'm glad we did though. I'd rather know what we're facing than wait for it to bite us in the ass."

"Amen," Sara said.

Brian smiled. "Tegan, is there anything else I need to know?"

"I don't think so. Garth, play the video. Let's see if Brian can see anything we missed before we penetrate the barrier."

Brian sat mesmerized by what he saw. "Play it again, please."

When it was over, Tegan asked, "What do you think?"

"From what I can see, there isn't anything I can add. I'm sorry."

"I guess we'll just have to take our chances," Cal said. "Are you ready to see the site in person?"

"Definitely," Brian replied.

"You do scuba dive, don't you?" Cal asked.

"Yes. My work sometimes requires it."

"We won't be going deep," Cal told him. "I'll stay with you the whole time. Since you can't give us additional insight, I think we need to get back to the site and breach the barrier."

"I agree," Tegan said.

The Pentagon — 1430 hours

General Stewart received the transcript of the second conversation between Dr. Lee and his wife. Why he hadn't received it sooner angered him. His teams had been on the ground for over an hour, and they were looking in the wrong place. Based on the intercept, he didn't think he'd need satellite coverage now that the search area had been reduced. He contacted both team leaders and redirected all but one two-man team to the Hole-in-the-Wall area. He ordered the teams to take both boats and search the area in grids. He wanted the south and west basins explored first. He called Stacy and told her the new target site was on the south end of Great Abaco Island and about his search plan.

"General Stewart, if you don't find anything in the next twenty-four hours, I want you to reposition your teams north and start asking questions," Stacy ordered. "The islands aren't that big, so they can't stay hidden for long."

"I'll have my people use their bogus law enforcement credentials to get interviews with friends and relatives," General Stewart said. "I'll have them imply that Garth Aldeberie and Tegan and Calvin Locke are harboring a fugitive involved in the shooting."

"Excellent. If you don't have any new leads by tomorrow at this time, you are authorized to bring in additional troops. At that point, it won't matter how many toes we step on. I'll contact the Bahamian Governor-General and the Prime Minister's office to advise them that we've learned the firefight was terrorist-related and that the team killed was part of a special unit that had been tracking the extremist cell."

"We'll find them. They can't hide forever," General Stewart said.

"Good hunting. We're counting on you."

CHAPTER FIVE

Great Guana Cay — The Marker Barrier — July 28 — 1530 hours

Cal motored the *Whispering Winds* to the site in order to make better time against the easterly winds. As they approached, Cal saw the *Deep Current* already tied to the mooring buoy. The seas were calm enough for him to tie up alongside her. Cal maneuvered the boat until he felt the gentle touch of the *Deep Current's* portside fenders, then shut down the engines. Tegan and Jessica secured the lines that Garth and Casey had thrown them, while Nate and Knolls stood at the stern of the *Deep Current* talking. Maggie, Edward, and Sara, had stayed behind at the house. If anything happened on MOW, Cal knew they would hear about it through their many contacts in the islands.

As Cal walked into the salon, Brian pushed the new drawings of the symbols across the chart table to Alex.

"Hell, I may be a grandfather by the time I solve this riddle," Brian said. "Even with Tegan's information, I'm still a long way from being able to decipher the message on the marker. I know you wanted me to come up with something before the dive, but I can't."

"Don't worry about it," Cal said. "We wouldn't have figured it out on our own anyway. Maybe we'll find some answers on the other side of the barrier." The boat rocked slightly when the others came aboard.

After everyone had gathered around the chart table, Cal said, "This is going to be a bit different from our other dives. I've also made some changes in the lineup. Tegan and I will stage on the platform that's next to the marker before we make entry. We will both have standard regulators. I don't believe the diver communication units will be of any value beyond the barrier. I think the signal will be blocked by the energy field.

"Nate, Garth, and Jessica, you'll be our safety divers. Jessica, I know you don't like using an FFM, but this time I think it would be a good idea for all of you to wear them in case there's a problem. Casey, you'll serve as our surface safety and communications officer so that Alex and Brian can continue working on the symbols. Rob, I want you to back up Casey on communications and be our relief diver. Perhaps you could look over what Alex and Brian have been working on and find a common point of reference they've missed to solve the puzzle. If you come up with something, relay it to Garth."

"Got it," Knolls replied. "I'll check in with our assets in New Mexico and see if our supercomputer has made any headway."

Cal saw the look of disappointment on Brian's face. "Brian, you'll go down next time. I'm planning two dives this afternoon."

"I may be of more value to you down there than I am up here," Brain said.

"Not for this dive. This is going to be a brief exploratory foray. We will go in, see what's there, and come back out. I'll handle the digital recorder. Garth, you will keep in contact with Casey. Any questions?"

Knolls asked, "Who's going down next with Brian?"

"It depends on what we discover. However, I think you and Alex should be next. Casey, you'll get your shot later."

"No problem. I'm in no hurry," Casey replied.

"Thanks, guys," Cal said. "Let's get the transducer over the side and get on with it."

Five minutes later, they were in the water and headed back to the marker. Tegan took the lead. From a distance, she couldn't see the portal. The only thing visible was rock and coral. She looked back at Cal. She could tell he was puzzled, too. She reached the marker before the others arrived.

The portal was once again covered by marine growth, but it didn't look right to her.

Cal swam up next to her and shook his head in disbelief as the others settled into a hover next to them. Tegan shrugged and touched the marker. A new sensation coursed through her body. She realized the marker was sending her a greeting. A moment later, the camouflage disappeared and the portal and platform were visible.

As Tegan and Cal settled onto the extended platform, she reached down and felt the texture of the black material. It was smoother than the other black composite material that surrounded the marker. It reminded her of polished quartz. It had a faint, reflective speckle running through it, unlike the material holding the marker, which was a matte black color. She inched toward the energy barrier with Cal at her side and tried to peer through the shimmering wall of water without touching it. She couldn't discern any details within the cavern. All she could see was a blue aura of light that faded into darkness. After a few moments, Tegan noticed what looked like a walkway on the other side of the barrier. She wasn't sure if it was only a reflection of the one she was standing on. There was only one way to find out.

Tegan took Cal's hand, extended her right leg through the barrier, and found a solid surface. She stepped through before Cal could stop her and immediately felt the full weight of the dive gear dig into her shoulders. There was a brief second of disorientation. It was unnatural to walk through a vertical wall of water onto a horizontal plane. Cal gripped her hand tightly, but he didn't pull her back. The massive cavern she had entered extended deep under the island. She tugged gently on Cal's hand, indicating it was safe for him to follow.

Tegan moved to her right as Cal came through the barrier. His grip tightened at his momentary disorientation. She looked back through the barrier and saw the distorted figures of the others swim closer. Water from their gear dripped onto the floor and evaporated instantly. The cavern felt cool, and if she hadn't been so enthralled with what she was seeing, she would have felt chilled. However, for now, the adrenaline racing through her system was enough to keep her mind off the cold.

They were both still breathing through their regulator. Their exhalations sounded loud, so Tegan knew they weren't in a vacuum. There was an atmosphere and positive pressure here. The question was whether the air was breathable. The sound of their breathing and the dripping water from their dive gear echoed across the massive cavern. As they stepped further into the cavern, a reddish-colored light suddenly enveloped them. Before they could react, the light faded away. The red light reminded Tegan of her days working in a sterile environment, and she wondered if their hosts had decontaminated them. That would make sense. The owners would want to keep out foreign biological agents.

Then a bluish glow radiated from the walls, making them appear to be moving. A strip of soft blue-green lights turned on, marking the edges of the gently sloping walkway that descended into the cavern. A moment later, the cavern was illuminated with a blue light, just like the walls nearest her. Now the light radiated from the walls, floor, and ceiling.

Tegan removed the regulator from her mouth and took a deep breath. The air was pure, clean, and heavy with oxygen, as it must have been the day the cavern was sealed. There was no smell of age or mold in the air. She took her mask off and looked at Cal. She could tell he was watching her for any sign of hypoxia or other adverse reaction. She smiled a reassuring smile and said, "It's okay. The air is good. It's slightly heavier in oxygen and surprisingly cleaner than we're used to breathing." From her work in clean rooms, she knew the smell of an oxygen-rich, sterile environment.

Cal took off his mask, removed his regulator, and took a breath. "You're right," he said, running a hand through his hair. "The air is pure."

"Would I lie to you?" Tegan unbuckled her buoyancy compensator and eased her tank onto the black floor. She removed her fins and weight belt, but left her rubber-soled dive booties on. Tegan motioned for Cal to do the same.

"I think I'll keep my gear on just in case I have to rescue you."

"Suit yourself, but you may want to take your fins off if you plan on walking around with me."

"You have a point." Cal removed his power fins and weight belt. As he poured the water from his fins onto the floor, it evaporated before his eyes. "That's a neat trick. We could use that technology on the deck of the boat. Whoever built this did a nice job. The camouflaging of the entrance was amazing."

The cavern looked as if it extended deep under Great Guana Cay, so far back that the blue-green glow from the floor lights vanished into the distant darkness. There were multiple levels below them. They stood at the highest point in the cavern.

"It looks like the ramp continues down from level to level until it reaches the floor of the cavern," Tegan said. "I'd guess it's at least a hundred feet to the bottom."

"At least," Cal replied.

"Look at the roof. It's domed."

"Black and sparkly like the floor and walls. I guess your friends like dark things and don't like stairs or squared-off corners."

"It looks that way." Tegan looked to the right. A smaller oval version of the marker was affixed to the inside wall next to the portal. As she examined it, she noted it had fewer symbols and lacked the darker background images. The marker appeared three-dimensional. It had depth, like a hologram. She wondered if her hand would pass through it if she touched it. Tegan placed her hand on it. It was solid. A blue glow surrounded her hand. She didn't feel any sensations as she did when she touched the marker outside.

"I wish I knew how to read this," Tegan said. She took her hand off the marker. "Let's take a look around." She started down the ramp.

"Hold up there, Pocahontas," Cal said. "Don't you think the folks outside will be concerned if they see us disappear? If we're altering our timeline and not coming right back out, we need to tell them."

Tegan gave Cal an evil smile. "What makes you think we can ever leave?"

"Humor is not your strong suit," Cal replied. "This isn't the Hotel California. But I have to admit, I didn't think about being able to get back out."

Tegan looked back through the portal. The energy field wasn't as opaque as when they'd entered. Jessica stood on the platform in front of Garth. She could see Jessica's features clearer now. Garth's facial features weren't as sharp. Tegan detached the writing slate dangling from Cal's BCD and scribbled a message, telling them they were okay, that there was fresh air inside, and that they were going to look around for a while.

"They may not let us back in if we leave," Tegan said. "I think we need to take this opportunity to explore as much as we can."

"I agree," Cal replied.

"Stick the slate through the barrier. Then we'll know if we can get out."

Cal pushed the slate through the barrier. There was no resistance.

Tegan watched as Jessica and Garth read the message. When Cal brought the slate back through the barrier, the red light illuminated the parts of his arms and slate that had been outside.

"That answers that question," Tegan said. "I guess we can leave. Do you want Jessica or Garth to come through?"

"I think all of them should stay outside," Cal replied. "We still don't know what we'll find. That red light thing could be dosing us with radiation."

"I think it's decontaminating us. I doubt it's radioactive."

"Well, hopefully it isn't sterilizing us. I would like to sire children someday."

"Are you implying I'm your mare?"

Cal laughed. "No. Forgive my choice of words."

"Whoever built this probably made sure everything that entered was decontaminated before they allowed anyone to go deeper into the structure or mingled with the aliens."

"Yeah, well, maybe it was designed for an alien physiology. If something comes out of my chest in few days, you'll know why," Cal joked.

Tegan could tell by Cal's wittiness that he was on edge. She wasn't. For some reason she felt at home here. She saw Jessica waving and point at her ear. "What does she want?"

Cal pushed the slate through the barrier for Jessica to use. When he pulled the slate back, Jessica's hand followed, and the red light illuminated the slate and their hands. "She says they can hear us talking, but they can't quite make out what we're saying. She wants us to speak louder, and she wants to join us."

"She's an adventurous one," Tegan said. "I think it best that she stays outside, don't you?

"I do."

Tegan shook her head at Jessica and yelled, "We want you guys to stay there." She could tell by Jessica's reaction that she was disappointed. "Don't be alarmed if we don't come right back. The cavern is huge, and it may take some time to explore it."

Cal shouted, "Garth, I want someone standing by at the entrance, so make sure you rotate the duty. Is that clear?"

Garth nodded.

"From what I can see, there're multiple levels connected by walkways that gradually slope down to the floor of the cavern," Tegan shouted. "The walkways are illuminated by green lights. The rest of the cavern has an eerie blue glow to it. Tell Alex and Brian there's another, smaller marker just inside the entrance with more symbols on it."

Garth nodded again.

"I'm all yours to go exploring," Tegan said.

"After you," Cal replied.

They started down the slope.

CHAPTER SIX

The Outpost — July 28 — 1600 hours

The tranquility of the cavern surrounded her like a blanket as she walked down the lighted path. Tegan could tell that Cal was very tense, and she didn't understand why she wasn't. She was in an alien place, possibly the first human ever to be here, and yet she felt at home.

"Cal, you can take off that tank." Tegan said. "Nothing is going to happen. The sea isn't going to swallow us."

Cal stopped and took off his gear, then said, "I'll be right back."

He walked back up the ramp and set his gear down next to hers. Standing at the entry portal, he turned on the digital camera and began recording the vast expanse of the cavern and the unnatural light illuminating the facility.

"The light in here doesn't seem to have a source. It's like it's radiating out of the walls and floor," Cal said.

"I noticed that." Tegan took a closer look at the symbols embedded in one wall. They glowed with a soft blue light when she stood in front of them. They were smaller than the symbols on the markers, but just as intricate. She ran her hand over them. Nothing happened. "Make sure you record the symbols on the walls," Tegan said. "And get a good shot of the new marker by the entrance."

"Will do," Cal replied.

Cal provided narration as he filmed. The walls, floor, and ceiling were all obsidian-colored, but they showed subtle differences. The walls appeared to have been constructed of the same material as the floor, but they had silvery-blue, crystalline particles embedded in them, giving them a slightly reflective appearance. As Tegan continued down the ramp, she noticed that the crystals not only refracted the light, but were the source of it. The blue light was being emitted through the crystals. *How was that possible?* she wondered.

Tegan knew that the islands were composed mostly of limestone, so apparently the builders had used their own composite materials to reinforce the structure. The floors and ceiling gently curved into the walls. There were no seams anywhere.

Tegan stopped to see what was keeping Cal. "What are you doing?" He had the camera pointed at her.

"I want to use you as a reference to provide a sense of scale when its reviewed later," Cal said, panning the camera around.

"Good idea, but let's not waste the battery or memory on me. We need to get on with exploring the facility."

"But you're the star of our Hollywood movie," Cal replied. "I think that's a line from the lyrics of a 60s song." He turned off the recorder and walked quickly down the ramp to join her. "I'm only going to record while standing still. I don't want it to look like a shaky reality film. It might take more time, but it should provide better detail and keep the people watching it from getting seasick."

Tegan nodded and led the way down. Cal stayed behind her, even though the ramp was wide enough for several people to walk abreast. The floor gradually leveled off. Tegan stopped when Cal turned to record the sheer size of the portal. She could see how the ramp widened as it went deeper into the cavern. It reminded her of a terraced hillside. After several levels, the ramp reached the floor of the cavern.

"It looks like there are two more levels before the bottom floor. Let's keep moving," Tegan said.

When they came to a branch leading away from the ramp, they stopped in front of a group of symbols. Tegan ran her hand over them. In an instant, a workstation materialized. The surface of the counter was composed of the same material as the wall and blended seamlessly into it. Three black oval panels appeared above the counter and glowed with fluctuating intensities of blue light.

"What did you do?" Cal asked.

"Nothing I haven't done before. I just touched the symbols." She touched the symbol above the center panel, and more panels appeared. It seemed as if the wall was interacting with her.

"Stop that!" Cal yelled. "There's no telling what you're activating."

"Okay, okay," Tegan said. "There's no place to sit. I wonder if they work standing up."

"How do you know it's a workstation?"

"What else could it be? Look, some of the symbols on the panels are larger than others, and several of them are changing to a different blue color."

"This is truly an alien place, and considering the energy flow around everything, it has to have a power source," Cal said as he filmed each of the symbols. "I imagine we're the first human beings to step inside this place. Let's just hope it's deserted."

"Now where would the fun be in that?" Tegan asked, examining one of the panels more closely. "This place is amazing."

"It's definitely different," Cal replied, turning off the recorder. "We need to stay alert. They could show up at any time."

Tegan glanced down at the dive knife strapped to his calf. "If they did, I doubt there's much we could do to stop them from having their way with us."

"Not funny. Let's keep moving," Cal said.

"Which way?" Tegan asked as she looked back at the workstation and watched it disappear as she moved away. "That's definitely a space saver."

Cal said, "We can take this corridor or continue down the ramp. Do you have a preference?"

"Let's take the corridor and see where it leads. Maybe we'll find something more interesting than symbols and walls that turn into workstations."

"What happens if we find other corridors?"

"We'll be systematic," Tegan replied. "I suppose we should be mapping all of this as we go. If this corridor becomes a maze of pathways, we could get lost."

"I don't think that will happen," Cal said. "I have a good sense of direction. All we have to do is play back the recording and backtrack."

"That will work if we can recognize a landmark. One black wall looks the same as another without reference points," Tegan said.

"We can match the symbols we've recorded so we'll know where we are."

Tegan cocked her head. "Unless they get absorbed into the wall like the workstation or they all look alike."

"I see your point. Next time we bring cave diving equipment, ropes, and lights to mark the paths. I think we should leave scuba tanks at various locations on each level just in case we need a backup air supply."

She walked toward a dark section of the pathway leading them deeper into the cavern. The green lights disappeared. As the passageway narrowed, the ceiling dropped to where it was only a few feet above their head.

"It looks like a tunnel and it's getting darker," Tegan said.

Cal turned on the digital camera light.

They moved deeper underground, passing several panels covered with symbols. Cal stopped to record each of them. Tegan refrained from touching any of them. Then the tunnel ended abruptly at a wall of panels.

"End of the line," Cal said. He began recording the symbols. When he finished and turned around, Tegan was gone. "Tegan!" he yelled.

"I'm over here." Tegan walked back into view. "It's an optical illusion. The wall turns to the right and goes further back, so get your ass down here." She disappeared again.

"God, you scared me," Cal said.

Past the turn, the bluish glow from the walls was more intense. The green walkway lights returned. The light created a dazzling aura, making it appear as if the tunnel narrowed toward where the light stopped.

Cal stopped and recorded the illusion. "It looks like we're entering a time tunnel."

"It does look futuristic," Tegan replied. "What purpose could this serve?"

"I have no idea."

As they walked farther into the tunnel, the floor sloped down again, taking them deeper into the cavern. Suddenly, Tegan stopped dead in her tracks. In front of her was another energy barrier, and beyond it, something she could hardly believe.

"Holy shit!" Cal shouted.

"That is impressive."

Beyond the barrier, the tunnel opened into a vast chamber, with a cathedral ceiling that was at least fifty feet high. Floating in the center of the chamber, defying gravity, was a large, opaque sphere. To their left was a large opening with another energy barrier. Tegan could see it led back to the main cavern and the ramp leading down to the next level.

At least twenty, large workstations were affixed to the wall. They were elaborate in design, and none of them had chairs. Lighted panels and metal markers crowned each station, all of them covered with symbols.

"This looks like a control room," Cal whispered.

"That would be my guess, too. It would explain the additional energy barrier."

Beneath the opaque sphere in the center of the chamber were four oversized recliners, each with a sculpted indentation in a shape that would allow someone to lie in.

"Those look interesting," Tegan said as she walked to the edge of the barrier. "Do you think the air is the same on the other side?"

"I can't imagine why it would be any different."

"Let's hope so." She tried to push her hand through the barrier, but met resistance. Although it shimmered like the outer barrier, this one felt solid. "Interesting. It seems we have been given another obstacle."

"It must be a security field. They don't want anyone getting in who isn't authorized."

Tegan looked to her right. Hidden in the shadow of the wall was a small metal plate. This marker was devoid of symbols. "Cal, you have to see this."

The plate had a depression shaped like a large human hand. Four fingers and an opposing thumb were distinctly visible.

"The good news is the aliens who built this facility appear to have humanoid features," Cal said, placing his hand into the indentation. A blue glow surrounded Cal's hand. The light danced up his arm to his shoulder and stopped, then blinked out. The barrier pulsed as Cal placed his hand against it. He pushed his hand through. "I guess you're not the only one with the magic touch."

"I guess not." Tegan touched the energy field. Again, her hand met with resistance. "Alright, let me try the palm reader." The blue glow came to life and she pushed her hand through the barrier.

"Maybe it keeps track of who enters, like a keycard system, only more sophisticated," Cal offered.

"Like the biometric marker outside. So why did it accept your signature?"

"Maybe it recognizes me. I think the next question is will we find good air on the other side of the barrier?" Cal asked.

"There's only one way to find out." Tegan grabbed Cal's hand and pushed her face through the barrier, then breathed in. The air was no different. Tegan let go of Cal's hand and walked into the control room. "It's good."

"Glad to hear it." Cal followed her through the barrier and stopped. He turned around and tried to push his hand back through the barrier. His hand met resistance. "Crap, that's not good."

"What's not good?" Tegan asked, turning around.

"It let us in, but I can't push my way back out."

Tegan tried to push her hand through the barrier, but couldn't get it through. Then she noticed a palm reader on the wall identical to the one they used to gain entry. She put her hand on it, it glowed, and she was able to walk through the barrier to the other side. In order to come back into the room, she again had to use the palm reader. "Well, that's not very efficient."

Cal said, "Someone definitely wants to keep track of who comes and goes in this room."

"Apparently, but if you've gained access to the facility already, what would be so important about this place?" Tegan asked.

"I don't know, but I'm betting your friends know we're here," Cal said. "Those four high-tech recliners in the center of the room look like command seats."

"They look like something that belongs on a spaceship," Tegan said, walking to the nearest one. She touched the fabric. It was soft, and as she pushed down on the material, it conformed to her hand. "I bet that would be comfy to sleep on."

"Or for marital pleasures," Cal said.

She grinned at his impish look and shook her head. Only Cal could be in an alien environment and still think about sex. She walked between two of the recliners and looked up at the gravity-defying sphere. A barely noticeable light blue glow of energy swirled inside it. It was too high for her to reach.

Cal looked up at it and said with a creepy voice, "It's alive."

She walked over to the workstations and said, "Alex and Brian are going to have a lifetime of work ahead of them. I hope they like living in the Bahamas, that is if the aliens who built this don't evict us."

"This may very well be one of the safest places in the world."

Tegan looked around the chamber. Everything felt disturbingly familiar to her.

After a few seconds of videoing the blue energy waves churning around inside the sphere, Cal said, "The sphere and workstations are recorded."

"Good," Tegan said. There was a slightly raised, hand-shaped pad on the surface of the counter at one of the stations. Tegan put her hand on it. Instantly, a humming noise resonated throughout the control room. A small seat appeared in front of her, floating in the air. She sat down, half expecting to drop to the floor, but the chair remained suspended. It adjusted to her weight, supported her back and thighs, and then moved forward until Tegan's legs were under the countertop. She was at a perfect working height. "Now that's ergonomically friendly."

"Easy there," Cal said. "We don't know how any of this works or what havoc we could cause by touching things. We just may launch ourselves into space."

She reached out, ready to touch one of the now glowing symbols.

Cal stepped back and began recording. "You sure you want to play with those?"

"Stop worrying so much." Tegan placed her hand on top of the lighted pad, and the control room came to life.

The floating sphere activated itself, and the screen that appeared reminded Tegan of a holographic plasma screen she'd once seen in a sci-fi movie. The sphere descended and enlarged, like a balloon filling with air. At the same time, the area in front of her workstation emitted random pulses of light. The panels lit up, and holographic images of symbols appeared in front of her.

As Cal recorded everything, a white light appeared above them, adding more illumination to the darkened chamber. Other lights flashed from various places and more holographic symbols materialized in the ether, each staying lit for a second, then morphing into a different symbol.

It reminded Tegan of a file selection menu. She touched one of the symbols.

"I will ask again, are you sure you want to play with those controls?" Cal said.

"If we don't explore and experiment a little, we won't know what works and what doesn't."

"I think you playing haphazardly with *anything* in here is a very dangerous and foolish idea. I am advising against it."

"Noted," she replied as she touched several more symbols. There was no reaction. "I guess it doesn't like me anymore. None of the symbols seem to be repeating, either."

"Good, but let's not say it doesn't like you. Maybe it just doesn't understand your commands."

Tegan spotted a raised, circular pedestal next to a far wall. "I guess it's time to try something new." She pushed back from the workstation and stood. The seat disappeared as she walked toward the raised platform.

Cal said, "Don't even think about standing on that thing."

"We'll have to test it someday. May as well be now." She stepped onto the platform before Cal could say another word and said, "Beam me up, Scotty." The base of the platform glowed, and alternating red and green lights pulsed in a blue aura rising from the base. It looked like water rising in a tube. The light pulses grew in intensity, and an electrical charge built up around her legs. She leaped up and over the blue light, which had reached knee height. She landed hard and sprawled on the floor. The lights disappeared just as quickly as they popped on when the platform had activated.

Cal gaped at her with both relief and disbelief. "Are you trying to kill yourself and give me a heart attack?"

"No, at least not yet. We just got married. I think giving you a heart attack comes later in our relationship. But I guess I could be more cautious."

Cal smirked and helped her up. "Are you alright?"

"I'm fine. We need to figure out what all of this is and how it works. Judging by the number of workstations, I'd say this was a busy place once and had quite a few aliens working here."

"You mean, NIBs. At least that's what Rob calls them, remember?"

"Yeah, Nonterrestrial Intelligent Beings."

"I think we've seen all there is to see on this level."

"Not so fast." She walked back to the recliners and knelt beside the one nearest the sphere to take a closer look. Each recliner was about eight feet long and three feet wide. There were arm-and-headrest indentations molded into the material "These look like they are designed to fit beings that are taller than us."

"I agree," Cal said.

"Why don't we head down to level three and see what's there."

"So this is going to be level two?"

"Yeah, but I think we should call it the control room. That'll make things clearer. The portal entrance will be level one."

"You're the boss."

They walked to the wider barrier that overlooked the cavern. Tegan put her hand on the palm reader and walked through.

"Are we just going to leave the lights on?" Cal asked as he followed her out.

"Unless you know how to turn them off."

The ramp continued to widen as they proceeded farther down. Once it leveled off on the third level, several passageways led back under the control room. The ramp continued down, curving slightly until it met the cavern floor on the fourth level.

"I guess we explore these corridors on the third level first," Cal said.

"None of these corridors has an energy barrier at its opening. I guess they aren't as important to operations as the control room."

They took the first corridor they came to and found door after door lining the passageway.

"There has to be at least fifty doors along this corridor," Cal said. Each one appeared sealed. The doors were a lighter shade of composite and lacked the crystals that were in the wall.

Tegan stopped in front of a door and placed her hand on one of the symbols on the wall next to it. The door disappeared, and the interior of a room became bathed in blue light. "The room is small," she said as she walked into the room.

Cal looked in and said, "A bit austere, but it matches the décor of everything else we've seen. Let me record it."

An oversized recliner was against one wall. It was smaller than the ones in the control room, but was made of the same formfitting material. It had a pillow on one end and indentations for a person's arms and legs.

"That must be a bed," Tegan said. "There are symbols on the walls. I imagine if I touch them, other furnishings will materialize like the chair did in the control room."

"Let's not do that just yet. We need to check some more of the rooms along this passageway, then the rest of this level. I don't want to spend too long down here. Let's just peek inside and move on."

They checked the next ten rooms and they were all the same as the first.

"I think we can skip the rest of the rooms," Tegan said.

"I agree," Cal replied and stopped recording to save the battery and memory in the camera. "Let's call this area the dormitory."

"Okay."

"I keep expecting to see something or someone lying in one of the recliners," Cal said. "This reminds me of walking through a Halloween house of horrors. All we need are bats, cobwebs, and human bones stacked in a corner."

"There's no one here."

"This corridor extends well past the back wall of the control room," Cal said. "I think we're close to being under the beach on the eastern side of the island."

"This place is definitely larger than I expected."

When they reached the end of the corridor, they discovered even more corridors. One looked as if it went deeper under the island. Another ran perpendicular to the one they had just exited.

"This could take hours to explore," Cal said.

"Yes. Let's see what we can see in the next thirty minutes."

They took the tunnel that went deeper under the island. There was less light here. Cal turned the light on the video camera. The corridor seemed endless. After several minutes, they stopped.

"I don't know how much further this goes, but I think we should check this one out when we have better lighting and more time," Cal said. "This is the type of place in the movies where the aliens grab you. Let's check the other passageways."

They retraced their steps and took another passageway. A few minutes later, they came to a triangle-shaped door. Tegan touched the symbol on the wall, and the door disappeared. The room was empty. "This could be a storage area," Tegan said.

"Did you notice the color of this door is different than those on dormitory row?"

"Yes. The variations in color and shape could signify they're used for different purposes."

They continued down the hallway until they came to an archway with nothing but darkness beyond. Tegan walked through the archway and into the room and ran into a wall a few steps in.

"Ouch!"

Cal snatched his dive knife from its sheath. "What is it?"

"I ran into a wall."

"Wait a second." Cal put his dive knife away. "Did you hurt yourself?"

"No, I'm fine. Shine the light in here."

When Cal walked through the archway with the light, he could easily see what had happened. The wall angled away from the opening. "No blue lighting in here either." He filmed the oddly shaped room. "So why do some parts of the facility have power and some don't? More importantly, where is all this power coming from?"

"I've been wondering that myself."

"And why is everything so clean?" Cal asked.

"If water evaporating when it hits the floor is any indication, I'd say it's self-cleaning."

They came to three more sealed doorways at the end of the corridor. When Tegan touched the symbols at the first door, it didn't open. She tried the next two and got the same results.

"That's interesting. Why won't these open?" Tegan asked.

"Maybe our sightseeing time has expired and the owners are telling us to leave."

Tegan shook her head. "Not likely."

The corridor widened as they approached the last group of doors along the way back to the ramp. The doors were huge and looked to have been made of white marble.

"Wow, these doors are different," Cal said. "They're the size of those on an airplane hangar." He recorded them.

Tegan touched the symbol by the first door. The white doors split apart at the center and retracted without making a sound. The room behind them was incredibly large—and empty. "Nothing. This is really getting boring," she said.

"These rooms had to be for storing very large items," Cal said.

"Let's check the other two."

They, too, were empty. As they continued toward the ramp they found another lighted corridor just before they reached the opening to the cavern. Inside were rows of small rooms. Each one had a small door the same color as those in the dormitory. Tegan touched the symbol on the wall by the first one, and the door disappeared. Inside, flat plates jutted from the walls at a forty-five-degree angle, with pinprick holes in the end of each of them. They were nearly eight feet high.

"Shower nozzles?" Tegan said, looking quizzically at Cal.

"That's my guess. Nice to know the aliens have good hygiene habits."

Tegan shook her head, and Cal recorded the room.

Farther down the corridor, the next series of doors also opened into small cubicles. Tegan touched a symbol just inside the door and an oval receptacle the size of a toilet appeared. "Well, if I'm right about what this is, then they have a digestive system."

"Yeah, but what do they eat?" Cal asked.

A few minutes later, they found the galley.

"You asked what they eat. Let's find out." Tegan touched the symbol by one of several recessed areas. Nothing happened.

"Maybe whatever you ordered takes time to cook," Cal said. A small opening appeared in the wall next to the symbol Tegan had touched. "See?"

Tegan looked inside. "Nothing there."

"Don't stick your hand in. It could end up being cooked." Cal filmed the area. When he was done, they worked their way back to the ramp.

"It looks like all the rooms are empty," Tegan said. "The galley didn't work, and what I think are storage rooms are all empty. That adds up to this being an abandoned facility."

Cal checked his watch and saw they had been exploring for over forty minutes. He figured the others would be getting worried. "I think that takes care of the tour of the third level. Let's check out the fourth level and head back up so the others don't become alarmed."

"I imagine they're getting low on air out there," Tegan said.

They walked to the ramp and started down. The ramp was wider and not as steep here. The bottom of the cavern flattened out nearly forty feet below the third level.

When Tegan reached the bottom, she turned and looked back at the portal, then said, "It looks like the portal extends up from the base of the third level."

"Yeah. This level is below the ledge that we saw outside the portal. We're definitely over a hundred feet below the surface. I wonder if we're under atmosphere and will need to decompress." Cal said.

"I don't think so. An alien species wouldn't design a facility which required them to decompress every time they left if they had a humanlike physiology. I also felt a change in pressure when we entered."

"I felt it, too. I think we'll be okay."

Looking around at the extensive floor area, Tegan decided this had to be where they docked their ships. "It looks like the rear wall on this level is still hundreds of feet away," she said, her voice echoing from the walls.

"It has to be four hundred feet from the portal to the back wall," Cal said.

They walked to the back wall and found all manner of odd-looking pieces of equipment stacked neatly. They were devoid of dust or dirt, as if they had been cleaned recently.

"Those large, triangle-shaped frames on the floor appear to be locking mechanisms," Cal said. "I think their spacecraft came through the barrier and landed on those frames. Then the aliens unloaded their cargo and stored it on the third level. Perhaps this area was also used like a dry dock where they could make repairs."

Tegan couldn't disagree with Cal's assessment. She noticed two silhouettes on the other side of the barrier. "Cal, turn the recorder light on and point it up toward the barrier."

Both figures waved back. "They can see us all the way down here. At least they know we're still alive," Cal said, then he began recording the area.

Tegan walked over to one of the landing platform frames. There were three in the center and three more spaced seventy to eighty feet apart, forming a large triangle. There was another set of six docking frames closer to the portal. "Well, if the positioning of the frames means anything, I'd say their spacecraft is triangularly shaped."

"I agree," Cal said. "The bay is designed to hold two ships of the same size."

Tegan looked closely at one of the docking frames and pushed down on it. The frame moved slightly downward, and then it returned to its previous position when she stopped pushing on it. "It senses weight and adjusts for it, like the chair upstairs. But if this moved under the little force I put on it, their ships must not be very heavy."

"Maybe the frames are designed to react to even a small weight difference. Who knows?"

They walked to the back wall again.

Cal looked up and said, "The hangar bay is at least 120 feet high."

Along the back wall under an overhang, several large storage bins were stacked on top of one another. They lifted one down and examined it. The sealed bin had symbols embedded across the top of it.

Tegan ran her hand around the edges, feeling for a seam, but there wasn't one. Try as she might, it wouldn't open. "There has to be a way to get this open," Tegan said, running her hand over the top of the bin for the third time.

"Maybe it's a magnetic lock or requires a special tool to open it."

Tegan spotted a dark opening hidden in the wall under the ramp. She walked over to it. "Looks like another corridor. I can't see the end of it. It's too dark in there." She walked into the corridor and said, "This may be the last area we need to explore."

"Or it could be linked to even more of the facility like the corridor that led into the void on level three," Cal replied. "Let's get it done."

They started down the dark hallway. After a few steps, the floor slanted downward, and Tegan could feel a pulsing vibration beneath her feet. "You feel that?"

"Yes, I do," answered Cal.

Tegan knelt and put her hand on the floor. "It feels like energy pulses under the floor."

"This could be what Casey found with those new sensors the Navy is testing. Let's keep moving."

They walked on.

"Down and down we go," Tegan said. "We must be getting closer to the source. The vibration is getting stronger."

At the end of the corridor was an intense blue glow. They approached it, and found themselves blocked by another energy barrier.

"This is like a maze," Cal said.

Tegan saw the palm reader on the wall and looked at Cal.

"You may have the honors," Cal said.

Tegan placed her hand in the indentation, and the barrier disappeared. She and Cal walked into the room and saw a massive circular ball of blue light embedded in the wall behind some type of containment field. Tentacles of light extended from the ball of light, and disappeared into the walls. There was a workstation next to it. "I think we found the power source."

Cal placed his hand on the translucent shield. "It's pulsing. The tentacles look to be contained in some kind of clear fiber tube—probably made of the same stuff that's keeping the ball of energy in the wall." Cal stepped back and began recording.

"I wonder if it's generating the power or receiving it from somewhere else." She walked to the workstation next to the containment field. When she reached out to touch a symbol on the desktop, a light barrier materialized and stopped her hand from reaching it. "I think only someone adept at operating the system can use the workstation."

Cal finished recording. "That's probably a good thing. The recorder's battery is almost dead. I think we should head back to the cavern."

"Sounds good. We may need an engineer to figure out how the power station works."

When they reached the cavern floor, Cal looked toward the portal, then said, "I don't see anyone outside."

"That's strange." Then the sound of shuffling feet came from the control room. "Stop," she whispered. "Listen."

"Damn it, I knew they wouldn't stay outside," Cal said.

Tegan grabbed Cal's arm before he bolted up the ramp. She put her index finger to her lips and stood still, listening to the sound of the movement. The noise was too loud to be coming from only one person's feet moving across the floor.

"My money is on Knolls and Casey," Cal whispered.

Tegan shook her head and looked back up to the outer barrier again. Now she saw two figures hovering outside. She pointed. "I don't think it's one of us."

Cal cocked his head and his eyes widened. "Are you telling me you think it's the aliens?"

"Shush!"

PART TWO

"Ex nihilo nihil fit —
Out of nothing, nothing comes."

PARMENIDES

CHAPTER SEVEN

Dr. Mike Peters waved as a large Navy helicopter took off from the pad and turned westward for Key West Naval Air Station. He smiled, then gave it the finger and walked across the field toward the research complex. He had endured a long day of meetings with the auditors from the Naval Audit Service. The group of micromanagers from Washington had arrived for a surprise visit earlier that morning. Everything had gone smoothly, with one exception. They had asked about the test results from the Sound Surveillance System sensors, known as S3. He hadn't seen any of the preliminary data, so he couldn't provide a response to their inquiry. He'd explained that the research assistant that was working on the project had taken a short vacation and was due back in a few days. He promised to provide them with a detailed report as soon as she returned and finished her analysis.

The Navy SOSUS S3 system consisted of a line of underwater sensors that stretched from Cape Canaveral to the Mona Rift off Puerto Rico. It wasn't scheduled to be fully operational for two more weeks and then, only if their tests proved the system was ready. If it tested out as well as he thought it would, nothing moving on the surface or underwater would be able to avoid detection. The system was capable of identifying any form of propulsion equipment, and it could detect water displacement and calculate the mass of a vessel. Knowing that any preliminary test data was probably still in Casey Lane's queue, he headed for her office.

Assigned to the Naval Sea Systems Command, Dr. Peters was, in title, a civilian acoustical engineer, although he was responsible for much more. Originally, he was on loan to the Navy from his tenured position at the University of Miami. Then the Navy had made him an offer he couldn't refuse. For the last three years, he had been in charge of all experimental research in acoustic intelligence, ACOUSTINT, that was conducted at the Atlantic Undersea Test and Evaluation Center.

AUTEC was the Navy's version of Area 51, and was chosen for its strategic location in 1958. It offered the ideal setting for conducting undersea testing of underwater vehicles, weapon systems, and acoustics. AUTEC was ideally located on the Tongue of the Ocean, the TOTO, which offered a deep-water channel that allowed submarines easy access to the facility.

Known to only a select few, the Navy had attached a special investigative unit to AUTEC to investigate unidentified submerged objects in the 1960s. It was simply known as DSI. All strange or unexplained anomalies involving USOs or unusual underwater events were sent to the DSI office.

The S3 system was only a small part of what Peters was working on, and he hadn't thought much about it recently. Casey's first report on the tests wasn't due for another week. Casey was one of his best research assistants, and he knew her intimately. Their affair had lasted a few months. She had been a wild woman in bed, and for a while he considered moving to Andros so they could be together more often. His home and family were in West Palm Beach, and every other week he commuted to Andros to be "hands-on," as he liked to say, especially with Casey. After he mentioned the idea of their living together on Andros, Casey had distanced herself. They remained friends, but the romance was over, and he had moved on to a new love interest.

He walked into her office, sat down behind her desk, and powered up the computer. He noted that Casey's desk didn't have any pictures of family or assorted knickknacks lying around. It was sterile compared to the other desks in the office. After the computer finished its start-up, he opened her queue and scrolled through the files until he found the folder he sought.

Peters noted Casey had forwarded the S3 test data to an unknown email address. His stomach turned over. Why had Casey sent a classified analysis to an unknown receiver? He saw that she'd reviewed the data on July 25, the same day she'd left on vacation and the same day she'd sent the file out. He went through her file history and realized it was the last file she'd looked at before leaving. She'd never mentioned that the test results were even available. Something wasn't right.

He couldn't believe it. He checked the data again. A signal had been detected on June 23rd. The frequency of the pulses recorded from the new sensors was extremely low on the ULF band, and they were pulsing across the harmonic spectrum. It wasn't seismic. It was a generated signal from an undetermined source. He pulled up additional data and discovered that the pulsating signal was intermittent. He picked up the phone and placed a call he'd hoped he'd never have to make. Peters had to report the anomaly and the breach in security. He knew what was required under security protocols. He couldn't believe Casey had done this to him. He also knew his day was about to become really bad.

Five minutes later, a tall, thin woman walked into Casey's office. "Good afternoon, Dr. Peters," she said.

"It's afternoon, but I don't think it's good."

"I think you're right. Show me what you found."

After reviewing the findings, seeing they were forwarded to an unknown email address and then hearing that Casey had left the island immediately afterward, the woman stepped away and made a call from her cell phone. Peters couldn't hear the conversation, but he could tell from the woman's tone it was an intense one. When she disconnected, she returned and said, "Could these signals be an NNEMP?"

"I hadn't thought about it being a non-nuclear electromagnetic pulse. Yeah, it's possible, but not likely. The wavelength is odd for it to be high-powered microwaves, but I can't rule that out. The data indicates the pulses do have a high-energy output, but it's an unusual reading."

"The Russians are extremely advanced in their HPM technology. This may be something new. How well do you know Casey Lane?"

Peters figured she probably knew about their affair. "I know her *very* well. Casey's not a foreign agent, if that's what you're thinking."

"She may have found a commercial buyer for the information. Thank you, Dr. Peters. We'll take it from here. If she checks in, order her to return, but don't tell her why."

"I could just call her cell now."

"No. We'll ping it and determine where she is. I don't want her to become suspicious. Continue to monitor the new signal and forward all the information to me." She wrote an email address and another phone number on the pad in front of him. "You are not to discuss this with anyone else. You are the only person to have access to this data. Is that clear?"

"Yes."

The woman left.

"Casey, what have you done?" he said in a low voice.

Marsh Harbor — 1700 hours

Sgt. Chad "Ram" Ramstein hit the disconnect button on his secure satellite phone. He ran his hand across his close-cropped hair and put on his ball cap. "General Stewart isn't pleased with our progress," he told Sgt. Phillip Stillwell. "He suggested we start interviewing people on Man-O-War Cay."

"You want to take the ferry or rent a boat?"

"Let's rent," Ramstein answered. "He sounded stressed, and made it clear he needed answers yesterday."

"So you're saying we don't need to be covert about what we're doing?"

"That's exactly what I'm saying. We have fake federal agent creds. General Stewart said the Bahamian authorities have welcomed us. I think that gives us the clout to rattle some cages. I recommend we get to Man-O-War Cay ASAP."

"Charlie Mike," Stillwell replied.

The Delta operators looked like the hardened military men they were. Both were twenty-nine years old, tall, and built of solid muscle. The ball caps they wore did little to hide their military haircuts. The two men had served together for five years in Delta, and they had been hand-selected by General Stewart to run his special operations. The rest of their team was at the Hole-in-the-Wall. The two men rented a small outboard boat using their newly minted IDs and headed for MOW.

The White House — 1700 hours

Stacy Preston walked into the Oval Office with purpose. TC was sitting behind his desk, staring at the wall. "I just heard from my source at DSI," she told him. "They're picking up an intermittent pulse deep in the ocean in the Bahamas."

"You could have told me that without barging in here. There are enough rumors circulating about us already, and I don't need to be fielding questions that will distract me."

"I'm sorry. I was nearby when I received the call, and I thought I'd tell you in person."

"The damage is done. Your source thinks these pulses are related to the site in the Abacos?"

"They have to be. The signal was first detected on July twenty-third. The information about the pulses went from AUTEC to General Westfield's node and terminated at his fail-safe. The person who sent them was a research assistant named Casey Lane. She left the island for a supposed vacation after she forwarded the information."

Stacy handed TC her cell phone with Casey's picture and file. "I just received this enhancement from the video captured during the firefight in Hope Town. She's the woman who was with Westfield. She used to be a special operator in the Navy. After she was discharged, Westfield got her a job at AUTEC."

"Based on the results in Hope Town, she's certainly efficient at killing. What else do you know about her?"

"I haven't reviewed everything, but I know she's fluent in five languages and was trained as an infiltrator."

"Which means?"

"She'd deploy into hostile territory, alone, blend in, and gather intelligence. Her last mission went sideways. The Navy presumed she'd been killed. Three months later, she resurfaced. During the extraction several local civilians were killed."

"She's a survivor and someone who can cause us problems if she isn't dealt with," TC said. "If she worked for Westfield, we can assume she's privy to what he did. What were her duties at AUTEC?"

"She was assigned to acoustical intelligence. That's why she told Westfield about the signal."

"So they think the source is alien, and we know it's not Antediluvian." TC stood and walked around the desk. "What is the source of the signal?"

"The best that DSI has been able to determine is it's located somewhere in the Abacos."

"That's not telling us anything new."

"I directed General Stewart to send more operators to the area. If we saturate the islands with our people, I'm certain we'll find the source of the signal and the artifact."

"Did you clear our increased presence with the Bahamian prime minister?"

"Yes, sir. He welcomes our assistance."

"Very good. Send however many troops you think it will take. I want that site found, contained, and if necessary neutralized before the Antediluvians arrive."

Stacy left the Oval Office. As soon as she was out of the White House, she called General Stewart.

Palmer Land, Antarctica – July 28– 1700 hours

Manatu stood on the bridge of his ship. He had been monitoring Cal's and Tegan's cautious movement through the Outpost remotely and noted the systematic approach they'd taken to explore it. Tegan seemed less cautious than Cal. The Outpost was programmed to function independently, but he'd already had to turn off the Dogita field to prevent Tegan from being harmed when she stood on the ritual platform.

Takatu approached, the rustling of his forest-green robe announced his presence. Manatu looked at him. Takatu nodded and emitted a short burst of clicks.

Manatu replied, "Yes, I believe it is time to make contact with them. I have already energized the monitor."

"Do you wish me to remain here?"

"Yes, but I will be the only one they see during the initial contact."

The Outpost — 1705 hours

Tegan slowly edged her way up the ramp until she could see into the control room. Even through the protective barrier, she could see shadowy movement reflecting off the walls. Cal stepped up beside her. The shadows danced around the room while odd sounds filled the cavern.

Cal whispered, "I think something else turned on while we were gone. It sounds like static. I don't see anyone walking around in there."

"Well, there's only one way to find out what's happening." Tegan walked to the barrier, put her hand on the palm reader, and entered the control room. The opaque sphere crackled and whooshed as intense light bounced around inside it. The sphere was generating the shadows and sounds.

Cal walked up beside her. "The hair on my arms is standing on end. Any idea what that is?"

Without telling Cal what she planned to do, Tegan walked over to the recliner nearest the sphere and sat down. She stretched out, filling the indentations as best as her smaller frame could and looked up into the sphere.

"Get off of that," Cal demanded.

She ignored him. The metallic fabric felt like course ridges against her exposed skin. She felt as if the recliner was molding to her body. The headrest supported her head and neck. She relaxed and focused on the light in the sphere.

"Comfy?" Cal asked.

She could tell he was annoyed with her. She couldn't blame him, but she knew this was important. "Very much so. You should try one."

Cal shook his head. "No, thanks."

Tegan felt a warming sensation on her back, and then the recliner's armrests and headrest came alive and encircled her forearms and forehead, locking her in place. A microsecond later, transparent keypads appeared beneath each of her hands with blue lights flickering across them. Symbols rotated in the holographic ether around her fingers.

"Are you happy now?" Cal asked. "Can you get out of that before you launch us into space?"

Tegan smiled at him as he knelt beside her. "I'm not sure. The armrests feel snug around my arms. There's no pressure or pain associated with the headrest that's encircled my forehead. I don't feel restrained. I guess you could say it's like being swaddled. It's as if the recliner has conformed to my physique." Tegan lifted her right arm, and the armrest released it. "Guess that answers that question." Tegan put her arm back down, and the armrest molded itself around it again.

She wiggled her fingers over the two keypads. Suddenly, a heads-up display materialized in front of her face. Pulsating lights flickered in her eyes, and frame after frame of symbols scrolled across the holographic screen. She looked down at the keypads and saw the same picture displayed under her hands. The new symbols were unlike any she had seen before, but then again, everything in here was unlike anything anyone had ever seen before. The symbols appeared and disappeared quickly. Even if she knew what they meant, she couldn't have read them. A moment later the sphere went dark and the heads-up-display vanished. Then the sphere came back to life and Tegan found herself staring up at the three-dimensional image of a wizard. It was the same image she'd seen in her vision after her encounter with the drone last night.

Tegan caught the combined look of astonishment and wariness in Cal's eyes when he saw the image. She'd seen that look before. He was trying to decide if the image was a threat. The being was human-looking, with an angular face and long white hair, and his skin was as white as a sheet of paper, almost translucent. He looked old, as if he possessed the wisdom of the ages.

Tegan inhaled sharply when the being opened his eyes and found hers. He had a mischievous sparkle in his emerald eyes. They were larger than hers but not grossly so.

The man looked at Cal and gave him an acknowledging nod. She realized this was a live feed, but it was on a more advanced level. After all the discussion over the last week, and even with Tegan's encounter with the drone, she wasn't prepared to come face to face with an alien.

"Tegan," Cal whispered. "He has your eyes."

She didn't respond. Not only did the being have her eyes, but he also had an uncanny resemblance to her. He could pass as a relative. Had they copied her eyes and facial features when they scanned her? Was she looking at an interactive computer image, or was this what the alien really looked like?

There was a burst of audio clicks followed by a rapid staccato of chirps and squeals. Tegan not only heard but also felt the intensity of the audio. She recognized the sounds, but didn't know why. Cal move closer to her.

"That sounds like a dolphin echolocating," Cal said.

"I've heard those sounds before. It was just after I was scanned, when I tried to talk."

"I remember."

The sounds stopped while the being turned his head away from them. Tegan saw that the alien's skull was slightly larger and more elongated than hers. The alien turned back toward them, and the next audio burst sounded much like the first but sharper, as if background static had been removed. The being had yet to move his lips. She couldn't tell if he was making the noises or if it was an audio signal being generated elsewhere. A moment later the control panel under Tegan's right hand pulsed, and the headrest emitted a dark blue and pale rose-colored light which surrounded her forehead like a fog. Her first instinct was to pull away, but she fought the urge, fearing the image would disappear if she broke contact. She looked at the being and simply said, "Hello."

The alien nodded, and a moment later the control panel under Tegan's right hand pulsed. She felt the energy enter her body through the head-rest and her arms. It wasn't an electrical shock, more like an energy wave, similar to what she'd experienced with the marker.

Then the being said, "Welcome, Tegan Leigh Strong Locke," speaking in English. The voice was monotone and low-pitched, with a melodic waver. She detected an accent or inflection in the voice, as if it was being computer-generated. Maybe the computer was translating his chirps to English.

"Alright, we just jumped way beyond spooky here," muttered Cal.

Cal stepped behind the recliner. Tegan knew he did it to conceal his movement as he grasped the handle of his dive knife.

Tegan focused on the image and said calmly, "It is nice to meet you. You know my name. May we ask who you are?" She didn't know what else to say, even though a million questions were running through her mind.

"I am Manatu. I am an Igigi."

"An Igigi." Tegan paused. "You know who I am from your scan, but do you know me?" Tegan asked.

"That's an odd question," Cal whispered.

The Igigi processed the question, appearing as if he was waiting for a translation, then slowly said, "Yes, Tegan, we know you. We know your essence from your interaction with the … with the Gatekeeper. The scout craft we sent confirmed your essence."

"By the Gatekeeper, are you referring to the marker?"

There was another pause before Manatu responded. "Yes, it is there to govern entry. In order to be allowed access to the Outpost, you must be … accepted."

"I was accepted, but why not the others?" Tegan asked, fearing the answer.

Manatu responded more quickly this time. "They are not relations."

"And I am a relation?" she asked, wanting to confirm her theory about how the marker was indeed a genetic biometric lock.

"Yes, you carry the essence of an Igigi within you."

Tegan smiled at the validation and heard Cal's indrawn breath. She could tell he hadn't been ready to hear Manatu's statement, even though they'd speculated that was possible. "By my essence, are you referring to my DNA, my genetic sequencing?"

Manatu nodded. "The Gatekeeper could not verify your essence because it lacked specific genetic pairings. We needed to better understand you."

The statement didn't sound quite right, but she understood his meaning. Tegan knew that Cal was growing more defensive. Manatu must have noticed this, too.

"You are in no danger, Calvin Alexander Locke," Manatu said. "The portal is stable, and no harm will come to either of you while you are here."

Cal looked up at Manatu. "How the hell do you know who I am?"

"You are in Tegan's thoughts."

Tegan understood that the scout ship had captured not only her physical composition but had also downloaded her thoughts, feelings, and memories, which meant they were vulnerable. Manatu probably knew everything she did.

"What do you want from us?" Cal asked rudely.

"We want nothing from you. You sought us out. You are an inquisitive species, which is what first attracted us to you."

"You mean there are more like you?"

"Yes. We are the Watchers. I know you have many questions. I will answer them in time. It has been a long time since I have communicated in this manner, and it is difficult for me. I may not express myself as clearly as I should or in proper custom."

Cal asked, "How many more are there like you, and where exactly are you?"

"There are enough of us to watch over you. We are in the place you call Antarctica."

Tegan decided to end Cal's line of questioning. "I think you communicate very well," she said softly. "You understand our language. How is that possible?"

The Igigi blinked slowly, and Tegan thought it might be the first time she had seen him blink.

"We have observed and studied your kind for many thousands of years. We can speak all the languages spoken here, or have ever been spoken, since we arrived. We seldom have need to speak any of the native languages. The human method of communicating is highly inefficient and tedious."

"Exactly how long have you been watching us?" she asked.

"Over thirteen thousand years."

Tegan nodded. "And the clicking noise we heard at first is how you normally communicate?"

"Yes."

"Your language sends bursts of information all at once, and your symbols represent more than just words or sentences. Is that correct?" Cal asked.

"Yes."

"You have my eyes," Tegan blurted. At first, she thought she'd offended Manatu. It was the first time the Igigi showed any sign of an emotional response. His smile appeared forced, as if he hadn't done it for some time.

"No, Tegan. You have ours. You are of our essence. Was I not clear?"

Tegan smiled back at him. "Yes, you were clear, but how is that possible?" Tegan asked. "My parents are human."

"Yes, as are you, but we are alike genetically."

Tegan thought about that briefly, then said, "How can we be related?" She sounded as though she was struggling with an ugly secret.

Manatu waited a moment, then replied, "You were created by nature."

Tegan nodded. "For that to be true, it would mean that an Igigi mated with one of my ancestors, and I'm blessed to exhibit those recessive genes."

"Yes. The scan confirmed you are descended from the first pairing of a human and an Igigi. You are descended from Ninurtu, the last of his clan. We believed his essence was lost forever, but here you are."

Tegan could hardly believe what she was hearing.

"We need to study you." Manatu continued to look at her and slowly blinked. "You are a genetic oddity which we cannot explain. Your genetic sequence is like no other human we have seen since the twins from the first pairing."

"Twins." Tegan replied, feeling excited. "I'm a twin, the oldest."

"Yes. We know. All of the first-born daughters have given birth to twins. Your mother was a twin, was she not?"

"Yes. My aunt died before I was born."

"And your mother's eyes were green?"

"Yes, but not like mine. They were a lighter shade. My sister's eyes were blue."

Manatu nodded. "All second born are blue. I felt her loss in you."

Cal asked, "What do you mean by needing to study her?"

"She is an abomination, Calvin Locke. She should not exist. Ninurtu and his kind were disavowed long ago."

"What do you mean by disavowed?" Tegan asked.

Manatu frowned. "Ninurtu was the leader of a clan that chose to disregard one of our primary tenets, so he was disavowed and cast out. After the dark times passed, he chose a human mate, Oda, and his descendants interbred with humans. After thousands of years of pairings, we thought the Igigi essence was lost in your species."

"You mean his DNA became part of my family's junk DNA." Tegan felt like a specimen in a petri dish. She shivered, and her cheeks grew hot with anger. "I'm not an abomination. I may be an anomaly by your standards, but not an abomination. I'm a human being."

"You are indeed. However, you also possess Ninurtu's traits. You are loyal, protective, and passionate. Your intellect is far above the normal range of most humans. And most interestingly, you are able to take human life without feeling remorse."

"Wait just a minute," said Cal. "Tegan didn't kill because she wanted to. She killed to save her own life and mine. She is a kind and giving person with a good heart. I don't appreciate your insinuation that she's a cold-blooded killer."

Manatu nodded. "I understand your emotional response. I meant nothing disparaging. I was only stating a fact."

Tegan knew that Manatu was right. She had killed without remorse. She did have all the traits he mentioned. Apparently, she was a descendant of a rogue and violent Igigi. "Can you be more specific about what tenet he violated?" Tegan asked, not really sure this was the time or place for this conversation.

"Like you, Tegan, he chose to act and kill rather than watch."

"Who did he kill?" Cal asked.

"The Etu Inu Idimmu. Translated to English from the language of the second civilization we created in Sumer, it means Dark-Eyed Demons. They came to this world over seven thousand years ago seeking to eradicate your species. Ninurtu and his clan could not detach themselves from your kind. Instead of watching, he and his clan waged war against them. There was great loss of life. We could not condone his behavior, nor could we take action to stop him."

Tegan was stunned. *Were these Etu Inu Idimmu the same creatures she knew as Antediluvians?* she wondered.

"Igigi are forbidden from killing any intelligent life form," Manatu added. "We watch, educate, and nurture the development of all intelligent life. We are a peaceful species. Ninurtu and his clan chose a different path."

Tegan didn't know what to say. Some part of her wanted to defend Ninurtu. She could tell that Manatu knew what she was thinking. "The Etu Inu Idimmu are coming back. They are the Antediluvians."

Manatu nodded. "Yes. We know what you are capable of doing, and if what we have seen through your eyes becomes a reality, then you and your offspring may offer the only hope for human survival. But your actions must be tempered."

"Are they your enemy?" Cal asked.

"No, Calvin Locke, they are not. We do not wish to abandon you, but unlike Ninurtu, we will not kill to protect you. We will not wage war against them. Ninurtu is responsible for teaching humans how to fight as a unified group. He and his human army slaughtered thousands of the Etu Inu Idimmu. If they are returning, it can be for only one reason, and that is a concern for both of our species."

"What kind of enemy are we facing?" Tegan asked.

"They are takers, users, and killers. They come from a dead, cold planet with a dying star. Earth is a suitable replacement for them. It is rich in resources, and human beings offer them a species to be subjugated."

"How many of them are there? Cal asked.

"I cannot say with certainty, but it will be all of them. More than a billion are possible."

"If you won't fight them, why would that be a concern of yours?" Tegan asked.

"We would have to leave before it was time."

"When is it your time to leave?" Cal asked.

"I cannot say."

Cal snorted. "Why not?"

"Our time to leave is now up to Tegan."

"Why would that be up to me?" Tegan asked, growing confused. This conversation wasn't what she had imagined first contact would be like.

Manatu didn't answer right away. He just stared down at her. Finally, he said, "There are many reasons that I may not speak at this time."

"What the hell does that mean?" Cal asked.

"Was I not clear? I cannot answer at this time."

"With your technology, surely you can confirm if the Antediluvians are coming back here," Cal said.

"Our scout ships are searching now. What little Etu Inu Idimmu activity we've seen since they left many millennia ago has not concerned us. They have always come in small numbers. We have watched them take samples and depart."

"So they've been here all along. I thought you said they were defeated and left. And what do you mean by samples?" Cal said.

"They return periodically in small numbers. A few ships a year, nothing threatening. The samples are human specimens."

"You just let them take people?" Tegan asked. She was outraged.

"Yes. We cannot interfere. I thought I had made that clear."

"You said you can't kill another species, but if you permit the Etu Inu Idimmu to kill us, aren't you just as responsible for the deaths of an intelligent species?" Tegan asked.

Manatu nodded. "That is the same argument Ninurtu once used. The answer is, no. We are the Watchers. Our goal has always been to improve your species, and we have done so in many ways. You were at one time peaceful and devoid of greed and personal ambition. You killed only to survive. Ninurtu turned you into warriors and spread the disease of greed and power among your factions. His actions brought about the failure of our primary objective."

Cal stood up. "I don't see how keeping us alive was a failure. From what you have told us, Ninurtu was our savior. It sounds to me like he gave our species a chance to survive and gave your kind a reason to stay behind and watch."

"Ninurtu did save your species, and he gave us a continued purpose. We are grateful to him for the outcome but not the means by which he attained it."

"Your species has a funny way of showing appreciation," Cal said.

Manatu looked back at Tegan and spoke in his melodic way. "We do not expect you to understand. If the Etu Inu Idimmu created modified human beings to assist them in their quest as your thoughts revealed, I'm not sure how they will be stopped. If it is possible to stop them, you will be the key."

"You didn't know about the Awakened?" Cal asked.

"No. Our first knowledge of their existence came from our scan of Tegan's thoughts."

Manatu's words resonated deep in her being. She didn't understand it all, but if they'd downloaded her thoughts, they knew about Deep Sky. She could tell there was an underlying message going unsaid. She sighed, then said, "You said Sumer was the second civilization. What was the first?"

"Twelve thousand years ago, the land above you gave rise to a harmonious human society. Then the sea took it from us as the ice melted. You still have many questions, and your friends grow concerned by your prolonged absence. You should return to them. They are welcome to explore this place. Nothing here can bring them harm. Tegan, I will come to you soon so we can speak at length."

A soft pulse of blue light flashed across her forehead. "Until then," she said, smiling, understanding the message she had received.

The sphere blinked back to its original state, the soft blue energy once again dancing around inside it.

"Hey, we still need to know some things, a lot of things, and I don't take kindly to him calling you an abomination. Why did you let him go? He said he's coming here when?" Cal asked. "How many of the Igigi are coming? How are they getting here? I have a lot more questions."

"Relax, Cal. He will arrive tonight."

"Now how would you know that?"

"He told me."

"What do you mean? You mean you received a message in the last flash of light?"

"Yes. Let's go back to the others and tell them what we've found." When Tegan thought about standing, the arm and head restraints disengaged.

"You seem rather calm about all this. You just found out you have an alien ancestor in your family tree. I'd be very unnerved by that."

"I'm not unnerved. It all makes sense to me now. You could have Igigi genes, too. My DNA just paired differently than others that carry the genes. I've always thought differently than most people, including my parents and sister. I envisioned things and saw things that I never quite understood. Coming here after my family was killed was one of those things I knew needed to happen, but I didn't know why. Now I do."

Tegan thought back to that day in Alessia's apartment and the strong pull that guided her to the Abacos. "Cal, I think I knew to come here because my DNA is hardwired to return here in a crisis. This is a sanctuary. It's like how salmon know where to return to spawn."

"So you think your alien genes sent you to me?"

"Something like that. Does my having dominant Igigi genes concern you? You know that our children will carry those genes."

Cal smiled and took her by the shoulders. "Are you kidding me? It just makes you more mysterious and intriguing. Besides, if the Igigi mated with humans back then and cross-bred over the too-many-to-count generations, then like you said, we all have some Igigi in us. You're just the lucky one who gets to express your dominant alien genome." He kissed her lightly on the lips. "Let's get back to the others before they panic. You want to tell them about the alien factor or should I?"

"I think I should be the one to tell them. I also think we should ease into the alien encounter after we're back on the boat." Tegan put her arms around Cal's waist and squeezed.

CHAPTER EIGHT

Man-O-War Cay — July 28 — 1740 hours

Ramstein and Stillwell tied up at the dock and stayed on the boat as they reviewed the new intelligence update packet from General Stewart. They studied the photographs and bios of everyone that was possibly involved as they went through the comprehensive files.

"It would appear that the place to start is the dive shop," Ramstein said, pointing down the dock. "Aldeberie owns it, and someone there has to know how to reach him."

"That's the kid's ferry tied up over there."

Ramstein did a quick check and confirmed the *Alde I* did belong to Edward Aldeberie. "Looks like it's out of service."

"Can I help you with something?" Hans Bechmeyer asked as he approached the men.

"We're looking for Garth Aldeberie," Ramstein answered, flashing his fake Homeland Security credentials.

"You're investigating the shootings?" Hans asked. His voice was deep and his German accent strong.

"We are assisting the Bahamian authorities. Our investigation has widened, and we understand Garth Aldeberie knows just about everything that goes on around here. We need to ask him some questions."

"I'm taking care of his business interests while he's on holiday. I'm Hans Bechmeyer. I don't know where Garth is right now. He may be on Treasure Cay or over on Grand Bahama. He said he was going to check on some property there. I doubt he would know anything about the shootings."

"That's his son's ferry, isn't it?" Stillwell asked.

"Yes."

"Is he around?"

"No. I thought you were looking for Garth."

Ramstein knew that the old man was getting suspicious. "Edward runs the ferry, so we thought he might have seen someone that fits the description of the woman that was involved." Ramstein pulled up a picture of Casey Lane on his tablet and showed Hans the picture. "You ever see her?"

Hans took a moment to study the photo. "Yes, I've seen her. I saw her leave yesterday afternoon. I think she went over to Treasure Cay. That little girl had something to do with the killings?"

"She was there. She may just be a witness, but we need to talk to her. You have any idea when Garth or Edward will be back?"

"Sure don't. If you leave your name and number, I'll have one of them call you."

Ramstein believed Hans really didn't know where any of them were, and he decided not to push any further. "I think we'll try over on Treasure Cay. If they aren't there, then we'll come back. We may need to ask you a few more questions."

"I'll be here. How about that number?"

"I can't give it to you. It's a confidential line. Just call the Bahamian authorities, and they'll contact us. Thanks for your help."

Ramstein started the outboard motor, and they headed for Treasure Cay.

The Outpost — 1750 hours

Tegan and Cal left the control room and walked up the ramp to the portal. She checked the time and saw they'd been inside the Outpost for almost two hours. She could see Jessica and Garth standing on the platform outside the portal. Jessica no longer wore the FFM and Tegan realized that she and Garth must have changed tanks. Knolls, Alex, and Brian floated behind them.

"Looks like Nate went back to the boat," Tegan said. She waved at them to come through the barrier.

Jessica came through first.

"Take your fins off," Tegan said as she took her hand and guided her away from the ledge. "There aren't any railings, so be careful."

Jessica spit the regulator from her mouth, and said, "Wow!"

"That was my first reaction, too, but it gets even better," Tegan said.

A few seconds later, Garth poked his head through the barrier.

Jessica said, "Come on in. The air's fine."

Garth retreated to the other side of the barrier and removed his fins. Tegan could see him motioning for the others to follow him. As the group entered the cavern, one after the other, Cal captured their first reaction using the remaining battery life on the digital recorder.

Tegan didn't realize until that moment that they hadn't recorded any of the exchange with Manatu. They gave the others an overview of what they would find on the different levels before escorting them down the ramp. As they explored, Tegan and Cal explained what they had tested already, giving everyone a brief demonstration. Tegan avoided the pedestal she'd tried earlier. The control room and the recliners seemed to be everyone's favorite.

Tegan checked her watch and said, "We should head back."

"I think we need to explore a little longer," Knolls said.

"Okay, but it's getting late," Tegan replied.

Treasure Cay Marina — 1815 hours

Sergeant Ramstein docked their small outboard alongside a floating dock.

"Ram, we have company," Sergeant Stillwell said.

Ramstein saw a man wearing a white, short-sleeve shirt and tan shorts walking toward them.

"Afternoon. What can I do for you?" Dock Master Howard Finley asked.

"We're looking for Garth or Edward Aldeberie. Hans Bechmeyer said they may be here," Ramstein answered, flashing his credentials. He could see Finley tense.

"You're American?"

"Yes. We're helping with the murder investigation."

"Why are you looking for them?"

Ramstein was tiring of the banter. "A young woman was involved in the shooting. We know she was on Man-O-War. Hans said she came over here. He also thought Garth and Edward might be here. We think they may know where the woman is."

"Why do think they would know her?"

Stillwell said, "Just answer the question."

Finley cocked his head and said, "I don't need to answer anything. You have no authority here."

Stillwell stepped between Ramstein and Finley, and said, "You're right. However, if you don't answer our questions, I'll have to call my boss. Then he'll call his boss, and eventually the Bahamian authorities will arrive and ask you the same questions we need answered. Then we'll have to decide if you're obstructing the investigation and possibly abetting a fugitive. I'm sure there will be more investigating and legal drama that'll take days to sort out. So, for the sake of expediency, we'd appreciate any help you can provide."

Finley looked at both men, then said, "You flashed those IDs pretty fast. All I had time to read was United States Government. You guys are FBI?"

"Actually, we're with Homeland Security," Ramstein replied. "What's your name?"

"Howard Finley. I'm the dock master here."

"The incident in Hope Town involved a terrorist cell operating in the islands. That's all I can tell you."

Finley shook his head and said, "A terrorist cell is operating here? That's unbelievable. I don't know where Garth is. He stopped by here earlier this morning. He and Cal were with a woman I'd never seen before. They went to the airport to pick someone up. I didn't see them come back."

"Is this the woman?" Ramstein asked, showing him Casey's picture.

"No. This woman was older, heavier, and wore glasses. Her name was Alex. Garth said she was staying with Cal on their boat."

Ramstein scrolled through the photo file and found Alex Hutchins-Winslow's picture. "Is this Alex?"

"Yes. I can't believe Cal and Garth would have anything to do with terrorists."

"We think the woman in the first picture I showed you is a terrorist. She's military-trained and has befriended Garth and his friends without them knowing her real identity. She's probably using them as cover. I doubt they know what she is capable of doing. She's very dangerous. That's one of the reasons we need to find everyone with Garth."

"I understand. Garth and Cal were on the *Deep Current* when they were here. Garth mentioned they were taking a holiday. He usually doesn't go very far from home. I imagine he's with Cal on one of the islands. Edward wasn't with them. He's probably running that ferry of his. Why don't you just call him?"

"We don't want them doing anything stupid like trying to apprehend her on their own. What's the *Deep Current* look like?" Stillwell asked.

Finley told him.

"Thanks for your help," Ramstein said. "I think we'll head back to Man-O-War and see if we can catch up to them there."

Once they left the dock, Stillwell said, "I think if we find one of them, we'll find them all."

"I agree. I'll call General Stewart and let him know about the second boat. I have a feeling they threw us a red herring. I think our men at Hole-in-the-Wall are searching in the wrong area. Let's check some of the other islands on our way back to Man-O-War. I have a feeling they're close."

Washington — 1850 hours

Stacy Preston was sitting at her desk when the phone rang. She sensed who it was. "Yes, General Stewart."

"I wanted to give you an update," Stewart said. "I have sent three more teams to Grand Bahama Island. We haven't found anything around the south end of Abaco yet. One team thinks there may be a second boat involved. They're checking the Out Islands now for it. I told the teams to focus on the marinas. There's a guy on Man-O-War who's taking care of Garth's businesses for him. His name is Hans Bechmeyer, but he didn't know anything."

"General, we need them found. Someone knows where they are. Put a team on Hans, and monitor all of his calls."

"It has already been ordered. We have tracers on every phone associated with any of them or their businesses. We'll find them."

"You'd better. If you have to, lean hard on the people who know them."

"Stacy, if I'd had the full intelligence packet sooner, my first team wouldn't have been ambushed and killed."

"You'll get the information we deem necessary when we want you to have it. Is that clear?"

"Yes."

"Good," Stacy replied, then hung up.

The Outpost — 1900 hours

Tegan was exhausted, and most of the group looked tired, too. Casey and Nate would have to wait until tomorrow for their turn to explore. She needed to tell everyone some things.

"It's time to go," Tegan said. They all looked disappointed, but there was no reason to stay any longer. She had watched Alex and Brian go from workstation to workstation, panel to panel, and they had photographed everything. They hadn't seen or heard the best part yet.

Tegan knew that Knolls had explored every room, and she could see the weight of responsibility weighed heavily on his shoulders.

"This facility belongs to the good aliens, right?" Knolls asked for the third time.

"Yes, Rob. I'll explain more when we're topside."

"So there's more to explain?"

"Yes. Much more. Now everyone, let's go!"

As Tegan went through the barrier into the ocean, she could tell the sun was getting lower in the sky. The light was subdued, and the colors around her were less vibrant. Once everyone was through the barrier, the camouflage hologram once again covered the entrance.

East of Great Guana — 1900 hours

Chris Ramstein first spotted the mast of a catamaran and then a motor yacht alongside. He slowed the boat and picked up his binoculars. The sterns were facing away from him. "I can't read the names. There's a dingy tied alongside the catamaran. We may have them."

Stillwell took the binoculars from him. "The boats match the description. I see a skinny, white guy sitting in the cockpit of the catamaran. We're too far away for me to ID him. Do we call it in?"

"Not yet. Let's see if we can get close enough to read the names on the boats."

Casey was in the salon when she noticed the small boat approaching. It slowed and stopped. She grabbed the binoculars from the chart table and trained it on the boat. Two men were looking in her direction, one with binoculars. She could tell by the haircuts and their mannerisms that the men were military. "Shit!" She shouted. "Nate, don't look around. Just keep doing what you're doing. Are you in contact with any of them below?"

"Not yet."

"Check and see if you can raise anyone. We've been spotted by hostiles."

"What do we do now?"

"We take them out before they can report our location. I'll get Cal's gun."

"It's in a drawer by the chart table."

"I know where it is." Casey opened the drawer and found the Glock 21. She checked the magazine and saw it was full and there was a round chambered. "Doesn't he have any more magazines?"

"I—I don't know," Nate stammered.

"I'll have to live with what's in the gun."

"Still no answer from the site," Nate said.

"Keep trying." Casey ducked below the gunwale and crawled past Nate. "Are the keys in the dinghy?"

Nate stood and walked to the side of the boat, then said, "Yup."

"Climb in the boat, start the engine, and leave it running, then untie the line and get back aboard. We need to warn the others, so keep trying to reach someone."

Nate climbed aboard *Little Breeze* and started the engine. "Okay, it's done. The line's off and *Little Breeze* is starting to drift away. Casey, what are you planning to do?"

"Attack." Casey jumped into *Little Breeze* in one fluid motion, then pushed the throttle all the way forward and turned straight for the enemy.

∞

Ramstein saw the auburn-haired woman jump into the dinghy. She matched the description of Casey Lane, and the way she had suddenly appeared told him she was going to attack them. "Got her, she's headed right for us." He knew there wasn't time to call it in. "Get ready, Phil. She doesn't look friendly."

"Do you think she knows who we are, or is she just coming out to warn us off?"

"Judging by how fast she's approaching, and the fact she crouched down, I'd say she intends to engage," Ramstein replied.

"Goddamn it! We got no cover in this boat, and the fiberglass hull isn't going to stop any bullets."

"This is gonna be a straight-up marksmanship exercise. I'll drive, you shoot."

∞

Casey saw the boat accelerate toward her. One of the men braced himself with one hand on the gunwale while holding a semiautomatic in his other hand. The boat operator steered so that they would pass on her port side. She knew she was outmatched. She couldn't evade them and shoot accurately at the same time.

As the boats neared each other, Casey made a decision. She couldn't let them escape regardless of the outcome of the firefight. She waited until they were only a few yards apart. Even with the din of the outboard, she could hear the bullets whizzing past her head. She raised her Glock and fired at the driver of the boat. He slumped sideways and fell over the side. She whipped her boat hard to port. The *Little Breeze* struck the men's boat at an angle with a deafening crunch, then flew over its stern, hitting the outboard motor hard enough to silence it. The force of the impact tore the Glock from her hand. She regained control of the *Little Breeze* and swung it hard to starboard as several rounds sliced through the air behind her, hitting the engine. She felt a searing pain in her left shoulder as a round tore through it. She ducked down behind the gunwale and screamed in anger. This was the second time in two days that she'd been shot.

Casey found the Glock just as the engine sputtered and died. She looked back at the outboard engine. It had two bullet holes in it, and gasoline spurted from the fuel line. The two disabled boats weren't far apart now. Another slug tore off a chunk of the gunwale near her. She belly-crawled aft, waited a few seconds, and took a deep breath. Then she popped up and fired twice. The man fell backward into his boat.

The smell of gasoline was growing stronger now. She worried about a hot casing igniting it if she had to fire again. She needed to find a way to stop the flow. The boats had drifted closer to each other. Just as they were about to touch, the man jumped up and fired. She saw the muzzle flash at the same instant she felt the pain in the right side of her chest. She fired two more times, but knew she'd missed. As she fell back, more rounds hissed over her head.

Cal had heard the collision above him, and he was close enough to the surface to hear gunshots. When he broke the surface, he saw the *Little Breeze* drifting toward another boat. As the others broke the surface, he yelled, "Dive back down and head for the *Whispering Winds!*" He didn't wait for a response. He dove and swam toward the two boats as fast as he could.

He knew who was on the *Little Breeze*, and he was certain she was outgunned. As he approached the unfamiliar boat, he pulled his dive knife from its sheath, swam under the boat, dropped his tank, mask, and fins, and surfaced quietly, the way he'd been trained to do. He grabbed the gunwale and pulled himself into the boat in one quick motion. The man at the stern was aiming his gun at the *Little Breeze*. The rocking of the boat caused him to turn. The man's eyes went wide. He aimed his gun at Cal.

Cal knew he a was dead man. Then three shots rang out, and the man jerked and his arm dropped. Cal rushed him and drove his knife into the man's chest just below his sternum and pushed it upward, slicing into his heart. The man dropped his gun and crumpled into the bottom of the boat. Cal jumped into the *Little Breeze*. Casey lay sprawled on her back, his Glock still in her hand.

"Casey, you're hit!" Cal said.

Casey grimaced and said, "No shit."

Cal quickly checked her wounds. He knew she wouldn't live long without help. "Casey, are there any more of them?"

She shook her head and tried to sit up. "Get me out of this damn gas."

Cal helped her up and onto the other boat, then laid her down gently. He applied pressure to the chest wound with his hand. "You need to be airlifted to a trauma center."

"Yeah, I know." She coughed up blood. "There won't be time for that. I wish I could be there with you for the fight to come."

Cal nodded, then said, "Me, too."

"I don't think they … had time to report our position. I was … on them too fast."

"There was more than one of them?"

"Yeah, two. I shot one." She coughed. "He fell over the side … before I ran into their boat." She gave him a brave smile, then said, "I like your gun. It shoots true." Casey coughed again.

Cal could tell she knew she was about to die.

She grasped his arms and said, "Finish the mission." Her eyes glazed over, and she let out one last breath.

Cal closed her eyes. He heard the *Deep Current* engines firing up. He rolled the dead man over and removed his knife from the man's chest, then leaned over the side and cleaned the blood from it and his arms and hands.

Casey had saved his life.

A moment later, he heard the *Deep Current* coming closer. He slid his dive knife back into its sheath. "Thank you, Casey, for your sacrifice. We will finish this," he whispered.

"Cal, are you okay?" Tegan yelled, her voice fraught with concern.

He stood up and faced her. "Yes. Casey is dead. She shot this guy and saved my life. There's another dead body in the water around here somewhere." Cal looked toward the beach. There was a couple walking hand in hand not the least bit aware of what had just transpired.

"We need to find the other body before it floats up or washes ashore, then dispose of the bodies and their boat," Knolls said. "Is that a satellite phone?"

Cal turned and saw the phone in the bottom of the boat. "It is. I'm sure it's being tracked, so we need to move it and these boats soon. Casey said she didn't think they had a chance to report they'd found us before she attacked. Tegan, throw me a line."

"What about the body in the water?" Knolls asked.

"I'll go down and find it. I need to retrieve my tank and gear. Someone throw me a mask."

Garth tossed him a mask.

"Thanks, Garth. Tegan, *Little Breeze* is loaded with fuel."

"I know. I can smell it." Tegan tossed him a line. "You sure you're alright?"

Cal tied the boat off. "Yes. I'm very grateful to Casey."

"Me, too," Tegan said.

"She had a final request that I intend to see fulfilled."

"What did she ask you to do?" Tegan asked.

"To finish the mission. Garth, take the slack out of the line. Rob, I'll need you to help lift the body out of the water when I bring it up."

"Roger," Knolls replied.

Cal put his mask on and dove over the side. He swam down and found his tank sitting on the bottom. He slipped the BCD on, put his regulator in, and took a breath. He found his fins and mask floating nearby. He started his search in the area north of the boats. He figured they'd drifted south. It took several minutes, but he finally located the body. It was resting on the coral, blood seeping from the holes in the man's chest and head. A large barracuda was already taking an interest. He grabbed the man under the shoulders, swam back to the boat, and passed the body up to Knolls.

Cal pulled himself into *Little Breeze* and assessed the damage. The outboard engine cover had two holes in it. Little wisps of smoke were still coming out of the holes. Gasoline was no longer leaking from the fuel line. He looked up and saw Tegan standing with Knolls at the bow of the *Deep Current*. There were tears in her eyes as she looked down at Casey.

"I thanked her for saving you," she said to Cal.

Cal nodded.

"Time to leave," said Knolls.

They tied the two smaller boats together and used a short towline for the trip back to the *Whispering Winds*. Nate stood on the flybridge of the *Whispering Winds*. Cal heard the engines running already. Alex stood on the trampoline with Jessica, and Brian stood in the cockpit.

"Tegan, get back aboard the *Whispering Winds*. Take her back to Scotland Cay. Garth, Rob, and I will take care of the other boats and bodies."

"What about Casey?" Tegan asked.

Cal looked at Knolls. "Does Casey have any family?"

"I don't know," Knolls replied.

Tegan said, "I'll ask the others if she mentioned any." She jumped off the *Deep Current* and swam to the stern of the *Whispering Winds* and climbed aboard. A few moments later, she yelled, "Cal, no one knows if she had family."

"Commander Knolls," Cal said, "she was Navy." He didn't have to say anything else.

Knolls nodded. "I think a burial at sea would be appropriate. She wouldn't want it any other way."

"Garth, let's head southeast. We need plenty of deep water. Tegan, we'll meet you back on Scotland."

Four miles east of Scotland Cay, Garth stopped the *Deep Current*. As it drifted, they wrapped Casey in a bed sheet and tied a thirty-pound toolbox to her legs. Cal and Knolls stood at attention and saluted as Garth released her over the side. She slid beneath the surface and disappeared into the abyss.

Cal wasn't sure what to say.

Knolls said, "We commit this body to the deep. Allow her to rest in peace until the resurrection, when the sea shall give up her dead."

"Amen," Cal said.

"We'll have to remember to mark this spot someday," Garth said. "I have the GPS coordinates."

Cal swallowed hard, then said, "Let's run south for a mile. We'll sink the boats and the other bodies there."

"I didn't find any trackers on them," Knolls said. "I think the only thing being tracked is the satphone."

"Good. I guess the president wants to find our site bad enough to keep sending troops. Any idea who these guys were?" Cal asked Knolls.

"I'd say they were Delta."

The satphone chirped. "You want to get that or should I?" Cal asked. He saw the name on the caller ID and recognized the routing number.

"Let me," Knolls replied, picking up the receiver and putting it on speaker. "Yes, sir."

"What's your status?" the voice on the other end asked.

"Southbound."

"I can see that. There'd better be a damn good reason for you being so far out to sea."

"Yes, sir."

"Well, did you spot one of the boats?"

Cal thought Knolls's voice must sound like one of the men Casey had killed. He motioned for Knolls to continue the conversation. The man had said "boats," so they knew about not only the *Whispering Winds*, but the *Deep Current*, and maybe even *Little Breeze*.

"We thought we found them, but it was just a charter boat," Knolls answered, holding the receiver pointed into the wind to help mask his voice.

"Anything on Great Guana?"

"Great Guana is clear. Nothing else to report."

"I want those people and that site found by daybreak tomorrow. Is that clear?"

"Yes, sir."

"Find one of those two boats, and you'll find them all. They have to be near there. Try pressuring Hans Bechmeyer if you come up empty. Maybe he's learned something new. We have sufficient resources south, and I'm moving a team back to Marsh Harbour. I also deployed three teams to Grand Bahama. You're my roving scout team for the middle ground. Don't let me down. We've been authorized to use forceful means if necessary to find them, but do not engage. I want them alive, especially the bitch that took out our other team. Do you copy?"

"Yes, sir."

They heard the line go dead.

"Well, at least we know what we're facing," Cal said.

"I'd say the president and the vice president are in search-and-capture mode," Knolls said.

"Cal, they know about Hans and the *Deep Current*," Garth said. "If they are going to use force to extract information, I need to warn Hans."

"I agree. It sounds like MOW is clear," Cal said. "Let's sink the boats and the bodies, but keep the phone, and then head for MOW. Garth, you can warn Hans in person. That call originated in the Pentagon."

"The ID said it was from General Stewart. How do you know that he's at the Pentagon?" Knolls asked.

"I recognized the encrypted routing code from the time I spent there a few years back."

"He'll know we're on MOW if we keep the phone," Garth said.

"I want him to know we're there," Cal replied. "It's where he expects his men to go. Hopefully, we can give him further misdirection. We'll leave the phone on the beach when we're done with it."

"Sounds like a good plan to me," Knolls said.

"We know they've got men headed for Marsh, and they've been to Treasure," Cal said. "They probably followed Dr. Lee there. We'll need to have Brian warn Crystal. I think we need to have them come out here."

"Why here?" Garth asked.

"For the same reason you wanted your family close, and they could use her to find us," Cal replied.

"What about the *Little Breeze*?" Knolls asked. "It's virtually unsinkable."

Cal looked back at the battered boat. "I don't know."

"She's still loaded with gas," Garth said.

"I see your point. We can use one of the engines to weight down the two bodies. Then we can sink their boat and set *Little Breeze* on fire. She'll burn to the waterline, and maybe the engine will drag her under."

"Let's get it done," Knolls said.

Twenty minutes later, the two bodies were on the ocean floor. Cal chopped several holes in the bottom of their motorboat and removed as much flotation material from the gunwales and seats as he could. It took a few minutes for the boat to settle at the stern, but then it went down.

As they motored toward MOW, Cal removed the metal plate with *Little Breeze*'s identification number.

"If you plan on setting her afire, you'd better do it soon," Garth said. "People ashore may see the smoke if we get much closer."

Cal hated to see the little boat go, but it had served its purpose. Cal poured the rest of the gas from the fuel tank around the inside of the boat, jumped aboard the *Deep Current*, then dropped a flaming rag into *Little Breeze*. The boat exploded in flames, the black smoke billowing into the evening sky.

"Let's get out of here," Cal said.

The fire went out a minute after they left, and Cal couldn't even see the remains of the boat after they were a mile away.

CHAPTER NINE

Scotland Cay — July 28 — 2030 hours

Tegan shut down the twin diesel engines just as the sun was setting. She stayed seated on the flybridge of the *Whispering Winds*, listening to the seagulls squawking overhead. Alex and Jessica secured the lines to the dock. Emotionally drained, with her stomach roiling, she ran the events of the day through her mind. She had made contact with an alien being, a fact she had yet to share with any of the others, and a team sent by the president had found them and killed Casey. No wonder her stomach wouldn't settle down.

She looked at the setting sun, stood, and climbed down the ladder from the flybridge. Jessica and Alex were talking about how lucky Cal had been. She couldn't agree more. Life without Cal would be unimaginable. When she walked into the salon, she was overcome by vertigo, and then everything went black.

When Tegan opened her eyes, someone's hand was under her head.

"Tegan, what's wrong?" Alex asked. "Talk to me."

As Tegan focused, she saw Jessica and Alex kneeling beside her. She tasted bile in her mouth and felt a wet stickiness on her hand. When she looked she saw that her hand was covered with vomit. As her mind cleared, she grabbed the edge of the counter and pulled herself up.

"Take it easy," Jessica said. "You need to sit down."

"I'm fine," Tegan replied.

"What happened?" Jessica asked.

"I'm not sure. I felt dizzy, and I guess I fainted."

Nate hurried into the salon. "What's all the fuss?"

"Tegan fainted," Alex replied.

Tegan hobbled to the sink, washed her hands and face, then grabbed a bottle of water from the counter and drank it all. "I'm just dehydrated. I haven't had much water to drink today. I'm good now." She glimpsed Maggie walking down the dock. "We need to tell the others about Casey."

"You stay put," Alex said. "I'll tell her what's happened."

"I don't want you telling Cal about this," Tegan said. "I'm fine, and he's under enough stress after everything that's happened this afternoon."

"I understand. I won't say anything, and neither will Nate," Alex said.

"My lips are sealed, too," Jessica added.

Man-O-War Cay — 2050 hours

Garth maneuvered the *Deep Current* into a slip. "I don't see Hans."

"He probably went home," Cal said. "It's late."

Garth called Maggie on a burner phone. When she answered, he asked, "Is everything alright there?"

"Yes. How about over there? I know what happened today."

"We're all fine," Garth replied. "Is there any more information about the investigation?"

"Nothing to report. No one saw the drone light show last night."

"That's good. I need to tell Hans about the new developments, and then we'll head back."

"Call when you're starting back."

"Will do."

Twenty minutes later, Garth found Hans at his home. Hans told him about the two men that were looking for him and Casey. Garth decided to tell him what had happened, but would omit the alien connection.

When he finished, Hans looked shocked. "Casey killed those two men that came to see me?" he said. "They told me she was either a witness or was involved in the shooting in Hope Town. Was she a terrorist?"

Garth sat down on the sofa. "No, she was one of the good guys. The men that came to see you were the bad guys."

"But they had badges."

"They weren't American law enforcement. They were American soldiers. They're trying to find something Cal and his friends found underwater down by the Hole-in-the-Wall. It's buried in the reef. A rogue faction within the United States government will do most anything to get us to show them where it is, and we can't let them have it."

"The men killed in Hope Town were all Americans. What the hell are you mixed up in, and what did they find?"

"I can't tell you," Garth said. "We're leaving here in a few minutes. We're heading for Florida." He hated lying to Hans. "They know who you are and will probably come back to talk to you again. You can leave the island, stay and tell them what you know, or make up some other story, but don't be a hero. These people are deadly."

"I'm not the kind of man to run, and neither are you."

"I have Maggie and the kids to think about, and this is really something we can't defend ourselves against. I want them safe. When they're settled, I'll call you or come back and tell you more. For now, the less you know, the better off you'll be."

"What about your businesses?"

"If you decide to stay, you can keep any profit they turn while I'm away."

Hans nodded. "I'll stay and take care of things. It's probably best that I don't know what's going on. I guess whatever it is you've found out there will remain hidden. If I'm asked, I'll tell them you left."

"Thanks. I doubt anyone will find what we found. It's well hidden." Garth stood, shook Hans's hand, and left.

As he approached the dive shop, he saw Cal sitting at the end of the dock and walked over to him. "Hans is staying. He'll tell anyone who asks that we left the island. Where's Rob?" Garth asked.

"He's disposing of the satphone."

"What do we do now?"

"Wait for him to come back, then head back to Scotland and regroup."

∞

Knolls walked along the beach, looking for a place to conceal the satellite phone, when it beeped. He saw it was General Stewart and decided to gamble. "Yes, General Stewart."

"What are you doing on the beach?"

"We're following up on a lead. According to a witness, Casey Lane is supposed to be out walking on the beach. We're checking it now."

"*And?*"

Knolls smiled and said, "Negative contact, so far."

"Stillwell, your voice sounds strange. Let me speak to Ram."

"He's up the beach. Do you want me to go get him?"

"You were instructed to stay together," Stewart said.

Knolls knew that the general was testing him. "General Stewart, I don't recall being instructed to be with him every minute."

"Are you questioning me?"

"No, sir. I'm looking for clarification."

"Have Ram call me when he gets back."

"Yes, sir," Knolls replied and hung up. "Time to permanently disconnect." Knolls muttered. Then he buried the phone behind some rocks and walked away.

Scotland Cay — 2145 hours

Everyone but Nate had found a place to sit in the living room at Base Camp Alpha. Tegan noted that Nate had found his way to the kitchen.

"I'm glad we're all here together," Tegan said. "Everything go okay on MOW?"

"Yeah," Cal replied. "I had to convince Garth that leaving the *Deep Current* there wasn't a good idea. The *Deep Current* gives us more options. It has speed and a long range if we decide to run.

"I listened, and I agreed," Garth said.

"We towed back one of Garth's rental boats," Cal said. "It's a twenty-one-foot Boston Whaler. It's white fiberglass hull and red Bimini make it easy to spot, but it's fast and seaworthy, and it'll be as useful as *Little Breeze* was to us."

"It may be a boat they don't know we have," Knolls added.

Maggie fidgeted, then said, "I called my cousin on Elbow Cay earlier. She said the authorities were questioning people in Hope Town. They were showing all of our pictures around the island. They mentioned that we may be involved with a group of terrorists."

"Bloody hell!" Garth said. "Well, it won't be long before they find someone who'll tell them where we are."

"Garth, people know we aren't terrorists," Cal said.

"I know that. I think it's time we push back. Tell some people what's really happening. I have a friend who can get me in to see the prime minister."

Knolls shook his head. "We'd be discredited. Even if we released the video of the interior of the Outpost and the news about the president and claimed there was a looming invasion, few people would take us seriously. The only thing our claims would bring is a full-blown military action against the Bahamas. The NSA would shut down all communications and create havoc until we were found or eliminated."

"By the time people realize we're telling them the truth, it'll be too late, and panic will ensue," Alex said. "So what do we do?"

"Dinner's ready," Nate said as he walked out of the kitchen. "I've made my specialty, spaghetti with sauce from a jar. It'll give us the carbohydrates we need for energy. No army can function without food."

"So true, Nate," Tegan said. "Let's eat and then decide what to do next. I'm starving, and there are some other things we need to discuss."

After dinner everyone reassembled in the living room. Tegan sat on the sofa next to Cal. She leaned into him and felt him kiss the top of her head softly. "Cal, I think it's time we told them the rest of the story."

"I agree. Everyone, listen up."

The conversation stopped.

"We need to tell you something, and you aren't going to like that we haven't said anything until now," Tegan began. "We wanted to tell everyone at one time. Cal and I made contact with the alien race that built the Outpost earlier today."

"You're joking, right?" Garth said, and smiled.

"She's serious," Cal said.

The smile on Garth's face disappeared. Everyone started asking questions at the same time. Tegan put her hands up to get them to quiet down.

"We didn't have direct physical contact. We only spoke to one of the beings through the sphere in the control room." Tegan cleared her throat. "The Igigi are the alien race who built the Outpost. They are the Nordics Rob told us about a few days ago. The one we spoke to is called Manatu, and he looks like the wizard I saw in my visions."

"They speak English?" Jessica asked.

"Yes. They speak all the languages of this world and even some that have been forgotten."

Alex glanced at Brian.

Tegan began explaining what she'd been told about the Antediluvians and their continued visits to the planet.

"So the Antediluvians have been here before?" Knolls said.

"Yes. The Igigi call them Etu Inu Idimmu."

"Dark-Eyed Demons," Brian said, drawing some looks. "That's what it means in Sumerian."

"Yes, that's what we were told," Tegan said. She looked at Cal, who gave her a nod of encouragement. "You know how the marker only reacts to me. Well, Manatu explained why. It seems that I'm related to the Igigi."

No one responded. Tegan didn't see any of them blink. The stunned looks on their faces said it all.

Alex said, "You have Igigi DNA?"

"Yes. According to Manatu, I'm a descendant of an Igigi called Ninurtu." Tegan realized just how strange all of this sounded, but went on. "After a war that happened thousands of years ago between humanity and the Idimmu, Ninurtu took a human female mate named Oda. My genetic sequencing is an anomaly. A freak act of nature."

"I always knew you were special," Garth said.

Everyone smiled at Garth's comment, except Knolls.

She continued, "They're intrigued by me. That's why they sent the drone to scan me and why they programmed the Gatekeeper to allow me to open the portal to the Outpost."

"Who's the Gatekeeper?" Jessica asked.

"The marker is the Gatekeeper." Tegan went on to explain what Manatu told them about the Etu Inu Idimmu and the history and actions Ninurtu and his clan had taken.

Brian said, "Interesting names they've chosen. They're all Sumerian-based. The translation of the word Igigi is 'those who watch.'"

"Manatu told us they're known as the 'Watchers,'" Tegan said. "He said the Sumerian civilization was the second one they developed."

"What was the first?" Alex asked.

"Alex, it's exactly what you suspected. It was here in the Abacos. The Outpost used to be above sea level, and a great human civilization developed in the surrounding area."

"Then the symbols are the template for all the written languages, and it all started here," Brian said, sounding excited.

"That's why they looked like a root language," Alex said.

"I believe so," Tegan said. "We didn't discuss the history of the languages."

"What about the Native American myths?" Jessica asked. "Are the Igigi the Star Beings and the Sky People Alex told us about?"

"Probably," Tegan replied. "Listen, there's something else. They're going to pay us a visit tonight."

Silence once again descended on them. Jessica looked excited by the prospect of meeting an alien. The others looked shell-shocked.

"You are just full of surprises," Knolls said. "How many are coming and how do we defend ourselves if they turn hostile? Are you going to protect us with some newfound latent alien power?"

"That's enough!" Cal bellowed. "If they were hostile they would've attacked us already. They know where we are and have for some time. They downloaded Tegan's thoughts and memories when they scanned her. If they wanted to harm us, they wouldn't have let us in the Outpost. For Christ's sake, they've been here since before the dawn of modern civilization."

"The Igigi know about the impending invasion," Tegan said. "They seemed very concerned about whether General Westfield's information was accurate. From my interaction with Manatu we know the Igigi are pacifists, and unlike last time, none of them will interfere to stop an invasion."

"Let's be clear," Cal said. "Tegan's ancestor, Ninurtu, and his clan saved humanity from extinction."

Knolls rocked his jaws and ground his teeth. "Is there something else, Rob?" Tegan asked.

Knolls nodded. "If they scanned your thoughts, then they also know about the synthetic virus you created. Did they happen to mention it?"

"No," Tegan replied. "However, I was thinking about biological counter-measures. I'm sure you noticed the red light you passed through when you entered the Outpost. I think it decontaminated us so we didn't bring any harmful biological agents into the environment."

Maggie said, "Jessica, did you get exposed to that light?"

"Yes. It didn't hurt or anything," Jessica replied, shrugging.

Maggie's face flushed. Tegan could tell she didn't like her daughter being exposed to an alien light beam. "Maggie, I'm sure it isn't harmful to us."

"If you say so."

"If the Igigi use a system that kills pathogens upon entry into their facility, the Antediluvians may have something similar," Knolls said. "Deep Sky may not be the weapon we thought it would be. The Antediluvians may be able to neutralize it."

"It may not work on them, but I think it could still be effective against the Awakened," Tegan said.

"I hope so," Knolls said.

"Manatu said I was the only hope of stopping them. He must've seen something in my scan that made him think that."

"Actually, Manatu said you and your offspring may offer the only hope for human survival," Cal said. "I'm not sure it had anything to do with Deep Sky."

"Anything else you both learned that you'd like to share?" Knolls asked.

"Yes," Tegan said. "Manatu thinks the invasion force will be the entire Idimmu population. Their planet is dead, and they have nowhere else to go."

"How many?" Knolls asked.

"I don't know exactly, and neither does Manatu. He thought it could be a billion or more."

Knolls shook his head in disbelief.

"Sara, you and Edward have both been very quiet," Tegan said. "Do you have any questions?"

"I'm just trying to take this all in," Sara said. "I still can't believe it."

Edward said, "Whatever you need from of us, we'll help."

"Cal, what do you think is the best option for Crystal and Katie?" Brian asked.

"I think they should fly to the Abacos," Cal replied. "Have Crystal call us when she knows where she's going and we can figure something out."

"Okay," Brian said.

"Where and when are you supposed to meet the Igigi?" Jessica asked.

"Sometime after midnight," Tegan replied, then looked at her watch. "We need to get back to the Outpost. It's later than I thought."

"We'll take both boats," Cal said. "Nate, Alex, and Jessica, you will stay with us on the *Whispering Winds*. Everyone else on the *Deep Current*."

"If Maggie, Sara, and Edward are coming, I think they should take the *Blue Angel* over and position it north of us," Garth said. "It'll give us more eyes to see trouble coming, and we'll have an extra boat to use for escape if we need it. They can tow the Whaler."

"That means leaving the house vacant," Knolls said.

"I don't think that's a problem," Cal answered. "In fact, it might be a good idea. They won't be checking Great Guana again for a while, but if they do recon Scotland Cay tonight, we won't be here for them to find."

"People on the island may tell them that we were here," Maggie said.

"If they do, they'll figure we left in the middle of the night to make a run for it," Cal said. "That could work to our advantage. Everyone, check your gear and make sure it's ready for a night dive. We need to load everything we can into the boats."

Tegan boarded the *Whispering Winds* and walked into the salon. She felt her stomach turn over, and she barely made it to the galley sink before she vomited. The stress was getting to her. She saw Cal jump aboard, and she hastily rinsed the sink. He didn't need anything else to worry about. When everyone was aboard, Tegan cast off the lines, and the *Whispering Winds* left the marina.

"I'm leaving the running lights off," Cal said from the flybridge.

"Good idea," Tegan replied.

The cool night air felt good against her skin. She looked across the dark water, and her thoughts drifted to Ninurtu. She wondered how he must have felt before sacrificing everything and everyone he cared about in order to protect the human race. Tegan wasn't sure if she had the fortitude to wage a protracted war with the Idimmu or whether she possessed the courage to kill millions or maybe even billions of them. She understood their need to find a new home. She wondered if there might be a way to reach a compromise and share the planet with them. Only time would tell.

She looked back and saw the dark silhouettes of the other boats leaving the marina behind them. All of her family and friends were with her. She had to find a way to succeed.

CHAPTER TEN

It was just after midnight, and the *Whispering Winds* and the *Deep Current* were dark smudges on a vast sea. At least that's what Tegan hoped. The *Blue Angel* drifted north of them, but she couldn't see it, which was good. The stars lit the night sky as she sat in the dark salon, watching Jessica as she slept next to her. Jessica would live in a new age. She would see a global war unlike any experienced in human history if they couldn't find a way to coexist with the Antediluvians.

Tegan could see Garth and Knolls sitting in deck chairs at the stern of the *Deep Current*. She heard Cal, Nate, Alex, and Brian, in the cockpit of the *Whispering Winds* embroiled in a discussion about how they could substantiate their claim of the coming invasion. Not knowing exactly when the Antediluvians would arrive or what President Collingsworth was going to throw at them made planning impossible.

Some form of Deep Sky could possibly be effective against the Awakened and the Antediluvians, but they would need a delivery system. To infect all of the Awakened and the entire alien population would require a mass dispersal. Not knowing how much time she had to work out the details was vexing. Cal said he was going with her to New Mexico.

Even if they could garner support and find a way to disperse Deep Sky, President Collingsworth would try to stop them.

The Antediluvians had been very crafty in their tactics. Flying sorties to Earth, snatching people, and modifying them to do their bidding. That must have taken centuries. Tegan didn't know how many Awakened there were, but she knew they would have been strategically placed around the world. If the Antediluvians attacked and gained a foothold, a protracted war would follow, and human blood would flow.

How could they ever convince the populace that the president and others like him were involved in an alien invasion? They had no proof. There were simply too many variables to contend with, too many unknowns to develop a real action plan. For now, all she could do was take it a step at a time.

First, she would meet with the Igigi and again plead the case for their intervention. She didn't think that would do much good, but she had to try. Then she'd find a way to prep Deep Sky. She knew there was also the possibility that the Antediluvians could unleash their own bioweapon on humanity. If that happened, she could use Deep Sky to find a cure, but getting it distributed worldwide would be nearly impossible.

Tegan stood and walked to the window and looked out over the black sea. What had Manatu meant when he said she and her offspring offered the only hope for humankind's salvation? She didn't possess any super-powers. *Why did he include my offspring?* she wondered.

When Brian and Alex entered the salon, Tegan raised a finger to her lips and pointed to Jessica. Even in the gloom, Tegan could see the frustration etched in Brian's face. "You're worried about Crystal and Katie."

"Yes," he said. "I want to keep them safe, but I don't know how to do that. I hope your friends can help us."

"Me, too," Tegan said. "Did you reach her?"

"Yes. She's going to try and find a way to the islands. She hasn't seen anyone following them, but she's going to take precautions."

"Good. Alex, you look worried, too."

Alex nodded. "I was just wondering if the *Whispering Winds* and these islands are going to be our home for the rest of our lives."

"I think they will be our home for a while." She checked her watch. The Igigi would arrive soon. Somehow, she knew they were near. She walked to the door and said, "Let Jessica sleep a little longer."

She opened the slider and walked into the cockpit. She walked past Cal and Nate to the stern and sat down on the dive platform. The humid sea air was barely moving. She leaned back against the fiberglass steps and looked up at the twinkling stars. They appeared brighter than usual in the moonless sky. The heavens took on a new sense of wonder and importance. Somewhere out there was where her ancestors had once lived. She had so many questions she wanted the Igigi to answer, and she was certain there would be many more questions generated from the answers she received.

Tegan felt drained, more so than she had ever felt in her life, and she knew her fatigue would only get worse in the coming weeks. Somehow, she'd become the tip of the spear, and the full weight of her responsibility overwhelmed her.

A part of her understood the needs and motivation of the Antediluvians. *Wouldn't we expect another species to welcome us to their world if our sun had died? But, wouldn't we attack them to insure our survival if we had superior firepower?*

Tegan remembered that Manatu said the Antediluvians were parasitic. It dawned on her that he was telling her there was but one option for the human race—kill, or perish.

The more she thought about it, the more she believed that Manatu wanted to intervene. She wondered if she could persuade Manatu to tell humanity what he knew about the Antediluvians. An alien being revealing the Antediluvian treachery should convince people. Just the arrival of an Igigi spaceship could convince everyone that they were telling the truth about the pending invasion. The Igigi didn't need to actively be involved in any fighting. Their mere presence could save millions, maybe billions, of human lives. How could he possibly object? How could they choose to remain hidden and simply watch? It didn't make any sense, unless there was a missing piece to the puzzle.

She leaned back, rested her head on the step, and closed her eyes. She focused on the warmth of the Atlantic water surrounding her legs and felt the motion of the *Whispering Winds* as it rocked in the low swells. The water lapped against the twin hulls. If only she could go back to the time before they found the marker. She imagined Cal and her taking a romantic swim. But even if she could go back in time, the Antediluvians would still be a threat. She just wouldn't know about it.

Tegan wondered if her family's and Alessia's death were preordained by the universe so that she would be here today. If they hadn't been killed, she would never have come to the islands and discovered her ancestral roots. She would not have met Cal. *Things always happen for a reason*, she mused. At least that's what her parents always said.

She wondered if Ninurtu had felt apprehension in this very place as he tried to decide what action to take. She smiled as she wondered if Jessica had the right answer after all. Maybe they should just tell everyone and see what happens. Even if people thought they were crazy, they may think twice about following the president's orders when alien spacecraft filled the sky.

She contemplated the possibility, selfishly, of all of them staying hidden and living in the Outpost, if the Igigi allowed them to, and do nothing. No, that wasn't an option.

Tegan opened her eyes and looked at the dark horizon. A black cloud masked the star field as it floated by. The wind had calmed. The shape of the cloud was too uniform, and the rate of its movement seemed too fast. It slowed, then changed directions, descended, and headed toward them.

Feeling a surge of excitement, Tegan stood and watched the dark shadow approach. She would have missed it if she hadn't been looking at that part of the sky. She called to Garth and Knolls.

"What is it Tegan? Do you see something?" Garth asked.

"They're arriving!"

Knolls joined Garth at the railing, and they both squinted into the darkness. "I don't see anything," Knolls said.

Tegan pointed. "There. See that black shadow low on the horizon? Just watch for the stars to disappear."

Garth grabbed the binoculars from the locker by the helm and returned to the rail. "I see it now. Bloody hell! That thing must be a good twenty to thirty meters across. Seems to be triangle-shaped." Garth handed the binoculars to Knolls.

"I see it!" Knolls cried.

Cal joined them and asked, "What's going on?"

Tegan pointed again and said, "They're here."

Cal squeezed her shoulder. "Yes, they are. Go tell the others."

Tegan tapped Nate on the shoulder as she walked past him into the salon. "Show time." She shook Jessica's shoulder to wake her up.

"What is it?" Jessica asked.

"The Igigi have arrived."

Jessica bounded out of the salon, nearly knocking Brian down. "Sorry," Jessica said, as she passed him and found a place at the stern.

It took Tegan a moment to find the alien ship again.

"That thing is well camouflaged," Cal said. "It's hard to see even knowing where to look. It doesn't look as big as the triangular craft reported years ago over Phoenix, but it's got to be seventy to eighty feet across at the beam."

"Maybe the one over Phoenix was the mother ship," Jessica said. "Was it, Rob?"

"We never determined what it was. Too bad Casey isn't here to see this," Knolls said.

The craft slowed almost to a stop, then hung in the sky as if it was waiting for clearance to land. It made no sound and had no lights. It was just a dark shadow floating over the ocean less than a mile away from them.

Then a small red orb appeared below the craft. It circled the ship once, then dropped and skimmed across the water toward them. Then it suddenly disappeared into the sea. A few seconds later, the Igigi ship disappeared into the ocean.

"I guess we better get our gear on," Nate said.

Tegan looked at Cal. "I should go alone."

"That's not going to happen. We go together or not at all."

Tegan bit down on her lower lip and said, "Okay, but everyone else stays here until we determine it's safe."

Garth said, "Fair enough for the others, but Knolls and I will follow you down and stay outside the portal just in case you need help. Nate, you have communications."

"As always," Nate said. "I'll protect the women folk and circle the wagons."

"We appreciate that, honey," Alex said.

"Do you think Maggie saw them?" Garth asked.

"Only if they knew where to look," Cal replied.

The Outpost — 0100 hours

Tegan entered the water, turned on her underwater dive light, then turned it off once she saw the white light penetrate the black water below her like a beacon. She checked the lithium glow light attached to the shoulder strap of her BCD. The light gave off a greenish-yellow glow, which reminded her of a night-vision image.

"You better dim that some," Cal said.

Tegan reached back and adjusted the intensity. Cal and Tegan had changed from the chemical glow sticks to the lithium lights months before. Not only did they maintain their night vision, they were more environmentally friendly, too. Night diving was always eerie, but tonight the feeling was especially strong. Even though she'd been on many night dives, she still had difficulty adjusting to the inky blackness. It was a foreign world, made more so by what lay ahead.

Knolls stepped off the dive platform and entered the water followed by Garth and Cal. They activated their glow lights and dimmed them.

Tegan couldn't see any reference points as she descended into the darkness. She didn't want to risk turning on her dive light, so she watched her gauges and estimated when she would be close to the marker. She felt Cal's hand touch her shoulder and knew she was on target. Cal had an incredible sense of direction and distance, especially when diving at night. It was a training benefit left over from his days in the Coast Guard.

She caught a glimpse of a soft blue light at the barrier. It was barely discernable. It appeared as if the glow was radiating from a narrow beam extending out from the portal.

"That's pretty," Garth said through the diver's communication unit.

"It's like they're guiding the ship in," Knolls said.

"Everyone stop," Cal said, reaching out to stop Tegan from swimming in front of the portal. She was the only one not wearing an FFM. "We can't see the Igigi ship. Let's wait here and see what it does."

When the pressure wave hit her, Tegan understood why Cal had stopped her. She couldn't see the ship yet, but the buffeting was a precursor to its imminent arrival. A moment later, the triangle-shaped craft passed just feet in front of her. It was so close she could have reached out and touched the side of it. The ship's hull appeared composed of the same black material used inside the Outpost. The craft emitted no light, nor did it have any visible windows. The ship effortlessly penetrated the barrier.

As the ship disappeared through the portal, the small red-glowing orb that dropped from the ship earlier followed it. Tegan wondered if the ship presented a radiation hazard or some other biohazard. Surely if it did, the Igigi would have warned her, she thought. She swam to the platform and took off her fins. Cal, Garth, and Knolls joined her on the platform.

"Garth, I'll wave to you if we need anything," Cal said. "Rob, I know you want to get a closer look, but I need you to stay with Garth until we know what we're facing."

"I understand," Knolls replied.

Tegan took her tank off and dropped it onto the platform. She pointed at the tank to let them know they could use the extra air if they needed it. Knolls and Garth nodded their understanding.

"I'll leave mine, too," Cal said. "See you in a bit."

Tegan walked through the barrier. The red light glowed as she passed through the portal. Her excitement spiked. She was about to come face to face with an alien being, but she didn't feel the least bit nervous. She waited for Cal to join her. When he stepped through the barrier, she pointed to his dive knife. "You won't need that tonight," she said.

"*Semper Paratus*," Cal replied. The water streaming from their bodies and swimsuits disappeared as it hit the floor.

"I know, 'always ready.' But tonight is different."

The black, triangle-shaped craft filled the front part of the void they had grown accustomed to seeing. The craft settled onto the first set of landing cradles at the front of the cavern. Tegan knew that no other ship would be coming through the barrier with it sitting there. The portal opening was only slightly larger than the width of the craft.

"It reminds me of a B-2 stealth bomber," Cal said. "It's bulkier around the fuselage, and the wings are more delta-shaped."

"It's a very beautiful ship," Tegan said.

The craft emitted no sound, and no water dripped from it. The hull was dry, as was the cavern floor below it.

"Let's go down to the control room," Tegan said. "I think they'll want to meet us there."

They walked down the ramp. Neither took their eyes off the craft.

Tegan prepared herself for an otherworldly experience. Seeing an alien on a plasma screen and meeting one in person were two different things. They avoided the tunnel entrance, instead using the hangar entrance. The energy barrier to the control room had been deactivated and they walked into the room. They were alone.

Tegan let out a deep breath not even realizing she'd been holding it.

"They're not here. Maybe they're waiting for the trumpets to sound to make an entrance," Cal joked. "Why don't you put the lights on to let them know we're here?"

"I think we should just wait right here and not touch anything. Besides, I think they can turn on whatever they want from the ship, and if they want the lights on, they will put them on."

"So now you decide not to touch anything," Cal said.

"I imagine they needed to secure the ship before they joined us. I'm sure they'll be here in a few minutes."

"I'm sure they will."

They waited nearly five minutes in silence beneath the sphere in the middle of the room. Then the sound of soft footsteps and heavy rustling fabric grew nearer. Tegan straightened. Cal inhaled, squared his shoulders, and locked his jaw. She'd seen him assume this posture before. It was a primitive male response. She was certain Cal's voice would no doubt be an octave lower than normal when he spoke. This reminded her of a gorilla posturing so as to appear larger and more intimidating to an adversary. In this case, Tegan didn't think it much mattered.

"Cal, they aren't going to harm us." Tegan's voice was calm and soothing. Then she froze at the first sight of movement on the ramp and squeezed Cal's hand. *This was really happening.*

Two Igigi walked into full view and stood at the entrance to the control room. Tegan recognized Manatu. The Igigi beside him was without doubt a female. She'd never considered what the female of the species would look like, but here was a female Igigi with prominent human features that were evident even beneath her robe.

Her appearance was very striking, Scandinavian-looking. She was tall with white-blond hair and fair skin. Her facial features were much like Manatu's, but softer. Both Igigi were easily a foot taller than Cal. They were clad in deep forest-green robes, which hung loosely to the floor. The material shimmered in the soft light, as if the garments were illuminated from underneath. Each of their robes was adorned with an ornate symbol, which reminded Tegan of something King Arthur would wear. The robes made them appear regal. Their body posture commanded respect. They looked omniscient.

"They look more like you in person," Cal said. "You were that pale the first time I saw you. They don't have weapons. That's a good sign."

"They're here to talk, not wage war," Tegan said softly. "They won't harm any living, intelligent creature, remember?"

"So they said."

After what must have been an appropriate length of time, the two Igigi entered the room. They stopped a few feet away from Tegan and Cal. Cal stepped forward to face Manatu. Tegan knew this was another protective gesture. She took a step forward and stood beside him so as not to offend the Igigi and faced the female. Cal took her hand.

Tegan felt the woman's eyes examining her as if she was a specimen in a zoo. Her facial expression took on the look of a future mother-in-law meeting the prospective bride for the first time and trying to decide if she was worthy of her son. Tegan remained calm.

The female Igigi uttered soft, rapid chirping sounds similar to those they had heard earlier when Manatu first tried to communicate with them. Manatu responded with several clicks. The two Igigi had two distinctly different tonal qualities and pitch levels. Both Igigi took another step toward them and stopped just far enough away so as not to violate their personal space. Tegan felt Cal's grip loosen, as if he wanted to have his hand free if he had to take action. She wondered if it was their custom not to get too close or if they sensed Cal's anxiety. Either way, she was fine with them keeping their distance, considering the surreal experience that was playing out.

Without taking his eyes off Manatu, Cal asked Tegan, "Do you know what to say?"

Tegan shook her head and then extended her hand to Manatu. "I can see my genetic resemblance even more clearly now." She wasn't sure why she'd said that as her opening line.

Neither Igigi reached out to take her hand. After an awkward pause, Tegan lowered her hand. The female Igigi chirped something, and then both of them bowed their head slightly, as if to formally acknowledge them.

Tegan returned the gesture and whispered, "Bow your head, Cal."

He nodded, but he never took his gaze off them.

"Greetings to you both," Manatu said in perfect English but with a lilt in his voice. "I wish to introduce, Makita. She is to me what Calvin is to you, Tegan."

Tegan bowed slightly to Makita.

Makita returned the greeting, then inspected Cal the same way she had Tegan. She fixed her gaze on the dive knife strapped to his calf and chirped. Manatu responded to her.

"Cal, bow again," Tegan whispered.

"Why?"

"As a sign of respect."

Makita remained focused on the knife.

Cal bowed.

Makita blinked, bowed in return, then looked at Tegan again.

Tegan couldn't believe she was staring into the faces of alien beings. She saw Megan's features in Makita's face. Her blue eyes were radiant. Tears welled in her eyes, surprising her. She quickly wiped them away and said, "I'm sorry. It's just that Makita's eyes look so much like Megan's did."

"Most of the women in our clan have blue eyes," Makita said in English. "All of the men have green eyes, like yours."

Tegan wasn't sure if Makita had just insulted her or not. "I don't know what to say or if there is a customary gesture or ritual we should follow. I guess I could start by saying thank you for allowing us into your outpost."

The two Igigi nodded, then walked past them toward the workstations against the back wall without any further exchange. Their hands deftly swept over the symbols that materialized from the ether. The equipment came to life.

"You have left two others outside. You do not yet trust us?" Makita asked accusingly.

"We wanted to meet you first." Tegan felt uncomfortable with Makita's directness. She felt as if their presence was annoying her.

Manatu faced them. His look reminded Tegan of how a father regarded a child. "You wanted to make sure it was safe."

"Yes, we did," answered Cal, while taking a step toward them.

"That is understandable. Inefficient and unnecessary, but very human," Manatu replied.

Makita asked, "Do you feel safe now?" Her gaze dropped to the dive knife again.

"Not really," Cal answered. "There are many questions we would like to have answered before we ask anyone else to join us."

"Certainly. I imagine you have a plethora of questions," Manatu said. "We will answer anything you wish to ask. Shall we sit?" Manatu gestured toward the recliners.

"I think we'll stand for now, thanks. But you all feel free," Cal said.

Makita gave a short snorting sound that Tegan thought must be a sound of derision. Makita approached Tegan and asked, "Do you also fear us?"

"No, I don't. We are just being cautious. This is all very hard for us to grasp. The better we understand you, the easier it will be for us to get others to trust you."

Makita simply nodded, then walked to one of the recliners and sat down. Manatu joined her. Even seated they retained their regal air.

Manatu said, "What would you like to know about us?"

"Everything," Tegan replied, sitting down on the end of the recliner across from Makita and Manatu.

"To tell you everything would take much time and would have little meaning to you," Makita said.

"I didn't mean it in the literal sense. I only meant we want to understand who you are. Where you're from and why you're here?"

There was a rapid exchange of chirps and clicks between the two Igigi. "You are quite correct. To earn trust you must first understand us," Manatu said, waving his hand over the armrest of the recliner. The sphere glowed.

Makita said, "Tegan, the quickest way for you to understand is to connect with the annals."

"Connect to the annals? What does that mean?" Tegan asked.

"It is an information archive."

"Ah, you mean like a library. How do I connect to it?"

"Sit back and I will activate the system. You may ask any question you have, and if the information is stored there, it will be presented."

"Presented where?" Tegan asked.

Manatu and Makita exchanged a short burst of chirps. Tegan got the sense that Makita was tired of having to explain everything.

Makita said, "It will be sent directly to your consciousness. I will adjust the system to display what you see on the sphere. We will watch and see what you are inquiring about so we can help you interpret anything you don't understand."

"I can interact with a database and the information will be sent directly to my mind? How is that even possible?"

"You are in essence one of us," Makita said. "Like the Gatekeeper, we can adjust the library interface so it can interact with you. Lie back and open your mind. It will seem odd at first because the information will bypass your normal senses. You will have to learn to process the information faster than you are used to, without any human filters."

"Whoa, not so fast," Cal said. "What do you mean open your mind? Why can't you just display the questions and answers on the monitor? Or better yet, let's just have a nice conversation."

"Conversing is inefficient, so it will require far more time for you to receive the answers you seek," Makita said.

"I understand your hesitancy and your desire to protect Tegan," Manatu said. "She will not be harmed by the experience. Once she understands how to interact with the annals, she will acquire the knowledge you seek. The quicker she understands, the better it will be for all of us."

"It's alright, Cal. I want to do this. The faster we learn the better." Tegan lay back on the recliner, and the chair molded to her form. Makita waved her hand over the control console, and the connection process began. A blue halo surrounded Tegan's head. She closed her eyes.

The connection Tegan felt was somehow familiar. It was reminiscent of her interaction with the Gatekeeper. She opened her mind as Makita had instructed and began making her inquiries. The library answered all of her questions in a way she understood, but she learned quickly that she needed to narrow her question parameters. Otherwise, the massive amount of information flittered away into the ether because she wasn't able to handle the volume of information entering her mind.

"I'm seeing what she is seeing?" Cal asked.

"Yes," Manatu answered.

"It's a blur of images and symbols. I can't tell what she's seeing," Cal said.

Manatu and Makita exchanged clicks.

"Are you following her questions?" Cal asked.

"Yes," Makita replied.

Tegan opened her eyes and disconnected. She felt as if hours had passed, but it had actually been only a few minutes. The halo around her head disappeared. She swung her legs off the recliner, stood up, and smiled at Cal. "That was amazing. Cal, go get Knolls and Garth, please. I'm sure they'll enjoy meeting Manatu and Makita."

"What questions did you ask?" Cal said.

"I'll fill you in later. I'd like a few minutes alone with Manatu and Makita."

"You're sure you're alright?" Cal asked.

She knew he didn't want to leave her alone. "Very much so. A little mentally fatigued by the interaction, but what I've learned is amazing. Please, Cal, give me a little time."

"You said it was amazing already. I'll be right back." He strode out of the control room.

Once Cal was out of sight, Tegan looked at the Igigi and said, "I have much to learn, don't I?"

"Yes, you do," Makita replied. "It will take time, but you will come to know us and our ways."

"Can we co-exist with the Etu Inu Idimmu?"

"No," Manatu replied. "We believe that you will lead the fight against them, as your ancestor did long ago. You and your offspring offer the only hope for humanity."

"You said that earlier. I don't know what you mean."

"There is more at stake than you can possibly imagine. It is not just about waging war and the killing," Manatu said.

Tegan thought his reply sounded cryptic. "I looked into the history and saw things that I'll need time to process."

"We know what you sought and what you saw," Manatu responded. "We are here to help you understand, but we cannot take part in your actions."

"You believe the Idimmu are coming for sure?"

"We have not yet found them, but we believe in your thoughts. You will lead your people, Tegan. Perhaps that is why you are here at this time."

"Perhaps this is what Ninurtu foresaw," Makita said.

Tegan understood. A wave of fatigue swept over her. The interaction with the alien system had been intense. From the brief time she'd looked at the files concerning the Antediluvians, she understood some of their strengths and weaknesses. She had learned the Igigi didn't think that the Idimmu possessed any advanced planet-destroying weaponry, which was a comfort. She understood that man-made weaponry would more than likely be the deciding factor in the battle to come, as it was eons ago. However, back then, the human race fought as one. This time the Awakened would divide humanity.

She had to find a way to break the Etu Inu Idimmu's hold on their human puppets, or else the war would be lost. She needed to dig deeper into the annals, but that would have to wait until after she rested. The library had responded with such intensity that it felt as if all of her brain synapses had fired at the same time. It was the most amazing intellectual experience she had ever known. Physically, she felt as if she'd run a marathon.

Tegan had been given only a glimpse of the reasons the Igigi didn't possess weapons and why they had chosen to nurture life. It was far more deeply rooted than she expected. The rationale ran to the core of universal existence. Images of formulas about the structure of light, the dimensions of time, and gravitational equations that Einstein would have needed a lifetime to comprehend still danced in her head. She was a medical doctor, not an astrophysicist.

Her learning curve was going to be vertical, but she knew she would begin using more of her brain as new neural pathways developed. Each of the eighty-five billion neurons in her brain were connected to thousands of other neurons. She learned that her connection to the library required the Igigi to rewire her brain, and when they were done, her connectome, the comprehensive map of her neural connections, would be unique. She decided not to tell Cal about this, at least not anytime soon. Perhaps the new neural net would allow her to process the math and physics she had seen and allow her to make sense of it. If not, she would press the Igigi for a better explanation. Tegan could tell they wanted her to discover what she needed to know on her own.

How odd it must be to know how to stop something, want to stop it, but because of a belief be restricted from doing so. They needed her to do what they could not. She felt that the Igigi wanted her to take up arms so they didn't violate doctrine.

She was too tired to think anymore. "I will do my best to learn as quickly as I can," she told the two Igigi, "but you will need to be patient with me. You will also need to be patient with Cal and the others. I think I know what you need from me, something that must remain unspoken. My husband and our friends won't understand what it is that I must do. I'm not sure I understand completely."

"We will be patient," Manatu replied. "You will understand in time what must be done."

Tegan smiled and stood.

Manatu and Makita stood and bowed more deeply than before. It felt more formal. The Igigi would light the path that she was destined to follow. This much she did understand.

CHAPTER ELEVEN

Vice President Stacy Preston moaned with ecstasy as waves of pleasure washed over her. Her skin glistened with perspiration. She sat across from the president on the floor in the sanctuary of the White House private gym. She was in a state of utter bliss as she communed with Trakar through the Orb that floated in front of her. For her, in this moment, she was in the presence of a god, and she soaked in all Trakar had to offer.

She'd just learned she was to be one of Trakar's disciples, and soon people would believe the Antediluvians were the only gods worth worshipping. TC was the strongest of the Awakened, the first disciple, and she was the second.

When Stacy cried out one last time, TC plucked the Orb from the air and concealed it. He didn't think his security detail would intrude, but with Stacy's loud moans, he didn't want to take any chances. He knew that the members of the POTUS detail believed he and Stacy were romantically involved, and he had done nothing to dispel that assumption. Stacy was seldom away from him for more than a day. Their closeness had forged an unbreakable bond. It was as if they were becoming one person, each knowing what the other was thinking, both acting on impulse without needing to speak. Trakar had just explained what he and Stacy were experiencing was the joining to the collective whole. Soon their thoughts would not only be one with each other but with all of those they chose to be with.

The look on Stacy's face triggered some of TC's old memories, but as soon as they flashed into his consciousness, they faded away. Still, they touched a part of him he didn't want to remember. Sandra had had that look after they'd made love.

TC suddenly winced involuntarily, as if a hot poker had touched him. Pressure built within his skull, as if it was about to explode. Information shot through his brain in waves. It was a sensation unlike anything he'd experienced before, but then it ebbed. He had just received his final instructions, and he passed them on to Stacy. The roles they would play in the upcoming first contact were carved into their minds. For the first time, the Antediluvians had shared their true intentions. They told him about a beast they carried with them that would help them change the world. In the farthest depths of TC's psyche, he felt a darkening of his mood, and he knew something wasn't right. Then the inner conflict abated.

Trakar shuddered, realizing that she had only just begun to grasp the nuances of the human spirit. Even after all the comprehensive studies, this was something they still couldn't understand. It was disturbing to know that a piece of humanity remained within TC, who was concerned about the people they would ultimately have to destroy. The anguish TC felt when he learned the truth had given her pause. It was an interesting development, but Trakar knew she could control him, and so long as she controlled him, she'd maintain control of all the Awakened. TC and Stacy were the first to know about their true objective. Having them understand the endgame would help guide their actions when the critical time arrived. They would act without hesitation.

She forwarded TC's latest information about the Igigi base to her command center. Moments later, Trakar received her instructions directly from the Monan. She was to direct TC to destroy the alien base by any means necessary. The Monan couldn't risk their arrival being interpreted as an invading horde. If the Igigi offered support as they had before, their losses would be significant. Trakar knew that their invasion strategy required that people accept them to allow them the time they needed to fortify their bases. The first few months were critical to their success, and the strategically placed Awakened would keep the nations of the world from attacking.

The new stealth technology they'd developed would hide their ships from detection by Earth-based systems. Only two ships would enter orbit around Earth. The remainder of the first-wave fleet would remain hidden. Both TC and Stacy would serve as their voice, as ambassadors of acceptance, and present an image of peaceful openness so that the humans would embrace the species from the stars.

Trakar would be their emissary. She would meet TC on Earth as the multitudes looked on. After their initial contact, Trakar, along with a selected cadre of Antediluvians that had been trained to ignore the offensiveness of humans, would share new technology and medical marvels the likes of which the world would hardly believe. They would bring gifts to the indigenous people and pretend to help them. Eventually, the human species would discover their true intentions, but by then it would be too late.

The Antediluvians planned to gain a foothold in Antarctica, where they would establish a protectorate. When that was completed, the first-wave fleet, with over a hundred million Antediluvians and a thousand ships, would land. Once concealed beneath the ice, they would dismantle their ships, and establish their underground city. At the same time, they would build a faux city on the surface. Trakar made contact with TC again and conveyed the Monan's command.

When he returned to reality, TC found he was covered with sweat, and he didn't know why. He understood the true nature of the future world. Stacy seemed to be bewildered. He sensed her conflicted feelings. They didn't speak as they stood up and looked into each other's mind now free of Trakar's thoughts. There was an undercurrent of misgivings about what was to come.

"Do they want us to destroy the Abacos?" Stacy asked.

"I believe so. To do that without knowing the exact location will require a nuclear strike." TC rubbed his temples.

"That can't be what Trakar meant," Stacy said. "I'm leaving now. I need to check in with General Stewart. Maybe he has found the site." She walked to the door and opened it, looked back at TC, cocked her head as if listening to something, then crumpled to the floor.

TC ran to her side and knelt beside her. He took her hand in his. She muttered strange, unintelligible words. Her face was pale, and her skin felt clammy. TC felt a sense of *déjà vu*. He thought of Sandra and the night he'd destroyed her mind. Then the thought passed, replaced by a sharp pain in his head. He heard the agents summoning an emergency medical response team.

Stacy opened her eyes slowly, her pupils dilated. "Xunta," she whispered. "The Xunta can't be allowed to come here. We have to stop them." She looked terrified.

TC reached out to her to establish a mental bond.

She closed her eyes and shuddered. A moment later she opened her eyes and said, "What happened?"

TC said, "You fainted. How are you feeling now?" The elevator doors whooshed open, and the medical team ran toward them.

"I'm fine."

Her color returned, and her pupils had contracted to their normal size. TC sensed her indecision and remorse. Something bad was going to happen, something they weren't supposed to stop. If fact, they were supposed to pave the way for it.

"What's a Xunta?" the closest agent asked.

"That's classified," TC snapped. "You're not to make reference to it again." TC looked at the other agents and the medical team. "None of you are to speak of this again. Do I make myself clear?"

"Yes, sir," they all responded.

$$\infty$$

After a medical evaluation, the attending physician agreed that Stacy appeared to be fine, but he still wanted her transported to Bethesda Medical Hospital for a complete examination. She reluctantly agreed, but refused to be wheeled out of the White House to the waiting ambulance. She stood up and excused herself, adjusting her clothing and buttoning her blouse. She walked to the elevator ahead of her detail, with the medical team in tow.

As the elevator closed, Stacy reached out and connected with TC. Their original mission was in conflict with their new orders. She knew something was wrong, but couldn't explain what it was. TC's thoughts seemed to be cloaked with a fog of doubt. She could feel a different person there, like someone she once knew. TC told her that he wouldn't launch a nuclear strike. He instructed her to expand the military operation to locate the base. A moment later, the sickening feeling hit her again. It was like a virus. She'd been infected by his doubts, his feeling that Trakar and the Antediluvians had betrayed them.

"What are we doing?" she asked aloud. Her pupils dilated again and the voices came. She looked around the small space and saw everyone staring at her. Feeling disoriented, with her mind reeling, she suddenly understood what the Awakened's real purpose was, and it was terrifying. Stacy shook her head, trying to clear her thoughts. Just as the elevator opened, an excruciating pain spiked in her mind. She screamed, grabbed both sides of her head, and collapsed.

The Pentagon — 0730 hours

General Stewart sat at his desk. He hadn't left his office since losing contact with Stillwell and Ramstein. He'd ordered a team to Man-O-War Cay. They'd found the satellite phone on the beach, and he knew he'd lost two more men. Another team had questioned Hans Bechmeyer at his home, but after nearly an hour of intense interrogation, he'd told them only that he thought Garth and his family had fled, possibly to Florida. He couldn't provide anything else of value. He was lucky they hadn't killed him.

Stewart ordered the same team to scour the south end of Little Abaco again to make sure they hadn't missed anything.

When the phone rang, he sensed it was the president. "General Stewart," he answered.

"General, I need an update."

"I've lost another team. All intelligence still points us to Hole-in-the-Wall, but we haven't found anything there. The subjects may have abandoned the site and may be headed to Florida."

"You will provide me with your reports from now on. Vice President Preston has taken ill."

Stewart thought that was odd. "What happened?"

"She collapsed after an encounter with Trakar. It was a very intense session. I'm still feeling the effects myself."

Stewart realized from the president's tone that he was struggling to maintain his composure. He'd never had contact with Trakar himself. Her instructions were always conveyed by TC or Stacy.

"I'll find the site, sir. Don't worry about anything." The line went dead. He contacted the team commander in the Abacos.

"Yes, sir," answered Captain Delbert.

"Pull everybody we have off Grand Bahama," Stewart ordered. "I want our people searching all of the Abacos. I'm ordering in additional personnel. I want every island checked and rechecked. If you meet resistance, use whatever force is necessary. I want that site located."

"And the subjects?"

"Check all boat traffic westbound from the Abacos. Intelligence indicates they may be headed in that direction, but I'm not so sure. Continue your sea search around the islands. Capture them if you can, but consider them enemy combatants."

"I understand, sir. Even with the additional teams, it will still take time to locate these people. Finding the site may be more difficult unless we can find the subjects involved and they cooperate. There's a lot of water and many places to hide out there."

"I understand that, captain. I've dispatched stealth drones to help with the search. However, don't expect immediate intel. I'll check back with you as soon as they're on station."

"Why haven't we had aerial surveillance before now?" Delbert asked.

"Because I thought you were good enough to find them without it and because we didn't want an international incident. I guess I was wrong. Any other questions?"

"No, sir."

"Call me at noon if you don't hear from me before then."

"Yes, sir."

The Outpost – July 29 – 0900 hours

Tegan had just completed her fifth interactive session with the annals. She swung her legs off the recliner and sat there for a while, letting her mind rest. With every session she was extending her interface time, and her speed of comprehension was increasing. Tegan understood the neurobiology of how the system was helping her build new neural pathways and allowing her to use her brain differently, more efficiently. She was keeping the information about her enhanced mental acuity to herself. She was just beginning to realize the seemingly unlimited potential capacity of her mind. It was both frightening and exhilarating at the same time, and the medical applications of what she was learning could change the way they treated neurodegenerative diseases and brain injuries.

The amount of information stored in the annals was incredible. Tegan knew she could easily spend the rest of her life combing through the vast archives in what she now thought of as the Universal Encyclopedia of Everything, the UEE. In the last session, she focused on the history and culture of the Igigi and its influence on humankind. By the time she'd finished the session, she knew she hadn't even scratched the surface of their extensive history.

She was surprised to learn that the Igigi's recorded history went back hundreds of thousands of years. Their society was utterly devoted to exploration and finding new life, and she'd been amazed at how prevalent life was in the Milky Way. The Igigi had cataloged thousands of life forms, most of them primitive or microbial, but there was more sentient intelligent life out there than she thought was possible. The UEE calculated that the center of the galaxy was heavily populated. The Igigi had restricted their exploration to the outer bands of the Milky Way. Even with their advanced technology, longer journeys weren't possible within a single lifetime.

Tegan had learned that the Igigi civilization was comprised of thirteen clans that lived on four home worlds. Regulus, the nearest of the Igigi planets to Earth, was only eight light years away. This had been Ninurtu's home world. Locked in orbit around Lalande, a red dwarf star in Ursa Major, Regulus had the same mass as Earth.

The planet's atmosphere was rich in oxygen and nitrogen, and the sky was pale blue, like Earth's. Azure seas surrounded the single continent, which was the size of all of the Americas combined. Even though Regulus was well within the habitable zone for life to exist, intelligent life had never developed there. The land remained covered with dense vegetation that was host to billions of microscopic beetles. The beetles and plants had found a balance, drawing nourishment from each other. Drawn by the uniqueness of the planet, the Igigi chose that world as their stepping-stone to exploring the outer rim of the galaxy, and in the process they discovered Earth over thirteen thousand years ago.

The Igigi had left most of the planet in its natural state. They farmed only what they needed to sustain the clans. Their main cities blended naturally with the landscape. The buildings were elegant, ultramodern structures that consisted mostly of transparent walls that allowed the dim light of Lalande to find its way into even the deepest nooks. The northern hemisphere was a vast frozen sea that never melted because of the planet's fixed axis. It reminded Tegan of what Earth may have looked like during the Pangea era. The southern hemisphere of Regulus was always warm, providing a temperate climate and harvestable land year round.

Tegan learned that Manatu's and Makita's clan were from Ceri, a planet circling the Dog Star in the binary star system of Sirius, located over eight light years from Earth. The intensity of light and the magnetic field surrounding Ceri's system kept the large planet hidden from Earth.

Ceri and its satellite moon, Danatis, were the center of the Igigi civilization and home to seven clans. Ruins from an advanced civilization that had once inhabited Ceri remained undisturbed. The fate of Ceri's original settlers remained unknown. They had left the planet before the Igigi arrived.

Tegan marveled at the images of the Igigi cities built on Ceri and the ruins of the first civilization. Even though the Igigi population on Ceri surpassed ten billion, the world retained its natural beauty. Nearly eighty percent of the planet was covered by land. The seas were small, but there were vast oceans of freshwater underground. Copses of trees standing hundreds of feet tall were incorporated into the cityscapes, shading the cities by day.

Danatis, nearly as large as Earth, was starkly different from Ceri. It was a rocky world that resembled Mars with a red sky. Its tide-locked, synchronous orbit with Ceri kept the same side of Danatis facing the planet. Nearly a billion Igigi occupied the satellite. There was an unfrozen sea on the daylight-side of the world.

Kalmu, the Igigi planet farthest from Earth, was the most densely populated. Bathed in the sunlight of Tau Ceti, the planet was twelve light years from Earth. The unique geology of Kalmu's surface, which was composed mostly of iron, heavy metals, and granite, somehow managed to support lush, dense vegetation. Deep oceans covered the majority of the world, and over half of the population lived on or beneath the sea in technologically advanced habitats designed to preserve the environment.

Kalmu had nearly twice the mass of Earth, with an oxygen, helium, and nitrogen atmosphere. The raw materials mined from the ocean floor provided everything the Igigi needed to construct their interstellar starships. The black composite material used to build their outposts and starships was manufactured there.

The first settled home world, Stanus, was a rocky, desolate place. Only the oldest of the Igigi clans lived there. They stayed more out of a sense of tradition and a need to honor their founders, than for any practical reason. The planet had few remaining resources of any value. Because the atmosphere had thinned, it was necessary to create an artificial environment in order to live there. Eventually, the world would have to be abandoned. Tegan found a plethora of information about the first three clans that had settled there, which was the first planet the Igigi discovered and developed. But she decided that exploring that much history would have to wait. There were other issues that were more important.

Tegan stretched and looked around the control room. Manatu and Makita had returned to their ship. They had taken time to meet everyone during the last few hours. She thought they'd demonstrated great patience with fielding a multitude of questions, especially the continuous barrage from Knolls. He had provided the Igigi with as much detail as he could about what General Westfield had learned from Senator Woodsman concerning the Awakened and the Antediluvians, some of which she hadn't heard before. Makita and Manatu seemed to enjoy their interaction with Jessica the most. Manatu described her as having "limitless bounds of inquisitiveness."

So far, none of the Igigi scout ships had made contact with any Etu Inu Idimmu ships. Manatu speculated they might have discovered a way to mask their ship's signature from Igigi arrays and sensors. They'd agreed that the Antediluvians would be referred to simply as the Idimmu for the sake of expediency in future conversations.

After much discussion, Manatu had finally agreed to modify one of the recliners so it could respond to human voice prompts. It had taken some time to simplify the system to interface properly, but it was finally operational. Brian and Alex had been studying all the information they could about the Igigi language. They were able to trace all of the known and ancient languages that had developed in the ancient world to the original Igigi symbols.

Tegan was glad that everyone now had access to the UEE, albeit at a much slower speed than what she was capable of achieving. Still, if the rest of humanity accessed the UEE, they could learn more in a few weeks than what had been discovered over the last one hundred years.

Tegan couldn't help but marvel at the amount of information she'd gleaned from each of her sessions. The medical annals revealed new treatment and surgical options she could apply in the neurosciences. Her foundational understanding of physics and math was now exponentially more advanced than her knowledge base was four hours ago, but she was still struggling to grasp it all.

Her interest in space flight had taken her into a realm that she couldn't fathom, at least not yet. She learned that the Igigi had many different types of interstellar ships. Their largest ship on Earth was in Antarctica, and it served as their base of operations. The ship resting on the cavern floor of the Outpost was one of their terrestrial explorer ships. It was their smallest interstellar ship, needing only a crew of two, but with berths for ten. The terrestrial explorer ships weren't as complicated to operate as she'd thought they'd be. Almost all the systems were automated. Tegan decided she would learn the basics of flying one of the ships when she had the time. She thought it might come in handy someday.

Tegan knew she needed to focus on the Idimmu physiology during her next session. She'd have to take on a leadership role in the battles to come, and she needed to know how best to kill them. It would take time to harvest the information she needed, but with her newly developed mental abilities, she was the only one that could use the knowledge and lead the fight.

Leadership had never been Tegan's strong suit. Cal was the real leader. She was more of a follower and a researcher. She preferred making decisions based on scientific evidence. Cal's forte was strategic and tactical warfare, and he had a knack for making split-second decisions. As he always said, "Making a decision and acting on it will be more successful than analyzing it to death and doing nothing."

Tegan confirmed what Manatu had told her. The Igigi possessed no special weapons for the defense of themselves or the planet. This piece of information had not pleased Commander Knolls and the others.

Tegan scratched her head and decided she needed to take a shower and grab a cup of coffee. Pulling all-nighters was something she hadn't done since medical school. She looked at Brian and Alex, knowing they wouldn't even notice if she left. When she reached the portal, she put on her mask and fins and dove through it, foregoing the scuba gear for the short swim to the surface.

When Tegan reached the *Whispering Winds*, she could hear Cal talking to Garth through the open doors of the salon. She stood there for a moment, looking out over the ocean and wondering what would become of them. Then she entered the salon.

"You look a bit tired," Cal said as she walked over and kissed him gently on the lips. "And you taste like saltwater. Did you learn anything?"

Tegan pulled back and said, "I learned a lot, and I'm very tired from my studies. I'm going to grab a quick shower before I brief everyone." She walked down the stairs to the head and showered. It was always a relief to wash away the stickiness the saltwater left on her body. She wrapped a towel around herself and decided to make coffee before getting dressed. As she climbed the short stairway, she tripped and nearly lost her towel. Only a last-second adjustment saved her from exposing her natural beauty. When she walked into the salon, Garth gave her the once-over and whistled.

"That's getting old, Garth," she said with an exasperated, dramatic emphasis. "You're a father figure to me. You walked me down the aisle. Would you whistle like that at Jessica?"

Garth flushed a deep red. "No, I don't suppose I would. I offer my most sincere apologies, and I'll do my best not to let it happen again."

Cal chuckled.

Tegan turned to look out the window and adjusted her towel. Another whistle. She spun around and saw Cal giving her his impish grin. "I can appreciate my wife's beauty, even if Garth can't."

"The hell you say. I can appreciate it," Garth said. "I just can't comment on it anymore."

Tegan poured herself a mug of coffee. "Boys will always be boys, I guess. I'm going to get dressed." As she walked away she gave them both the finger over her shoulder. "The shower woke me up, so let's gather whoever is available, and I'll run through my briefing."

Tegan entered the stateroom, put her mug on the dresser, dropped her towel, and rummaged through a small drawer under the bed for something clean to wear. She picked out a blue tank top and a pair of white shorts. Just then a wave of nausea hit her, and she nearly became sick. She sat on the bed and waited for her stomach to settle down. After a few minutes, she dressed and decided not to drink the coffee.

When Tegan walked back into the salon, only Alex and Brian were missing. She put the coffee mug in the sink and made a cup of tea, hoping it would settle her stomach. She briefed the rest of them on what she had learned from her last interaction with the library. She told them about Igigi history, culture, and their home worlds. Of key interest was the substantiation of their interaction with Native American cultures. Tegan wound down the briefing with a sobering reminder of just how primitive the Igigi thought humankind was.

"The Igigi are still waiting for us to grow up," Tegan said.

She sipped her tea and nibbled on a cracker. Her stomach was still bouncing around, but it seemed a little better. "The Igigi became discouraged with us many centuries ago. We've developed the technology to reach for the stars, but we allow war and starvation and disease to run rampant on our world. Some people have riches they couldn't spend in a lifetime, while others are barely able to survive in perpetual poverty. It's their opinion that unless we face a major crisis, we will only continue looking out for ourselves.

"They have witnessed humankind face major disasters and have found that we can be compassionate and that our generosity is overwhelming under those circumstances, and yet our greed, lust, and corruption results in unnecessary loss of life at other times. I got the impression they think the Idimmu arrival could be a good thing."

"Why would they think that?" Nate asked.

"Because it will present a common threat that forces us to work together. It could move us toward actually becoming civilized."

"I wouldn't count on it," Nate said. "My guess is someone will try to capitalize on the situation and find a way to make a profit or broker it into a political power base."

"You got that right," Knolls said. "The Igigi informed me that they have doubled the number of scout ships deployed along the Idimmu's usual routes. I hope that they find them while they're still far enough away so that we can at least have some time to prepare. Since none of their ships have been detected, Manatu thinks they're either still weeks or months away or they've found a way to shield their ships from being observed."

"Why would they use the same approach route every time?" Cal asked. "In any military action, you change routes and times to avoid detection or ambush. It doesn't make sense they would use the same route, unless they've been conditioning the Igigi all these years for this moment."

"According to Manatu, they travel the same route because it's safe," Knolls said.

"But how do we know they haven't found another route which is just as safe?" Cal asked.

"I guess we don't," Knolls replied.

"Rob, did Manatu explain how they will detect the ships?" Nate asked.

"He did, but I'm not a physicist, so a lot of his explanation went over my head. From what I did understand, the Igigi detection system has something to do with tracking particles of light and gravity displacement. Anything that gets anywhere near one of the remote sensors will be detected, analyzed, identified, tagged, and tracked. Whether it's an asteroid or a ship, they claim they will see it. When the Igigi scout ships make contact, we will also know how many are coming."

"Well, at least their arrival isn't imminent," said Nate.

"It's imminent, Nate," Tegan said. "Whether it's a day, a month, or a year, they're coming, and they mean to kill, conquer, and enslave us. We have to have the resolve to fight them, and we have to understand that the battle will be long and hard unless I can figure something out."

"What makes you think you're the only one that has to figure out a plan of attack?" Knolls asked.

"Because I'm the only one that can absorb the information we need fast enough to come up with a plan and because Manatu said I'm the only hope." Tegan took a breath. During the last few days she had been snapping at people, and she didn't know why. She suddenly felt an intense wave of exhaustion hit her.

Knolls said, "I wasn't attacking you. We're here to help you. Don't feel like this is all on your shoulders."

Tegan said, "I know. Thank you." She looked at Cal, and he nodded in agreement.

"If they bring some new form of disease or have weapons of mass destruction, we will need to use Deep Sky and every other weapon in our arsenal against them," Knolls said. "When they arrive, our modes of transportation will be restricted, so we need to get assets and equipment prepositioned. I imagine they'll take out our satellites so we won't have communication, GPS, or targeting capability. I have a feeling this will come down to an old-fashioned slugfest."

Cal said, "Tegan, assuming we can use Deep Sky as a weapon, what will you require to modify it as the battlefield environment evolves?"

Tegan gave his question some thought. "Ideally, I'll need multiple lab sites or a mobile lab with enough programmable nanocytes to create the Deep Sky virus medium. If I have transmission capability, I can modify the program of any virus I create."

"That's a tall order." Knolls shifted on his seat cushion and leaned forward, looking at each person in the room. "If there are a billion Idimmu, then the number and size of their ships will be large enough that our radio telescopes and sophisticated observatories can detect them. We just need to know where to point them."

"We're back to the key issue. Where are they coming from?" Cal said. "I'm not convinced the Igigi haven't been duped. I think the Igigi are looking in the wrong place."

"I guess we'll just have to wait and see," Knolls said. "If their strategy is to overwhelm us with numbers, a billion Idimmu landing anywhere on Earth would be like an unending tidal wave. The Chinese human wave attacks during the Korean War were very successful with gaining territory. This enemy has nowhere else to go, so they will be determined, and we still don't know what kind of weapons they have."

Cal said, "Even if we get lucky and Deep Sky kills half of them, which I would consider a success, it still leaves a formidable number of Idimmu to contend with, not to mention the asymmetrical threat from our own kind. We have to stop them before they can dig in."

Knolls scratched his head. "True. This will be a genocidal war. It'll be us or them, and only one species will be left standing to inherit the Earth. It's vitally important that when someone learns something, we all need to hear about it as quickly as possible. The smallest detail could make the difference in our survival."

Tegan understood his concern. She and Cal hadn't been overly forthcoming with sharing information in a timely manner.

"Rob, Cal and I fully understand the need to share information," Tegan said. "But keep in mind that what I'm learning in my sessions can't be regurgitated verbatim. There's simply too much detail, so there may be gaps." Tegan looked at Jessica. She could tell Jessica grasped the true gravity of the situation. Something had finally burrowed through her youthful facade of innocence.

"We can't save everyone, can we?" Jessica asked.

"No we can't," Tegan replied. "Millions, maybe billions of people are going to die."

"What about us? Where will we go?" Jessica asked.

Garth put his arm around his daughter's shoulder to comfort her. No doubt he was very concerned about how he could protect his family.

"Jessica, I can only tell you this," Tegan said. "I promise all of you that I will do everything I can to find a way to stop them. I may not have all the answers right now as to how, but I will not stop until we succeed. I will need your help."

Cal leaned forward. "As Rob said, the burden isn't yours alone to bear."

Jessica nodded, and said, "I'll do my part. What do you need me to do?"

Tegan smiled at her. "You've already been doing your part. Rob just made it seem more real." Tegan's nausea returned, and she grabbed another cracker. "As to the small details, we know the Idimmu world is, or was, a very cold place. They come from the Kapteyn's star system, which is almost four parsecs away in the southern part of the constellation Pictor."

"I also learned that from my inquiries," Knolls said. "The records the Igigi have on the Idimmu portray them as galactic parasites. They take whatever they want. There was limited information on their weaponry and tactics."

"Maybe they rely on their overwhelming numbers," Nate offered.

"How far away is four parsecs?" Jessica asked.

"Around thirteen light years," Cal answered.

"That's a long way to travel," Jessica said.

"Yes, it is," Knolls said.

"I found little information about their ships," Tegan said. "but I learned their propulsion system is gravity-driven and that some of their ships are triangularly shaped, like the Igigi ship. I didn't understand the mathematics of how their propulsion system works, but I do know it will move a large mass at a phenomenal speed."

"I saw that, too," Knolls said. "There's still no way to know how long they've been traveling toward us, so we can't extrapolate a time of arrival. It's very frustrating."

"Did Manatu give you any idea about where he thought they will land?" Nate asked.

"Manatu believes they will most likely land in either the Arctic or Antarctic," Knolls replied. "They're both sparsely populated and remote."

"My money's on Antarctica," Nate said.

"I wish I could determine what the president and his kind are planning," Knolls said. "They could prevent any military action being taken against them."

"They could even provide military protection after they arrive," Cal said. "They may not need weapons. They could just use ours."

"Why can't we just nuke them?" Garth asked.

"That's what I was wondering," Cal said. "If the Idimmu are clustered together when bombed, the fallout from tactical nukes would be minimal. Didn't Casey tell us Westfield had launch codes?"

Knolls said, "Yes, he did. The codes were on his laptop. The one Casey gave you and was tossed into the water."

"You told us you couldn't unlock his laptop," Cal said.

"That's true. The only way I can get the codes is by using my terminal in New Mexico, which is biometrically locked. Even with the codes, I'm not sure I can access the missile defense system and select targets. I don't think Westfield had enabled it for me to execute a launch."

"So the nuclear option is off the table," Cal said. "Tegan, can you infect the Awakened with something that would lay dormant but still be infectious and harmful to the Idimmu?"

"I don't know. What are you thinking?"

Cal rubbed his chin, then said, "That our vector—the organism that transmits the disease for Deep Sky—could be the Awakened. Instead of building something to kill the Awakened outright, the president and others could spread an infectious agent by contact with the Idimmu. Perhaps the Idimmu wouldn't detect it or be able to counter it before it was too late."

"Now that's a good idea. Can it be done?" Knolls asked.

Tegan thought about the idea. "It could work, but I don't know if we could get close enough to infect the Awakened without being discovered."

"You could infect everyone," Cal said. "Something that is benign for people but fatal for the Awakened and Idimmu over time."

"We still can't rule out that the Idimmu might have advanced biohazard protocols in place to detect infectious agents," Tegan said. "We may want to just stick with killing the Awakened."

"How close would a host have to get to infect them?" Nate asked.

"It depends on the environment, the infectious agent, and the vector," Tegan replied.

"What if we attacked on multiple fronts simultaneously?" Knolls said. "Use the Awakened as the vector. You could program Deep Sky to be an airborne agent and have it stay active indefinitely. We could disperse it globally using aircraft."

"We'd need a lot of it to cover the globe," Tegan said. Then it came to her. Why hadn't she thought of this sooner?

"Rob, I could program Deep Sky to be a self-assembling virus. It would transform itself as the Idimmu developed counteragents. That doesn't solve the delivery problem, but Deep Sky would continuously mutate to ensure serial infection. The downside is it could take years to spread through their populace, and it still might not kill them, but it should keep them busy."

"That sounds like an option," Rob replied.

Cal said, "If we know where their center of operations is, we could strike there first. We may not need to go global."

"A saturation bombing campaign," Knolls said.

"Exactly. We spray everything within miles of their bases or where they decide to strike from," Cal replied.

"My concern is if they discover the virus is synthetic and programmable, they may be able to reverse engineer it and attack us," Tegan said. "I don't think we could immunize the world's population fast enough to keep up with the mutations they could throw back at us."

"If they did find a way to use Deep Sky against us, we'd need a kill switch of some sort to neutralize it," Knolls said. "You used a kill switch program when you tested the first generations during testing, didn't you?"

"Yes."

Knolls said, "And if they choose to deploy an alien virus as a first-strike weapon, you could use Deep Sky to develop a vaccine. That's what it was designed for, wasn't it?"

"Yes. Programming a kill switch is easy," Tegan said. "Reaching the population with a cure to an alien infectious agent is another thing. And if they reverse engineer Deep Sky and discover how the kill switch works, they could program it to be useless." Tegan rubbed her temples. "I could program it to self-destruct if it's removed from a host. I'd need some time to work out how to do that."

"I think it's a good idea," Knolls said.

"If they deploy an alien virus, I may not be able to identify or sequence it in time to be effective, even with the best lab, production, and distribution available," Tegan said. "Isolating the reproduction variables would be a major undertaking. An alien virus could also use a completely different infectious medium. Programming Deep Sky to imitate something alien may take more time than we have."

"How about developing something new?" Jessica asked. "Like an acid bomb that melts their skin."

"I couldn't even begin to know how to develop a chemical agent to do that. I could modify Deep Sky to attack as an immediate contact agent. The downside to developing a contact virus is having a sufficient amount of Idimmu DNA to test the efficacy. We could use live subjects, but that may be even more difficult to obtain."

Tegan realized that everyone was looking at her, as if she could pull a magic potion out of thin air. "Guys, it doesn't work like in the movies. Deep Sky took me years to develop with the best equipment available. Let me explain some basics about virology.

"Viruses are infectious agents that are only able to replicate inside the living cells of another organism, at least the viruses found on Earth. In addition to animals, a virus can live in plants and bacteria. That's why I thought of using it on their food supply. If we could figure out what they eat and get to it, we could attack them that way."

"Makes sense," Garth said.

"Virus types vary, but they all work on the same principle. Briefly, their genetic structure actually takes over a host cell, and then when it's able to replicate and infect another host cell, it moves on. A virus can manifest and present differently in people. An infected person can spread the bug without even knowing they themselves are infected, like the Zika virus. Others are deadly, like the flu pandemic of 1918, which killed fifty million people. As you know, there are some nasty viruses out there. Ebola and the virus variant that decimated most of the Anasazi civilization are two viruses with a high mortality rate. The Anasazi virus was more contagious than the common cold and far deadlier than Ebola, and it wiped out a whole civilization."

"That's exactly what we need now," Nate said.

Tegan took a sip of tea as her stomach turned over again. "What you all don't know is that Deep Sky behaves like any other infectious agent, but with one big difference. It doesn't need a host to replicate. I can control the replication process artificially. Just for clarification, Deep Sky is a synthetic life form that operates at a nanomolecular level."

"You mean it acts like a nanobot?" Jessica asked.

Tegan nodded. "Yes, that's a pretty good description. I won't bore you with the medical descriptors of each virus type or subtype, but all viruses have their own lifecycle, with six distinct stages of life. They just need a host cell in which to live, and like I said, it doesn't even have to be an animal."

"How long can a virus live?" Jessica asked.

"Every virus has a different lifespan. Some can live eons if frozen and thawed correctly, while others live for just a few seconds outside of the host. A virus is actually very fragile, even the deadliest of them."

"Deep Sky isn't fragile," Knolls said. "Tegan's creation is truly a work of genius."

Tegan wasn't sure how to respond. She felt somewhat flattered but at the same time wished she could crawl into a hole. "No, it's not fragile. It can survive in minus two-hundred-degree temperatures and in boiling water for years."

Jessica asked, "Where do viruses come from?"

Tegan took a bite of a cracker. "That's a good question. Virologists are still debating the issue. There is some evidence to support the theory they evolved from bacteria emerging from the primordial soup billions of years ago. Another theory postulates they evolved from plasmids."

"From what?" Garth asked.

"Plasmids. They're pieces of DNA which move between living cells."

"Whatever you say, Doctor Locke," Garth said.

"How many types of viruses are there?" Jessica asked. She never seemed to run out of questions.

"There are literally millions of different types, but only about 5,500 have undergone genomic identification. A virus can have either RNA or DNA genes with single- or double-stranded genomes, and they come in all shapes and sizes. Deep Sky can replicate any of them. The largest known viruses are the mimiviruses and the megaviruses. The mimivirus is a double-stranded DNA virus measuring four hundred nanoparticles in size, with a genome size of over 1.2 megabases, with over a thousand protein variables. Ironically, it's found in the smallest single-cell organism on the planet, the amoebae. The megavirus, discovered off the coast of Chile in 2011, is slightly smaller than the mimivirus, but its DNA genome is larger. The smallest virus decoded so far is in the Circoviridae virus family. It has two coded proteins and is only about two kilobases in size." Tegan stopped. She could see by the looks on everyone's face she'd gotten too technical.

"What's a megabase or a kilobase?" Jessica asked.

"A megabase is a measurement used to describe DNA fragment size. A million base pairs make a megabase. A thousand base pairs make up a kilobase."

"Not helping," Jessica said.

"I'll make it easy for you," Garth said. "They are really small, like the size of an atom."

"Jessica, you could be a future scientist," Tegan said. "You keep asking questions until you understand. Don't ever lose that trait."

Jessica smiled proudly and looked at Garth.

"Bottom line, whatever I create will need to find its own way to infect the Idimmu for it to be of value."

"I understand," Knolls said. "Let me think more about our options."

CHAPTER TWELVE

Aboard the Whispering Winds — July 29 — 1100 hours

"You hear that?" Tegan asked, leaning toward the salon door. "I hear a faint banging noise outside."

Everyone quieted and listened.

"It's only Alex and Brian," Cal said.

A few seconds later, Tegan watched Alex climb onto the boat and drop her dive gear onto the deck. Brian followed a moment later.

Alex beamed as she walked into the salon. Brian fidgeted with nervous excitement as he followed her in.

Cal threw them both a towel. "You both look like you've discovered something. Did you decipher the meaning of the marker?"

Alex said, "Yes, and we learned so much more about the Igigi from the UEE."

"So what do the symbols mean?" Cal asked.

"It's a history lesson," Brian answered. "It tells the story of why they sent thirteen clans here. It describes where they came from and why they're here."

"Jessica was right about the marker being a representation of the universe," Alex added. "It's a star map. The center of the marker depicts the Milky Way."

"But that's not the best part," Brian said. "I discovered a symbol that the UEE wouldn't translate, so I asked Manatu about its significance. At first he didn't answer me. I got the feeling he wasn't sure if he should."

"Brian, please get to the point," Tegan said.

He picked up a pen from the table, drew a symbol on a piece of paper, and circled a section of the symbol. When he was done, he panned it around the room. "This is what we found."

"Okay, so what is it?" Cal asked. "The symbol looks like many of the others I've seen."

"The piece of the symbol you've circled looks like it could represent an Egyptian ankh," Tegan said as she looked closer.

"Exactly," Brian said. "Manatu said there isn't any translation that can truly define its meaning. It's apparently too complex of a concept for us to grasp. He said Tegan would understand it in time."

Tegan felt uncomfortable.

"Manatu gave us a general explanation," Alex said. "He told us you were the only one with whom he'd share the full scope of its relevance."

"I don't understand," Tegan said.

"You'll have to ask him," Brian said. "Let me tell you what he told us. The symbol refers to life, just as the ankh symbolizes. But it also refers to an emergent power that is the source of all life in the universe."

Alex said, "The word we came up with that best describes what Manatu explained is *Arklight*. Like in the story of Noah, the ark held life. In this case, the symbol represents the power that's considered to be the light of life."

Nate shrugged. "Still not getting it."

Brian cleared his throat. "When Manatu spoke of Arklight, it sounded like it was something he held in reverence, so much so that we thought he was referring to a religious deity at first, but it's not. It's much more. Arklight is the wellspring of all things. It's the ultimate cosmic power, and without it nothing in the universe would exist."

Alex said, "From what I gather, if it didn't exist, there'd be no universe."

"What does it do?" Knolls asked.

"It powers everything. The sun, their ships, their equipment, and it's used to create energy fields like the one holding the water at bay at the entrance to the Outpost. It's also a source of cellular nourishment. It cleanses and regenerates living tissue. The Igigi can go without food for extended periods so long as their tissues are rejuvenated by Arklight energy."

"That would certainly cut down on the food stores needed for long interstellar travel," Nate said, drawing a chuckle from Jessica.

"Is it a living entity?" Tegan asked, believing she already knew the answer.

"I didn't get the impression it was an entity, but it could be," Alex said. "From what Manatu explained it's the source of the energy that governs everything. Matter, antimatter, dark matter, dark energy, gravity, and even time were all created within the Arklight field. From what we could understand, Arklight surrounds and flows through everything. All of the physical laws that govern the universe exist because of it."

"Sounds like the basis of Core Theory," Cal said.

"Possibly," Alex replied. "It appears to have been the spark for the Big Bang thirteen-plus billion years ago and is the fabric of the universe. Arklight could very well be considered … God."

"Are you talking about the God particle, the Higgs boson?" Nate asked.

"The Higgs field and the Higgs boson owe their existence to the Arklight field," Alex replied.

Brian said, "From what we could determine, it may very well be the missing piece of the puzzle Einstein sought for his Unified Field Theory and what has eluded physicists in the search for the final answer to why everything behaves as it does. Manatu wouldn't take us any further than what we've told you. He seemed unsure about telling us as much as he did."

Knolls said, "And the Igigi have harnessed it?"

"Yes. We have all seen its signature. The soft blue light we see surrounding the marker and the glow from the barrier and around the workstations in the Outpost. The blue glow is the byproduct of the harnessed energy of the Arklight field as it converts to visible ions."

"In his pursuit of truth and knowledge, the Roman poet and philosopher Lucretius challenged the religious beliefs about the origin of life during the first century BCE," Cal said. "He wrote his famous poem *De rerum natura*, meaning 'On the Nature of Things.' I believe we may be walking up the same slippery slope as Lucretius did.

"Very profound, Nerd Boy," Tegan said.

Cal smiled, then added, "We obviously need to know more about Arklight, but I think it's going to alter the way we think about life and the cosmos. It would explain many things we don't understand about the interaction of dynamic energy fields. As to the Higgs field, it would explain how mass is created in bosons and fermions and the reason for quantum fields."

"Are you sure that Igigi drone didn't do something to Cal?" Garth asked, looking at Tegan. "He sure has smartened up over the last few days."

Cal said, "I've told you, I'm educated, but I hide my geek side to avoid this type of ridicule."

"Well, it's out in the open now," Garth said, chuckling.

Jessica asked, "What's quantum?"

Tegan raised her eyebrows at Cal, then said, "Well?"

"By definition, a quantum is the minimum amount of anything involved in a physical interaction," Cal replied. "Quantum theory explains how a field is composed of particles. The particles are the smallest amount of something that can exist. However, the Higgs field is different because it's the only known field that doesn't carry an electromagnetic charge. It's considered nonzero. Therefore, the Higgs field has to have special properties that allow the bosons and fermions to interact. The Higgs bosons are the quanta of the Higgs field."

"I understand, I think," Jessica said.

Cal added, "From what I remember, fermions make up matter. They provide the foundation for things we touch and see every day and can be broken down into different types. Bosons create force-carrying particles, which in turn create gravity and electromagnetic fields. I won't bore you with the science of quarks, leptons, or the various types of bosons and particles. Just understand that the microscopic particles and fields we can't see all interact so as to bring about the macroscopic world that we live in."

"You're well-versed on the subject," Tegan said. "You surprise me with something new every day. Maybe Manatu should explain Arklight to you."

"I like to keep it interesting, but that's the extent of my knowledge of the matter," Cal said.

"Interesting you mentioned nonzero," said Alex. "Manatu said that the Arklight field is at absolute zero on the energy scale."

"I thought it was the power that gave life to everything." Nate said. "Now you tell us it isn't energy at all. How can something that has no energy be the source of all energy and be responsible for the creation of all things?" Nate asked.

"Good question," Cal said. "It must be something entirely different than what we think of as energy or having mass. Maybe Tegan will be able to tell us why after she speaks with Manatu."

"If they have the ability to alter and control the Arklight field, I think that they would be able to create a powerful energy weapon," Knolls said.

"Maybe Deep Sky isn't the answer. Maybe we should explore Arklight as a solution," Tegan said. She stood and was nauseous.

"Tegan, are you alright?" Cal asked, hurrying to her side.

"I'm okay. I'm so sorry. I think the stress has gotten to me."

Cal said. "You sit back down."

The Outpost — 1230 hours

Embarrassed by being sick in front of everyone, Tegan wanted some time to herself. She went to the head. When she returned topside, she walked past everyone, went to the dive platform, and sat down.

Cal followed her. "You sure you're alright?"

"I'm okay. Cal, I just need some time alone to think. Can you give me some space?" Her tone was biting.

"Sure. But if you need me…"

"I know where you'll be."

The slider scraped open and closed behind her. Alex had said Manatu wanted to speak to her about Arklight, so now seemed like a good time. Tegan grabbed a mask and slipped into the calm water without making a noise. She knew that the others would be eating lunch and figured she'd have a little time before anyone came out to check on her.

Tegan penetrated the barrier, and as the red light fell across her body, she realized it was abnormally quiet. This was the first time she'd been here alone. She dropped her mask, walked down the ramp, and entered the control room. Finding neither Manatu nor Makita there, she sat down in the recliner and connected to the system. The number-one priority was to learn how Arklight could protect them from the Etu Inu Idimmu.

Once connected to the library, Tegan began her inquiries. The first responses from the UEE confirmed what Alex and Brian had told her earlier. Arklight was indeed the reason the universe existed and the conduit by which the known forces of nature interacted in the physical world. She confirmed that the Arklight field governed all universal laws and space-time. Arklight was the fifth and final fundamental cosmological force, but she soon learned there was more to it than that—much more.

As she probed deeper into the Arklight layers she was stunned by what she discovered. Theoretical physicists were right about the multiple-dimensional aspects of M-theory and curved space. The infinitely expanding cosmic habitat, bathed in the Arklight field, allowed for the existence of an unfathomably larger number of universes. The conceptual aspects of it all were overwhelming.

Arklight was not only the foundational building block of the universe, it also provided a plasma boundary that protected the expanding universe from the infinite cosmic fabric of other universes surrounding it. The plasma acted like a cellular wall. It provided structure and kept the universe separated from the other systems. The known universe, as infinitely large as it seemed, was but a microscopic speck in the cosmic realm of a supersystem.

The UEE couldn't provide any information about how expansive the superverse was or whether the adjoining universes were replications of other universes or something completely different. What the UEE did provide was a flood of equations, so many that she felt as if the information was going to drown her. All she could tell was that there wasn't just a single mathematical model to define Arklight.

A multidimensional image surfaced in her mind, as if the UEE was trying to help her grasp what it all meant. She saw multiple universes stacked in succession. Different cosmic realms extended to infinity in all directions until everything became so small that they faded into the void. *Was it possible that the other universes had an infinite number of alternate universes?* she wondered.

She asked the UEE what, if anything, lay beyond the Arklight sphere of the superverse. It told her that could not be determined. Once again, every answer only brought more questions.

Tegan asked the fundamental question of why Arklight existed and why it had chosen to create life in the first place. Again, mathematical equations spiraled through her new neural pathways. So much of the information she didn't understand. Her frustration grew as she struggled to grasp the quantifiable blueprint presented. She was only able to ferret out tidbits of knowledge that she could comprehend. She wasn't sure if any human being could truly understand the enormity of what it all meant. It left her feeling as insignificant as a microbe, but she was undeterred.

She learned that each universe provided a construct for the other universes. It was a synergistic system of perpetual life. The Igigi theorized that each universe ultimately reached a critical point of negative return during its lifetime. When that occurred, the Arklight field of the adjoining multiverses somehow detected the failing system and created a singularity that replaced the failing system. This resulted in the spontaneous creation of another universe, and a new member of the cosmic family was born in its own Big Bang.

Tegan queried the UEE about the origin of Arklight. The response was that Arklight existed because it could. It had always been there, and it always would be. Arklight was ever-present, and its only purpose was to create and nurture life as it interacted with the collective consciousness of all things. Tegan couldn't help but wonder if the Arklight field had its own consciousness.

She understood that the Igigi belief system emulated the very heart of the Arklight field's existence. It was there to provide for the creation of all things. Then it, in essence, watched what it had created to see what happened.

Tegan shook her head. The Igigi's greatest technological triumph was discovering, harnessing, and understanding the source of the universe. She needed to learn how the Igigi manipulated and controlled Arklight if she was to use it. She knew that Arklight was devoid of energy and had no mass. She thought about Nate's question. How could something without energy or mass create something with energy and mass?

The paradox reminded her of a passage from an ancient Chinese text, the Tao Te Ching. "Something undifferentiated was born before heaven and earth; still and silent, standing alone and unchanging, going through cycles unending, able to be mother to the world, I do not know its name; I label it the Way."

She wondered if the Igigi had given the old Chinese master Lao Tzu some insight into the nature of Arklight over twenty-five hundred years ago. Tegan decided that the Tao was Arklight.

When Tegan asked how she could harness Arklight to create a weapon, the UEE shut down. She opened her eyes and saw Manatu standing behind the recliner, looking down at her.

"You have questions?" Manatu asked.

"Yes, I do. I somewhat understand what Arklight is, but I was denied access to learn how it's harnessed."

"You sought not to determine how to harness Arklight but to determine if it could be used as a weapon. Is it not enough for you to know Arklight exists?"

"Can Arklight be used to provide Earth with a defensive shield to repel the Etu Inu Idimmu like it protects the boundaries of the universe?"

"Arklight will not be used as a weapon." His voice was firm. "Arklight is the source of life, and you will not use it to destroy life."

"I seek not to use it offensively. I only wish to find a way to stop the invasion. A protective shield would not bring death. Can it be used that way?"

Manatu didn't respond.

Tegan exploded with anger. "Why would you allow people to die if you have the means to prevent it without killing intelligent life?"

"Arklight is sacred. If we use Arklight to defend you from the Etu Inu Idimmu, they will discover we have harnessed the power of the universe, and they will want to do the same. If humanity learns of its existence, they too will want to turn it into a weapon. This we will not permit."

Tegan shook her head in disbelief. "You had the ability to stop them when they came before, but you allowed Ninurtu to sacrifice himself and members of his clan in the defense of our lives when it wasn't necessary. You could have shielded humanity then. Your reasoning doesn't make sense to me."

"We could not allow the Etu Inu Idimmu to discover Arklight. If we used it for defense as you suggest, they would not stop looking until they discovered how to use the power."

"Share with me the knowledge of how to shield ourselves."

"No!" Manatu exclaimed. "Long ago, we tried to demonstrate the power in the pursuit of advancing and saving human lives, but the knowledge of how to use Arklight to heal was corrupted, so we withdrew the gift."

"Is this the magic you gave ancient tribal chieftains?"

"Yes, and they used it for their own gain."

Tegan understood. She decided to change her path of inquiry. "I thought you said I offered hope to save our world. Couldn't the knowledge I seek be my path?"

Manatu looked away from her, then said softly, almost in a fatherly way, "Long ago, conflict existed between many of our clans. Like your people, we fought devastating wars. When we discovered the source of all things and came to understand the nature of the universe, we learned to value life and put away our aggression. But even among our clans, we restricted the knowledge of harnessing Arklight to only a select few. Only those who passed the test were permitted to possess the knowledge."

"And you are one of those?"

"Yes, and so was Ninurtu, but he chose not to use the knowledge to defend humanity. I respect his decision. He knew that humanity wouldn't stop killing and that you, in your primitive state, would have destroyed your world if you had the knowledge of Arklight."

Manatu stepped around the recliner and sat next to her. "I have studied Ninurtu's actions, and I understand why he did what he did to protect you. Humanity isn't ready to stop killing. It seems the more technologically advanced you become, the worse you become as a species. Throughout history, humans have taken what we have given and turned it into a means to kill one another. I'm sorry, but I cannot permit you to go any further in your knowledge of Arklight."

Manatu looked up at the sphere. For a moment, Tegan thought he was waiting to receive a divine message. "Perhaps in time, I will test you. If you pass, then we will talk again."

"Manatu, without your help humankind will most likely perish. You know my essence. I won't give up Arklight's secret. You've seen my thoughts.

You know who I am. You know I created Deep Sky to preserve human life, not to take it."

Manatu stood. "Yes, we know that your heart is pure, but so was Ninurtu's, and look what he did. Arklight is ours to keep hidden. To know about it and understand it is one thing. Harnessing and using it is something else entirely."

It was the most passion Tegan had seen him show. She knew deep down that Manatu was right. Human beings had always found a military purpose for any new technology. The need to control the high ground of space had sparked the race into space. In harnessing the power of the atom, Einstein's work, and that of his colleagues, ended up becoming the most destructive weapon on Earth.

She locked her gaze with his. "You don't care about individuals, do you? You only care about the survival of the species as a whole." She could tell by Manatu's expression that she was right. "How can you guarantee the Etu Inu Idimmu won't destroy us all?"

"The human race will not be exterminated."

Tegan crossed her arms. "I'm not going to give up and become a slave. You should know by now that the human spirit requires free will to survive. It's what makes us who we are as a species."

Manatu stepped back. "I know that." He took a deep breath, then said, "We will offer sanctuary to as many people as we can."

"Where?"

"There are other outposts like this one scattered around the world."

"How many?"

"Twenty-seven. Some are larger than others, and all of them are still operational and well hidden. Most of them are located in the northern hemisphere. Then there is our city. We can conceal many people there. This place is but the outer chamber to the city."

"The city is beneath the first civilization you helped to create?"

"Correct. The city has three main clusters. The southern cluster connects to this outpost on the third level. You and Cal found this corridor during your first exploration. Farther north is the largest part of the city. It lies beneath North Abaco. There is another city cluster beneath Strangers Cay, near Grand Bahama Island."

"Strangers Cay is at least sixty miles from here."

"Correct. There is another access portal and outpost there. I believe there is ample housing within the city clusters and the outposts to hide over a million people."

Tegan sighed. "Why didn't you tell us this before?"

"I needed time to convince the others to allow it. We will seal this outpost's access portal once everyone is inside the city. The outpost will remain active so people can still live and work here. Once sealed, the portal will be impenetrable until we choose to open it."

"Do the other outposts have cities?" Tegan asked.

"No. This was our only city, however the other outposts are much larger than this one. Each of them can accommodate several thousand people comfortably, except for the one beneath Bimini."

"There's another outpost on Bimini?"

"Yes. The one beneath Bimini is larger than most. We started building another city there, but when we determined there was no stopping the rise of the oceans, we stopped construction before it was completed, but it is still habitable and fully operational."

"Are all the other outposts around the world connected?"

"No. Only the two below Bimini and Strangers Cay are connected to the city center. There is a tunnel that extends deep beneath the ocean floor from Bimini and connects with the clusters here in the Abacos. All of the other outposts are independent."

"Where are the other outposts?"

"The UEE can provide you with a list of their locations."

Tegan said, "Give me an idea of where they are."

"There are outposts in Antarctica, in Egypt at Abydos, and one beneath the great pyramids and the Sphinx. One is located off Yonaguni, Japan, and another is buried deep under the jungle along the eastern shoreline of Mexico near Cancun."

"And the others?"

"There is one on a mountain peak in the Himalaya Mountains of Tibet and another one in the Kunlun Mountains in Western China." Manatu stopped. "Tegan, this is inefficient. The library provides a complete list and their specifications."

Tegan had heard of the fabled magic mountain legend of Kunlun. It was a sacred place. Now she knew that the Igigi were the immortals of legend.

Manatu put his hand on her shoulder. It was the first time he had made physical contact with her. She didn't move.

"Your anger and worry serves no purpose," Manatu said. "The future is uncertain. If humanity loses the war to come, in addition to the outposts, we are willing to transport as many people as we can to another world."

"You mean you would move us to a new world?"

"Yes, or you could live on one of our home worlds. I know you would like Regulus. Your husband and friends would be welcome, too."

Tegan shook her head emphatically and said, "No. I will stand and fight for what is ours. Not interested."

"You are very special, Tegan. We need to explore what your presence means. It would be a tragic loss to both of our species if you perish. I have gone to great lengths to convince the others that you, Cal, and your friends will have sanctuary under my protection."

"Under your protection? What does that mean?"

"It means my clan will see that you, your offspring, and your friends will survive and live full lives."

"How many others could you take off-world?"

"A few thousand."

"That's not nearly enough. That was all the people left seventy thousand years ago, and we almost became extinct."

"That it is all we have room for on our ships. You must develop a way to select those who will occupy the city and the outposts and, if necessary, those that will be taken off-world. You will need to be cautious so as not to allow any Awakened to join you."

"That's impossible!" Tegan shouted. "I couldn't begin to decide who lives and who dies. Even if I had the resources to screen them, I couldn't communicate with them. Not from here."

Manatu responded with only a benevolent look.

Tegan let out a deep sigh. "I'll tell the others about your offer." She could see that Manatu was sincere. However, she could also see that he wasn't telling her everything. "Why have you decided to help us hide?"

"It is important that *you* survive. If I can't persuade you to leave, then I will stay until you have no other choice."

"Why?"

"That will be explained in due time. Let me tell you what good can come from Arklight."

Manatu explained the rejuvenation ritual involving exposure to an Arklight field adjusted to an Igigi's specific cellular needs. The Ritual of Dogita was an annual event. The field realigned and nourished the cells in the body, preventing cellular entropy. As Manatu explained the process, Tegan likened it to a medical checkup but with added benefits. It could extend life indefinitely.

"You can live forever?" she asked.

"Yes. But we may request the physical release when it is our time."

"Why?"

"Even the stars have a limited amount of fuel to expend, and so does the living spirit of an Igigi. When we reach a point in our life cycle where we are no longer productive, we store our memories in the Kalu Darisam."

"What's that?"

"It's a virtual vault of life where our essence is retained. You see, all intelligent beings create electrically charged molecules within the neural structure of their brain. These molecules in turn generate a magnetic field. Memories are retained in that field."

"You mean you can visit the memories of your loved ones or other Igigi?"

"Yes, if granted permission."

"Could I access Ninurtu's memories?" Tegan asked, hoping she could learn something from his experiences to help in the coming fight.

"Ninurtu was disavowed, so his memories are lost to us."

For some reason Manatu's comment stung her. "Is that how you captured my thoughts?"

"Yes." Manatu looked at the platform she'd stood on when she and Cal first visited. "You stood there once."

"So?" Tegan replied.

"That is where you will stand when you undergo the Ritual of the Dogita. You may undergo a partial ritual if you like. It may help you with your sickness."

Tegan could tell that Manatu knew she wasn't feeling her best. "So the ritual isn't restricted to Igigi physiology?"

"I have adapted the ritual for your unique physiology."

"You can take away my pain and prolong my life?"

"Yes."

"For how long?" Tegan asked, more out of curiosity than consideration of the idea of extending her life. Any life without Cal would be meaningless.

"For as long as you wish to live."

"And what about for other human beings?"

"We could adapt it for them as well."

Tegan wasn't expecting eternal life as an answer. "Can our consciousness be saved like yours?"

"We have never tried that before, but it may be possible. Arklight is all-knowing. Your thoughts are there even as we speak. The Igigi are prepared from birth for the process. Every neural connection is cataloged. I cannot say with any certainty if the human consciousness would remain whole."

"If our thoughts are being trapped by the Arklight field continuously, why wouldn't they be retrievable? Why couldn't you find Ninurtu's essence?"

Manatu shook his head. "You have so much to learn. There must be pathways and storage receptacles, just as you must have a place to store information on a computer. Without the pathways and compartmentalization, it would be like trying to extract information from the ether. All knowledge is out there, but it is scattered. You will never find what you want without the proper address of where it has been stored."

Tegan understood what he said. It would be like searching for data files in different programming languages. Unless the system recognized the language or knew the location of the information, it would remain on the drive, but unreadable.

"I get it." Tegan said, lowering her head, feeling weary. She closed her eyes and pinched the bridge of her nose. There was genius in the Igigi system. She had a new thought. If people could extend their life to travel many thousands of light years to find a new world to begin life anew, they could be on another world within one generation, maybe sooner, depending on the speed of the Igigi ships. The ability to save some people did hold promise. She would recommend to the others that they accept Manatu's offer as a last resort.

She became nauseous.

"I can help you with your sickness, if you will permit it," Manatu said matter-of-factly.

"I haven't been feeling my best lately." Tegan breathed in slowly. Her stomach seemed to have a mind of its own, and right now it wasn't happy. "I've been under a lot of stress."

"That's understandable."

Tegan decided to let down her defenses and open up. "All of this has been a lot to absorb. Meeting you and Makita, discovering there's an alien race about to invade the planet, and learning I'm a descendant of an … Igigi." Tegan had almost said alien. "So much has happened over the last week, so I'm not surprised that I feel a little run down and sick to my stomach."

Manatu motioned her toward the Dogita pedestal. "I can help you."

She looked at the pedestal and said, "That would be wonderful."

Tegan walked to the pedestal, stepped up onto it, and turned to face Manatu as he sat down at the control station nearest the pedestal. When he connected with the system, the pedestal came to life as it had done before, but this time she allowed the tingling sensation to course through her body. She stiffened with apprehension, and she was about to step down from the pedestal when Manatu spoke.

"There is nothing to fear. What you are experiencing is normal. It will not take long. Please extend your arms to the side."

A moment later, a blue glow enveloped her. She thought she could actually feel every cell in her body interacting with the energy force. It lasted only a few seconds, and then the light faded.

"You may step down," Manatu said. "Come here, and I will show you what I did."

Tegan stepped down from the pedestal, feeling refreshed. She breathed in deeply, realizing the nausea had passed. "Thank you. I haven't felt this good in weeks."

Her holographic image hovered above the station. She realized that with her arms extended and the glow surrounding her, she looked like the ankh symbol. It was clear to her now why the Egyptians built the pyramids and worshipped as they did. They must have seen the ritual performed, and they were trying to emulate what they'd seen the Igigi do to extend their life. The ankh was the breath of life.

Manatu appeared to be transfixed as he scrolled through the symbols on the screen as he worked the holographic controls.

"I've never seen anything like this," he said. "I want to compare the results of your scan from the Dogita to those we did earlier." He forwarded the information to Antarctica for Takatu's review.

"Did you find something wrong with me?"

"No. But there is something I do not understand. I needed to compensate for your offspring, so I focused on only alleviating your symptoms. The treatment will only last a few weeks, but by then the time of sickness will have passed."

"What?"

Manatu frowned at her. "To prolong your cellular life now could potentially alter the development of your offspring. I must wait until she enters the world before I can provide you with a complete rejuvenation."

It had never occurred to Tegan that she could be pregnant. She recognized the symptoms now. The nausea, the mood swings, and her breasts were tender. She'd attributed it all to the physical and emotional demands of late. She needed to hear confirmation. "Manatu, are you saying I'm pregnant." She paused then said, "I'm with child?"

"Yes. Did I not communicate this correctly? You must have known."

"I had no idea." A wave of emotions overwhelmed her. Tegan felt a moment of pure joy, but then reality struck her. The positive benefits of what she'd experienced only moments before faded into oblivion. Pregnancy meant more complications. What would Cal think?

"Is the baby healthy?" she asked with mixed emotions.

"The child is very healthy, and she is the source of my puzzlement."

"Why?"

He remained silent.

"Okay, if you're not going to tell me what you've found, Manatu, I'm going to return topside. I'll come back later. I need some time to think. Thank you again for sharing the news and for trusting me with the knowledge of Arklight."

"A moment," Manatu said.

Tegan stopped and turned back to face him.

"There is something else."

Tegan could feel the rumble of the train coming down the tracks at her. She wasn't sure what else there could be. "What is it?" she asked tentatively.

"I would normally wait until the results I forwarded were confirmed and the council agreed with my decision, but I feel compelled to tell you. Your child possesses a genetic signature that is unique. She has changed dramatically since you were first scanned."

Tegan felt the train race by, brushing her psyche. That was something she hadn't expected to hear. However, it was consistent with how unexpected everything had been this past week. "In what way is her genetic signature unique, and how has it changed? You said she was healthy."

"Yes, she is perfect. All I can tell you is that she is a very special specimen. She will need to be studied, protected, and watched very closely."

Tegan didn't like the ominous sound of that. "What do you mean by studied?"

"I should not have spoken of this until my findings are confirmed."

"Until what is confirmed?"

"Her genetic structure is remarkable. Her mind is already absorbing information, and she will undoubtedly have an intellect that will surpass any of your kind and probably ours. She will have gifts that very few of us have ever possessed. She could be the … next evolutionary leap."

Tegan struggled to understand how Manatu would know what her child's potential intellect and abilities would be or that she was learning already. Even knowing her complete DNA sequence wouldn't provide enough detailed information about what learned behavior the child would display and how she would develop. "What aren't you telling me? What kind of gifts?"

"All I can tell you is that your daughter will play a significant role in the future of humanity. Believe me when I say that she will be very special."

Tegan stared at Manatu, knowing she wasn't going to get any more specific information from him, at least not now. She bit her lower lip, then said, "I need to speak with Cal." That was all she could think to say as her emotions crashed over her. She fled the control room with tears streaming down her cheeks.

CHAPTER THIRTEEN

Tegan swam back to the *Whispering Winds*, lost in her thoughts. When she reached the stern, she pulled her mask off and looked up to find Cal standing at the rail. She could tell he was angry. She climbed the boarding ladder, and when she reached the top, Cal turned away from her and threw his mask onto the cushioned bench seat in the cockpit. He didn't throw it hard enough to break it, but it was hard enough to send a message. Everyone was watching them through the windows of the salon, and by their looks of relief they were obviously aware of her secret disembarkation.

Tegan decided to deal with the problem directly by taking the offensive. "Cal, we need to talk, privately, and it can't wait," Tegan said forcefully, grabbing his hand as she walked past him and led him into the salon. She looked at everyone and said, "Cal and I need a moment alone, please excuse."

Tegan led Cal to their cabin and closed the door.

"You asked for this meeting. What is it?" Cal said.

Tegan stood there for a moment, looking into his deep blue eyes. She was happy to be pregnant yet conflicted because of what lay ahead. What hadn't Manatu been able to tell her about her daughter's genetic signature? How could she fight a war, do the work that needed to be done, and protect her child? Nowhere in her research had she seen that the Igigi could adjust time, so how did Manatu know with such certainty their child would be so special? She suddenly realized that Manatu had said child, not twins. All of the first-born women on her mother's side of the family had twins. What did that mean?

"What did you want to tell me?" Cal asked again, still looking angry.

Tegan wondered if the baby would have his eyes or hers. Somehow she knew their baby would have her emerald eyes, the eyes of an Igigi.

Cal grabbed her by the shoulders. "Tegan! What's wrong with you?"

His forceful voice and touch pulled her back. "I just spent time with Manatu and poked around in the library and learned some disturbing things…" Tegan lowered her head, then added, "and some wonderful things."

"And that required you to break protocol and disappear without telling anyone?"

Tegan ignored his sarcastic bite. "I told you I needed some time alone."

"You didn't mention leaving the boat," Cal countered.

"First, the good news," Tegan said. She took a deep breath and held it for five seconds. "Cal, we're going to have a baby." She knew that wasn't something he'd expect to hear.

Cal looked dumbfounded. "You're pregnant?"

"That would be correct," she replied, smiling.

Cal's face flushed with excitement. He took Tegan in his arms and hugged her tightly, nearly crushing the air out her lungs. "That's fantastic!"

With her ear pressed against his chest, she could hear his heart racing. After another squeeze from his powerful arms, she pushed away. "Manatu didn't tell me how far along I am, but I'd figure at least two months. That explains my fatigue, the periodic nausea, and the emotional roller coaster ride I've been on lately."

Cal said, "Manatu told you? How would he know?"

"He knew from my scan. In case you're interested, it is a girl, and we're both healthy."

"I'm sorry. I didn't mean to sound accusatory. This is wonderful news. We're going to have a little girl! We need to tell everyone."

"I need to tell you something else about our little girl." The words sounded strange as she spoke them. She was going to be a mother! That very instant she felt it. She and her little girl bonded. It was an odd sensation, but she felt her presence.

"And that would be?"

"Manatu told me she will be highly intelligent, with gifts he wouldn't describe."

Cal cocked his head. "And how exactly does he know all of this, and what does he mean by gifts?"

"Do you remember the pedestal I stood on in the control room?"

Cal nodded.

"Well, it turns out the pedestal is a medical diagnostic and healing device. It's called the Dogita. He scanned me again and confirmed the pregnancy. As to her gifts, he said he couldn't tell me anything else until he spoke with the others. He needed to verify something. Cal, I was so stunned, all I wanted to do was come back and tell you that you're going to be a father."

Cal hugged her again, but not as tightly this time. "I'm going to be a father! Wait a second. If Manatu has to have a meeting about the results of the scan, that doesn't sound good. Is that the bad news?"

"I would reclassify it as being more strange than bad. According to Manatu, our child needs to be studied. He says she's unlike any human he's ever seen."

"What did he mean by studied?"

"I don't know."

"They will not turn our child into a science project."

"Cal, he said she was perfect, and they need to protect her from the Idimmu."

"She's that important?"

"Yes. He claims she may be the future of humanity and much more."

"Coming from our gene pool, she'd have to be perfect. I only hope our baby girl will have your eyes."

Tears rolled down Tegan's cheeks as she hugged him. "I'm almost certain she will. Let's get everyone assembled so we can give them the news."

She took Cal's hand and walked to the salon. It was empty. She looked through the windows. Everyone was looking back at them.

"Now I know how animals at the zoo feel," Cal said.

She motioned for them to come into the salon. Tegan waited while the others settled around them. The suspense hung in the air.

Tegan said, "Cal and I are going to have a little girl."

Garth slapped his leg and shouted, "Bloody hell! That's great news!"

There was a flurry of congratulatory remarks and well wishes from everyone. Jessica approached Tegan and patted her belly.

Tegan told them how she'd learned about the pregnancy, omitting the parts about the child's special attributes. She told them about Arklight and the need to keep its existence secret. She left out some of the details after seeing the look on Knolls's face. Then she told them about the Igigi's offer to conceal as many people as they could in the great city and the other outposts scattered around the world.

"How many people?" Knolls asked.

"At least a million. Manatu needs us to select and screen those we're going to admit."

"How do we do that?" Knolls asked.

"That was my question. He said it was up to us to figure out."

"At least he's given us hope," Maggie said.

"Yes, and there's something else." Tegan explained the Ritual of the Dogita and told them about the possibility of extending human life. "That's all I can tell you. I want to take a break with Cal before I head back down."

"I'd like to know more about the rejuvenation process," Knolls said. "That sounds like it could be useful if the Idimmu release a bioattack against us. I want to talk with Manatu about its healing qualities."

"I'm sure he's expecting you," Tegan said. She knew that Knolls would get no further with Manatu about the use of Arklight than she had.

Knolls left the salon, put on his dive gear and headed for the Outpost.

Alex cleared her throat. "Brian and I have some questions and an observation. Tegan, was there any more information about the outpost buried in the desert near Abydos?"

"Why is that of significance to you?"

"It's a mysterious ancient Egyptian city that was once known as Abdju. It's the site of many ancient temples and where the royal necropolis is located. It's also where fourteen boats were found encased with brick under the desert sands. The ships were believed to have been left to carry the pharaoh into the afterlife, but the shape of the hull has left many archeologists puzzled."

"Why are they puzzled? The Nile River is there. Pharaohs used the river."

"It's not that they found boats, it's the style of the vessels that's intriguing," Alex replied. "The vessels' construction indicates they were designed for long ocean voyages."

"We're wondering if the boats were left by the people taken from here," Brian said.

"Why don't you just ask Manatu or check the UEE."

"We intend to, but there's something else of interest," Alex said. "Have you ever heard of the Book of the Celestial Cow?"

"No," Tegan answered.

"The Book of the Celestial Cow describes the destruction of mankind. It's written on the walls of many of the Egyptian pharaohs' tombs, including Seti I. We think it might have relevance."

"Why?"

"Because the goddess Hathor was sent to Earth by Atum," Brian said.

"And who was Atum?" Tegan asked, starting to feel impatient.

"Atum is the supreme god of the sun, more commonly referred to as Ra, the self-created god of all things," Brian said. "The text of the destruction of mankind found on the walls of many of the tombs describes Atum sending the goddess Hathor to Earth to destroy the people that had rebelled against him. According to legend, she succeeded, and Ra returned to the sky, where he now lives on the back of the goddess of the sky, Nut, whose body forms the heavens."

"Brian, do you have a point here?" Tegan asked.

"Yes. On one of the walls in Seti's tomb there is a hieroglyph above Hathor's skyward extended hands that looks like a wave. It's supposed to be a water sign, but I'm wondering if the hieroglyph could mean something other than water." Brian drew the hieroglyph on a piece of paper. "I think this symbol is a depiction of the invisible power of the universe—Arklight."

"You think the Igigi shared the existence of Arklight with the Egyptian pharaohs?"

"Exactly," Alex replied. "Arklight is a source of unimaginable power. They may have seen it as the only power they could understand—the sun.

It's the bringer of life. It provides the 'breath of life,' which they represent with the ankh. They built their tombs above where they saw the harnessing of the power of the sun. They could have seen the Igigi come from the heavens and return to the stars. The myth fits."

"I guess that's possible."

"Do you know about the controversy surrounding the picture of the light bulb found in the underground tomb of Dendera?" Brian asked.

"Yes," Tegan said, rubbing her temples.

"The tomb is hot, dark, and dank, and it has a very low ceiling. It would be a reasonable assumption to say that the Igigi may have provided the Egyptians with a source of light. Perhaps that picture is what the builders of the tomb left as a way of acknowledging their assistance. They were trying to leave a message behind that the gods had the power of the sun and life."

"Perhaps they hoped to find eternal life through the power of Arklight like the Igigi do in the Ritual of the Dogita," Alex said. "Maybe the journey through the underworld was a description of their knowledge of an outpost buried beneath the desert. If they buried their pharaohs near them, they probably thought it would make the journey toward their rebirth easier. Perhaps the boats found in Abydos were left for them to use."

"Another interesting fact is that the location of the other outposts you described are in geographical line with other temples found around the world," Brian said.

"And within a narrow band of latitude," Alex added. "The Mayan ruins in Mexico, Japan's underwater pyramid in Yonaguni, and the other locations you mentioned all have some type of ancient structure or monument built over or near them."

"So we're back to where we began on this journey." Tegan felt weary. They seemed to be covering the same ground without purpose.

"Yes, but now we have a clearer picture of why ancient civilizations were built where they are and why they worshipped gods from the heavens. If we tell the world about the outposts, combine that with archeological facts, they will serve as proof of our story and give us credibility if we go public."

"Manatu doesn't want anyone knowing that Arklight exists," Tegan replied. "If we go public with the location of the outposts, the Etu Inu Idimmu and the Awakened will know where our sanctuaries are. If anyone outside of our group learns about Arklight, it could have disastrous results."

"I was just thinking we may not have time to secretly select, screen, and direct everyone to safety," Alex said.

"Going public is not an option," Tegan reiterated.

"So how do we select and tell a million people where to hide?" Brian asked. "Showing the world the outposts will give us an opportunity to save as many as we can and take the fight to the president."

"All that will do is put targets on potential places of refuge," Tegan said. "Don't you get that?"

"So we don't tell the world about all of the outposts," Alex said. "Just show them one or two so that when the Idimmu arrive, people will fight back."

Tegan could feel the discussion turning argumentative. "The outposts belong to the Igigi, and they have offered them to humanity as a sanctuary, conditionally. I will not risk compromising the existence of Arklight. End of discussion."

Tegan took Cal's hand and led him out of the salon. They climbed up to the flybridge.

"Are you okay?" Cal asked as they sat down.

"Yes, just frustrated."

"I understand, but I think Alex and Brian have a point. There's no way we can covertly relocate a million people into the outposts."

"Don't you think I know that?" Tegan snapped. "I think Manatu has a plan, but he can't share it with us yet."

"I think he wants us in a position where we have no other option but to go along with him."

"You think he's trying to manipulate us?"

"Why don't we ask him?"

The Outpost — 1500 hours

Tegan and Cal walked down the tunnel to the control room. The sound of a heated discussion met them as they entered. Makita glared at Knolls. He was in turn doing his best to intimidate her by staring back at her. Manatu held his hands up as a way to calm Knolls and to stop his shouting.

"What the hell is going on here?" Tegan shouted as she walked toward them.

Knolls glanced at Tegan, then looked at Makita again. "Why don't you tell them?"

Tegan turned to Makita. "Tell us what?"

"The scout ships have reported that the Etu Inu Idimmu ships will be here late tomorrow or the following day," Makita answered. "Commander Knolls has once again demanded that we use Arklight against them. We have once again refused." Her voice was cold.

"Perhaps we should not have told you about Arklight," Manatu said.

Tegan didn't think he meant it. She was sure he wanted them to know. She could see that Knolls was growing angrier by the second.

Knolls rubbed the back of his neck. "We can't get to New Mexico and get Deep Sky into production in time to stop them. Game over."

Makita gave a chirp, which Manatu acknowledge with a nod, and then they both abruptly turned and marched out of the room.

"Where are they going?" Cal asked.

Tegan shrugged. "I have no idea." She looked at Knolls. "You know, Rob, we may not agree with them or understand them, but they're our only ally and source of intelligence. It wouldn't hurt for you to be less confrontational."

"Being nice hasn't gotten us anywhere. They've got the technology to save our asses, and they're refusing to use it."

"I have to agree with Rob," Cal said.

"I don't disagree with either of you, but it's their technology, and they don't have to share," Tegan said. "Sometimes you can get further with honey than with a hammer."

"I wonder if they'd feel the same way if their planet was going to be attacked," Knolls said. "What if I give myself up and cut a deal with the president?"

"What kind of deal?" Cal asked.

"Tell them about Arklight and where they can find it in exchange for our safety. It could force the Igigi to fight with us or lose control of the secret of Arklight."

"Don't be obtuse," Tegan said. "The president wouldn't keep any agreement and you know it. All you'd do is destroy any hope of us saving anyone and give the Idimmu a new weapon."

"How many ships did they spot?" Cal asked.

"Over three thousand, so far," Knolls replied. "Manatu said the ships are larger than anything he's seen before. God only knows how many Idimmu are on each one. Manatu said they're using a new type of stealth technology. That's why the Igigi network didn't spot them sooner. I don't think our telescopes will detect their ships until they block out the stars when they enter orbit around the Earth. The Igigi scout ships are heading deeper into space along the azimuth of the fleet's route to see if there's any more of them. I think we're screwed."

"We still have time to get some people to safety," Tegan said.

"Maybe, but nowhere near the numbers we could hide," Knolls said. "I'm going back to Marsh Harbor and find a way to take Westfield's plane to New Mexico. Casey said nothing to the flight crew, so they may still be on the island. I'm sure they would have left contact information at the airport. Tegan, I still want you to come with me. In fact, everyone can come. I have a feeling the facility in New Mexico is going to be safer than here."

"Bad idea," Cal said. "The president will have you shot down before you reach the coast or follow you to New Mexico. You know he's watching everything leaving here by air or sea, and I'm sure he knows where Westfield's plane is sitting by now."

Tegan looked at Cal. "I think we should take Manatu's advice and stay in the city below us."

Knolls looked puzzled, then said, "Why do you say that? Manatu made it very clear we can't use Arklight, and that's the only weapon we have that can stop them. Don't tell me you're advocating we just sit back and watch."

"I don't want to sit and watch. I believe I can contribute more by learning as much as I can from the UEE. I know the answer to our survival is here. I just need to find it."

Knolls frowned.

Tegan sighed and said, "Like I told Cal, I think Manatu has a plan, but I don't think he can share it without breaking doctrine. Somehow, I'm the key."

"Okay. Then we stay," said Cal.

Tegan took Cal's hand and looked at Knolls. "I don't want to run from the fight, but I think Deep Sky is of little value to us in the short term. It's simply too late. Perhaps later we can find a use for it."

Knolls nodded. "If I can't leave the island, maybe we can bring the Dark Moon teams from New Mexico here. We can create a lab for you in the city. I'll make some calls when I get topside."

"Won't that put everyone in the crosshairs?" Cal asked. "I think we should start moving local people to the city first. I'm sure Garth will need some time to wrap things up on Man-O-War and decide which of his relatives and friends he can trust to bring with him."

Tegan realized everyone else had family to think about except her.

"Not everyone will be able to make it to the sanctuary," Knolls said. "And we can't just have people disappearing into the sea. Someone will notice. My teams can be here in twelve hours."

"Cal, I think bringing the lab here is a good idea," Tegan said. "Brian's wife and daughter could get here in a day. They could charter a small plane to Bimini and wait for us there. Manatu said there was a tunnel connecting the city to Bimini."

Her head began to pound, and she felt something move within her. She closed her eyes and felt the movement again. This wasn't possible. The fetus was too small. She couldn't be feeling her yet. But something was telling her otherwise.

Tegan walked out of the control room and stood at the edge of the ramp and looked at the Igigi ship in the cavern. She felt the baby stir again. It wasn't her imagination. She felt as if her baby was communicating with her, maybe trying to comfort her. How could that be? She placed a hand on her belly. *Be still now, you're safe,* she thought.

Just then, an image exploded in her mind. Tegan saw a young woman standing on a red, sandy beach. She appeared to be Jessica's age. The woman was about Tegan's height, and had her figure. She was as pale as an Igigi. Her long, blond hair blew straight out behind her in the wind. To the young woman's left, a heavy surf battered an outcropping of rocks. The woman turned and she knew that the woman wanted her to follow her gaze. When she looked, she saw a shining marker covered with symbols attached to a large rock. It looked similar to the marker they'd discovered, but it was much larger. Behind it was a reddish sky, and dark water rose as if trying to conceal it with every wave. *Was this a warning?* Tegan thought.

The woman turned back and faced her. An aura of blue light now surrounded her head like a halo. The woman smiled. It was a confident and comforting smile. She recognized a hint of Cal's facial features, and there, gazing at her, were her own emerald eyes. Tegan cried out.

"What's wrong?" Cal asked as he rushed to her side.

"Nothing," Tegan said, deciding not to tell Cal what had just happened until she knew what it meant. She wondered if she had really seen the future. *Had she actually glimpsed the image of their daughter when she was grown? Had her child really sent her a message, or was this the result of having undergone the Dogita treatment?* She touched her belly, and a warm sensation cascaded through her body. Their child was indeed going to be very special. She knew she must protect her at any cost, even if it meant leaving Earth.

Cal said, "It sounded like you were in pain."

"I'm not in pain. Just let it go. We need to get over to Bimini and check it out. Manatu said it was the largest of the outposts. I think we should start using that portal for access to the cities once this one is sealed. It's far enough away that it won't be under observation. I don't think we should use the Strangers Cay portal unless it's an emergency. No sense drawing attention to it. Are you going to call your parents?" Tegan asked.

"Yes. I'll call them. I'm not sure how Garth and Maggie are going to deal with this. They have extended family and deep roots in these islands. I'll tell him to start thinking about who he wants to join us."

Knolls approached them and said, "Let's get to it then," using his voice of command.

Tegan nodded, then said, "Rob, is there anyone you need to get to a sanctuary?"

"No immediate family, but I just thought of someone who could help us, if I can locate him, General Bishop, the former director of the NSA. We're going to need all the help we can get to fight this war, and he has contacts that would help us convince the military to intervene once the Idimmu arrive. In less than forty-eight hours the people of Earth are going to have their way of life disrupted beyond comprehension."

Cal said, "Alex and Nate will need to decide who they want to bring here."

Tegan said, "We need to get word to Garth about the new timeline."

"I'll tell him," Cal said.

Knolls said, "You and Cal should see what you can do to smooth over the Igigi feathers I ruffled. They didn't look very happy, and we can't run the risk of alienating them. Tegan, maybe you could use some of that honey you talked about."

"I'll see what I can do. Cal let's go pay them a visit."

"I've wanted to have a look inside that thing ever since it landed," Cal said.

Tegan took Cal's hand, and they walked down the ramp toward the ship. When they reached the cavern floor, Tegan looked back. Knolls was staring up at the sphere. Then she heard him say, "I'm going to need your help, too." She wasn't sure if he was talking to God or to the sphere. Maybe in this case they were one and the same.

She felt resigned to the fact that the inevitable was upon them, but a glimmer of hope appeared in their plans and her resolve. Knowing the time had come to make a stand weighed heavily on her. She knew they would have to hide for the time being. She would work on Deep Sky as she worked to uncover more about Arklight. Pregnant or not, Tegan would fight the good fight, just as Ninurtu had done.

CHAPTER FOURTEEN

The bridge of the Igigi ship was larger than Tegan had expected. The interior was dark, and a small sphere floated near the forward viewport. Although there were no windows visible on the outside, Tegan could see out. Holographic screens covered two sides of the bridge. Symbols and images appeared and disappeared so fast that only an Igigi could understand their meaning. Tegan stood next to Manatu as Makita studied the holographic displays while Cal looked on.

"There isn't enough time for us to get everyone to shelter, so we want to get those we can into the city," Tegan said. "We can start with the people living in the Abacos."

"Moving so many people in such a short time will draw attention to the Outpost," Manatu replied.

"True, but we can shuttle people over on different boats, using a staggered schedule. That may help keep our efforts concealed for a while."

Manatu nodded and said, "We will prepare the city and provide a temporary staircase to the surface. It will be faster that way, but it will also make it easier to detect us. Understand that we will seal the portal at the first sign of a threat. We will remove the marker and camouflage the entry."

"You said once you sealed the portal that it's impenetrable. Can it be reopened?"

"Yes. I won't do it unless there is an extreme necessity. If the Etu Inu Idimmu gained access to the Outpost, they could discover Arklight. If this portal is compromised, we will need to use one of the other outpost portals for access to the city."

"I understand," Tegan replied.

"The president knows we're somewhere in these islands," Cal said. "Before Casey was killed, she told us she'd picked up a signal from new sensors the Navy's deployed. It won't be long until the president figures out there's a connection and starts probing the reef."

"You were able to detect the Arklight resonance?" Manatu asked, sounding concerned.

"We believe that's what Casey was talking about," Tegan replied. "The signal was detected after my first contact with the marker. She described the signal as a pulse."

"Most extraordinary. We will need to make adjustments." Manatu looked at Makita and let out a series of chirps and staccato clicks. She responded in the same way. After a few more exchanges, Manatu walked forward to the sphere. A moment later, the sphere shimmered, and a new Igigi face appeared. A brief exchange transpired, and then the sphere turned opaque again.

"What was that all about?" Cal asked.

"I'm not sure," Tegan replied.

Manatu chirped again, and Makita nodded.

"Our scout ships report the rest of the Etu Inu Idimmu fleet are yet deeper in space."

"You said earlier they'd found thousands of ships," Cal said. "You mean there's thousands more?"

"Yes. The first fleet is composed of three thousand two hundred ships. The second fleet has over twelve thousand ships. The ships in the second group are large enough to contain well over one hundred and fifty thousand Idimmu each, but these are just rough estimates."

"That means there could be close to two billion Idimmu," Cal said.

"That is correct. Also, ten ships have separated from the first group. They could enter orbit as soon as tomorrow evening. The rest of the ships in the first group are decelerating. We believe they are going to join the second group."

"They're only going to show us a small number of ships so we don't feel threatened," Tegan said. "If they need the Awakened to pave the way, they don't want to appear as an invading hoard until they're certain they can control our response."

"I agree," Cal said. "It would make sense to acclimate us to their presence, and then, once they establish a base, bring in the other ships."

"We concur with your assessment," Makita said.

"Good. Then while they land we'll have more time to get our people into the city," Tegan said.

"Time is short. I suggest we get started," Cal said. "We only have about twenty-four hours before they arrive in orbit, which means Maggie and Garth somehow have to convince people to leave their home before first contact."

"I will prepare the portal," Manatu said.

"Thank you, Manatu," Tegan said. "And thank you, Makita. We'll get as many as we can to safety."

Manatu and Makita spoke briefly, and then Manatu said, "Tegan, you and your child must be protected. We recommend you join us now."

Tegan shook her head. "I know you want to protect us, and we appreciate it, but we must fight as long as we can."

Whispering Winds — 1900 hours

There was a sense of renewed optimism among the group even after learning about the number of Idimmu approaching. Cal had Garth radio Edward with the news. They'd decided that they would first contact only those people they believed they could convince to seek shelter. Once the Idimmu ships orbited above Earth and the news spread, they'd have plenty of believers.

Cal knew that telling people there was going to be an apocalyptic invasion by an alien species and that their only hope for survival was living in an alien facility was pushing the bounds of reality. However, if anyone could convince people of an alien invasion based on faith alone, it was Maggie and Garth. Once people arrived and saw the hole in the ocean leading to the Outpost, they would be believers and reach out to others. Cal figured there would be a surge of islanders once the word got out.

Knolls had already used up two of their burner phones looking for Director Bishop, without success. But he'd managed to get the rest of Dark Moon mobilized. What remained of S-3, Signal Intelligence Analysis (SIGINT), Human Intelligence (HUMINT), and Technical Intelligence (TECHINT) staff would be packed and airborne within the hour. People knew the drill. General Westfield had ordered them to leave Maryland under operation Flash Burn just a few months earlier.

The teams and their family members would travel by different routes on different types of aircraft and converge on Treasure Cay and Marsh Harbor. From there a flotilla of boats would shuttle everyone to the Outpost and into the city. The Medical, Biological Research, and Genome Team (MBRG) and all of the Deep Sky material based at the Los Alamos National Laboratories facility in New Mexico were the priority. They would arrive first.

Cal heard some of the exchanges as Garth and Maggie reached out to people. Geoffrey Crane, the owner of Base Camp Alpha, was one of the first to believe them. He had even arranged for the Dark Moon executive jets to land thirty minutes apart on Treasure Cay. Cal was glad to hear Geoffrey had agreed to join them in the city. Bahamian customs at Treasure Cay airport was notified to expect more air traffic than usual. Geoffrey told them he was bringing in a large group of investors to look at several of his properties. It wasn't much of a cover story, but it may hold long enough to get everyone into the city. Their original plan to use Scotland Cay had to be scrapped because the runway was too short to handle the jets.

Cal figured that with Geoffrey spreading the word that they would reach more people. Geoffrey had many friends and extended family in the islands. A little over an hour later, Geoffrey confirmed that twenty families would be joining them and that he would shuttle them to the portal using his yacht.

"Did anyone ask the Igigi about food, pharmaceuticals, and other supplies?" Garth asked.

"We didn't," Cal said. "Just have everyone bring as much as they can carry."

"I wonder if they intend to feed us something edible," Garth quipped. "I'll have Edward and Hans bring all the food supplies they can carry. If they want bottled water instead of the water the Igigi can supply, they'll have to bring that, too."

"I'm glad Hans believed you," Cal said.

"Hans wasn't a hard sell after I had Edward show him the video I took of the entrance. He's going to approach some others on MOW—discretely."

"I'm still concerned about using the *Alde I* to move people to the site," Cal said. "They know the ferry belongs to us."

"I was thinking of having Edward use it as a decoy. Run it over to Treasure and leave it there and grab another boat from Howard Finley to shuttle people over."

"Does Howard know what's going on?" Cal asked.

"Yes, and he said he'll be joining us."

"I'm glad to hear it," Cal replied. "I'm amazed that so many people believe us."

"Quite frankly, I am too. I think they trust Maggie more than they trust anyone. If she says something is going to happen, it does. She has the whole Aldeberie clan convinced, and they're heading this way."

"Too bad the rest of the world doesn't know her. She could spread the word."

"Right now, I'm just happy we're reaching the ones we can in the short time we have to get them to safety," Garth said, then sighed. "There are so many more we could save."

Cal knew that his friend was struggling with abandoning the people of the Abacos, but they could only contact those people they could trust. Everything Garth and his family had worked to create was going to be gone. "We're going to survive this, Garth. Then we'll rebuild. It may take us some time, but we will survive."

"I wish I was as optimistic as you. I'll have Howard move the *Alde I* over to Green Turtle Cay while Edward runs everyone back here. Then I'll have Edward go to Green Turtle to fetch Howard and his family with the *Blue Angel*. Did you reach your parents?"

"Yes. It took some time to convince them that I wasn't drunk or insane. My dad said they'd leave for Bimini tomorrow morning. He's decided to sail over on his Catalina. It'll be nice to have a boat near the other outpost until we can get ours moved."

"That area is going to be busier than usual," Garth said.

"And it will draw some attention for sure," Cal said. "We'll have to get everyone underground as fast as we can."

"We'll work through the night. Maggie still has people to round up. They can use their own boats to get here."

"What are we going to do with all of their boats? We can't have it look like a convention."

"Maggie says she's going to have them towed to surrounding island marinas. Some they'll beach or anchor. She plans to have Edward pick up the captains and bring them back here."

"Did Sara reach her family?" Cal asked.

"She did. They decided to stay on Elbow Cay. They swore they wouldn't tell anyone about what's going on. Even Maggie couldn't get them to budge from their homestead. Sara is upset, but believes that when the invasion starts, they'll have a change of heart."

"I hope we can get them safely below after the Idimmu arrive. Any word on Brian's family?"

"I heard they're flying to Bimini," Garth said. "They'll stay put until we can get to them."

"I'll have my parents find them and get them aboard the *Tranquility*. I don't think any of us are going to get any rest for the next few days," Cal said.

"Your wife needs her rest. Don't put too much pressure on her. She's in a delicate condition."

"God, you're a dinosaur," Cal said. "She's fine. She was already pregnant when she killed Grant, and she survived all of the other things that happened to her. I think she and the baby can handle it."

"It's still hard to believe that you're going to be parents."

"Yeah, I know. I'm excited and scared shitless at the same time."

"Welcome to my world. Wait until they get older and decide you're no longer relevant."

Cal gave a sorrowful nod. "I only hope we live long enough to see that day."

Great Guana Cay — July 29 — 2330 hours

Three Gulfstream G280 jets had landed on Treasure Cay, and all of the personnel had been transferred to the Outpost and were moving into the city under Tegan's watchful eye. Two larger jets carrying the MBRG team, their families, and equipment had arrived before them. Cal knew that moving large numbers of people through Treasure Cay at odd hours was sure to draw the attention of not only the locals but also the president. The number of aircraft alone would be a sure sign something was happening, and he didn't think Geoffrey's ruse would hold up to scrutiny for long.

The S-3 personnel and assets hadn't been the logistical problem Cal had thought they would be. The equipment they'd brought with them wasn't as bulky as he'd expected, and the use of Geoffrey's yacht expedited their transfer. The biggest issue—something they'd all taken for granted—was connecting to a power supply. The equipment used plugs, and there weren't any in the city or the Outpost. Cal asked Nate to work with Makita to solve the problem.

Edward arrived bearing grim news. The president's search teams were methodically working their way north through the islands. Cal knew it was only a matter of time until someone pointed them to Great Guana. He looked at the hole in the water. Even in the darkness, it could be seen. Several boats lay alongside the opening, and Sara, Jessica, Alex, and Maggie were escorting people down into the Outpost.

Brian jumped aboard the *Whispering Winds*. He looked panicked.

"What is it?" Cal asked.

"Crystal and Katie ended up flying to Treasure Cay. The charter pilot said he wouldn't land on Bimini after dark. She said they just landed and that there are two men at the airport asking questions. Crystal said there's only one customs agent there and just a handful of other people that are leaving. She thinks the airport is about to close."

"Have they drawn any attention?"

"She doesn't think so. Crystal said she heard the two men asking about all the jets sitting on the apron. She said they haven't approached her."

Knolls walked up and said, "Looks like we have a mission."

Cal turned to Brian and said, "You're staying here. Rob and I will get Crystal and Katie."

"I need to go," Brian replied.

"I know how you feel, but we're taking the Boston Whaler, and we won't have enough room for everyone," Cal said. "Rob and I can get in and get out faster without you. Trust us."

"Just bring them back safely," Brian said, his eyes tearing up.

"We will," Cal said.

Treasure Cay Airport — Midnight

Thirty minutes later, Cal and Knolls pulled into the airport parking lot. The two-man element wasn't hard to spot through the large windows at the front of the building. They stood next to a uniformed customs agent at the counter. It looked like Crystal and Katie were being questioned.

"Shit! Rob, I'll lure the two guys away. You grab Crystal and Katie and get them to the car. Wait for me on the main road that goes back to the marina."

"That's risky."

"A little, but we're out of options and time."

"What if one of them stays with Crystal and Katie?"

"They won't. They're trained to operate as a team. I have no doubt they'll leave her with the customs agent." Cal checked his Glock, jumped from the car, and jogged across the parking lot. He stood in front of the window just long enough for the two men to see him, then bolted for the abandoned hangars. The two men raced after him. Cal knew by their reaction that he was high on the president's target list.

Once the men cleared the front entrance to the airport terminal, Knolls pulled up to where Crystal and Katie had walked out to see what was happening. The customs agent at the counter picked up a phone.

Knolls yelled, "Crystal, Katie, get in the car! Brian sent us. We don't have much time. Let's go!"

"What about our luggage?" Crystal asked.

"Grab a bag. Hurry!" Knolls looked into the darkness. He didn't see Cal or the two men, then he jumped out to help Crystal with the bags. Once they were in the car, he gunned the engine and headed for the airport exit.

∞

Cal jumped a fence and ran to the large, rusted hangar doors that were open at the end of the tarmac. He hoped to use the hangar as cover and escape. He ran through the old hangar to the back door. It was chained shut. So was the side door. It was too late to run back out the front doors. He glanced around, then ducked behind an old empty gasoline drum. He'd hoped to outrun the men back to the main highway, and then speed back to the marina. Now he had only one option.

He drew his Glock just as the two men appeared at the hangar doors. Both men carried a handgun. There wasn't time to line up a shot before one of them bolted across the open doorway. The other one slipped around the doorframe and scurried to a darkened corner. Spray and pray shooting wasn't an option for him. The light coming from the terminal only illuminated the front part of the hangar. He'd have to wait for them to fire first in order to get a good shot at them.

"Come out, Mr. Locke," one of the men shouted. "We just want to talk."

Cal stretched out on the floor, making himself the smallest target possible. When his foot hit a piece of metal, both men fired in his direction. Each round fired sounded like a bomb exploding in the empty metal building. Cal spotted the muzzle flashes from the first man's gun. He fired at his position twice. The man grunted and fell to the floor with a thud.

Cal rolled just as the second man fired again. Three rounds punched into the gasoline drum where he had been a second before. Cal fired repeatedly at the second man until he stopped shooting and fell to the floor. Cal crept forward in a crouch and found both men dead. He hid both bodies under an old tarp. He stepped to the doors and looked out. There were only two cars in the parking lot. A customs agent stood at the front door of the terminal. *He had to have heard the exchange of gunfire,* Cal thought. It didn't appear that he wanted to come any closer to investigate.

When the customs agent went back into the terminal, Cal ran for the highway. As he crossed the field, he saw the car parked on the side of the road. Knolls was standing by the driver's door. When Cal reached the car, he jumped into the passenger seat and shouted, "Go! Go! Go!"

"Trouble?" Knolls asked as he jumped into the driver's seat and stomped on the accelerator.

"A little, but our six should be clear."

"Were those gunshots?" Crystal asked.

Cal turned to look at her, then at Katie. "I'll tell you about it later. You're safe now."

"Where's Brian?" Crystal asked.

"He's in the city," Cal replied. "We'll have you there in less than an hour."

Forty minutes later, Crystal and Katie were back with Brian and ensconced in the city.

"Did you kill both of them?" Knolls asked when they were alone.

"I had no choice."

"I'm happy you did. I wouldn't want to be the one to tell Tegan you'd gotten yourself killed. Glad you made it."

Cal nodded. "Let's not tell Tegan about this, if we can avoid it."

"Agreed. But Crystal or Katie might mention it."

"Maybe. Right now, I think they're just happy to be with Brian."

"How many more do you think Maggie and Garth will get into the city?" Knolls asked.

"I'm not sure, but I figure that by noon tomorrow, everyone that's going to be in the city will be there." Cal knew they needed to head for Bimini in the morning and get the outpost ready. Everything was falling into place, and he thought they might just make it before the skies filled with alien craft.

Washington D.C. – July 30 – 0800 hours

"We found them, positive ID," General Stewart said excitedly over the phone. "Both boats are anchored together off Great Guana Cay. They're grouped with several other boats."

"Excellent," President Collingsworth replied.

"How did you find them?" Stacy Preston asked. She'd been released from the hospital and now sat across from the president.

"A stealth drone picked up a cluster of heat signatures, and we were able to read the name of *Deep Current* on the transom of one of the boats. There's a catamaran sailboat anchored next to the *Deep Current* that matches the description of the *Whispering Winds*. The drone is still orbiting at fifteen thousand feet. I have three teams headed for them now. I expect to have them ready to make contact in less than two hours. I'm going to make sure they're boxed in before I commit the teams. By the way, how are you feeling, Stacy?"

"I'm much better now," Stacy replied. "I guess I was just overwhelmed by the enormity of what I'd learned."

"Let's get back to the topic," TC said. "Do you think they're throwing us another red herring?" He was annoyed with both of them.

"I don't think so," Stewart answered. "There's also been a surge of unusual activity in the area and at the airport on Treasure Cay."

"What kind of unusual activity?" TC asked.

"Boats arrive, stay a few minutes, and then depart. Recent infrared imaging shows people getting into the water and disappearing. At first we thought they were just diving the area, but the number of people that have returned to the surface is less than the number of those that went down. There's also a darkness just beneath the surface we haven't been able to identify. There has to be something down there."

"Why didn't you tell me about this sooner?" TC shouted.

"I just received the information before I called."

"You're telling me all of this was just reported? What the hell have you been doing?"

"Mr. President, remember, I just got the drones over the Abacos a few hours ago. If I'd had the resources sooner, I may have found them faster. As it is, I think we were lucky to find them when we did. We'd searched the area around Great Guana Cay earlier with negative contact, so it was low on our priority list."

"And the activity at the airport?" TC asked.

"I was advised that Calvin Locke was seen at the Treasure Cay airport last night and that a team went after him."

"I'm assuming Locke wasn't taken into custody," TC said.

"I haven't heard from the team since they reported the sighting. A second team is checking the area now."

"Your team at the airport is probably dead," TC said.

"That hasn't been confirmed," Stewart replied. "The jets parked on the tarmac were supposed to have brought in investors looking at property on one of the islands. We checked the registration numbers this morning and found them listed to shell companies."

"They're probably government aircraft," TC said.

"They are. We were able to track them down through a classified file at the General Accounting Office. They're listed as being assigned to the Department of Energy."

Trying to calm himself, TC said, "Focus on securing the site."

"Yes, sir."

"Is there anything else?" TC asked.

"Yes, two more things. Our NSA sources confirmed a flurry of cellular activity in the Abacos area late last night and earlier this morning. In addition, Dr. Mike Peters at AUTEC said the sensor buoys are no longer picking up the strange acoustical signatures in the area. They went quiet late yesterday."

TC banged his fist on the desk. "You've failed me, General Stewart. Have all of your teams go to the site, now. I want that location secured. If you have to, you're authorized to launch a full-scale military assault. Blow that site and anything near it to hell! Is that clear?"

"Yes, sir."

"I'll forward your update to Trakar." TC disconnected and stared at Stacy. "I have a bad feeling."

"Why?"

"There are some hidden forces at work here. This isn't how it was supposed to happen."

Stacy nodded. "Would it be a disaster if we didn't succeed?"

TC closed his eyes. Something gnawed at his spirit. He replied, "We have to succeed, don't we?"

Little Abaco City — 0930 hours

Tegan was tired. Bone tired. Jessica and Sara had helped her usher people into the city all through the night. For the first time in thousands of years a part of what was now known as Little Abaco City was once again alive with the sounds of inhabitants. Manatu had given Tegan instructions for where the people were to reside. They planned to keep everyone in Little Abaco, the southernmost city in the massive city complex.

The residents had renamed all four of the cities within the complex, mostly because no one could pronounce the Igigi name for them. Tegan felt that by letting the people rename the cities after the places they'd left behind that it would make it easier on them. The Igigi hadn't minded.

Tegan stood at the entrance to Little Abaco where the shimmering blue-white glow of the three-mile passageway from the Great Guana Outpost changed to a daylight-like luminosity. She was pleased when Manatu had reenergized the transit system to carry people from the Outpost to Little Abaco. Moving equipment and people without the shuttle would have been arduous. As she watched Jessica walking toward her, a shuttle car shot out of the tunnel startling her. The portal flashed red as the shuttle passed through it.

"Hi, Tegan," Jessica said, waving to her.

"Good morning. Why aren't you in bed?"

"I'm not tired. Too many things to do and see. Why are you standing out here?"

"I enjoy looking at the city," Tegan replied. "The architectural design is captivating and so different from the Outpost. It's Zen-like. The buildings remind me of the Elion-Hitchings building in Durham, North Carolina." She pointed to the first cluster of structures along the west wall, then said, "See how the exterior walls interlock and jut out from each other creating a negative space between them?"

"It just looks like a badly assembled condo to me."

Tegan chuckled. "I agree. The buildings do have a modular shape to them, but look at the angled lines of the building around the edges and near the dome over the city. What the Igigi have done is elegant."

"The buildings certainly are otherworldly looking. Especially the way the blue light radiates from the outside walls around those huge windows."

Tegan looked at the opposing seven-level buildings that were located along the east and west walls of the city. She imagined just how magnificent this must have been when the Igigi had lived here.

Several buildings towered over a common area near the center of the city. There were smaller buildings grouped along a main passageway that was wider than a six-lane highway. The passageway vanished into the darkness to the north. Tegan could see the shuttle that had blasted by her was stopped near a pedestrian mover station. The pedestrian movers ran adjacent to the faster shuttle cars, and then branched off periodically near the buildings.

Manatu had told her that the entrance to the main city was twenty-five miles farther on. The passageway that continued north, to what the residents called Sanctuary, was dark. She couldn't wait to see Sanctuary. It had once been the central hub of the entire city complex. Manatu had described it as having rings of buildings that stretched three miles across and stood fifteen stories high in some places. From Sanctuary another passageway continued north for another thirty miles to North Abaco City. It was located beneath Strangers Cay, and was the same size as Little Abaco. The Strangers Cay Outpost was a few miles farther north and was built on the southern edge of the Blake Plateau just before the ocean floor swept downward for thousands of feet.

The Bimini Outpost and the unfinished city to the west had been dubbed Bimini Station. Based on the size of the Bimini facility, and the fact the city had never been completed, they'd decided to call it a station rather than a city. Bimini Station and the outpost were connected to Sanctuary by a single one-hundred-fifty-mile tunnel. Transport cars could travel the distance beneath the ocean floor in twenty minutes. Each transport was fitted with comfortable seats and was large enough to hold twelve people.

Tegan had already heard a few people discussing the need to establish rules during their stay in the city. One man suggested they create an interim government if they were sequestered in the cities for any length of time. People would be living a communal lifestyle in a new environment, cut off from the outside world, and she was certain the stress of not knowing what was happening outside would elevate tensions. She knew that people needed guidance, but creating any type of government was going to be an interesting endeavor. For now, she figured Knolls was in charge of S-3 and Dark Moon personnel, and Garth would lead the others.

Tegan and Manatu had agreed that keeping people busy doing research on the UEE would help them adjust more quickly. Manatu agreed to provide additional access stations. Tegan thought it best for every family to have a specific occupation, which would give them a sense of purpose. She planned to recommend establishing educational forums that would meet every evening for the exchange of information gleaned from the UEE. The new residents would have to adjust to using Igigi technology, especially when it came to hygiene. Considering the city could accommodate over a million people, at least they could find privacy. *If only they could have gotten more people to safety,* Tegan thought.

"Are all the supplies stored in the two dining halls on the second level?" Tegan asked Jessica.

"Most of them. There's still some bottled water cartons stacked on the first level."

"It looks like the labs are nearly set up on the main level. I think that the small cluster of buildings adjacent to the main commons was a good place for them. The Dark Moon technicians' families are settling in on the first level near them."

Tegan found it strange that there was no substantial light emanating from any of the occupied rooms or offices. The windows when viewed from the outside were opaque with a subtle white luminosity, but from inside, they were clear and easy to see out.

"Manatu thought it best for the other inhabitants to find quarters on the third and fourth floor levels," Tegan said. "But I think having all of the Dark Moon people in one area will make it easier for them to live and work." Tegan looked up. "The communications and research centers are going to be on the east side of level five. The west side of level five will house the operations and information center. The top two floors of Little Abaco will remain closed."

"I hope we get more people to come here," Jessica said.

"I think we will. Food and water won't be a problem, but the Igigi will need to adjust the food preparation systems. The basic nutritional bars and cakes they're accustomed to eating don't taste very good."

"I know. I tried one of those bars last night and nearly gagged," Jessica said.

"The Igigi diet was designed for ingestion efficiency and nutrition, not for taste or smell. All of the necessary proteins, fats, carbohydrates, amino acids, minerals, and other chemicals and enzymes required to maintain health are synthesized at a molecular level."

"They still don't taste good."

Tegan knew that the Igigi nutritional processing system took organic chemistry to a new level. The basic chemicals were taken from the sea and the environment, then assembled into micro- and macronutrients and infused with bacteria to create their food. "The Igigi can exist on the synthesized bars and cakes, but our diet requires more variety. Even though they're flavored, it still isn't the same as eating a big plate of spaghetti or a steak."

"That's for sure. I don't know what flavor the bar was that I ate last night."

"For now, the extra Earth-based provisions in the dining halls will help smooth the transition while modifications are made to the food preparation system. At least the drinking water is okay. It's made from the desalination and purification of ocean water."

"The water's fine, but some people still prefer their bottled water," Jessica said. "How's Nate coming along on getting power to the lab equipment?"

"Makita was, as expected, reluctant to use Arklight to power anything not of Igigi origin. Nate managed to convince her it was necessary. He pointed out they'd have to explain the power source if the equipment wasn't plugged into a socket. All the labs now have makeshift power receptacles as do most of the housing areas."

"I imagine that not having any outlets would have been hard to explain."

Tegan was amazed by how easily people seemed to be adapting to the alien facility and at how calm they were. The novelty of what they were discovering and the presence of Manatu and Makita greeting them had seemed to help. There was, as expected, continuous discussion about the pending invasion and about ways to stop it. Several people had already complained about not having cell phone service.

Only eighteen hours had passed since they started the exodus, and they had already accomplished so much. Once they were able to establish secure lines of communications without having to return to the surface, Tegan knew they would reach many more people. Things were moving fast, and she couldn't help but wonder if they'd overlooked something.

"Jessica, I need to head back to the Outpost. Why don't you see if you can't get some sleep?"

"Okay, I'll try."

Tegan walked to the shuttle, boarded, and was whisked back to the Outpost.

Great Guana Outpost — 0950 hours

She found Manatu gazing up at the sphere in the control room. It looked like an aerial view of the Abacos. "Is that Great Guana?" she asked.

"Yes," Manatu replied. "We thought it best to dispatch one of our observation drones at sunrise to monitor the portal and surrounding area while the portal was visible. Several vessels are approaching from the north at high speed and two more are coming from the south. All are occupied by armed men. There is also a small, unmanned aircraft circling above us. I believe our operation has been discovered. We secured the staircase to the surface."

"Everyone we expected from the islands is already in the city. We just got them settled. Where's Cal?"

"He and Commander Knolls are with your friends on the surface. They went to retrieve some personal belongings. Tegan, it is time to leave. We cannot be trapped here. We must leave. Our latest reports indicate the Etu Inu Idimmu ships will be in orbit within the hour."

"What?" Tegan shouted. "You said they wouldn't be here until later today at the earliest."

Manatu stared at her. "We feel you should remain within the Outpost. It is not safe to return to the surface."

"But Cal and the others need to be warned about the boats that are approaching and the advanced Idimmu arrival." Tegan felt panic taking hold of her.

She ran from the control room and headed up the ramp for the portal before Manatu could react. His protests echoed across the room and into the hangar bay. She dove headfirst through the barrier and swam for the surface. The drone of the high-speed boats grew nearer. Just as she surfaced, she saw that Garth already had the *Deep Current* churning south. Maggie was at his side. Edward, aboard the *Blue Angel*, had just untied the line holding it to the *Whispering Winds*. Cal stood in the cockpit. "Cal, they're coming in from both directions," she yelled.

Cal looked up and shouted, "We see them. Go below and have Manatu seal the Outpost."

Bullets spouted the water near the bow of the *Whispering Winds*, where Knolls was feverishly working to free the line from the anchor buoy. They were warning shots. Alex and Nate stood next to the window in the salon, then they disappeared as Cal opened fire from the stern with his Glock. They wouldn't be able to fight off two boats filled with well-armed men, and more were coming. There was no way Cal could get underway in time, much less outrun the faster, smaller craft. Spray flew up in front of the bow of the *Whispering Winds* as more rounds hit the water, only this time the bullets struck closer to her twin hulls.

"Get the hell off of there," Tegan screamed.

The *Blue Angel's* twin engines fired up and then they roared as Edward rammed the throttles full forward. The boat turned south and accelerated taking the route the *Deep Current* had taken. She thought Edward had made a smart move by using the bulk of the *Whispering Winds* as cover while he fled, but she didn't like that it put Cal and the others in the line of fire.

Tegan felt a twinge in her abdomen and sensed danger. She spun around and saw a boat coming directly at her. The two men seated in the bow of the rigid-hull craft had their weapons aimed at her. She dove beneath the surface. She'd gone down only a few feet when the water above her was churned into a white froth by bullets. She dove as fast as she could for the portal. When she reached the entryway and stepped onto the platform, a sense of calm replaced her fear. She looked up and saw the wake from the attacking boat pass overhead. The sound of their engine grew weaker as it continued on. Her thoughts went to Cal. Had he meant for her to seal the Outpost without them?

She pushed through the barrier and found Manatu standing there. "Cal said to seal the Outpost."

"We will. Please come with me." Manatu turned and walked away.

Tegan took a step, then decided she'd rather be with Cal and her friends than be left here alone. "I can't leave them."

She dove back through the portal. Her heart raced as she swam toward the surface. When she broke the surface, the shockwave hit her. Roaring flames lifted pieces of burning debris into the sky. Her heart sank as her deepest fears rained down on her like the falling pieces of the *Whispering Winds*. Three boats circled the burning wreckage as men repeatedly fired into the fractured hulls with automatic weapons. She didn't see Cal or the others. The heat melted the trampoline, and later the mast toppled into the ocean.

She was about to call out when she saw Cal surface for a second to gulp in a breath of air. Then Knolls's head popped up and went back under right behind him. One of the boats broke away from the pack. A man pointed and shouted as it accelerated toward her. She dove back down. A second later, bullets once again tore into the water, making white, bubbly trails all around her. She swam hard for the portal. When she reached the platform, she looked back, and to her relief saw Cal swimming toward her, with Knolls right behind him. She didn't see Alex or Nate yet, but they couldn't be far behind.

Tegan went through the portal just before Cal reached the platform and plunged through the barrier. He sprawled on the floor, gasping for air. Knolls appeared a few seconds later. Then came the rumble of another explosion.

"Cal, where's Alex and Nate?" Tegan asked.

He shook his head, gulped more air, then asked Knolls, "Did you see them jump?"

"No."

Cal looked around and grabbed a mask from the floor, took another breath, and dove back through the barrier before she could stop him.

"What happened?" Tegan asked.

"We didn't identify them as hostile until they were on us," Knolls replied. "We thought they might be late arrivals. Alex and Nate were gathering up notes and packing clothes to take down to the city. Then the bullets started flying."

"Rob, do you think Alex and Nate got off the boat?" Tegan fought a deep sense of dread.

"The last time I saw them they were in the salon. I didn't see them after that. As I was casting off, I was blown over the side when the SMAW rocket hit the superstructure."

"A SMAW?"

"A Shoulder-launched Multipurpose Assault Weapon. In this case, it looked like a Serpent, one of the newer versions."

She just stared at Knolls. She didn't need a lecture on the weapon. Just then Cal came back through the barrier.

"Did you find them?" Tegan asked.

Cal shook his head. "No. All I saw when I surfaced was one burning hull. The rest of our boat was gone. There were more boats headed my way, so I came back down. Tegan, I don't know if they made it off of the *Whispering Winds*."

A wave of emotion engulfed her. Cal looked devastated. Then a pain in her abdomen brought her back from her feeling of despair. "Ouch!"

"What's wrong?" Cal asked.

"Just some pain. I'll be alright."

"The baby?"

"The baby is fine. I think she's trying to tell me something. I had the pain just before the men opened fire on me." Movement outside the barrier caught her eye. Two figures hovered in front of the portal. "Is that Alex and Nate? What are they doing just staying there?"

"That's not Alex and Nate," Cal said. "Manatu, seal the portal. Now!"

Tegan watched as the two figures ascended. A second later, her view of the outside world was replaced by a black wall. The Outpost was sealed. And Nate and Alex were missing—or worse.

Deep Current – 1000 hours

Garth had the engines of the *Deep Current* at full throttle. The fifty-foot yacht was a mile south of the *Blue Angel*. He watched as Edward swung west through the shallow waters between Great Guana and Scotland Cay. He was confident Edward wasn't going to be cornered anywhere. The *Blue Angel* could make over thirty knots and was faster than most boats her size.

Garth watched as two small powerboats passed a mile to their starboard. Choosing to stay on the Atlantic side of Scotland had been a good decision. The boats continued north at a high rate of speed toward the smoke on the horizon. They wouldn't be a factor in a few more minutes. What concerned him most was the explosion he'd heard and the possibility they were being watched from the sky. He knew from the amount of smoke that the *Whispering Winds* had been destroyed. "I pray everyone got away," he said to Maggie. "I'm glad we left Jessica and Sara in the city."

"I'm sure everyone escaped," Maggie said. "Where're we headed?"

"I plan to run south, staying well offshore. There aren't many boats that could catch us, and we have full tanks, so our range even at maximum speed will be over five hundred miles."

"That should get us just about anywhere we need to go to hide."

Garth said, "We need to head toward Bimini and link up with Cal's parents."

"Is that smart? If they're tracking us, wouldn't it be better to head into a harbor and switch boats?"

"I have a better idea," Garth replied.

"I hope it's a good one."

"I think so."

"Do you know the name of Cal's parents' sailboat?" Maggie asked.

"Yes, it's called the *Tranquility.*"

"What kind of boat is it?"

"Cal said it's a Catalina 445, a single-mast sloop. It should be easy to spot."

"Do you know where the portal is on Bimini?"

"I haven't a clue," Garth replied. "I'm sure Tegan or someone will open it for us."

"I don't see the *Blue Angel* or the other two boats now. I'm worried about Edward."

"Edward won't let them catch him. When the time is right, he'll make a run for Bimini."

"I hope so."

Garth said, "Cal and Tegan will use the transit system and probably beat us to Bimini."

"Did you tell Howard about Bimini?"

"Edward did. Howard couldn't leave for Green Turtle until nearly five this morning, so he told Edward to go without them. He's been a big help. Edward thought he should be given an alternative if he didn't make it to Great Guana in time."

"That was the right decision. But what if he's stopped while he and his family are on the *Alde I* and they take them into custody? He could give up the other outpost location. I would if I thought it would save you."

Garth thought for a moment, then said, "If he's stopped, he'll spin some story. He can usually talk his way out of anything. He can always tell them he was moving the *Alde I* for us and deny knowing anything. After all, he's a harbor master, and that's something he does occasionally."

"How's he going to find us?"

"The same way everyone else is going to. Get to the area and wait for someone to find him."

Maggie said, "I'm just glad the rest of our family is safe."

"I think there's a world of hurt headed our way. Hand me the burner phone. I have some calls to make to put our evasion plan in motion so we can head for Bimini."

CHAPTER FIFTEEN

The phone rang in the Oval office. TC knew it was General Stewart.

"Yes, General Stewart."

"The teams have confirmed the location of the artifact. There's an underwater facility there. The situation is contained."

"Good. What about the people? Did we take them alive?"

"We didn't have a chance to get them. Our team put warning shots across the bow of the boats as they approached. The people on the sailboat fired at our teams. The men were forced to neutralize the threat and fired a rocket into the sailboat. Several of the people on the sailboat were blown into the water. The boat was completely destroyed. Two of our men went down to search the area and found an entrance to an underwater facility. They could see people on the other side of a blue force field that kept the seawater out."

"A force field?" TC muttered. "So these people are being aided. Trakar told me there was another species involved."

"Several vessels that were anchored near the *Whispering Winds* made a run for it. We have a drone tracking the *Deep Current*. Our teams will intercept it shortly. I'm still receiving reports, but I knew you wanted to be advised immediately of any developments."

TC said, "Keep me advised, but don't attempt to enter the facility. I want to advise the Antediluvians before we go any further." He didn't wait for General Stewart to reply. He disconnected and looked at Stacy. "They've found not only the marker but an underwater facility. We can destroy it whenever we need to, but I want to make sure that's what the Antediluvians want us to do."

"They will be pleased with our progress."

"Yes. I think they will."

TC focused his thoughts and connected with Trakar. He could tell she was closer than the last time he made contact. He relayed the information about the underwater facility and the events of the last few hours. Her response shocked him. She told him to do nothing. They would be in Earth's orbit within the hour. His priority was preparing for their arrival. For now, he was to keep the area secure.

The Outpost – 1000 hours

"Cal, we can't just leave them out there!" Tegan exclaimed.

"We don't have a choice. The area above us is under the president's control. We're outgunned and outnumbered. Even if they made it off the boat, Alex and Nate will have already been captured."

Tegan could see the frustration on his face.

"I have things I need to do," Knolls said. "I'm sorry, Tegan, but I agree with Cal's assessment." He walked down the ramp.

She couldn't believe what the two of them said. Alex and Nate were more than friends. They were like family, and they knew about the city. "Cal, they know everything. We have to rescue them."

"I know that." His voice cracked, and his eyes teared up. "Tegan, I'm not sure they'll be telling anyone anything."

It was the first time she'd seen him cry. "You think they're dead, don't you?"

He wiped the tears away. "They were still below when the rocket hit. I don't know how they could've gotten clear. The salon was completely destroyed. Unless there was a hole blown in the hull, I don't see how they could have made it out through the flames."

Tegan hugged him. He squeezed her back. "How will we know for sure?"

"We'll search the area, but that isn't going to happen anytime soon, by then…"

"I know," Tegan said. She felt a presence behind her, but didn't want to let go of Cal. "What is it, Manatu?"

"Your friends no longer live in this world," Manatu replied.

Tegan spun around. "How do you know?"

"Makita monitored the battle with the boats using the drone. She informed me that only Calvin and Commander Knolls left the sailboat. Your two friends did not survive."

Cal pushed Tegan aside. "This is your doing!" he shouted, jabbing his finger at Manatu's face. "You let them butcher my friends, and you could have prevented it."

Manatu remained calm. "There was nothing we could do to stop what was to occur. I warned Tegan of the vessels' approach. We feel the pain of your loss, Calvin. And yours as well, Tegan." Manatu bowed slightly and walked away.

Tegan clutched Cal's arm and said, "I don't know what to say, but I can tell you I'm tired of hiding, and I'm pissed. You know what I can do when someone has hurt my family. The president had Alex and Nate killed. I think it's time we take the battle to them."

Tegan felt the movement in her abdomen. She nodded her understanding, not knowing how she understood her daughter's message. She started down the ramp toward the control room.

"Where are you going?" Cal asked.

"To engage the enemy."

Dahlgren, Virginia — July 30 — 1010 hours

Jacob Miller parked his black Toyota Tundra in a secure parking lot and locked it out of habit. There was no chance anyone would steal the truck from the lot that was adjacent to the base. It was under constant surveillance, surrounded by concrete and steel barriers, and protected by armed military personnel.

Jacob was a civilian contractor assigned to the US Air Force 20th Space Control Squadron. His official job title was Technical Tracking Trajectory Operator and Analyst, or as he was known in the "Trench," a T3OA. As part of an around-the-clock team, he was responsible for tracking and monitoring every object in orbit.

Jacob's position was one of many in the Space Surveillance System, more commonly known as the Space Fence. The command tracked and collected data on all Near Earth Orbiting Objects, NEOO's, using radar tracking stations around the globe. Any object larger than four inches in diameter was tagged and monitored. With the recent system upgrades, detection capability and tracking now extended thirty thousand miles into space. The Joint Space Operations Center, JSpOC, at Vandenberg AFB in California, received daily updates from the Space Fence and then passed the information on to the Integrated Global Space Command.

The IGSC was the central command for all space operations and was linked to NORAD. It received information from an assortment of specialized space operations and tracking commands. Months earlier, the Deep Space Object Tracking Command and the Missile Defense Early Warning system became a part of the IGSC. The commanders knew that President Collingsworth had ordered that unification, but they didn't know the real reason behind it.

Jacob made the short walk from the parking lot to the facility entrance. He started to sweat the minute he left his air-conditioned truck, and by the time he reached the entrance to the annex, his blue shirt bore the telltale marks of heavy perspiration. He knew that the hot and humid air would be worse in another month, but he still preferred the heat to the incredibly cold weather he had experienced the past winter.

After passing through security screening, Jacob entered a biometrically controlled elevator. The fingerprint scan allowed him to descend to the third subbasement of a ten-story structure buried beneath the Virginia landscape. The Trench was an electronically shielded, high-tech operations area, located sixty feet underground. When the elevator opened, Jacob breathed in the familiar smell of the operating electronic equipment housed in the large command center. He felt the chill of the sixty-eight-degree temperature against his damp shirt.

Jacob took two steps down to the tiered, semicircular aisle where his workstation was located. His console faced multiple massive screens that lined a large wall beneath a thirty-foot-high ceiling.

Neela Anderson, a short, attractive woman sat at his console. She was Jacob's nightshift counterpart. To provide continuous coverage at the center, the T3OA's worked in two-person teams on twelve-hour shifts, three days on and three days off.

"Morning, Miss Neela," Jacob said in his Georgia drawl. He sat down next to her for the handoff briefing. "Sorry I'm a bit late."

Jacob always tried to get to the center early, but this morning he couldn't seem to get out of the house.

"Ally had a clothing crisis," Jacob said. "Can you tell me why a seven-year-old cares so much about coordinating her school outfits? This morning she discovered the matching top to her skirt had a stain on it, and you would've thought the world had come to an end."

"You'd have to be a girl to understand," Neela said. "What'd your wife do to resolve the issue?"

"Why do you think I didn't fix the problem?"

"Because I know you. You should have had boys."

"Tell me about it. Christine found her a clean outfit and promised they'd go shopping for some new clothes. Then we had to put Ally on the school bus, which you know she hates."

"Yes, I do. Christine's car broke down again?"

"Correct. I had to scramble to get her to work in Yorktown before driving here."

Neela chuckled. "No problem, Jake. I covered for you. Being a single woman, I don't have the luxury of blaming my tardiness on the family." Neela started the briefing before Jacob could respond to her good-natured sniping.

"Nothing of major interest to report. All systems are nominal, as usual. No tests are scheduled, and every piece of space junk is orbiting where it should be. There was some chatter an hour ago from GEODSS about spotting something unusual beyond the outer marker, but I haven't heard back from them yet. They're trying to decide if they have optics or software issues on Maui. Imaging produced some anomalous returns with undifferentiated spectral waves which they couldn't interpret."

The Ground-based Electro-Optical Deep Space Surveillance system also operated under the IGSC umbrella. GEODSS used multiple optical telescopes located around the world to track deep-space objects. These telescopes augmented, overlapped, and looked farther into space than the Space Fence. GEODSS telescopes operate only at night and during clear weather, which was why the observation sites were scattered all over the globe. When the telescopes were working, they worked very well. They were capable of tracking as many as four thousand objects each night. The telescopes could observe objects ten thousand times dimmer than what the human eye could detect and track something as small as a baseball in geosynchronous orbit. The Space Fence and GEODSS mission parameters also ensured that the International Space Station wasn't struck by any wayward objects.

"Did they report any information about what they saw or in what sector?" Jacob asked.

"Actually, the conversation was a bit odd. Those guys are always on the money with their information, but they seemed perplexed by whatever they were trying to sort out. Weather over Diego Garcia looks good, so they'll take a closer look when they can. It's something beyond our tracking range. That's all I've got."

"Thanks, Neela. You stand relieved," Jacob said with a smile. After Nella cleared, he plugged his headset into the VOX. Jacob checked in with the other stations, and once he was on-line turned to Neela and gave her a thumbs-up. "See you tonight."

Neela stretched. "Yes, you will, but I may be a little late. You know, to make up for the extra time I worked today."

"That only seems fair," replied Jacob, focusing on the multiple display screens in front of him. "Christine is going to get a ride home from work."

The alert tone sounded. It was the Large Mass Object detector proximity alert warning. The alarm's strident tone was different from the customary proximity alert for small space junk or meteors. The LMO detected any object entering Earth's orbital plane closer than thirty thousand miles and with a mass capable of causing severe destruction if it struck.

In all the time Jacob had worked at the facility, other than standard drills, he had heard the LMO alarm sound only twice without warning. Both times it turned out to be an unseen asteroid transiting within the

Space Fence boundary. Jacob focused on the data scrolling across his center screen. The system highlighted the object with a bright red tracking box, indicating that it was on a collision course with the planet. Jacob's blood ran cold. His thoughts went to his wife and daughter. The NEO was at the outer marker, the OM, and was large enough to be an extreme threat.

Jacob's fingers flew over the keyboard as he tried to verify the trajectory. He knew that an asteroid this massive should have been spotted and cataloged long ago. Jacob ran another set of diagnostics and reviewed the data stream. The object measured over two miles across by a mile deep, and it was three miles long. Jacob couldn't believe what he was seeing. The data had to be wrong.

"Christ, what is that?" Neela asked.

"I'm hope this is an unannounced drill," Jacob replied. With trembling hands, he tested all the systems for malfunctions three times. He found nothing to indicate the object wasn't real.

"Shit! The NEO appears authentic. I wonder if this is what GEODSS was looking at earlier," Jacob said, cycling through the array of analysis layers available to him. Jacob routed his data to the big board as he tried to make sense of what he was viewing.

"The object doesn't appear to be an asteroid," Jacob said, feeling almost thankful.

"The speed doesn't make sense. It's too slow," Neela added. "Do you think this is what I think it is?"

Jacob concentrated on the object's track. "If it is, then it's the biggest alien ship I could ever imagine, even in my worst nightmare."

Neela sat down at the empty station next to Jacob, plugged in her headset, and brought all the terminals online.

"I have a positive track," Jacob shouted. "Kickapoo, Gila River, and Jordon Lake have confirmed it and are tracking."

"Christ, I think the world is going to be in for a rude awakening," Neela said.

Jacob grabbed the phone. "Neela, I want you on the line with GEODSS. See if they have a visual and then let the boss know. I'll contact the duty officer at Vandenberg. He's probably going to keep me on the line for a while." Jacob punched in the short series of numbers that connected him instantly with the officer of the day at the JSpOC at Vandenberg.

"Major Sanderson," the duty officer answered immediately.

"This is T3OA Jacob Miller at Space Fence. We have a high-confidence profile on an unidentified object at the OM. It registers as an extreme threat. Its speed is steady at ten thousand KPH. Current trajectory puts the object on a direct impact path with Antarctica in less than three hours."

"Say again the threat level?"

"Extreme! Level Black!" Jacob shouted. "If it continues on course and speed … it's a planet killer, Major Sanderson. We're working on mass and possible composition. I have no visual confirmation yet from GEODSS."

There was a short pause at the other end of the line. "Is this a joke?"

Jacob heard shouting in the background from Sanderson's phone.

"I guess not. Space Fence, we confirm your NEO. Continue tracking and report back in ten Mikes. You are designated primary." The line went dead.

Jacob looked at Neela and said, "They see it, and somehow we became the primary. We need to report back in ten minutes. Has the box estimated a mass or composition yet?"

Neela looked more distressed than she had a few moments earlier. "Negative on mass, and we aren't receiving any density reflections."

"Did you call Captain Spriggs?"

"Yes. He was indisposed. I took that to mean he was in the restroom."

"Call his office again. Tell whoever answers to drag his ass out of the can!"

A few moments later, Jacob heard the sound of someone running in his direction. "Neela, I need you as communications liaison. I want to stay focused on the target."

Captain Spriggs slid to a stop behind him, and plunked down in an empty chair.

"Put *all* the feeds on the big board and transmit them to JSpOC and IGSC Command," Captain Spriggs ordered.

"Already being sent," Jacob said. "Have you ever seen anything like this before, Captain Spriggs?"

"Never. There will be hell to pay for why no one picked up this object until it was at the OM."

"GEODSS at Garcia confirms they have a visual on the object," Neela said.

The fright in her voice caused gooseflesh to stand up on Jacob's arms.

"Put up their optical feed. I want to see this thing," Spriggs ordered. A moment later, the image appeared on a screen.

"Dear Mother of God," Jacob said when he saw the object. He dialed Major Sanderson, deciding what he was looking at didn't warrant waiting the full ten minutes.

"This is Sgt. Johnson," the voice on the other end answered. Jacob thought for a moment that he'd keyed in the wrong number in his haste, then realized Major Sanderson was probably needed in ten different places at once.

"This is Jacob Miller at Space Fence. I have an update for Major Sanderson." Captain Spriggs motioned for him to put it on speaker.

"Stand by one. He is on the other line."

The sounds of a commotion came over the open line. Jacob knew that everyone in the Joint Operations Command was scrambling around. For some reason Sgt. Johnson hadn't bothered to mute his end. The speaker picked up the din of activity. Jacob looked at Spriggs and smiled. "At least our people aren't in a panic."

"Give it a few minutes," Spriggs replied.

The hardline crackled to life with a booming voice. "This is Major Sanderson. Any change on the track?"

"No, sir," Jacob replied. "The track remains the same, as does the speed. We're unable to provide mass or composition yet. The thing's bouncing everything back at us. The visual feed is being routed to you now, and we'll keep working it."

"Very well," Sanderson said.

"Whoa, that's not possible," said Jacob.

"What's not possible?" Sanderson asked.

Spriggs leaned forward. "Major, this is Captain Spriggs. The object has reduced its approach speed by half."

"How can it be slowing down?"

"I don't know," Spriggs replied.

Jacob looked at the big screens on the wall in front of him as the GEODSS images appeared and were enhanced. The object had a smooth surface and was as black as space. There was no doubt in Jacob's mind what he was seeing.

"Neela, you see that?" Jacob asked.

"I most certainly do. That's not a spaceship, that's a space station."

"We have an aspect change on the object, and it's continuing to reduce speed," Jacob announced. "It looks like the object is aligning itself to enter a polar geosynchronous orbit."

The proximity alert tone wailed again. Jacob turned it off, thinking it was responding to the object changing direction. Then he saw a new object highlighted on his screen.

"I have a second NEO coming in from the same quadrant. It's at the OM. The new object has the same approach speed as the first one." Jacob was sweating again despite the chilly air in the room.

"Copy, you have a second NEO," Sanderson's voice boomed over the speaker.

After a quick analysis of the new object, Neela said, "Object two is identical to the first one."

Captain Spriggs said, "Major Sanderson, I recommend we designate these objects as targets Alpha and Bravo. These are controlled NEOs."

Jacob heard Sanderson yelling to his staff. "Why the hell aren't we seeing these things until they're at the OM?" His voice echoed through the speaker. "I concur, Captain Spriggs. GEODSS has visual on your second target. Continue to monitor and notify me of any changes in Alpha or Bravo or if you see any new targets."

"Understood, will do," Spriggs replied. The line went dead. "Good work, you two. Stay on it. I need to make some calls. I'll post runners with you. I have a feeling this is just the beginning, and you're going to need all the help you can get. It's about to get really crazy around here."

Jacob looked at Spriggs and said, "I think we passed crazy ten minutes ago."

The Outpost — 1020 hours

Tegan lay in the recliner, connected to the UEE. She was looking for something in the archives, something she'd seen before when she was exploring Arklight. Cal had gone into the city to tell Jessica and Sara what had happened. Suddenly, the UEE went offline, she looked up and saw Manatu standing there.

"The Etu Inu Idimmu ships have arrived. It is time for you to go into the city with the others and for us to leave," Manatu said.

"I don't understand why you need to leave." Tegan said, sitting up. Manatu didn't answer. He just stood there. Tegan thought his emerald eyes reflected a hint of anger. "I'll ask again, why must you leave?"

"It is time," Manatu replied. "You must get to the safety of the city before we leave." Manatu started to walk away.

Tegan jumped to her feet and blocked his path. "I'm not going anywhere until I figure out how to stop this invasion." A tingling sensation spread through her. Tegan sat back down on the recliner, then laid back as if she was being commanded by something she couldn't explain. The system connected to her, and she felt her heart begin to pound. She suddenly found herself cocooned in the Arklight field, and she knew who was controlling it. That really frightened her. Tegan focused her thoughts and saw what she must do.

Makita walked up and stood beside Manatu. They exchanged high-pitched chirps and whistles.

"It's too late to stop her," Manatu said. "She's found a pathway to the Arklight field."

"The child is more resourceful than we imagined," Makita replied. "We must depart, or we will be trapped here."

"It's not just the child."

"What do you mean?"

"Look," Manatu said, then pointed at the sphere. "They are working together as one entity. I've never heard of this being feasible. They're taking control of the system."

"That isn't possible, not without access to the controller," Makita said. "Tegan has never even seen it or been given instructions for its use."

Manatu studied the sphere. "We must hurry to the ship. We cannot be here when she activates the field."

They ran down the ramp, boarded the ship, and began the preflight.

The Arklight field surrounding Tegan continued to intensify. The light was so bright she couldn't see out. The energy began to pulse rhythmically, matching the rapid heartbeat of her unborn child. Streams of Arklight energy flowed through their bodies. Tegan enlarged the field until it filled the control room. She knew that her daughter was linked into the field. The neural pathways in Tegan's mind exploded with a newfound prowess as she made the final connection to the knowledge that governed the universe. The information streamed into her brain like a flooding river after a dam had burst.

She felt the power on a molecular level. Every cell in her body energized, and she was one with the universe. Deep within her she found her daughter's consciousness. The Arklight field was giving her a gift she gladly accepted. Tegan was forming a bond unlike anything she'd felt before. She was the vessel through which the power and knowledge of Arklight was being channeled. Had Arklight sought her daughter, or had her daughter summoned it? All of Tegan's thoughts and experiences passed to her child. Her daughter gave her the insight she needed to share control with the Arklight field.

As the power grew within them, she felt her child's warmth and love as she discovered more of Tegan's essence. They would have no secrets between them. They couldn't. They were dependent on each other for surviving what was to come.

The Arklight field intensified further. Tegan felt as if she'd slipped into a different realm. Nothing could stop them. Their essence was woven into the fabric of the universe. Tegan had all she needed at her fingertips.

She commanded the Arklight field to respond. There would be no loss of life because of the action she was about to take. She knew that what she was setting in motion wouldn't stop the Etu Inu Idimmu from landing, but she would be able to isolate the Awakened and stop their madness. She thought that Ninurtu would be proud of what she was about to do.

The water above the Outpost looked as if it was in a sonic mixer. Ripples widened out from the center of the vibration, and the waves steadily grew larger. The teams in the boats, feeling the pulses intensifying, had wisely left. The tremors from the power buildup rocked the city like an earthquake. Many were panicking, thinking that an attack had begun.

Cal hurried back to the Outpost. As he ran from the city tunnel and onto the third level ramp, the intensity of the light coming from the control room above him forced him to shield his eyes. The Igigi ship hovered free of the docking cradle. Tegan was nowhere in sight. He sprinted up the ramp toward the control room. He slammed into the Arklight barrier as if it were a brick wall. The entry barrier had been reenergized, but he hadn't seen it. He felt for the palm reader. He placed his hand on the palm reader as he'd done many times before, but the barrier remained sealed.

Squinting, he saw Tegan lying on the recliner. She appeared to be at the core of the power source. Tendrils of light radiated from her like sunbeams piercing the clouds of a new dawn. Every control panel in the room was alive with multicolored lights. Symbols flashed within the holographic sphere so fast he couldn't begin to keep up with their changing forms, but he somehow knew that Tegan understood what they all meant. Cal beat his fists against the barrier and screamed at the top of his lungs. She didn't respond to him.

The floor trembled beneath his feet as he watched helplessly as Tegan manipulated the holographic controls under her hands. A basketball-sized sphere of blue energy appeared over Tegan's head. Then the energy sphere shot upward and passed through the ceiling without leaving a mark. A moment later, the tendrils of Arklight coalesced into another sphere of energy above Tegan, and it, too, shot through the ceiling. The control room continued to shake as one after another sphere appeared, enlarged, and ascended. He lost count of how many balls of energy Tegan sent from control room. Then the shaking subsided, and the tendrils of light disappeared. All that remained was a bubble of Arklight surrounding Tegan.

When the last sphere reached the troposphere, Tegan sent the execute command, and the energy contained within the spheres ignited. The intense blue glow of each sphere expanded and lit the sky as if a thousand meteors had entered the atmosphere at the same time. The glow faded as the energy interlaced itself with the atoms of the thinner atmosphere. Now, Tegan thought, the Etu Inu Idimmu could no longer control the Awakened. The people of Earth would see the truth. Tegan felt elated.

She touched her belly and smiled, knowing that she and her daughter had struck a significant blow.

∞

Manatu and Makita were aboard their ship, ready to leave the Outpost, when the energy spheres ignited in Earth's atmosphere. Manatu felt pleased with Tegan. He had counted on her visceral reaction to the invasion to awaken the entity she had developing within her. The loss of her friends only helped push her forward. She held the only solution to the catastrophic problem they faced. Now, both of their needs were satisfied without his compromising an inviolable law. What surprised him was how advanced Tegan's child had already become and how much power they wielded together.

The life form growing within Tegan was an amazing specimen. The new entity would be human, but she would be far superior to any other intelligent being they'd ever encountered. The child would be the Mitochondrial Eve of the next evolution of the human species. Manatu knew that another species was responsible for altering the genetic structure of the precursor to the modern human. They had moved humanity forward in one quick leap nearly a quarter of a million years ago. He was certain they, too, had understood the nature of life in the universe and the need to nurture it. Some Igigi speculated that the species responsible had once lived on Ceri and its moon Danatis, and it was their ruins that remained there.

But Tegan's child was not something the Igigi had chosen to create. She was something else entirely. Perhaps a quirk of nature, a random mutation, or maybe something more. Manatu pondered whether it was possible she was a gift, something created from the Arklight she so easily interacted with now. They would monitor her development closely.

Manatu would make sure that the child survived. It was his duty to protect her and Tegan. He hoped only that if it became necessary to leave Earth that Tegan would voluntarily join them. But that would be decided in the future. For now, he was certain that Tegan and her child would remain safe within the city walls.

He unsealed the portal and moved the ship toward the opening. He caught a glimpse of Tegan in the ship's viewer. She was still bathed in the Arklight field. The purity of the field was something that he always regarded with reverence. Now it meant even more to him.

Cal walked up to the palm reader again, placed his hand on it, and said a quick prayer. The portal opened. He ran to Tegan's side. When he reached her, he knelt beside her and looked at her face through the glow of the blue light that still encircled her head. When he touched the ball of light surrounding her face, it pulsed. The vision that penetrated his mind would have dropped him to the floor if he hadn't been on his knees. He could not only see his daughter, but he could feel her, too. It felt as if she was reaching out and touching his heart and mind. He sensed her love. It was pure and unconditional. Then the light around Tegan dissolved, and the connection with his daughter vanished.

Cal said, "Tegan, can you hear me?"

She opened her eyes. "Of course I can hear you. You're right next to me."

"Are you alright?"

"Yes, Cal, I'm very alright. Did you enjoy my gift to you?"

"I saw our baby girl. I could feel her, but how?"

"It's a secret. She wanted to meet you."

"The light didn't harm either of you?"

"No. The power of the universe is so beautiful, yet so complex." Tegan replied. Her emerald eyes enlarged, flashed at him, then returned to normal.

"What the hell was that?" Cal asked.

"A glimpse into our future, and it's looking up. The Idimmu are in orbit."

Cal felt dumbstruck. "How can you say things are looking up? We need to get back to the city."

"There's no hurry now. Our daughter and I have severed the connection between the Idimmu and the Awakened. The Idimmu don't control them anymore. There will be no further deception, no peaceful landing, no assimilation. The world knows they're here, and the people will rise up and fight them."

Cal wondered if the energy field had scrambled Tegan's mind. "How did you do all of this?"

She smiled. "Our daughter is very special. She's beyond anything I would have ever believed a human being could become. She's the most perfect being that has ever existed." Tegan stood up. "I see your look. I'm not delusional, and I'm not just saying this because she's our child. In a few minutes, everyone will learn that many of the world's leaders are no longer under the Idimmu spell. I'll explain it in more detail when we meet with Knolls and Brian. They'll want to hear the details." Tegan looked away.

"What is it?"

"I only wish I could have told Alex and Nate what happened. I wanted them to meet our child."

Cal didn't know what to say. He felt the loss of his friends deeply. Movement in the cavern caught his attention. The wall dissolved back to a portal, and then the Igigi ship glided through it. The ship stopped just outside the Outpost. "Where are they going?"

"Probably back to Antarctica. They know what we did," Tegan said, rubbing her belly. "And I think Manatu knew all along what our daughter and I were capable of doing if given the right motivation."

"That seems deceptive and more than a little chickenshit if you ask me. Letting you do what they wouldn't." Cal looked at the ship again as the marker slid into the ship. "They took the marker."

"That'll make it harder to find the portal. They plan to camouflage the entrance after they reseal it." She smiled at him. "Let's get to the city. We have lots of things to do. We'll see them again in a couple of days at the Bimini outpost."

"You're sure about that?"

"Yes. Cal, they want to help us. At least Manatu does. I could see it in his eyes, but he has a fine line to walk."

"So you don't feel like you're being used?"

"Not in the least. I can't explain everything now."

As they walked toward the tunnel, Cal thought Tegan was different somehow, but he wasn't sure how exactly.

Washington D.C. — 1020 hours

TC felt the closeness of Trakar. Stacy sat beside him on the sofa in his private office. He could feel Stacy's excitement. TC knew there would be no offensive military response from any nation against the Antediluvian fleet. Trakar had instructed TC on what he was to tell the world when he addressed the public in a few hours. Now all they had to do was await the official notification of the Antediluvians' arrival. He had to somehow convey a semblance of shock during his announcement. A moment later, there was an urgent knock on the outer door of his private office. Two Secret Service agents entered, both men looking distressed.

The senior agent said, "Sir, we have been advised to move you and the vice president to the DSCC immediately."

The Deep Secure Command Center was located three hundred feet under the West Wing of the White House. In Washington and the surrounding area, all of the most important things were secured deep underground. The hardened DSCC complex had taken over four years to construct. The outer shell of the structure could withstand a direct nuclear strike, and the facility had the most advanced electronics and communications systems imaginable. The DSCC was a labyrinth consisting of several floors. The President's Command Center was on the deepest level. The DUCC, the Deep Underground Command and Control Center, was connected to the DSCC, and together they had three times the square footage of the White House.

"What's so important that you have to barge in like this?" TC asked, feigning displeasure for the interruption.

"Sir, I haven't been informed of the reason for you having to be escorted there. You must come with us."

"Very well," TC said. He stood and took Stacy by the hand, then walked casually from the Oval Office as if he was going to get a snack.

"Please, Mr. President, we need to hurry," the agent said as more agents rushed toward them. "The VP has to go to a separate bunker per protocol."

"I think not," TC stated matter-of-factly. "Protocol may require her to be elsewhere, but that isn't what we'll do. She will stay with me."

The agent just nodded and hurried them onto the elevator.

TC and Stacy walked into the DSCC. The massive outer door remained open so that key staff could get in. Senior military personnel arrived from the Pentagon, accompanied by armed military personnel. Marines wearing combat fatigues took up positions at all the entry points. TC sat quietly in a luxurious mahogany leather chair and looked at the twelve large monitors suspended across one side of the room with insincere interest. Only one was operational, with a link to the Pentagon. Several communications specialists rushed to activate the video conference system. The other screens suddenly came to life with static, startling him.

The Air Force officer carrying the forty-pound portable launch code briefcase sat quietly behind him. TC thought his presence was redundant since he could launch weapons from the command center without using the "nuclear football."

"Sir, we have General Stoddard on the line at IGSC," one the communications technicians said. No one spoke. TC nodded for him to make the connection.

When General Eli Stoddard's face appeared on the screen, TC could see the strain etched on it.

Stoddard said, "Mr. President, less than fifteen minutes ago we began tracking two unidentified objects as they crossed the Space Fence Outer Marker. For unknown reason, the objects went undetected until they reached that point."

"What are these objects, and where are they headed?" TC asked, starting the charade.

"We aren't sure what the objects are, but all monitoring systems agree they seem to be under intelligent control."

"Did you say intelligent control?"

"Yes, sir. One of the objects changed course as it decelerated and is now moving into a stationary orbit five hundred miles over Antarctica. The other object is slowing, and it appears that it's heading for orbit over the Arctic. Both objects arrived within minutes of each other."

"You mean to tell me that these are alien spaceships?" TC asked with mock disbelief.

"That's correct. Neither object has displayed any act of aggression. Both have enormous mass. Their hull composition is unknown, but the material is light-absorbing. This could account for our long-range sensors not picking them up. The hull is black and makes them nearly impossible to see. We've detected no heat signature, and their source of propulsion is unknown."

"Exactly how big are these things?" TC asked, truly not knowing. It wasn't something he ever thought to ask Trakar.

"They're three miles long, two miles wide, and over a mile top to bottom. They have been designated targets Alpha and Bravo."

"Does anyone know what the protocol is for dealing with this type of situation?" More monitors came to life with the serious faces of the Joint Chiefs, several of the commanders of the Unified Combat Command, and a few Cabinet officials. TC noted that General Stewart was among the many faces on one of the screens linked to the Pentagon.

"Mr. President, we have already taken the initial steps to secure all military installations and sensitive facilities," the commander of the United States Northern Command, General Donald McLaughlin, said. "All military units have been placed on high alert, NORAD is at DEFCON 2, and General Stoddard at the IGSC is ready to launch Sprites on your orders. We may lose satellites soon, depending on their intentions. Secondary communication networks have been placed on standby."

TC knew that the Sprites were new missiles capable of carrying tactical nuclear warheads into deep space. Designed without the public's knowledge, they could intercept large earthbound space objects. They had the power to destroy an asteroid as large as the Antediluvian ships. The missiles, located at Vandenberg AFB and on the new specially equipped Neptune Class stealth submarines, could be airborne within minutes of his ordering it. He knew that wasn't going to happen. He'd never asked Trakar about their defenses, so he didn't know if the Sprites could destroy the Antediluvian ships. But that was a moot point.

"Thank you, General McLaughlin. I believe the prudent thing to do now is to wait and see what their intentions are," TC said. "I believe the last thing we should do is provoke them with a preemptive aggressive military action. I want to make myself perfectly clear, if military action is warranted, it will come *only* on my orders."

"Yes, Mr. President," McLaughlin replied. "The missiles are ready if you choose to initiate Operation Orbital Punch."

"Since no one has answered my question, I will assume there's no protocol for this situation," TC said in a louder voice. "General Stoddard, what's the response time if I order a launch?"

"Less than two minutes until the missiles are airborne, and four minutes to impact."

"Very well, then we'll wait," TC said. He knew that his role was to be the voice of reason in order to give the Antediluvians the time they needed to establish bases of operation. Still, TC felt conflicted, and he sensed that Stacy was having the same misgivings now that the Antediluvian ships were in orbit.

The rest of the leaders of the Joint Chiefs, the Unified Combat Commands, and the intelligence community began offering opinions on how best to deal with the developing situation. TC felt sick as he listened to all of the recommendations. Sharp pangs radiated through his head. The pain felt as if someone was stabbing him repeatedly with a hot knife. He glanced at Stacy and could tell she was experiencing the same physical discomfort.

"Mr. President," General Stoddard said, "I have just been informed that several smaller ships have launched from the Alpha craft."

"Where are they headed?" TC asked, genuinely caught off guard. He rubbed his temples. Trakar never mentioned anything about smaller craft being involved. They were supposed to wait in orbit. *What's happening?*

"Tracking trajectories are varied."

"How many of them are there?"

"There are seven small ships, all the same size. The smaller ships have been designated Alpha one through seven. They're moving erratically as they approach the atmosphere. They seem to be taking evasive action. Their destinations are unknown. Alpha one will penetrate the atmosphere over Antarctica in less than one minute."

TC squeezed the sides of his head as the pain grew more intense.

"No doubt the ships know we're tracking them," General Stoddard said. "Once in atmosphere we can't use the Sprites. Mr. President, do you wish to engage?"

TC grimaced. Something wasn't right. He reached out to Trakar and felt the connection, but it wasn't clear. Trakar told him what she wanted him to say. "No. I believe they're only demonstrating their superior technology and abilities. Will these craft be visible upon entry into the atmosphere?"

"Yes, Mr. President. In fact, several of them are lighting up the night sky like meteors over China and Eastern Europe now. European, Russian, and China space commands are reportedly tracking them. They haven't launched anything at them. I think they're waiting to see how we respond."

"General McLaughlin, do we have aircraft that can intercept them once they're in atmosphere?" TC asked.

"Yes, sir. Fighters are already airborne and ready to intercept the craft if they penetrate our airspace. Admiral Putnam, what's your status?"

Admiral James Putnam's face appeared on one of the monitors. "We have alerted all of the carrier and missile cruiser groups. All of US Fleet Force Command is ready. Navy fighters and electronic countermeasure aircraft are getting airborne. We don't have air support over the polar regions, but we do have submarines there. Two of them are Neptune-class."

TC looked at the monitors. They appeared blurry to him. He rubbed his eyes. "I believe the time has come to address the nation and the world to inform them that we're monitoring alien spacecraft attempting to land. I'll stress the need for calm. I'm sure the leaders of the other nations will follow suit. I don't want any of them getting trigger-happy and start shooting at these emissaries if they land in their backyard." His words were slurred.

"Mr. President, are you okay?" McLaughlin asked.

He closed his eyes and felt many of the Awakened around the world calling out to him. Some seemed more frantic than others. All of them were confused. He couldn't communicate with them. He thought about using the Orb. *What was happening?*

A nightmarish image appeared through the pain in his head. He saw the world in chaos. Industry and finance ceased to exist. There was no food for the people. Then came the images of mass suicides.

TC fought the pain and nodded. "Yes, I'm okay. Just a headache. General McLaughlin and Admiral Putnam, I want both of you here at the DSCC."

Both men acknowledged him and their faces disappeared from their respective screens.

He stared at the monitors. So many people waited for him to decide their fate, and all he could see was death. He'd already lost contact with many of the Awakened. His thoughts slowed, and then something snapped in him.

Billions would die if he didn't act soon. All of humanity would be lost. He couldn't allow that to happen. He slumped in his chair. He thought of Sandra. He suddenly felt the guilt of taking her life, and for what? These things were coming to destroy humanity. TC sat up, wanting to speak, but couldn't. Then he saw nothing as he lost consciousness and toppled from his chair.

A moment later, Stacy collapsed and landed on the floor next to him. General Stewart and the Secretary of Defense went next. The Awakened were collapsing all around the world.

General Stoddard didn't know what was happening. He needed direction, but the people responsible for giving it to him were either down or unavailable. The Speaker of the House was next in the line of succession. "Someone connect me with the Speaker of the House or the SecDef."

One of TC's protective detail agents appeared on the screen. "We are trying to locate the Speaker now," the agent said. "I was just informed that the SecDef has collapsed."

"What the hell is happening there?" Stoddard shouted.

"General Stoddard, Space Fence advises that additional ships are launching from the Alpha and Bravo targets," a communications specialist announced.

"How many?" Stoddard asked.

"Unknown, sir. Information is being forwarded through channels."

"I want a direct link to whoever is tracking these things. Now!"

"Yes, sir," the specialist said. A few seconds later, the connection was made.

"T3OA Miller," Jacob answered.

"This is General Stoddard. Are you tracking the targets?"

"Yes, sir."

"How many of them are there?"

"They are tightly bunched together, so I can't give you an exact count."

"Guess," Stoddard said.

"Over a hundred have launched from each ship, sir."

"Their location?"

"They are tightly grouped around the Alpha and Bravo ships," Jacob said, clearing his throat. "They look like they're providing a defensive shield."

"Thank you, T3OA Miller. Stay on the line."

Stoddard looked around the room and then at the monitors. Exigent circumstance required an immediate response. He had the authority and he issued the launch order.

Trakar felt the connection with TC fade away. She'd lost control of him. She reached out to Stacy to do what needed to be done. Trakar felt her presence for a moment, and then that connection was gone. Slowly and steadily, Trakar's connections to the other Awakened disappeared. Like dominos falling. All they had planned for eons was falling apart. Trakar advised the Monan about what had happened. Something was blocking their connections. Something unseen.

The Monan acknowledged the receipt of her message and ordered the first wave of ships to advance and take up stationary orbit. Trakar monitored the smaller sentry ships as they reached the atmosphere. Then all communications were lost. She sat motionless, feeling useless as hundreds of additional ships flew from the hangar bays of the two larger craft and took up positions for deployment once the first wave of ships arrived to reinforce them. There was nothing for her to do but continue to monitor everything and try to reach an Awakened.

A moment later, Trakar saw faint streaks of fire moving skyward through her optics. Missiles rose from the surface of the planet in search of their targets. She didn't know what they were called, but she knew they brought death. Trakar sensed the Monan ordering the two large ships in close polar orbit to take evasive action, but a check of her monitor told her the action would be futile. The smaller ships began pulling away.

The Sprites locked on to their targets. The mass of the two mother ships prevented them from maneuvering quickly enough to avoid the missiles. Trakar noted that several of the missiles were coming directly at her ship. She sent her final message to the Monan, knowing her fate. She felt a wave of comfort from the Monan and her appreciation as she bid her farewell. She had done all that had been asked of her. Trakar bowed her head and closed her dark eyes just as two Sprites struck her ship's hull. The energy shields they used to prevent damage from space debris were no match for the power of the missiles.

Moments later, mere fragments of the Alpha target floated where the massive ship once orbited the planet.

The Monan closed her mind to those aboard the two doomed ships. As the nuclear warheads exploded, each one added a new sun to light the darkness around the planet. When the light of the explosions faded, she could see only pieces of the two ships. Many of the smaller ships, she knew, had joined them in oblivion.

The war they'd planned to avoid had begun. All of their efforts had been stopped by a force unseen. She glanced around the command deck and saw the others awaiting her orders. With no place else to go, they would fight using their overwhelming numbers, their new weapons, and the Xunta. They would survive, and humanity would perish.

She sent only one order. "Prepare to attack!"

PART THREE

"The reason why the universe is eternal
is that it does not live for itself;
it gives life to others as it transforms."

LAO TZU

CHAPTER SIXTEEN

Washington — DSCC — July 30 — 1045 hours

Pandemonium had erupted in the Deep Secure Command Center. The medical response teams tended to President Collingsworth and Stacy Preston. Neither of them had regained consciousness. An assortment of generals, directors, and admirals, shouted at General Stoddard through the communications link. Some supported his action, while others condemned him.

Operation Orbital Punch was the only nuclear response option that didn't require the president to provide the launch codes. The Sprite missiles couldn't be used to strike ground-based targets. Once out of Earth's atmosphere, the Sprites would go active and self-destruct if they reentered the atmosphere. The system was designed to permit the commanding officer at the Joint Space Operations Center, JSpOC, or the Integrated Global Space Command, IGSC, to respond immediately to any Near Earth Object that had gone undetected until the last minute. NEO's appeared from time to time without warning, but usually they were too small to cause an alert. However, protocols changed when an asteroid that could have destroyed a continent had gone undetected until it passed within thirty thousand miles of the Earth.

"General Stoddard, we need you to keep us informed about the location of the smaller ships," Admiral Putnam said over the conference video. He and General McLaughlin had just walked into the DSCC having made the trip from the Pentagon in record time.

"I'll have the tracking centers relay the information to your combat command centers directly. It'll cut down on the confusion."

"Has anyone located the Speaker of the House yet?" Admiral Putnam asked.

"I haven't heard anything," Stoddard replied. "General McLaughlin, I'm glad to see you're at the DSCC. I recommend you take command until the Speaker of the House is located."

"You just declared war on an alien species," the Director of National Intelligence, Melvin Kotter, shouted as he joined McLaughlin and Putnam. "You weren't authorized to launch those missiles at that kind of target. General McLaughlin just can't assume command. There's a line of succession."

"Someone better, Director Kotter," Stoddard said, "since no one can find the Speaker. I don't think we have time to go any further down the line of succession looking for someone to be in charge. We need someone who can make a decision and act on it." Stoddard was accustomed to stressful situations, but this was something else. He turned to his aide, who stood off-screen and said, "I need an update on the damage we inflicted, and I need to know if there are any more of those ships out there."

"Director Kotter," General McLaughlin said, "General Stoddard's actions were appropriate for the threat level. Until I'm informed that Speaker McFarland has been located, or the SecDef is revived, I will coordinate all military actions from here."

It seemed as if everyone had an opinion, and they all continued voicing it at the same time.

Stoddard clenched his jaw and shook his head in disbelief at the new report he'd just been handed. "I've just been advised the Sprite missiles destroyed both of the larger ships that were in orbit. Space Fence is now tracking over a hundred smaller craft. Some were destroyed when we took out the larger ships, but the surviving ships are entering the atmosphere. Eight more ships, the same size as Alpha and Bravo, have appeared outside the orbital plane and are moving to bracket the planet."

"Your assessment?" General McLaughlin asked.

"The ships are positioned far enough away and far enough apart that they can maneuver to avoid the Sprite missiles if we launch again. We caught them with their pants down the first time. I don't think we can do it again, even with the advanced target-seeking guidance system. The tracking system on the Sprite wasn't designed to intercept anything that changes direction quickly."

"Great! So now we're facing a pissed-off enemy," Kotter said. "Any chance of a peaceful relationship has been obliterated."

"Perhaps," General McLaughlin said. "At least they know we won't go down without a fight."

A messenger handed a report to Stoddard. He read it, then said, "Space Fence is reporting targets Charlie through Juliet are launching smaller craft. It appears we have kicked the hornet's nest."

"How many?" McLaughlin asked.

"They can't provide an accurate count yet, but they're estimating well over a thousand."

Little Abaco City — July 30 — 1050 hours

Cal and Tegan walked out of the tunnel and onto the city commons. Tegan could tell that the people were scared. She wanted to tell all of them what she'd accomplished to allay their fears, but then thought it best to keep that a secret. They would have wanted her to destroy them all, but Tegan hadn't been equipped to do that.

Brian, Crystal, and Katie stood in front of one of the doorways, watching the others mill around. She could tell they still didn't know what to do with themselves. She made eye contact with them.

"Is it true?" Brian asked as he approached her. "Are Alex and Nate dead?"

"We believe they are," she replied.

"How did it happen?" Crystal asked.

"The president's teams blew up our boat while they were still in the cabin," Cal answered. "Rob and I were lucky to be on deck. We went over the side. Manatu said Makita was monitoring the battle, and she saw no one else leave the boat. I can only presume the worst." Cal swallowed hard.

"I'm sorry," said Tegan, seeing the pain on their faces. "I know they were good friends."

Brian nodded and said, "Yes, they were."

"Then the invasion has started?" Crystal asked.

"The Etu Inu Idimmu have arrived," Tegan replied. "I don't think they've started landing yet."

"Here comes Rob," Cal said, pointing.

"Good, you found them," Knolls said as he approached. "By the look on everyone's faces, I take it you told them what happened."

"Yes, some of it anyway," Tegan replied. "The Igigi have left the outpost, and they've sealed it. I managed to disconnect the Awakened from the Idimmu."

"You did *what?*" Brian exclaimed.

"I severed their connection. They can't communicate. So the Awakened are in the dark and can't assist the Idimmu as planned. It won't stop them, but it certainly made the Idimmus' life a lot more difficult."

"Just *how* did you do that?" Knolls asked.

Tegan shrugged. "I created an energy field of Arklight-charged particles that blocked their ability to communicate within Earth's atmosphere."

"You created a communications barrier around the entire planet?" Knolls asked. "How is our military supposed to talk to each other? They rely on satellites."

"All of our communication systems will operate normally, including GPS and weather satellites, at least until the Idimmu destroy them."

"But how?" Brian asked.

"What I did wasn't all that difficult once I understood how the Awakened were communicating. Remember, Casey had mentioned that the president communicated using an orb, but he didn't have to speak into it?"

"Yeah," Knolls said. "Casey said Westfield got that information from Senator Woodsman during his interrogation."

"Correct. So I figured they had to be communicating by some means other than traditional wave transmissions. I reviewed what little data was available on the Idimmu and decided they must have modified the Awakeneds' brains so they could communicate telepathically. I think the orb was some type of amplifier."

"You think they communicate telepathically, an actual brain-to-brain connection?" Knolls asked.

"Yes. I researched the possible wavelengths they could use. You see, molecular stimulation creates a charged electromagnetic field that's the basis for all communication. Whether it's your neurons talking to each other or some other form of wave communication, a field is created. I decided they couldn't be using radio waves, microwaves, infrared, light-waves, or even sound waves to send their messages to the president. It had to be something completely unknown to us. I created an energy shield that would disrupt the molecular flow of anything other than normal electromagnetic radiation communication systems."

"I'll ask again, how?" Brian asked.

"Brian, you've heard of a transcranial magnetic stimulation system, a TMS, correct?"

"Yes."

"I think they're using a more sophisticated version of one. Turn off the TMS, and the Idimmu lose the ability to stay connected, and their hold on the Awakened. The energy field I created blocks their brain-to-brain pathway. Not only will their messages not reach the Awakened, but their sensory control is disabled. I imagine for the Awakened this would be like a television losing a signal. They would get only static."

"Why won't that disrupt our brain waves?" Knolls asked.

"Because the Awakened brain EMFs would have to be different from the rest of us now. They were genetically altered. Their brains create a different electromagnetic field. One that I could disrupt. They've grown to rely on their connection to the Idimmu and to each other."

"How do you think the Awakened will respond?" Cal asked.

"My best guess is that they will be very confused, and some may become catatonic. Undoubtedly, they will be disoriented, at least until the Idimmu find a way to get around the shield."

"Will they be able to reestablish contact with the Awakened once they land?" Knolls asked.

"I believe they'll have to be very close to an Awakened to send any type of signal. Even near the surface, there will be residual effects caused by the energy shield. I'm not sure if it will impact the Idimmus' ability to communicate with each other at longer distances. I suppose it's possible if their brains are wired the same way they could experience some disorientation while in the atmosphere."

"Why didn't you create a force field to keep them from landing?" Brian asked.

"Because we couldn't control the kind of energy we needed to do that."

"Who's we?" Knolls asked.

"My daughter and I."

"*What!*" Brian said. "You and your unborn child tapped into the Arklight field? But the Igigi were quite specific that they wouldn't give us that knowledge, and how could your baby be involved?"

"It's difficult to explain. Let's just say I found something that could help us, and I gave that knowledge to my daughter, and she made the connection to Arklight."

Everyone looked stunned.

"All I can tell you is that our daughter is very special," Tegan said. "I'm just beginning to comprehend what she will be capable of doing." Just then, Tegan's abdomen glowed blue. Brian and Crystal took a step back. Katie seemed enchanted.

"Nothing to be frightened of, she's just saying, 'Hello.'" Tegan said.

"Good Lord in heaven," Crystal said. "Is she an alien?"

Tegan smiled. "She's human, just a very advanced model."

"We don't have any way to confirm that you actually blocked their communication, do we?" Knolls said.

"No. But I know it occurred."

"I need to get to the surface and make a call," Knolls said. "I have the contact number of a friend of Westfield's at the Pentagon. Westfield told me he could be trusted."

"Did you already try making a call from here?" Cal asked.

"Several times," Knolls answered. "Many of the others have tried as well. There's no signal."

"The portal is sealed," Tegan said. "All outside communications have been blocked. The Bimini and the Strangers Cay portals haven't been opened yet."

"Is the transit system to Bimini operational?" Knolls asked.

"Not yet," Tegan replied. "But I think I can get it operational in a few minutes."

"Sounds good, but do you think you can open the Bimini portal?" Cal asked.

"I'm sure the information is in the UEE. I should have it open by the time you get there."

"Bimini it is then," Cal said. "I'll take a phone and go with Rob. I can check on my parents' progress, too."

"What can we do?" Brian asked.

"Brian, you come with me," Tegan said. "Crystal, have you met Jessica?"

"Yes."

"Take Katie and find her. Tell her what we're doing, and then all of you meet us back on level five in thirty minutes."

"I love it when she's in command," Cal said, loud enough for everyone to hear.

Tegan smiled and walked away.

Washington — 1110 hours

"The president and vice president are in the infirmary, both still unconscious," General McLaughlin said, sitting down in the president's chair at the table. "Is there any word on Speaker McFarland?"

"No, sir," Admiral Putnam replied.

"Why can't anyone locate him?" McLaughlin asked. "He does have a security detail, doesn't he?"

"He does," Kotter replied. "I have a bad feeling our leadership has been compromised. I was also just advised that General Stewart was found unconscious at the Pentagon, and there are additional unconfirmed reports of several other high-ranking military and political officials in Europe and China who are unresponsive. Those that are conscious are talking gibberish."

"General McLaughlin," Stoddard said. "I've just been told that my Russian counterpart has been found unconscious, as well as several of his top aides."

"What the hell is going on?" McLaughlin shouted.

"This appears to be a coordinated attack," Putnam said. "They've disabled the heads of state around the world to create chaos."

"That's not entirely accurate," Kotter replied. "The Russian president, the British Prime Minister, and several others are still behaving normally. It's as if they're targeting only select people. There's something else going on here."

"If we can't hit them, we can't stop them," Stoddard said.

Director Kotter's secure line chimed, and he answered. A moment later, he said, "Are you shitting me?" His face flushed with anger, and he disconnected.

"What is it now?" McLaughlin asked.

"Speaker McFarland has been located. He's on his way."

"So he's conscious. Where was he?" McLaughlin asked.

"He was in the arms of his naked executive assistant. It seems the only thing elected Washington politicians do besides campaign and lie to the public is screw around. He should be here in a few minutes."

Ten minutes later, Speaker of the House Theodore "Teddy" McFarland walked into the secure facility.

"Mr. Speaker," McLaughlin began. "The president and vice president are unable to perform the duties of their office. You are now our commander in chief." He pointed at the president's chair.

McFarland crossed the room and sat down. "What's happened? I haven't been briefed. General McLaughlin, can you bring me up to speed."

A few minutes later, Speaker McFarland looked ten years older than his fifty-two years and much paler. He struggled to stand. "You're telling me we're under attack by an alien species?"

"Yes," McLaughlin answered. "They've strategically placed their ships around the planet. We can't hit them. Several of their smaller ships are in atmosphere but at an altitude we can't reach with our aircraft or air-to-to-missiles."

"We attacked them first?" McFarland asked.

"Yes, sir. Based on the reports and the number of ships they'd launched, combined with POTUS and the VP being unconscious, General Stoddard ordered the Sprite missiles launched. I support his decision."

"How many ships are there?" McFarland asked.

"General Stoddard, do we have an updated count?" McLaughlin asked.

General Stoddard reappeared on the screen. "Yes, sir, we do. There are eight larger ships and over two thousand smaller craft at various altitudes and locations in orbits ranging from two hundred to twenty-thousand miles out. There are nine small ships in high atmosphere with at least one over each continent. The closest ship to us is off the coast of Maine."

"When you say smaller ships, how big is that?" McFarland asked.

"They vary in size. Some are as small as a B-2 bomber, some as large as an aircraft carrier," Stoddard answered, then went on to explain the size of the eight main ships.

"My, God. I've never been briefed on how to deal with this kind of threat. What do you recommend, General McLaughlin?"

"We're all in new territory, Mr. Speaker. There are some scenarios we've played with over the years for an alien encounter, but no one ever took them seriously, nor were they of this magnitude. I believe if they don't destroy everything on the surface of the planet, then our biggest concern will be biohazards."

"How so?"

"Mr. Speaker, these creatures probably carry germs we've never encountered. Even if we can blow them out of the sky, their dead bodies could spread new strains of diseases. We also don't know what weapons they have. Their manner of attack is something we never anticipated. The only thing we agree on is that their ships are positioned for an attack."

"What is your recommendation, General McLaughlin?" McFarland asked again.

"The only thing we can do for now. We wait. When they're low enough in our atmosphere to engage, we should hit them as hard as we can. If they land forces, then we counterattack."

"Has anyone tried to communicate with them?" McFarland asked.

"Yes, sir," Stoddard answered. "They haven't responded. We aren't detecting any chatter between their ships, but we believe they're communicating based on the fact that they are coordinating the positioning of their ships. The only anomaly is that the nine ships in the atmosphere haven't changed locations since the Alpha and Bravo ships were destroyed. They stopped moving immediately."

"They were already in the atmosphere when we nuked the larger ships?"

"Yes, sir. There were seven smaller ships discharged from the Alpha ship and two from the Bravo ship that reached the upper atmosphere before the Sprites hit their targets."

"I wonder why the ships aren't moving," McFarland said.

General McLaughlin shook his head. "We don't know."

"And we had no warning at all they were coming?"

"No, sir," Stoddard answered him. "The first we knew about them was when the Alpha and Bravo targets crossed the Space Fence barrier."

"Was there any chatter intercepted by NSA before the ships arrived?" McFarland asked. "Could another foreign government be in contact with them?"

"No, Mr. Speaker," Kotter replied. "There was no unusual signals traffic."

"Any other unusual incidents prior to their arrival?"

Kotter said, "The only thing of interest is that NSA Director Bishop resigned abruptly and disappeared shortly after General Cecil Westfield vanished."

"Who is General Westfield?" McFarland asked.

"He was with the NSA. I don't know much about him. I do know that the president was very interested in finding out what General Westfield did for the NSA. He had tasked Senator Woodsman to discover what he could."

"And?" McFarland prompted Kotter, wanting more of an answer.

"Senator Woodsman has also disappeared, so I don't know what he learned. I questioned Director Bishop about Westfield, and he told me that I didn't have a need to know. Shortly after that conversation, Bishop disappeared."

"How could you not have a need to know?"

"Some things within the intelligence community are compartmentalized and restricted even from me. The president wasn't happy that I couldn't provide an explanation, which is why he had Senator Woodsman look into it."

McFarland could tell that Kotter was uncomfortable disclosing the information in front of everyone. It made him appear weak, but at least he was honest.

"I know I'm not the smartest pumpkin in the patch," McFarland said, his Georgia drawl more pronounced, "but I'd say there's got to be some connection between all of these people disappearing and what we're facing. Don't you think so, Director Kotter?"

"Yes, sir. I already have people tasked with finding a link, Mr. Speaker."

A moment later, the medical doctor tending both TC and Stacy entered the room under military escort.

"Tell me some good news," McFarland said.

"I'm afraid I can't," the doctor replied. "Both the president and vice president are stable, but they remain unresponsive. We've conducted a battery of neurological tests, including an MRI, a CT scan, an electroencephalogram, and a PET test. Both of their brains are functioning normally without any sign of disease."

"Then why are they unconscious?" McFarland asked.

"That's what has us stumped. Their brain activity is abnormal … it's higher than usual. Blood test results are preliminary, but there doesn't appear to be any toxins, drugs, or any other substances that can account for their mental state. I'm running genetic DNA tests to determine if they share a commonality that may react to certain stimuli that could cause a seizure."

"Doctor, this may sound odd, but is it possible to determine if they're using the same part of their brain?" Kotter asked.

"Yes, they are. We've noted that the same areas of their brain are more active."

"Meaning?" McFarland asked.

"To keep it simple, let me put it this way. The frontal lobes control motor function, among other things. The temporal lobe handles our auditory and communication functions, minus our visual stimuli. Both patients are registering hyperactivity in both the frontal and temporal lobes. This may sound crazy, but it's like they're talking to each other."

"Can they hear us?" Kotter asked.

"I believe they can."

"Doctor, I'd like you to run the same tests on the SecDef and General Stewart," McLaughlin said. "They're also unconscious. I need to know if their brain activity is like the others. I've been advised that there are other leaders around the world that have collapsed. There has to be a common thread. I want the DNA test results as quickly as possible. I'm wondering if they share a common trait that the aliens were able to use to turn them off, so to speak."

"I see what you're driving at," the doctor answered. "The DNA tests on the president and the VP should be done within the hour. I'll start the tests on General Stewart and the secretary of defense as soon as I can."

"Thank you, doctor," McLaughlin said, dismissing him.

As the doctor left, McFarland turned to McLaughlin and said, "You believe the unconscious people have a genetic trait that the aliens used to shut them down and cause confusion?"

"That's exactly what I'm thinking. When I heard General Westfield's name, I started to put some things together."

"You know General Westfield?" Kotter asked.

"We go way back. He was involved in some very strange shit, and I know he had a long reach. His work was always considered dark for as long as I can remember."

"What kind of strange *shit* did he work on?" McFarland asked.

"I'm not sure. But I think the alien presence explains a few things about his mission scope."

"He was working on aliens?" Kotter asked, sounding incredulous.

"That was my guess years ago. No one would, or could, talk about things like that back then. Your career would be over in a heartbeat if anyone thought you took that alien crap seriously."

"That might explain why Director Bishop left," Kotter said. "If what they were involved in was that secret and they knew something was going to happen, they might have had to go to ground."

McFarland said, "What if our president and the VP are involved in some type of alien conspiracy?" He could tell by the look McLaughlin gave him that that possibility couldn't be dismissed.

"Let's wait for the DNA results," McLaughlin said.

Bimini Station — 1130 hours

Cal was amazed by how quickly Tegan found a way to access the Bimini out-post. She had already energized the facility and even opened the small portal that was concealed nearly half a mile south of the famous Bimini Road, an anomalous underwater rock formation on the west side of North Bimini.

Cal and Knolls rode the transit system to Bimini Station. The outpost and portal were located two miles south of the station. Marble slabs, visible on the ocean floor, marked the rooftops of the northern part of the unfinished portion of the facility.

The transit system was a marvelous piece of engineering. The transport traveled deep beneath the ocean along a one-hundred-and-fifty-mile tunnel at an incredible speed. The car was comfortable, and they'd felt only the slightest vibration along the way. There'd been no change in pressure on the twenty-minute ride from Sanctuary.

Arriving at the end of the line, they exited the windowless transport. Cal looked up at the familiar obsidian walls and the ever-present soft, blue glow that illuminated the interior. Cal had brought scuba gear, knowing that the portal barrier was still thirty feet beneath the surface.

"Tegan said there's a small portal that will give us access to the surface," Cal said. "It's only ten feet in diameter, and its positioned horizontally. There's a larger, vertical portal further west of us that's in deeper water so their ships can access the hangar bay. That portal is inconvenient for our purposes, so Tegan has secured it until the Igigi pay us a visit."

"I can't wait to see them again," Knolls said sarcastically.

"You need to cut the Igigi some slack. They're doing what they can for us under the circumstances."

"If you say so."

"Since this is unfamiliar territory, and the portal we need to use is camouflaged, I thought I'd stay submerged at the portal entrance while you make your call topside."

"That works for me," Knolls replied. "I need to make a call, but I think we can take a quick look at things on the way."

"Alright. Tegan said there are seven levels. The hangar bay is on level seven. Transit is on level six, and the portal we need to use is on the first level."

They walked up the ramp to level five. There they found the galley and several storage areas. Adjacent to the ramp, a corridor led to two large open areas that were large enough for several teams to play football.

"I wonder what purpose these two rooms serve," Cal said.

"I'd say either for storing something really large or for having some serious room to party," Knolls replied. "Let's move on."

On level four they found the housing units. Unlike the Great Guana outpost, the first few rooms they looked into had their own shower and bathroom.

"Looks like housing for twenty," Cal said. "It appears they wanted more privacy here."

"They all look the same. Let's head up."

On level three they found a control room with workstations, recliners, and a small gravity-defying sphere. Another ramp ran along the back wall. "It's smaller than the Great Guana outpost."

"Yup. Looks like they wanted two paths to get up to level two," Knolls said. "That could be where the real action takes place."

"Let's stick to the central core ramp. When we have time, we'll check out the back ramp. There could be more rooms back there with additional workstations."

Level two was a duplicate of level three, only much larger.

"I think you were right," Cal said. "This appears to be the primary command and control center. It has more workstations and recliners than Great Guana and a much larger sphere."

Knolls stopped and said, "I don't see any security stations barring access like those at the Guana site anywhere."

"Yeah, I noticed that, too. Maybe they didn't think they needed them here since the outpost wasn't going to be operational for very long," Cal replied as he stepped into the control room. "The workstations and sphere look like the others. It looks like they built a redundant control room down below."

"I wonder why," Knolls said.

"We'll figure it out later. Let's go take a look at the portal. This gear is starting to get heavy."

They found the portal on the first level. The barrier was in place, just as Tegan said it would be. There was a steep ramp leading up to a platform that was directly below the shimmering barrier. The platform reminded Cal of something you would find in a car repair shop, and the portal looked like a skylight. The lift was perfectly round and matched the barrier opening above. A thin control stanchion rose from the floor on the far side of the platform.

"Looks like the platform will take us up through the barrier," Knolls said. "The controls are simple enough."

"Let's hope it'll work without Tegan's biometric signature." Cal walked over to the edge of the ramp and looked down. The ramp gradually spiraled down to each of the six levels below them, widening as it descended. "It didn't look that high when we were coming up."

Knolls walked over and took a look. "No, it didn't."

"This area looks like it's also used as a reception area for greeting those entering through the portal," Knolls said. "There's more workstations around the central core and along the outer walls, and there's the access to the other ramp that leads down to the control room."

"Strange waste of space unless they planned to move a lot of people in and out of here," Cal said.

"I want to explore the main part of Bimini Station that we passed on the way to the outpost, but I need to make that call," Knolls said.

"And I want to check on my parents," Cal said, picking up his scuba gear.

Knolls said, "This outpost doesn't feel lived in."

"This one was built after Great Guana. Tegan said they stopped construction on Bimini Station when the ice age ended. The outpost was complete, but wasn't operational for very long. There's probably updated technology here, but the workstations look the same from the outside. We'll have to ask Manatu about it later."

"The one thing that remains is that blue ethereal glow. I don't know if I'm ever going to get used to that," Knolls said.

When they reached the platform, they put on their scuba gear, stood on the platform, and Cal placed his hand on the control panel. "Here goes nothing," Cal said, activating the lift.

They rose slowly toward the barrier. Cal and Knolls started breathing from their tanks as the lift pushed them through the barrier into the warm Atlantic. Transitioning from this portal seemed less disorienting to Cal than the one on Great Guana.

Cal pushed off the platform, established neutral buoyancy, and explored the area around the portal. There was no marker marking the entrance. The camouflaged portal reflected the sandy bottom around it from the outside. If you didn't know where it was, you wouldn't find it. He picked up a handful of sand next to the portal and allowed it to drop, noticing that the current wasn't as strong as he'd expected. Cal looked up at the surface and watched as Knolls slowly drifted away from the portal.

Thirty minutes later, Knolls swam back down and gave Cal a thumbs up sign. They swam to the center of the camouflaged platform, and as their feet touched it, the platform slowly descended without Cal having to use the control. A red glow enveloped them as they entered the outpost and were decontaminated.

"Did you get hold of the guy you wanted to talk to?" Cal asked, taking his mask off and watching the water droplets evaporate from the floor.

"I did. It took some work to get to him. He's in the presidential bunker under the White House."

"That's an interesting place for him to be. You must have contacts in high places. Did he confirm anything?"

"He did, and Tegan accomplished what she set out to do. The POTUS and VP, along with many others around the world, are taking a nap. According to General McLaughlin, they were still trying to figure out why. I told him that we were responsible. I didn't tell him about Tegan."

"Thanks. Maybe we should've talked to your friend earlier."

Knolls shook his head. "He was Westfield's friend, and he never would've believed me if the Idimmu hadn't arrived."

"Well, it's good that we have someone who believes us."

"Yes. The bad news is they launched a nuclear strike at the Idimmu ships and only managed to destroy two of them. There are eight more big-ass ships sitting just out of range, and they have launched thousands of smaller ships that are orbiting."

"That isn't good."

"No, it's not. He wants me in Washington as soon as possible."

"You told him where you are?" Cal asked.

"Only the general area. I figured if Westfield trusted him, I could, too. He's sending a Coast Guard Jayhawk to pick me up."

"Where?

"I'm going to swim toward shore and wait until I hear the chopper. Then call in and guide them to me."

"Good idea keeping the exact location of the Bimini facility secret even from our own people. At least until we know for sure what we're facing."

"That's what I was thinking."

"Did General McLaughlin know you were floating around in the ocean when you called him?" Cal asked.

"Yes. I told him. I said I'd explain everything after pickup. I'll give it another half hour and then head up."

"Okay. Once you're clear, I'll head back to Sanctuary. Communications are going to be a bitch. I'll try to reach you on the burner six hours after you leave. Let's say 1800 hours."

"Sounds like a plan. I should be in Washington by then. If I can't be reached, try again at 2000 hours. If I still don't answer, assume the worst. This could be a trap."

"I doubt it, but I respect your paranoia," Cal said, then extended his hand. Knolls shook it.

Cal smiled and said, "I better make my call."

"I'll take you up." Knolls put his hand on the control, and the platform responded, taking them up.

"I've marked the portal with several rocks," Cal said. "If you know what to look for, you'll be able to find it."

"You'll have to show me."

A moment later they went through the barrier, and Cal headed for the surface. Knolls remained standing on the platform. When he broke the surface, Cal placed his call. Reaching his parents, he learned they were already at the Bimini marina. They'd left before dawn. He instructed them to wait there until he contacted them again. Cal provided his father, Jeffrey, with the general area they'd need to find if he couldn't get someone to meet them. Next, he called Garth's cell phone, hoping he could reach him.

"Hello, Cal," Garth answered. "Where are you? Are you okay?"

"I'm fine. Knolls and I are at Bimini. How is everyone there?"

"Edward was headed west the last time I saw him. Maggie and I are heading southwest now. No one behind us. I'm not sure if they're tracking us, though. Are Jessica and Sara safe?"

"Yes."

"Maggie and I saw the explosion. Is everyone alright?"

Cal felt the grief roll over him like a tidal wave. It was odd how it hit him without warning. "Alex and Nate were killed in the explosion," Cal replied, his voice cracking. "The *Whispering Winds*, or what's left of her, is on the bottom. Everyone else is safely sealed away."

"I'm sorry for your loss, Cal."

"I'll miss them. Listen, a lot has happened in the last few hours. I have much to explain, but right now I'm treading water, so I want to keep it brief."

"Treading water?"

"Yes, I need to get back down to the outpost. Knolls has been in contact with Washington. The president and the other Awakened have been put out of commission. Don't ask me how right now. You should have safe passage at least until the Idimmu start to land. I need you to head for the marina on Bimini."

"Will do. I guess I won't have to use my escape plan after all. So the Idimmu are here now?"

"Yes. All military operations are now focused on them. They won't land without a fight."

"That's impressive work in such a short time."

"I'll explain everything in more detail later. Just meet with my parents and get Edward headed this way, too. Open communication is safe again."

"We'll see you soon," Garth said.

Cal disconnected, sealed his phone in the watertight bag, and dove to the barrier, where Knolls was waiting. They reentered the outpost.

"You get through?" Knolls asked.

"I did. Garth, Maggie, and Edward are headed this way. My parents are already at the marina. I'm going to go get Tegan and some supplies. I think we'll operate from here from now on. It has easier access to the surface. I don't like being around lots of people."

"Alright then, I'm headed out. I'll keep my phone handy."

"I do have one concern," Cal said.

"What's that?"

"Are you planning to tell them about the other outposts?"

"Let me find out what's going on and what their plans are for dealing with the Idimmu. If the military can't stop them, then I'll tell them about the outposts."

"Did you tell him about the Igigi?" Cal asked.

"No. I thought it best I tell General McLaughlin in person and in private after I assess the situation."

"I'll let you decide what's best. I trust you."

They stood there for a moment. Cal knew they both understood that the past was in the past.

CHAPTER SEVENTEEN

Washington — July 30 — 1230 hours

General McLaughlin shared the information Knolls provided in his report to Speaker McFarland, the Joint Chiefs, and other military and government leaders. He planned to have Knolls explain everything in more detail when he arrived in Washington, which he hoped would be before the alien ships took any aggressive action.

Speaker McFarland had ordered him to remain at the DSCC and coordinate all military operations. McLaughlin figured it was because he was in command of NORAD and USNORTHCOM, and because he was already at the DSCC. McLaughlin had recalled General Stewart's special ops teams from the Abacos. He also put the president and the other Awakened under guard and had them taken to a medical facility away from the White House.

McLaughlin was amazed that the president had ordered General Westfield killed. Knolls claimed that the communications between the Awakened and the Etu Inu Idimmu had been severed, but he hadn't gone into detail about how he'd accomplished that feat. Knolls had also been vague about the nature of the creatures they were facing, the operational aspects of his group, and how he'd come by the knowledge in the first place. He didn't mind letting Knolls keep some things secret, at least for now. His having called him while floating in the Atlantic indicated the situation was fluid.

"General McLaughlin," General Stoddard said, interrupting his thoughts. "There's been no change in their positions. They may have gotten their noses bloody, if they have any, and are now trying to decide how to procced."

"Thank you, General Stoddard. Keep me informed," McLaughlin replied. "Admiral Putnam, has the Coast Guard found Commander Knolls yet?"

"Just received word from the Coast Guard that he's on-board a Jayhawk and is headed to Miami. I have an F-18 ready to bring him to Andrews. A Marine chopper will ferry him to the White House lawn."

"How long until he arrives?"

"Less than two hours."

"Thank you, admiral. I want a secure link established with Knolls while he's in flight in case I have questions. Can you coordinate that with everyone?"

"Yes, sir."

General McLaughlin sat down in the president's chair and looked at the monitors, then looked around at the people still in the room with him. There was no longer panic on their faces, only resolve. He knew this was the calm before the tempest.

The Monan's ship

The Monan paced the command bridge, looking from one tactical display to the next. They were making their final preparations for the assault. The remainder of the fleet would arrive in twenty hours. She'd decided to wait to attack until the bulk of her fleet was within striking distance. Until then, she planned to analyze the reaction to their presence by monitoring the movements of the human military aircraft and ships. So far, they hadn't sent many assets to the polar regions. The humans appeared to be preparing to defend their most densely populated urban areas.

She planned to land the first wave on Antarctica tomorrow. She would position her suborbital ships to act as a shield against any aggressive human response. As much as she wanted to avoid a conflict, they were prepared. The humans had used their nuclear missiles to destroy their ships in orbit, but she didn't think they would use them once they landed.

Communications with the Awakened and the ships in the Earth's atmosphere needed to be reestablished. She knew that the Igigi were somehow responsible, and once she found them, she planned to make them pay for their interference.

Construction of the Protectorate at the South Pole would begin as soon as the first of the ships burrowed under the ice. If the enemy launched missiles at them, the ships would be protected from a nuclear strike by the thick ice. Within days of landing, the Protectorate would be impervious to any physical attack. The surface city would be protected from conventional weapons by strike ships and the Xunta on the ground. The ships that had been their home for so many years would already be dismantled to make their new homes, and when complete, millions upon millions of her kind would land and take refuge there. Within a week all of the underground cities would be interconnected. Then she would unleash the Xunta and push their territorial boundaries outward from Antarctica.

The Xunta stood seven feet tall and were bipedal, with brown, armored hides and large, red, binocular eyes set far apart in their pumpkin-sized head. They were the perfect killing machines. Equipped with genetically engineered, fear-inducing pheromones, they were capable of immobilizing a person within twenty feet. Their large jaws sported an array of prehistoric-looking teeth, with overlapping canines that were as large as a saber-toothed tiger's, and their eyes gave them perfectly clear vision for hunting both day and night. They could eviscerate a person in less than a second. The creatures feared nothing, and they followed the orders of their keepers with blind loyalty. Their dense, thick hide and skull were impenetrable by conventional firearms, and they could run forty miles per hour across any terrain.

The Xunta on board had been designed to control humans once the planet was conquered, but the Monan realized that she needed to use them as a weapon. Knowing they hadn't manufactured enough to use as offensive weapons, she ordered a new batch to be produced. The new Xunta would have different coding with only one focus—to hunt, kill, and devour any human encountered. She would produce millions of them to be their primary ground combat force.

The Xunta would strike terror into any human unfortunate to encounter one. The Monan decided to have them programmed to hunt in packs so she could release them in the major cities of the world and create utter panic. They would be ideal for fighting an asymmetrical war.

Her ships were in position and poised for the assault. She glanced at the monitors again. Her forces would prevail. She sent her divine message to the others of her kind.

Little Abaco City — 1330 hours

Cal found Tegan and the others in the operations center on level five exactly where the message she'd left said they'd be. Not only had Tegan activated the outpost, she'd also found a way to send messages without using a cell phone from one location to another within the city. Cal had seen her holographic message flashing beneath the sphere in the control room. Several of the workstation displays had the same message on them.

"I got your messages," Cal said. "How'd you pull that off?"

"I knew there had to be a way to communicate within the city and the UEE provided the answer," Tegan replied. "I've already briefed some of the others. I'm sure they'll share the information."

"Can they contact the Igigi?"

"No. What I provided only gives them the ability to contact each other. They can send and receive messages from workstations in the common areas and their individual housing units. It also gives us an opportunity to leave general announcements."

Cal gazed at Jessica as she entertained Katie. He wondered if the world Jessica, Katie, and his daughter inherited would look anything like what it was today. What he really hoped was that there would be a world for them to see.

"So Knolls has left for DC?" Brian said.

"Yes," Cal replied, still watching Katie playing. "He should be there shortly. With what he knows, the military won't hesitate to use all their resources to get him where they need him."

"And the POTUS and VP have been disabled?" Tegan asked.

"Yes. You disrupted their communication link just as you thought."

"Did you speak to your parents?" Tegan asked.

"Yes. They're at the marina on Bimini. I spoke to Garth, too. He's going to join my parents and wait for Edward."

"How do we reach Knolls again?" Brian asked.

"I'm going to call him at 1800 hours. I'll need to go back to Bimini Station to reach the surface. I'll also check in with Garth to see if he's linked up with my folks and Edward. If they have, I'd like to get them settled in at Bimini Station."

"It's operational enough for people to live there?" Crystal asked.

Cal glanced at Tegan.

"It is," she said. "All of the systems seem to be operational."

"I told Knolls that our group would live and work at the Bimini Station," Cal said. "I think it best if Tegan's belly didn't draw any attention. We also need to reduce the possibility that one of us will let our knowledge of Arklight slip out. Bimini provides easy access to the surface for communications with the outside world. There's plenty of room there, it's a short trip back to Sanctuary or Little Abaco, and we can message one another."

"I think some people already know there's more to the Igigi power source than what they've been told," Tegan said. "Walking through a magic tunnel from the surface to the portal has been a focus of discussion."

"I thought we made it clear that it was a force field," Cal said.

"We did, and most people bought the story. There are a few MBRG techs that know there is something else to it. Fortunately, our child hasn't shown herself to anyone but us."

Sara asked, "Who's in our group?"

"Everyone that's been involved from the beginning and my parents," Cal replied.

"It would be nice to have a place where we can talk openly," Brian said. "I've seen people hanging around us when we're talking. I think they're trying to eavesdrop."

"We'll want some private time with the Igigi, too," Tegan said.

"Good point," Cal said. "Then we're all in agreement that Bimini is our new home?"

Everyone nodded.

Crystal said, "I've heard people talking about how long we'll be here. Some think they'll be able to return to their homes in a week. They believe that the military will destroy all of the aliens by then."

"I wish that were true, but I don't think so," Tegan said.

"I'm surprised that the Idimmu haven't attacked already," Cal said. "Knolls said they're in position but haven't made their move because the military destroyed two of their ships with nuclear missiles."

"You didn't tell us we already attacked them," Tegan said.

"Sorry."

"Having those ships destroyed probably made them less enthusiastic about proceeding," Tegan said.

"They will strike," Cal said. "The question is how and when."

"Did Knolls tell the military about the Igigi?" Tegan asked.

"No, and he didn't say anything about the other outposts, either. I'm sure once he gets to Washington that they'll press him for more answers. Especially about Dark Moon."

"I think our next step is to establish a regimen that will keep everyone busy," Tegan said. "They won't be seeing any sunrises or sunsets for a while. Life underground can be disorienting. Studies have shown that people living in subterranean abodes tend to suffer from disrupted sleep patterns. We don't need a bunch of cranky people. They're under enough stress already."

"I can help with that," Brian said. "It'll help me, too."

"Brian is very organized, so that will be right up his alley," Crystal said. "When do you think you'll hear from Manatu again?"

"I'm not sure," Tegan replied. "I think he wants to see what the Idimmu do and whether we can hold our own against them. He's very interested in our daughter's abilities and all of our safety. He's offered to remove us from the planet if it comes to that."

"Are you serious?" Jessica asked. Her voice carried a hint of excitement.

"Yes. We'll talk about that option later," Tegan said.

Cal said, "I think you're right about him knowing all along what you and our daughter are capable of. He just wanted to give you some motivation."

"Rather sneaky if you ask me," Brian said. "Cal, I think it would be proper to have a memorial service for Alex and Nate."

"That would be nice," Cal replied. Tegan's hand touched his. He took it in his and squeezed. "But I think we have other things to deal with first."

"You guys get word to everyone to gather on the main level," Tegan said. "I think we need to brief them all on what's happened. We probably need to have two full briefings a day so people aren't left in the dark."

"Is there an intercom system or something we can use to make an announcement?" Brian asked.

"Not that I've discovered yet," Tegan replied. "I'll query the UEE, but for now I think building a directory and training everyone on how to use the messaging system will help. Until then, it's word of mouth."

"In that case, I'll take level two, three, and four west," Jessica said. "Sara, you take the east side."

"I'm on it," Sara said.

"We'll take the first level then," Brian said. "That will give Tegan and Cal a chance to scout for a place to brief everyone."

Cal nodded. "The more we keep everyone in the loop, the better."

"I agree," Tegan said. "I think we're going to need each other to survive, so there shouldn't be any secrets."

Cal raised an eyebrow at her and pointed to her belly. "I think some things should remain classified."

Tegan smiled. "Okay, then let's just say most secrets."

Everyone hurried off in different directions.

Washington DC – 1500 hours

Commander Robert Knolls walked into the secure presidential bunker, wearing a pressed, white naval uniform. Admiral Putnam had seen to it he had a change of clothing when he landed at Andrews. He figured Admiral Putnam didn't want him briefing anyone in his shorts and an old T-shirt. Image was everything, so he needed to exude confidence and credibility as the leader of Dark Moon.

"Welcome, Commander Knolls," General McLaughlin said, greeting him with a warm smile.

"Thank you, sir."

"I need you to brief Speaker McFarland, who's our acting Commander in Chief, the Joint Chiefs, the Unified Combat Commands, and most of the agency heads, all of the NATO heads of state or their representatives, and other world leaders. Is there anything else you want to tell me before we go in?"

"General, there are many things that we need to discuss in private. I can certainly give everyone a general overview in the interim. I'm sure there will be many questions."

General McLaughlin nodded. "As you wish. Just be aware that anything you say is being recorded and will be analyzed later. If there's a question you don't want to answer until you have a chance to brief me, just glance at me, and I'll run interference. I want you to know I was sorry to hear about General Westfield. If he left you in charge of your secret group, he must have truly believed in you, and so will I."

"Thank you, sir. Let's get this started."

General McLaughlin led Knolls into the secure conference room, and they stood in front of the camera. The A/V technician queued them when they went live.

McLaughlin said, "Good afternoon. Standing next to me is Commander Robert Knolls. He is the leader of a covert group specializing in the field of operations that we now face. I suggest you listen to what he has to say, regardless of how far-fetched you may think it is. Commander, the floor is yours."

"Thank you, General McLaughlin. Let me explain what I know. Please hold your questions until I've completed my briefing. It may save us some time." Knolls spent the next forty minutes explaining the operational directive of Dark Moon and some of the events that had transpired in the Bahamas. He glossed over how he'd learned about the Etu Inu Idimmu and how the connection between the Awakened and the Idimmu had been severed. He described what he knew about the physical attributes of the Idimmu. He told them about the Tonopah, Nevada, crash and the recovered fragment of the arm found in the debris. He explained that this wasn't the first time the Idimmu had tried to conquer Earth, leaving out his source of the information or any reference to the Igigi. He emphasized how humanity had fought back, using primitive weapons, and had prevailed.

He also made it clear that present-day humanity faced a much larger and more motivated group than the last time.

Knolls detailed what he knew about the president and the other Awakened and what they'd been tasked to do. He explained Senator Woodsman's role and the circumstances surrounding his demise. He only briefly mentioned Tegan's bioweapon that could be used, highlighting its possible limitations. He chose not to go into detail about Deep Sky or its design. He told them about the team he had assembled, but not their location. When he completed his briefing, he opened it up for questions.

The first one came from Admiral Putnam. "Commander, first let me thank you for the sacrifices you and your team have made all these years. I would like you to tell us more about the Etu Inu Idimmu ships."

"Unfortunately, sir, I have limited technical information at hand. The debris from the Tonopah crash is at Wright-Patterson. I will authorize access." Knolls decided not to tell them about the metal plaque they found in the ship. It was of Igigi origin. He didn't want to go down that path, at least not yet.

"Can we have access to the specimen?" Admiral Putnam asked.

"Yes, sir. In fact, Dark Moon is going to be an open book. All of our files will be accessible." Knolls took a breath. "As I said earlier, Dark Moon was created to combat this very threat. You will know what I do."

"Thank you, I have no other questions at this time."

"How do you know these creatures were here once before?" Director Kotter asked.

"We have accounts from ancient records," Knolls answered, without having to lie. He just didn't tell them they were from Igigi ancient records.

"What records?" Kotter asked.

"The information was only recently deciphered from a lost ancient text." Again he didn't lie. "The war took place over seven thousand years ago."

"Where?" Speaker McFarland asked.

"The final battle of the war took place in Sumer, ancient Iraq. But there was fighting just about everywhere in the world."

"And you just now decided to tell us about this?" Kotter asked.

"I didn't know the threat level until recently. I would have provided the information sooner if I hadn't been hiding from President Collingsworth's teams that were trying to kill me. I doubt that any of you would have believed my story until the Idimmu arrived anyway."

Silence.

"If I may ask," Knolls said.

General McLaughlin said, "Yes."

"How have you kept the invasion fleet secret from the public? There are several ships in atmosphere, and the nuclear missile explosions must've been seen by almost everyone on Earth. Surely, with the president not addressing the public, there has to be some concern."

Speaker McFarland replied, "So far, our cover story is that the missiles successfully intercepted multiple asteroids. The president's press secretary has been handling the media by telling them the president is still assessing the results."

"Mr. Speaker, I believe it's in our best interest to tell the people about the Awakened and what's coming."

McFarland cleared his throat, then said, "The public does have the right to know what's really happening, but the announcement must be coordinated. We also wanted to wait until we heard what you could tell us about these creatures. We want to offer a solution so we could reduce the panic of knowing an alien species was poised to attack us."

Knolls nodded.

The aging Russian president said, "Commander, can you tell us if you can destroy these creatures?"

"Mr. President, I don't know. What I do know is they are mortal, but we aren't convinced Deep Sky will work for a number of reasons, but it remains an option. From what I know of these creatures and their previous tactics, they will try to use their superior numbers and technology to establish a beachhead on the planet. I don't know for sure where they will land, but my best guess is in the unpopulated polar regions."

"Speaker McFarland, are you willing to use nuclear weapons in unpopulated areas?" the Russian president asked.

"I haven't decided yet," McFarland replied.

"Well, I am willing to use them, and so are the Chinese."

"Mr. President, if we decide to launch a nuclear strike, we will need to agree on a common strategy," McFarland said.

Knolls said, "I believe we can defeat these creatures using conventional means. Our ancestors were able to defeat them with spears."

"Thank you, Commander Knolls, for your opinion," McLaughlin said, cutting him off.

Knolls nodded, realizing he'd overstepped his bounds. "Yes, sir."

"I have a question," Kotter said. "Commander, how did you cut off their communications with the Awakened and from where are you operating?"

Knolls looked at McLaughlin. Now was the time for him to run interference.

McLaughlin said, "There are some things we need to verify before we accidently release any misinformation. I'd appreciate everyone giving me some time to confer with Commander Knolls. Then we'll share everything we have."

Surprisingly, no one objected.

More than an hour later, and after many more questions, the briefing ended. McFarland and the others decided to make a joint worldwide announcement about the alien presence at 1800 hours. In an effort to reduce the inevitable panic, the people would hear for the first time in history that all military operational commands would work together to keep the world safe. Knolls wasn't sure if that would offer hope or frighten the people more.

Knolls was escorted from the bunker by two Marines after he'd met with McLaughlin privately. He'd started to brief him on the communications shield, but the general was called away before he got into any details. He thought that was a good thing. He wasn't sure how much more he wanted to tell him. McLaughlin told him to get some rest and that he'd call him later.

Knolls felt exhausted. He stood on the back steps of the White House. He checked his watch. Cal should check in with him in thirty minutes, the same time as the announcement about the alien threat would be released to the world. He looked up at the sky and sighed, knowing the challenges ahead. So many things had happened in the last week, and already so many had lost their life. He knew this war could become one of attrition, with fighting street by street and door to door in every city on the planet.

A Marine lance corporal approached him and said, "Sir, I will escort you to the helicopter for transport to a secure facility."

Knolls glanced at the helicopter sitting on the lawn. He knew that meant they wanted him accessible to other members of the military, scientific experts, and the intelligence community leaders. He needed to stall them so he could take Cal's call and get some time with General McLaughlin.

"I need a few minutes before we board the chopper. It's been a real shitty week, and I still need to get with General McLaughlin and take some calls. I can't do that while airborne."

"I understand, sir," the corporal replied. "My orders are to stay with you at all times until relieved. When you are ready to leave, just let me know."

"Thanks." Knolls walked to a bench and sat down to await Cal's call. He didn't care to listen to the worldwide announcement. He already knew what was going to happen.

Bimini — 1800 hours

Garth Aldeberie caught sight of the *Tranquility* in the North Bimini harbor, east of the island and Alice Town. He thought the sailboat had quite striking lines. At a little over forty-four feet, the *Tranquility* rode at anchor in the shallows adjacent to the marina. Her white hull had blue stripes running down both sides, and the matching colored bottom paint was visible above the waterline. Garth knew his sailboats, and this one was a beauty. The Catalina sailing yacht had been well maintained from the top of her sixty-four-foot mast to the waterline. Considering that Cal's parents owned her, he wouldn't have expected anything else.

Maggie stood on the bow of the *Deep Current* with line in hand when Jeffrey Locke came up and stood between the twin helm stations under the navy blue canopy that covered the cockpit. He stood six feet tall and had a muscular physique, and at a hundred and eighty pounds, he could pass for a fifty-year-old. He stood slightly hunched under the canopy.

"Ahoy. You must be the famous Maggie my son's told me about," Jeffrey said.

"I don't know about being famous, but I'm Maggie. That's my husband, Garth, doing the steering. Do you mind if we tie alongside?" Maggie asked.

"Not at all. Let me kick some fenders over the side. Jule, we have company," Jeffrey yelled.

Jeffrey made his way to the bow and caught the line Maggie tossed him, tying it to the bow cleat. Garth expertly maneuvered the *Deep Current* until it was within inches of the *Tranquility*, then cut the engines. Garth walked aft and tossed the stern line to Jeffrey.

"Nice bit of seamanship, Garth," Jeffrey said.

"Nothing special," Garth replied. "Who's Jule?"

"That's me," Juliana Alexander-Locke said, stepping up on deck. "No need to be modest. Nice to meet you."

"Same here," Garth replied, as Maggie walked back to stand next to him.

Garth could see the familial resemblance. Cal had Jeffrey's bone structure and physique, but Jeffrey's full head of hair was stark white. Jule was, about five foot five, and she couldn't have weighed more than a hundred pounds. She gazed at him with deep blue eyes. Cal's eyes were the same color.

"Why don't you come aboard," Jeffrey said. "I believe we have some things to discuss. I want to know if my son's gone nuts."

"Don't mind JR's strange sense of humor," Jule said.

Garth chuckled. "No, Cal hasn't gone nuts. I wish he had."

"Should we call you Jeffrey and Julianna or JR and Jule?" Maggie asked.

"Just call me Jule, and JR is short for Jeffrey Richard. You can call him by either one. So where's our son?"

"That may take some time to explain," Garth said. "He could actually be under you." Jule and Jeffrey gaped at him in disbelief. "I'm serious. We have much to discuss."

A cacophony of noise coming from the docks drifted across the water. Garth knew something had happened.

"Sounds like a party has started," Jule said.

"Not a party. I have a feeling the news media just broadcasted the reason for your being here," Garth said.

"The alien thing. They're really coming?" Jeffrey asked. "Cal didn't make that story up just to get us over here?"

"They're real alright. Do you have a television aboard?" Maggie asked.

"Yes. Let's get into the saloon and turn on the news," Jeffrey said.

"The *saloon*," Garth said. "Only old salts call it that. I could never break Cal from calling it a salon."

"I know what you mean. I think he did it to aggravate us," Jule replied. "I call it a salon myself sometimes."

They went below, and Garth noted the teak deck and trim, all of it in perfect condition. The Locke's sat down in the chairs by a small table, which made into a settee, while Maggie and Garth sat opposite them on the portside U-shaped couch that surrounded a dining table. They turned on the small television, tuned to a Miami station, and saw Speaker McFarland talking.

"Who is that?" Garth asked.

"That's Speaker of the House Teddy McFarland," Jeffrey replied. "I wonder why he's speaking and not the president." He turned up the volume.

Garth and the others sat in silence and listened. They'd missed the first part of the speech, but the gist of the message was that aliens had arrived and that they were at war. McFarland announced that the president, vice president, and several other officials around the world had been involved in a conspiracy to aid the aliens.

That wasn't the smartest thing to tell them, Garth thought.

McFarland gave an accurate description of the events, minus the Igigi and Tegan's work. When he concluded his talk, the news station recapped the story and then reported on looting at a Miami grocery store.

"And so it begins," Garth muttered.

"You knew about all of this?" Jeffrey asked.

"Yes. We've been involved since the beginning." Garth spent the next twenty minutes going over the highlights of all that had happened, taking care to leave out any details about Tegan and her past. He focused on the aliens, the outposts, the cities, and the people that had been involved, some of whom had died. "I know you have questions," Garth said.

"You said we need to take shelter in an underground city?" Jule asked.

"That's the plan until we can determine what to do next. Staying hidden seems like the best option for now."

"What about our friends? If we can reach them, can we invite them to join us?" Jeffrey asked.

"We'll need to decide that after we meet with Cal and Tegan. We can't have a throng of people arriving all at once. We did that already, and it cost the lives of two of our friends."

"I understand," Jeffrey said.

"We haven't met Tegan yet," Jule said. "What's she like?"

Garth smiled. "She's very special, and she's given us some surprises. I think we should leave it at that. It wouldn't be proper for me to say anything else. I can tell you that Maggie and I love her to death and that our daughter, Jessica, looks up to her."

"We look forward to meeting her," Jeffrey said. "So when do we leave?"

Garth's cell phone rang. It was Cal. "Timing is everything. It's Cal. Hello."

"I'll keep this brief," Cal said. "I'm in the water above the Bimini portal. Is everything okay there?"

"It's all good. Your parents are here and ready for the move. But I still haven't heard from Edward. Did you know they've made the announcement about the alien threat?"

"No. Remember, we can't receive TV or radio signals here. What did they report?"

"The Speaker of the House talked about the president and the other Awakened, the pending invasion, and in general started a mass panic," Garth replied.

"I figured that would happen if they went public. What are they recommending everyone should do?"

"Your Speaker of the House, who's in charge now, by the way, is telling people to take shelter where they are, for whatever good that will do."

"I hear ya. I need to call Knolls. I'm late checking in with him. You know the general location of where we are, so start heading this way. I'll guide you in when you get closer."

"Your parents are sitting right here. Do you want to talk with them?"

"I do, but not now. I'll talk with them at the outpost. I've got to reach Knolls."

"I'll start your way. We should be there in twenty minutes."

"See you then," Cal said.

Garth looked at Cal's parents and said, "We need to get going."

"I didn't mean to eavesdrop, but I couldn't help hearing him say he was in the water," Jeffrey said.

"He's above the portal."

"And we'll have to dive underwater to get to this portal?"

"Yes. It's the only way into the outpost and the city. When the Igigi built their outposts and the city, they were still above ground. Then the ice melted and everything became submerged."

"The Igigi are the friendly ones, right?" Jule asked.

"Yes. It's a complicated story."

"And I think one that Cal should explain, don't you think, Garth?" Maggie asked.

"That probably would be best."

"What about the boats?" Jeffrey asked.

"We'll leave them anchored near the site," Garth replied. "Someone will stay aboard to keep an eye on things and to answer the phones. We've done this before."

"I'll volunteer to stay on the *Tranquility*," Jule said.

"And I'll stay with her," Jeffrey added.

"Let's get to the site, and I'll let you and Cal sort this out," Garth said.

CHAPTER EIGHTEEN

Washington — July 30 — 1825 hours

"I was beginning to think you forgot about me," Knolls said when he answered the call from Cal.

"We've been busy. I understand everything has gone public."

"It was the consensus of the world's leaders that they be open about what was about to happen. I wasn't in a position to stop them. I'm listening to the blaring sound of car horns as we speak. It's utter pandemonium around here."

"I can hear the horns. Did you tell them about Tegan and what she did?" Cal asked.

"Not entirely. General McLaughlin knows I'm not telling him everything, but I didn't get a chance to brief him in private. I didn't want to out Tegan in a public forum, so I omitted some details."

"That was smart."

"Yeah, you're welcome. They're setting me up in a secure facility. Anything new from the Igigi?"

"No contact yet. Where are you?"

"I'm sitting on a bench in the Rose Garden at the White House."

"How nice for you. What are the Idimmu doing?"

"Watching us watch them. They haven't moved since we destroyed their two ships, which is a good thing. It's giving us time to solidify our defenses."

"What's your role looking like?"

"At the moment, I'm a consultant and information source," Knolls replied. "Dark Moon is an open book now."

"Any chance you'll get back here anytime soon?"

"Not likely. How are the new digs?"

"We're getting settled," Cal replied. "My parents and Garth are on their way here. I'll check in when I can, probably late tonight or early morning. If anything happens, we're in the dark. I hope we can work something out with Manatu."

"Just so you know, I didn't mention anything about the Igigi. I couched my responses about how I knew what I did concerning the Idimmu. I only told them about Tegan creating Deep Sky. No other details."

"Good. We're not even sure about what she and my daughter are capable of doing yet. I don't want them becoming lab rats."

"I won't say anything."

"I think I see my folk's sailboat and Garth headed this way. I need to guide them in. Rob, we'll post someone topside with the phone so you can reach us."

"I'll let you go. Be safe." Knolls disconnected and sat staring across the lawn. It was surreal to think that just a few hours ago he was in the Bahamas and Dark Moon's mission was still hidden. In some respects, he wished he were back there. He stood up and waved at the corporal. He was ready to leave for his new quarters and glad he was going by helicopter. The blaring sounds of the snarled traffic echoed across the lawn.

Bimini — 1835 hours

When the *Deep Sky* and *Tranquility* were anchored and moored together over the portal, Cal climbed the boarding ladder at the stern of the *Tranquility* and greeted his parents with hugs.

"Good to see you, son," Jeffrey said.

"It's been a while," Cal replied.

"Where's your bride?" Jule asked.

"Tegan's waiting in the outpost."

Jule gave him a look that only his mother could give to conjure up feelings of guilt. "You said she worked for you for a few months before you got married, or was that Alessia?"

"You know she's the same person. Stop with the guilt trip. I should have invited you to the wedding, but it was kind of a spur-of-the-moment thing, and we didn't want to make the wedding a big deal. Can you just drop it? We have much more important things to discuss."

"We look forward to meeting her in person," Jeffrey said.

"She's looking forward to meeting both of you. We need to get you below for orientation."

"What kind of orientation?" Jule asked.

Cal looked at Garth. He was smiling at him. "I thought you would've briefed them."

"I gave them an overview," Garth said. "I thought it best if you told them the particulars."

"Thanks. Did you get ahold of Edward?"

"He's on his way. I'll stay topside until he arrives. Why don't you take Maggie down with your parents? She'll need the orientation, too."

Cal nodded, then said, "You sure you don't want to take her down?"

"You're a better guide than me. Besides, someone has to stay here."

"Sounds good." Cal faced his parents and pointed to the cushion on the bench. "You'll need to sit down for this."

After they sat, he said, "The place you're going into was built over ten thousand years ago. It's part of a vast complex that's beneath the Bahamas."

"Garth said it was built by the friendly aliens, not the ones that are going to invade," Jeffrey said.

"That's correct." Cal told his parents the history of the Igigi and how they'd saved humanity, then briefed them as best he could on what they would see and experience, omitting the details about Arklight. Then he told them about Tegan—who she once was, her professional training, her recent actions, and her connection to the Igigi. Both of them looked aghast.

"And this is the *lovely girl* you married?" Jule spit out with derision. "You let Emily get away and fell in love with a weapons-maker, a killer, and someone related to an alien?"

His mother had loved Emily, his first wife, and she had been the most upset of everyone when they divorced. "Tegan's intelligent, beautiful, and ... she's carrying our child." Cal figured if his parents were going to explode, he'd rather have them do it away from Tegan and the others, and he hoped this bombshell would stun them enough to end the discussion.

"She's pregnant!" Jule shouted.

"Yes."

"Is that why you got married so fast?" Jeffrey asked.

"No. We found out she was pregnant after we were married."

"Are there any more revelations you'd like to tell us about before we meet her?" Jule asked.

Cal looked at Garth and Maggie, who pretended they weren't listening. "There is one other thing. Our daughter will be someone very special. She will be different, but in a good way."

"It's a girl!" Jule cried. "But how could you know that so soon? How far along is Tegan, and what's the child's disability?"

"She's not disabled. In fact, our daughter is quite the opposite. She will be far brighter and more gifted than any other human on the planet. There's much more to tell you, but I'd rather Tegan be present. We'll answer all of your questions then."

Jeffrey said, "You mean she's going to be like her mother, like this other alien species?"

Cal clenched his jaw. "She's not an alien. She's human, but she will be capable of doing things beyond anything you could imagine."

"Like a superhero?" Jule asked sarcastically.

"Look, we don't know for sure what gifts she will have, but I will tell you she and Tegan stopped the Awakened by using Igigi technology in a way I don't think even the Igigi thought was possible." His parents looked stunned.

"I think maybe you should introduce them to Tegan and their granddaughter," Maggie said.

Jule faced Maggie and said, "You know about this?"

"We do. I can tell you, Garth and I adore Tegan. She's like another child to us, and we're very happy to have her in our lives. We can't wait to meet their daughter."

"Maybe we'd better go and meet her," Jeffrey said. "I guess I'll need to wear a swimsuit."

"A pair of shorts will do just as well. Whatever clothing you wear will dry quickly once you're in the outpost."

Ten minutes later, Cal, his parents, and Maggie were in their scuba gear, in the water, and ready to make the short dive.

Garth leaned over the railing and yelled, "Edward just checked in. He'll be here shortly. Will he be able to find the entrance on his own?"

"I doubt it, it's camouflaged," Cal replied. "I've marked it with a cluster of rocks, but if you don't know what to look for you won't find the portal. I'll come back up and show him the way in. Maybe I can get Nate to stay with the boats." Cal couldn't believe what he'd just said. "I mean Jessica or one of the others."

"It's okay, Cal. It'll take time for you to come to grips with what's happened."

Cal nodded and turned away.

"What happened to Nate?" Jule asked. "I always liked him."

Cal dipped his face into the water to hide his tears. "I omitted that part of the story. Nate and Alex were killed on Great Guana by President Collingsworth's assault team. They blew up the *Whispering Winds* and Alex and Nate were trapped below when the missile struck."

Neither Jule nor Jeffrey said anything. Cal could tell the circumstances surrounding them had suddenly become very real.

"I'm very sorry, son," Jeffrey finally said. "I know they were close to you."

"Especially Alex," Jule offered.

"Yes, they were good friends," Cal replied. "It's time to get below."

Bimini Station — 1855 hours

The platform retracted and settled into place. Cal helped his parents and Maggie step down, then helped them remove their gear. Tegan walked up with Jessica and Sara. Brian, Crystal, and Katie followed and stood behind them.

Cal gave Tegan a hug. "Tegan, these are my parents."

"It's nice to finally meet you both," she said.

"Likewise," Jeffrey replied.

"Welcome to your new home, at least for a little while," Tegan said.

Jule looked at Tegan as only a mother-in-law could, then said, "So you're pregnant."

Tegan smiled, "Yes, we're expecting. It's a girl."

"Cal told us," Jule said, then brushed past her and stopped at the ramp and looked down. "And I hear she's *special.*"

"Yes, Mrs. Locke. She's very special," Tegan replied with a sharp edge in her voice.

Cal could tell she was starting to boil.

Without turning to face her, Jule said, "Please, call me Jule, and you can call Jeffrey, JR. Since we're related now, we don't need any formalities, do we?"

"I guess not," Tegan replied. "Jule, JR, would you like to meet your granddaughter?"

Jule spun around. "What do you mean, *meet* her?"

A soft blue glow lit up Tegan's belly.

"She's saying, hello," Cal said, as if what they were witnessing was a common occurrence.

"And how do we say hello back to her," Jule asked.

"You just did," answered Tegan, giving her a sweet smile. "Please come and sit."

"I don't believe we've been properly introduced," Jeffrey said, looking at Brian and his family, then at Sara and Jessica.

"My apologies," Cal said. "Dad, Mom, this is Dr. Brian Lee, his wife, Crystal, and their daughter, Katie. And this is Jessica, Maggie and Garth's daughter, and this is Sara, soon to be Edward's wife."

"Brian, are you a doctor like Tegan?" Jule inquired.

Brian shook his head. "I'm a professor at Arizona State University. I specialize in archeology and linguistics. Alex asked me to join them to help decipher the symbols they'd found on the marker."

"That's the marker you said you found off Great Guana?" Jeffrey asked.

"That's the one," Cal answered. "Alex couldn't decipher the meaning of the symbols, and Brian's an expert in ancient languages. She thought he could help."

"I'm sure you have many questions," Tegan said. "We want you both to know that you'll be safe here. If you have questions, ask any one of us."

"Thank you, *dear*," Jule replied.

"You can call me Tegan. Everyone else does." Her belly glowed again.

Cal knew by his daughter's reaction that she understood the nature of the dialog. It was cordial, but with an underlying bite. "Let me show you around," Cal offered.

Jeffrey patted his shirt and shorts. "Wow, Cal, you weren't kidding when you said everything would dry fast. My shorts and shirt are bone dry already. Was it from that red light?"

Jule patted her clothes. "Mine are dry, too. What was that light anyway?"

"The light decontaminates whatever comes into the outpost. The air in here is as pure and contagion-free as in any clean lab. It's an alien thing." Cal could see that his mother wanted to ask about something else, but had decided against it.

"If you're wondering if the light will harm you, it won't. There's nothing in any of the facilities that can hurt you. Come on, I'll show you around the outpost." Cal walked his parents, Brian, Crystal, Katie, and Sara, down the ramp to level two.

Tegan whispered to Maggie and Jessica, "I don't think Cal's mother likes me. I guess I can't blame her."

Maggie put her arm around Tegan's shoulder and said, "She doesn't know you. Give her time. When Edward brought Sara home, it was easy for us. We already knew her and her family. Cal's parents just found out who you are, who you were, and that you're carrying their son's child. They're also in a strange environment under extraordinary circumstances. I'd say they're a bit rattled."

Tegan nodded. "I know. I just want them to like me. Maybe I need them to like me for Cal's sake."

"They will," Jessica said. "You're easy to like."

"Thanks. I'd be lost without you two. Since I met Alex, I realized I was missing close female companionship. Now that she's gone, I miss that connection."

"I understand," Maggie said. "You have us."

"I don't mean to imply that since she's gone that you two will have to do."

Maggie laughed. "I know what you mean. No need to explain."

"I guess I'm just a bit hormonal. I can't seem to keep my emotions under control."

"I was the same way when I was pregnant with Edward and Jessica. It's natural."

Tegan nodded. "Especially with this special bundle." She rubbed her belly, and the blue glow returned. "I just wanted you both to know how much you mean to me."

"I always wanted a big sister to look up to," Jessica said, giving Tegan a hug.

Tegan beamed at them. "I think we better catch up to the group."

"Cal, are these the symbols you've been talking about?" Jule asked, pointing at the symbols above a workstation in the control room.

"Those are just a few of many thousands."

"What does this say?" she asked.

"I have no idea," Cal answered.

"Your parents are probably hungry," Tegan said. "Can I bring you anything?"

"We're fine for now," Jule replied. "When we get hungry, we'll just go back to the boat. We'd like to see the rest of the outpost. From what Cal's told us so far, it's quite the marvel."

"Is it alright if we tag along?" Jessica asked Cal. "We didn't have much time to explore before your parents arrived."

"Why don't we all explore it together?" Brian said.

"Alright," Cal replied.

As they walked, Cal explained to his parents what the rest of Bimini Station and the cities looked like, and how they all connected to Sanctuary. Brian and Crystal added their comments about what they'd experienced so far. Katie was excited to tell them about all the places and things she'd seen. Cal showed them the communal dining hall, galley, and quarters. For something so foreign, he thought they were accepting it all well. He wondered if their composure would be the same when they came face to face with Manatu or Makita. On level six he showed them the entrance to the transit system and explained how it worked, at least what he knew of it.

Tegan had said little during the tour and Cal wondered if that was a good or a bad thing. "I think we've covered what there is to see here," Cal said. "Level seven is a small hangar bay. There's nothing to see there."

"When you say hangar bay, you mean where they park their spaceships?" Jule asked.

"Yes."

"And you've seen their spaceships?"

"Yes. Mom, Tegan and I have been aboard one of their ships." Cal described what they'd seen and what the Igigi craft looked like.

"And they'll be coming back in one of those ships?"

"Yes. "Mom, Dad, we can run over to Sanctuary if you like. It'll take us twenty minutes to get there."

"Let's save that for another time," Jule said. "I want to sit and talk with Tegan for a spell." She looked at Tegan, then said, "Alone."

Cal glanced at Tegan, and she nodded. "I guess we can all go back up to level one. I need to go topside to check on Garth and see if Edward has arrived."

"That's good, Cal," Tegan said. "I'm sure Sara would like to go topside with you."

"I would indeed," Sara said.

"I think it will be good if your mother and I spent some time to get better acquainted. We'll be up shortly," Tegan said.

Cal caught a look from Maggie. "Let's give them some privacy," she whispered, taking him by the arm and leading him away.

The group started up the ramp. Tegan walked to a workstation, touched a symbol above it, and a chair materialized from the wall, then repeated the process at another workstation.

"That's convenient," Jule said.

"It's a real space saver. I wished I'd had that technology for the sailboat. What did you want to talk to me about?" Tegan sat on the chair and it automatically adjusted itself to her weight.

Jule tested the chair, then sat down. "I want to get to know you. Cal's told me a little about your life. How your parents died, how you came to be here, and that you worked for the government."

"There's not much else to tell."

"Do you love my son?"

Tegan smiled. "More than anyone can imagine."

"But do you love him for who he is, or do you love him because he was there when you needed someone?"

"You mean is this a love of convenience?"

"Yes."

"Jule, when I met your son, I was on the run. At first, I did use Cal and the *Whispering Winds* as an escape. But in some ways I think our meeting was preordained."

"You mean it was fate?"

"I believe so. I'm a reasonably intelligent person, a scientist, and a medical doctor. I'm spiritual, but not religious. What I feel for Cal is something I can't quantify or explain. It didn't take long for me to fall deeply in love with him. He was like a piece of my life that had been missing, and I was that piece of his life he needed. Together we made a whole. We just fit. He understands me. He understood me even before he knew about my past and who I really was."

Jule nodded.

Tegan continued, "When I told Cal who I really was and that it would be safer for him without me, he wouldn't hear of it. When they came for me that day in Garth's dive shop, I thought they were going to kill him, and I wasn't going to lose the man I loved more than anything else in this world."

Tegan took a breath. "I killed a man, the same man that killed my family, and I did it without any remorse. I would've killed Commander Knolls if Cal hadn't stopped me. I felt something primal erupt within me that day. I needed to protect my family at any cost."

"Cal told us about what happened that day. Commander Knolls is the man that's helping you now, the one that's in charge of the secret organization you used to work for, correct?"

"Yes. He's in charge of Dark Moon. I didn't know I worked for them. I thought I worked for the CDC."

"Let's back up a second. Why do you think your union with my son was preordained?"

Tegan sighed. "You may think I'm crazy after I tell you. When my family was killed, I was somehow drawn to these islands. I didn't know why at the time. All my life I've felt as if something was missing. I've since learned this was where my ancestors once lived."

"You mean you were drawn here like a sea turtle knows where to return to lay its eggs?"

"Exactly. I had memories of a place I'd never been to before. I saw images of people I'd never met. If I hadn't met Cal, we never would have discovered the marker or made contact with the Igigi. We wouldn't have learned about the Awakened. I wouldn't have become pregnant, and what my daughter and I did wouldn't have happened. The alien invasion would have been unopposed. Don't you see, there are too many variables that had to come together to stop them. That all couldn't have happened by chance."

Jule leaned back and nodded.

Tegan said, "The Igigi are thousands of years ahead of us in development. They are incredibly intelligent, but even they couldn't have planned for all of these events to align. They didn't even know that the Etu Inu Idimmu had created the Awakened. In my opinion, that leaves only fate."

Jule shrugged. "It could also have been just luck."

Tegan shook her head. "The odds are too extraordinary to measure for all of those pieces to have fallen into place. What's happened was meant to be. Our daughter is to be the next step in human evolution. She will advance human civilization beyond anything we can imagine. I know this to be true, but we must survive to see it come to fruition." Tegan's belly glowed. She placed her hand over it. "Without Cal, none of this would have been possible. But it's only now when I can look back on what's transpired that I see it was arranged by something greater than any of us."

"You mean, God?"

Tegan stared at her for a moment and decided to tell her. "It's called Arklight. It gives life to everything. It's the fabric of our universe and the multiverses that make up an infinite number of galactic systems. I believe Arklight has a consciousness, and it decides what our purpose is in this world. I can't begin to describe it."

"You think Arklight is God."

"If it isn't God, then it's the reason God exists. I felt its raw power when my daughter tapped into it. I could feel it in every cell of my body as it ran through me and my daughter. I felt as if it approved of what we were doing. Crazy, right?"

"No. I don't think so. It's just something that we can't explain, yet. I have to ask you something. Please don't take offense."

"I'll try not to," Tegan replied.

"My son is a normal man. How could he have produced this child?"

"I've wondered about that as well." Tegan sighed. "I'm the first twin daughter of a first twin daughter, in an ancestral line going back thousands of generations, not to be blessed with twins. You have to understand, there is more at work here than we can comprehend. There is a reason Cal and I are joined and that he is her father."

"How can an unborn child interact with this power? Are you certain she's the one responsible?"

"Yes. She was the catalyst that allowed us to connect to the field. It runs through both of us in a way that's different from other humans. I wish I could explain it better. The blue glow you see everywhere is the Arklight field. It is the source, and somehow we are able to interact with it."

"I see," Jule said.

Tegan stood. "I love your son, and we will love your granddaughter. I will do everything in my power to protect them. Now, is there anything else you'd like to know about me?"

Jule stood, took a step forward and hugged her. "You've told me what I need to know."

"Why don't we rejoin the others?"

Even before Cal surfaced, he knew that Edward had already arrived. The shape of the *Blue Angel's* hull appeared as he approached the anchor site. Sara surfaced behind him, and they swam toward the stern of *Tranquility*. Jessica had tagged along, claiming she needed fresh air. Cal figured she had another reason.

"Garth. Edward," Cal yelled as he reached the stern of the *Tranquility*.

Edward and Garth emerged from the cabin of the *Deep Current*. "Hey," Garth shouted. "I see you brought my daughter and Sara with you."

"Sara wanted to see Edward, and Jessica needed some air. Did you want me to set another anchor before getting out?"

"I don't think so. Edward was just saying it might make for a quicker departure if we keep the *Blue Angel* tied alongside."

"Good thinking," Cal replied.

A few minutes later, Sara was in Edward's arms. Jessica jumped over to the *Deep Current* and hugged her father. Cal hadn't seen her show any affection toward her parents for some time. He wondered what had gotten into her. He could tell that Garth was taken aback, but he squeezed her tightly and kissed the top of her head.

"What's this all about?" Garth asked.

"Can't I hug my father without an inquisition?" Jessica answered.

"Certainly. I'll take a hug whenever you want to give one."

"I think life has taught her some lessons over the last week," Cal said.

"Indeed. She's matured."

"I'm standing right here," said Jessica.

"I need to check in with Knolls and see if there's been any change," Cal said.

"If you don't mind staying topside for a bit, I'd like to see the new place," Garth said.

"Jessica can show you the way. There's a platform. The controls are simple to use. Take my tank."

"We might need to find a way to fill the tanks in a few days."

"I think we'll have enough air to get up and down without any problems for a while, but I see your point," Cal said. "The sun's going to set shortly. We'll need to leave someone topside."

"After I have a look around, Sara and I can spend the night on the *Blue Angel*," Edward offered.

"That'd be great. I'll wait here until you come back," Cal said.

"You want me to send Tegan up for a few minutes?" Garth said. "You guys could watch the sunset together."

Cal shook his head. "I think it best she spends some time with my parents."

"Okay."

$$\infty$$

As soon as Garth and the others had left for the portal, Cal made his call.

"Hey," Knolls answered.

"Everyone is where they need to be," Cal said. "Anything new there?"

"All of the Idimmu ships are still stationary. We've seen no activity, which concerns me."

"What about the Awakened?"

"They're all still the same. I've been sequestered in a building only minutes by air from the White House. If anything happens, I'll be notified. I briefed General McLaughlin in private. I still haven't told him everything."

"For now, let's keep them in the dark unless something's essential for him to know."

"I agree."

Cal said, "Edward has arrived. He and Sara have the evening watch. If anything happens, call them on this phone and one of them will come fetch me."

"Believe me, if anything happens, you'll be the first to know. How are your parents doing?"

"Getting settled. When I left, Tegan and my mom were having a chat."

"That would have been interesting to watch."

"My parents were shocked to hear about the baby."

"I bet they were."

"Nothing else to tell you. Be safe, Commander," Cal said and disconnected.

CHAPTER NINETEEN

Bimini — July 31 — 0600 hours

Tegan surfaced behind the *Tranquility* with Cal at her side. She was amazed there hadn't been some kind of a crisis during the night. The sky was lighter, but the sun had yet to make its appearance in the eastern sky. This used to be the time of day when she liked to meditate. Cal's parents had found the accommodations to be more comfortable than they had expected, and they had stayed below instead of swimming back to the boat in the dark. Cal had pointed out that South Bimini was known for its shark activity.

Garth and Maggie had retired early that evening, and Jessica had taken the opportunity to sit with Tegan. Jessica had asked some very insightful questions during their discussion, especially about her ever being able to go to college. Tegan had done her best to offer her some hope, but Jessica had seen right through it. She knew that Jessica would eventually adapt, and Tegan promised to help her find her way.

Tegan and Cal climbed *Tranquility's* boarding ladder, took off their gear, and dried themselves with the towels that had been left on the bench.

"Should we wake Edward and Sara?" Tegan asked.

"We're up," Edward shouted from the small cabin on the *Blue Angel*. "It's hard not to be with all the noise you two made getting aboard." Edward stepped out on deck and stretched, wearing a pair of shorts and an old, wrinkled T-shirt.

"You look like you were up most of the night," Tegan said.

"I was. I didn't want to miss a call. Sara relieved me at four."

"Where is she?" Cal asked looking around.

"She's on the *Deep Current* taking a shower, which is what I'm going to do in a minute." Edward jumped aboard the *Deep Current*. "I saw a few ships headed north, freighters by the look of their lights."

"Any local traffic?" Cal asked.

"I saw some boats heading west toward the mainland. Mostly they were the bigger motor yachts, and they were all running dark. The residents of Alice Town kept their lights off."

"That's good thinking on someone's part. No need to draw attention to the island."

"A few sailboats are still in the harbor," Edward said. "You can see their masts if you look between the buildings over there." He pointed. "No one has shown any interest in us."

"That's good news," Tegan said.

"Are my folks up yet?" Edward asked.

"I'm not sure," Cal replied. "I know that Jessica is still asleep. Brian took his family back to Sanctuary early this morning, and I haven't seen my parents yet."

"What do you think about me running into Alice Town to get some additional provisions after my shower?" Edward asked. "You can never have too much food."

Cal nodded, then said, "What we really need is a source of air to refill our scuba tanks."

"I can check on that. If the shops are still open and there's power, I'll get what you have topside filled."

"If the shop owner is there, see if you can buy us some more spear guns, fishing poles, stringers and nets, and anything else we can use to live off the sea. If he has extra tanks, get those, too."

"*Semper paratus.* Isn't that what you used to tell me?" Edward said.

"That's correct. We need to plan for all possible contingencies."

"If someone is there and asks about why I need all the stuff, what should I say?"

Cal thought for moment. "Tell them that you just heard the news about the aliens and you want to store a few weeks of provisions."

"And how should I pay for all these items?"

Cal said, "Give me a minute." He disappeared below deck. A few minutes later, he came back holding two credit cards wrapped in a fifty-dollar bill. "This should work."

"Don't those belong to your dad?" Tegan asked.

"He won't mind." Cal handed them to Edward.

"I'll see what I can scare up. I think Sara should stay with you two."

"I think that's a good idea," replied Tegan.

The slider to the salon opened, and Sara walked out with her hair in a towel, wearing a yellow, one-piece swimsuit. "I heard my name."

"I was just telling Tegan and Cal that you'll stay here with them while I scout Alice Town."

"We're not married yet and already you're bossing me around."

Cal smiled. "Edward, you need to be careful how you phrase things. Why don't you get started for Alice Town? I'll cover the phones."

"Cal, I doubt anyone's open yet, and I want a shower. I haven't had one in days," Edward said.

"Okay. When you get over there, see if you can get us some extra fuel."

"I already planned to do that. I burned at least seventy gallons just getting here. The fuel tanks are nearly dry."

"What happened to Howard and his family?" Tegan asked.

"Howard ended up taking an old, thirty-six-foot Gulfstar trawler over to Green Turtle Cay. He said the owners wouldn't be coming for it. The Gulfstar is slow, but seaworthy, and it has a lot of range. I told him to meet us in this general area."

"I don't think having another boat tied up next to us is a good idea," Cal said.

"He may not show up for a while," Edward said. "The Gulfstar cruises at about eight knots. From Green Turtle to here, that's a full day's run."

"I believe if we anchor within sight of each other that we'll be fine," Tegan said.

"Alright," Cal said. "When he arrives, we'll get him and his family into the city and then anchor the Gulfstar a few miles north of us. The boat's too slow to use to run from anyone, but it could serve as a lookout post if we need one."

"Shower time," Edward said.

"Go easy on the fresh water," Sara said. "We may not have an opportunity to refill the tank for a while."

"Where's the phone?" Tegan asked.

"You got it, right?" Edward said.

Sara replied, "I put it on the dinette. I'll get it while you shower. I'll be right back."

"Thanks," Tegan said. She was tired from lack of sleep. Everything had caught up with her. Last night she'd tried to decompress by meditating, but it hadn't helped much. She wished she could use the Dogita platform again, but she didn't want to risk exposure without Manatu's supervision.

"You okay?" Cal asked her.

"Yeah. I'm just trying to put things in perspective. I have you, and that's all that matters."

"Here's the phone," Sara said coming back on deck.

"Sara, do you want to go down to the outpost?" Tegan asked.

Sara shook her head. "Not right now. I just got the saltwater off me. I'll wait here with you guys for Edward to come back, if that's okay."

"That's fine by us," Tegan said. "Do you want to come over here?"

"No. I'm good right where I am."

Edward came on deck a few minutes later, carrying his T-shirt. His hair was wet. He still wore the old shorts. "Was that fast enough for you, Sara?"

"Perfect," she answered, then gave him a kiss. "Be careful."

"I will be. Cal, I'll take one of the old phones and call to let you know what I found."

"That's fine. We'll need to keep the line free, so your report will have to be short."

"Just like my shower," Edward replied.

Edward jumped over to the *Blue Angel* and went below. When he reappeared, he wore a clean shirt, one with his dad's dive shop logo on it. After venting the bilge, Edward cranked the engines, then checked the exhausts at the stern to make sure that they both had water coming out.

"Later, guys," Edward yelled. He pulled away.

"Do you think everything will be alright?" Sara asked.

"He'll be fine," answered Tegan.

"I didn't just mean Edward's trip to Alice Town," Sara said. "I mean with all that's coming. My family stayed on Elbow Cay, and I'm worried."

Cal said, "The Abacos are not what you'd call a strategic objective. The only thing of interest to the Idimmu is the outpost. I think your family will have a change of heart and join us. Why don't you call them?"

"Okay, I'll be just a sec." Sara disappeared into the salon.

Tegan sat down next to Cal. He took her hand in his and kissed it. "I love you," he said."

"I love you, too." The soft glow in her belly appeared. "I think someone else is agreeing."

Cal patted her belly. "I love you, too, little one. I guess we need to start thinking about names."

"I think we have some time. Besides, she may already have one that she'd like to use."

Cal wrinkled his brow. "I hadn't thought of that."

The Monan's Ship

The Monan stood before the view screen, looking at the Earth. The others around her were waiting for her to give the order to advance. She'd learned there was a way to circumvent the communications barrier by using a particular microwave frequency to contact their ships in the atmosphere. She still didn't have an explanation for what had blocked them from using their telepathy- and pheromone-based systems. The Monan believed the Igigi had intervened yet again, but that wouldn't change the outcome. After some consideration, she thought the Awakened could still be of value. If nothing else, they could become a distraction and slow any response to their advance. That would reduce her losses. The problem was that even if they could reach the Awakened, they'd lost most of their best controllers when the two advance ships were destroyed. But she had more controllers on other ships.

She felt the presence of her most senior advisor, Dractor, standing behind her. He was awaiting her orders. She decided to seek out the source of the interference. She would direct him to investigate the islands where

Trakar had said the Igigi artifact rested. Xunta would be aboard their contact ships. She would deploy them to test their proficiency against the populace. If they found the Igigi stronghold, the Xunta would attack it and kill everyone there.

"Millions of our collective will die before this ends," the Monan said, using her pheromones.

"Yes. The nurseries will make up for our losses," Dractor responded.

"For too long we have only been able to produce nurslings to replace those of us who died in transit. That's what we were forced to do to make our journey. The new ones that we bring into this world will not face the hardships we have endured. They will know a new life and remain safe under Xunta protection."

"It will be a good life," Dractor replied. "We make the sacrifice so that they may live, and our kind will grow stronger. You have led us well."

She turned and faced him. He bowed his head. "Dractor, you will lead the first ships down to our new home and oversee the establishment of the Protectorate. You are directed to first find the Igigi stronghold and the source of whatever blocks our normal channels of communication."

"It will be my honor."

Dractor was one of the very few that she'd taken as a mate. He was of good stock, with the suitable qualities of aggressiveness, intelligence, and loyalty. Their offspring had proven to be some of the finest specimens of their kind. Many of them would be on the front lines when they landed and would command the Xunta in their sectors. She also knew that some of their offspring would die in the coming days. That was the way it had to be. They all understood the sacrifices they had to make so that the collective could flourish.

The Monan conveyed the revised plan of attack to Dractor in detail, along with the timeline for their advance. The first wave fleet would attack instead of waiting. The second fleet would join them thereafter. The majority of the first wave of ships, under Dractor's command, would land in Antarctica. The remainder of the first wave would land all across the northern hemisphere in Greenland, Russia, Alaska, and northern Canada simultaneously. Twelve of their smaller contact ships would land in the largest population centers. She would test the humans' resolve as they encountered the thousands of the Xunta she planned to release. The Xunta would have only one objective, "kill anything human."

Dractor nodded, backed away, and left to carry out his orders. The tactical screens came to life. She only needed to issue the final command. She looked around the command deck and sent the message that all of her kind had waited so long to hear. "Execute!"

The fleet began to move toward Earth, and she sent her orders to their ships in Earth's atmosphere. When she reached out to the new Awakened controllers, she could feel the apprehension in many of them. Some had never interfaced with a human before. It took but a moment to allay their fears. They would obey her command when the time came.

The Monan anticipated that their ships would be subjected to aerial intercepts, but she had the advantage of numbers. Many of the larger ships could withstand an aerial assault by aircraft. From the intelligence she'd received over the last year, it was unlikely that the humans would employ nuclear weapons over land. The destruction of the areas they planned to inhabit would be environmental suicide for the planet. There was still a possibility that they could lose a few heavy carriers as they approached the atmosphere and had to face the nuclear missiles like the ones launched earlier, but now that they had encountered the weapon, she calculated that they could avoid most of them.

Once the Protectorate was established, she'd reinforce their foothold and bring in the second fleet. The Xunta nurseries were already producing more of the beasts, and they would continue to do so for a long time. They would be their most valuable weapon. She knew this was going to be a protracted battle, but unlike the last time, they would succeed.

Deep Secure Command Center — July 31 — 0630 hours

General Stoddard had awoken an hour earlier and was reviewing the latest readiness reports on his computer when he heard someone shout, "Movement!" He changed screens and analyzed the tracking of the multitude of ships.

"Confirm!" Stoddard shouted.

He hurried to the command center. A moment later, he had confirmation. He put on his headset and linked to the DSCC bunker. When General McLaughlin's face appeared on the monitor, he said, "General McLaughlin, we have incoming. Do I have your permission to launch the Sprites?"

General McLaughlin rubbed his bloodshot, tired eyes and said, "How many ships are we facing and from where?"

"Seven of the larger ships are closing. They are discharging thousands of smaller vessels."

"Give me a second to look at the tracking feed and brief Speaker McFarland."

McLaughlin's face disappeared from the screen. Stoddard looked around his command center as more and more people scurried back and forth.

A few minutes later, McLaughlin said, "General Stoddard, Speaker McFarland is on his way and has authorized you to use the Sprites. Your primary targets are the mother ships."

"Yes, sir. The Sprites are ready, and will be airborne in less than two minutes. We should be able to engage all seven of their bigger ships. It appears one of the larger ships is holding station. The smaller ships are scattered too far apart to target individually, so any of those we hit will be pure luck."

Alarms sounded.

"General Stoddard, is there something new to report?" McLaughlin asked.

"One moment, sir."

"Someone get me through to Commander Knolls. Now!" McLaughlin shouted.

A minute later, Stoddard said, "General, we have a problem."

"Not the words I like to hear."

"We have additional large mother ships crossing the Space Fence. Jesus, that can't be right. Verify."

Speaker McFarland appeared on Stoddard's monitor. "General Stoddard, are those new ships I'm seeing on the tactical display?"

Stoddard held up a finger and said, "Mr. Speaker, give me a moment." Jacob Miller's face came on the monitor in front of Stoddard and on one in the DSCC.

"Miller, can you confirm those ships?" Stoddard asked.

"Yes, sir. They just crossed the outer marker."

"How many more?" McFarland asked.

Jacob looked pale. "Mr. Speaker, we're tracking over three hundred mother ships. The number of smaller craft is too high to obtain an accurate count. All of them are earthbound."

"Over three hundred of the bigger ships?" McFarland asked.

"Yes, sir. They have begun to divide into two groups. If they maintain trajectory, they will either enter orbit or punch through the atmosphere over the polar regions."

Stoddard said, "We can't bring down that many before they reach the atmosphere. We don't have that many Sprites."

"How many do we have?"

"I have fifteen land-based left and twelve sea-based," Stoddard replied.

"That's it?" McFarland yelled.

"The Sprites were designed to intercept space rocks, not stop an invading race of aliens."

"Hit the ones you can, Eli," McLaughlin said. "Mr. Speaker, I recommend we initiate Operation Global Freedom."

McFarland said, "Jesus, you guys have an acronym or operational name for everything. What's Operation Global Freedom?"

Just then, General Stoddard yelled, "Sprites are away, and we have positive tracking on all of the mother ships."

"Advise when they impact," McLaughlin said.

"Aspect change by several of the smaller ships," Jacob said. "They're accelerating."

"Looks like the smaller craft are moving to intercept the Sprites," Stoddard added. "They'll probably intercept the missiles just after they leave the atmosphere."

"No doubt a defensive action to protect the larger ships," McLaughlin said.

Two minutes later, Stoddard said, "All of the Sprites have detonated. Negative impact on any of the mother ships. The smaller ships took the missile hits. I held six Sprites in reserve. They're aboard a submarine on station under the Arctic. I see no reason to launch those."

"I agree," McLaughlin said. "Maybe we can hit the bigger ships when they enter the atmosphere. Mr. Speaker, to answer your question, Global Freedom is a response scenario designed to protect the United States from multiple attacks from diverse enemies. It seals our borders, establishes martial law, and activates every military reserve unit in the country, including civilian auxiliaries. We assume control of all media outlets. Everything in the country is federalized and at our disposal. All federal agencies and resources are under the president's command. Congress is no longer a factor. You will have absolute authority to take any action necessary."

"Let me think about this for a minute."

"We don't have a minute!" McLaughlin shouted. "Why the hell isn't Knolls here yet?"

Deep Secure Command Center — 0650 hours

Knolls jumped from the helicopter that had just landed on the White House lawn and ran. He had no doubt that the Etu Inu Idimmu were advancing. By the time he reached the secure elevator, he was out of breath. He descended into the bunker. As he entered the presidential secure room, he could tell by the looks on everyone's face that it was bad. He approached General McLaughlin.

"You asked for me, sir."

"The shit has hit the fan. I suspected that you weren't telling me everything last night. I need to know exactly what assets you have available and what information you haven't disclosed. *All* of Dark Moon information needs to be shared, now!"

"What's changed?" Knolls asked.

"When I called fifteen minutes ago, we had over three hundred mother ships headed this way. The latest report puts their number at nearly six hundred, and there are so many smaller ships that we can't even count them all. No way we can stop them in space. The smaller ships formed a picket line to shield the bigger ships and prevented our Sprite missiles from getting to the them. So tell me everything."

Knolls nodded and said, "Before I left Bimini, I was advised that there were two groups of Idimmu ships headed this way. The first group has over three thousand ships like the ones you destroyed. The second group has over twelve thousand. The second group looks to be the bulk transports. Much larger than the others. You're facing as many as two billion Idimmu, maybe more."

McLaughlin shook his head in disbelief. "Why on Earth didn't you tell us that yesterday during the briefing or in any of our conversations?"

"I wasn't in a position to disclose the information. I shouldn't be telling you this now."

"You said yesterday that you didn't know what kind of weapons they have. Is that accurate?"

"Yes, sir. The weaponry they used the last time they attacked Earth wasn't enough to bring us down. Our tactics and superior numbers prevailed. It's different this time."

"No shit! If we'd known about their numbers yesterday, we could have planned for a different defense. What are you hiding?"

"General, with all due respect, I need to make a call before I can provide you with any additional information."

"You're kidding, right?"

"No, sir. The party I need to speak to is on Bimini and she offers the greatest hope of preventing our genocide. There are several factors at play that I will brief you on when I'm authorized. It sounds crazy, but as I said, there are other factors involved."

The general's eyes widened, and the veins on his forehead enlarged.

"Make your call," McLaughlin said, through clenched teeth.

"Yes, sir.

Tranquility — 0700 hours

The cell phone chimed, and Sara ran to grab it. Tegan and Cal jumped to their feet and went to the railing.

"Hold on, Rob. They're right here," Sara said. She tossed them the phone. "He sounds frazzled."

Cal caught the cell phone and put it on speaker. "What's happened?"

"They're advancing, many hundreds of mother ships, and tens of thousands of smaller ones."

"We knew they would," Cal said. "So what's the problem?"

"I want to brief the Joint Chiefs and the other world leaders about what else is in play."

"You mean the Igigi."

"Yes. And about Tegan and Arklight."

"Hold on. Tegan, I think you need to field this one."

Tegan took the phone. "What is it?"

"Tegan, I need to tell my new boss about you and everything else. They need to know how you can help. And not just Deep Sky, but Arklight as well."

She felt torn. Of course, she wanted Knolls to tell them about anything that would help the cause, but she didn't want anyone knowing about Arklight or her child's abilities. After a moment she said, "Rob, give them the location of the outposts and the city. You can tell them about the Igigi, but not about Arklight. No one can know about what I've done or about my daughter. Is that clear?"

"Perfectly. Any chance you've learned about anything else that you can weaponize?"

"No. I haven't even heard from Manatu," Tegan replied. "What is all that noise I hear in the background?"

"I'm not sure," Knolls replied. "Let me call you back."

Five minutes later, Knolls called her. "It seems the Idimmu have found a way around your dome of silence. We're detecting microwave transmissions between their ships in the atmosphere and space."

"Like I said, the Arklight shield I put in place wouldn't work against normal communication frequencies."

"Apparently, but here's the even better news. The POTUS is awake and demanding to return to power. The VP claims they will release something called a Xunta if we don't let them back in power."

"How is that possible?" Tegan asked. "I don't think it's likely they could have been genetically altered to communicate on a microwave frequency."

"We have no idea. It seems the president's orb came alive. The best I can figure is he and the VP are getting instructions from it again."

"Well, shut the thing down," Tegan said. "Why didn't they seize that earlier?"

"Good question. No one knew what it was when they found the thing in his pocket at the hospital, and it found its way outside. We can't shut it down. It went airborne just after activating."

"So it's active. How many other Awakened are functional again?" Tegan asked.

"I don't know. I believe the Idimmu were waiting to find a solution to their communications problem before they attacked. Any chance you can shut down the microwave and other radio frequencies?"

"I could try, but that will shut down our ability to communicate. That would be worse. What's a Xunta?"

"We don't know. I was hoping you could do some research on the subject."

"Okay," Tegan replied.

Knolls said, "I'll brief the general. You need to get to the new lab and prepare Deep Sky and find a way to use Arklight to our advantage. We need to throw everything we can at them, and soon. Stay available for a few. I'm sure the military and other folks here are going to have more questions."

The line went dead.

"I don't know if he hung up on me or the signal was dropped," Tegan said.

"I don't think the military will be able to stop them before they land," Cal said.

"What's happened?" Sara asked.

Tegan looked at her. "Call Edward and tell him to head back at top speed."

Sara nodded and grabbed the other phone.

"Tegan, I want you back in the outpost," Cal said. "I'll stay here and talk to Rob if he calls back."

Tegan shook her head. "No. I need to be here." She looked at Cal. "The Idimmu have found a way around our communication blackout. The Awakened are causing trouble."

Cal nodded. "So I gathered. You figured they might find a workaround. What next?"

Tegan's belly glowed. "We find a way to contact the Igigi, and then our daughter and I need to get back to work. I need Deep Sky ready to go, and I need to find an Arklight solution, neither of which is going to happen quickly."

Deep Secure Command Center — 0715 hours

"Let's talk," said Knolls as he walked up to General McLaughlin.

"In a minute," McLaughlin replied tersely.

Knolls sat in the nearest chair and listened to the inane discussions going on around him. McFarland didn't want to authorize Operation Global Freedom, because only the president could do that, and the president was awake and demanding he stand down. McLaughlin reminded him that the president was one of the Awakened. The president demanded that he be allowed to address the nation and the world. The media had already learned that he and the VP were awake. Knolls figured it wouldn't be long before the rest of the world knew this, too. The Idimmu were using the Awakened even if it wasn't how they'd planned.

General McLaughlin turned to face him. "Commander Knolls, I need to know if the president is still a threat."

"Absolutely. He is an Awakened and the enemy. He only wants to cause turmoil so we can't react. That's why the Awakened were put here."

McLaughlin walked over to McFarland and said, "Mr. Speaker, you need to listen to me. You are the president. We have nothing else to throw at them while they're in space. President Collingsworth and Vice President Preston are the enemy."

"General, the president is claiming that the Antediluvians aren't hostile," McFarland said. "There is no threat. He said the Antediluvians have assured him that they will forgive our actions against them. They are here to help us."

"Wake up, you're being played. Give the order to launch Operation Global Freedom or everything and everybody we know and love will be lost."

McFarland still looked torn.

Knolls said, "Mr. Speaker, if I may offer a suggestion."

"Certainly."

"Check and see if General Stewart has become conscious again, then ask him if he wants to send our forces back to the Abacos to locate an alien artifact. I'm willing to bet he is, because that's where an Igigi city is located."

McLaughlin looked confused. "What city, what artifact, and what's an Igigi?"

"This is the rest of the story," Knolls said. "The Igigi are an alien species that have been watching us for over twelve thousand years. They helped us successfully defeat the Etu Inu Idimmu over seven thousand years ago. Humanity was led by an Igigi that taught us how to fight." He paused, realizing that the room had gone silent.

"I've met with two Igigi representatives," Knolls continued. "They're humanoid, a bit taller than us, and incredibly advanced. The downside is that they can't take direct action to help us this time. I can assure you that the Idimmu and the Awakened they control are the enemy. Over the past several thousand years, they've abducted human beings and modified their genetic structure so they can be controlled to help them. The president and the others like him will say and do whatever the Dark-Eyed Demons tell them. The Awakened became comatose after we were able to sever their connection."

General McLaughlin turned to a colonel sitting at one the desks and said, "Find out if General Stewart is awake and if he's issuing orders."

McFarland said, "Tell us about the city."

For the next few minutes, Knolls told them about the outposts and their locations and about the Igigi and the city they'd built. He said that it was Igigi technology that was responsible for the communications interruption. He explained that it was his team, not the Igigi, that had found a way to send a signal to block normal Idimmu communications within the Earth's atmosphere. Knolls refused to disclose any more details.

McLaughlin said, "I've just been advised that General Stewart wanted to send Special Forces back to the Abacos, just as Commander Knolls said he would."

"So this underwater city can hold almost a million of these Igigi, and it's impregnable?" McFarland asked.

"The city and the outposts can give us a fighting chance of surviving as a species. The Igigi have offered to take some of us off-world if it becomes necessary."

"But they won't fight the Idimmu," McLaughlin said.

"No, sir. I've argued with them several times and they won't budge. They're bound by a sacred covenant that won't allow them to kill an intelligent being."

"But you said they helped before," McFarland said.

"And the clan that helped us was disavowed. It's a long story. Bottom line, we can't count on them to defend us."

"Why would the Idimmu want to land in the polar regions?" McLaughlin asked.

"That climate is much like the one on the planet left behind, and it's remote enough that we would have difficulty fighting them there."

McFarland said, "What if we let them land and then nuked them all?"

McLaughlin shook his head. "They may not land everyone all at once. Also, there's the environmental concerns and collateral damage that could result from melting that much ice in Antarctica. And I don't think we or the Russians want to light up the Arctic Circle. We could end up with a nuclear winter."

Knolls said, "It's going to be hard to stop them once they land. Deep Sky is a viable option for slowing them down once they're here, and I have the creator of the virus working on it in the Abacos as we speak. Under Operation Global Freedom, we can deploy Deep Sky quicker and more effectively. I just don't know if it will be enough. I suggest we begin sheltering people in the outposts as soon as possible, but they'll need to be screened. We can't allow an Awakened to compromise an outpost and the technology that's there."

"How do you propose we screen that many people?" McFarland asked. "What selection criteria do we use? Just announcing that there are these outposts will create global chaos."

"You can't announce the existence of the outposts or the city or where they're located. It will have to be done quietly, and it will take time."

"Which we all know we don't have," McLaughlin said.

Knolls looked at McFarland. "Mr. Speaker, you need to act. The Etu Inu Idimmu are determined to take this planet from us, and they'll kill everyone they don't need when they're done. You have to issue the order immediately."

"I appreciate your opinion, Commander," McFarland said.

Knolls knew there was a *but* coming, so he cut him off by saying, "Mr. Speaker, many brave people have sacrificed their lives to get this information to you."

In the silence, Knolls could see that the others in the room and by the faces of those on the monitors that they agreed with him. McFarland clenched his jaws for a while then stood.

"General McLaughlin, you have my authorization. Let's stop these bastards, even if it means launching limited nuclear strikes on our own soil."

"Yes, sir." McLaughlin looked at Knolls and smiled, then turned to the monitors. "I need a sit-rep, General Stoddard."

"The alien ships are continuing to advance. The nine ships in atmosphere are also moving again. Tracking analysis indicates additional landing locations, but it still looks like the majority of their fleet is converging on Antarctica and the Arctic Circle."

"What are the other locations, General Stoddard?" McFarland asked.

"It appears they intend to land in some larger population centers, but you have to understand that these are only preliminary projections. They could alter course at any time."

"Admiral Putnam, how long would it take to get Focused Starlight operational and positioned to defend the larger cities?" McLaughlin asked.

"We have two units off North Korea, two in Alaska, and one in Hawaii. There are four units with the B-2s in Missouri and four more in Germany. We can have all of them airborne in twenty minutes. We also have several more advanced prototypes in Nevada, but they aren't flight ready."

"So all you need is a target?" McLaughlin swept his hand across the bank of monitors. "Pick one. Let's see how effective they are."

"Yes, sir."

McFarland said, "What is Focused Starlight?"

"SDI Star Wars laser weapons. The most advanced weapons system we've ever created. I'm sure the Russians and Chinese have something similar. They tend to steal our technology, so they may have the same capability."

McFarland said, "Why don't we ask them?"

A technician connected them to the Chinese and Russian representatives. When their faces appeared on the screen, McFarland asked them about the weapon. The Chinese representative only smiled.

The face of a Russian general replaced that of the Russian delegate on the monitor. "We do indeed have a prototype laser cannon, but they are all land-based. They are very effective against armor. They can be operational in a few hours."

"That's excellent. For once, I'm glad you stole our design."

"We did not steal it, General McLaughlin, it was given to us, and we have improved the power and range."

"I won't ask by whom," McFarland said. "I wonder if they'll be able to bring one of those ships down."

The Russian smiled, then said, "We will see. I suggest we coordinate the use of these weapons so we can hit them at the same time."

General McLaughlin said, "I agree. Our operational commanders will contact you to coordinate."

Antarctica — Igigi Command Ship

A battery of holographic screens illuminated Manatu's face. He was intently watching the movement of the Idimmu's armada. Only a quarter of their fleet was unmasked. He knew what they were doing. He'd studied military tactics. Probe the enemy defenses, test for their weaknesses, force them to expend what assets they had, then commit your main force. A group of symbols flashed on the screen.

"So that's how they're getting around the communication block Tegan created," Manatu chirped.

"They're reawakening their puppets," Makita replied, standing next to him.

"I see that. This may be over before it has a chance to begin."

Makita said, "You can't possibly be thinking about interfering. Tegan and her child's impulsive action only gained them a day's reprieve from the inevitable."

"No, we will not interfere, at least not directly."

Makita made a scornful sound.

"I have done additional analysis of how Tegan and her daughter created the communications barrier. Her child has to survive, no matter what the cost. She must be studied and given the opportunity to mature."

"You've said that already. Are you beginning to have protective feelings?"

Manatu turned to her. "I want to provide a nurturing environment for the next evolution in human development. She is a fascinating creature. Watching her grow will be most enlightening."

"Has Tegan's actions brought attention to the city?" Makita asked.

"I don't know. Perhaps we should send another masked drone to watch it more closely."

"That would be prudent, but we cannot take action regardless of what we see."

Manatu didn't respond. He knew he would risk his life to save the child. A strange feeling came over him. He uncharacteristically shuddered. Now he understood completely how Ninurtu must have felt. For the first time in his life, he felt the rage building. He turned to the monitor next to him and opened the channel to the outpost.

CHAPTER TWENTY

Deep Secure Command Center — July 31 — 0800 hours

Knolls stepped out of the secure bunker and called Tegan.

"Yes?" she answered.

"The information has been passed along. I told them I had the creator of Deep Sky working on it. They're going to put Operation Global Freedom into play."

"I don't know what that is," Tegan said.

"It's our opportunity to launch Deep Sky globally if you can't come up with an Arklight solution. The Idimmu are targeting the polar regions, as expected, for most of their landings. They may hit some of the larger cities."

"Are you safe?"

"As safe as anywhere, I guess. I wish I was back with you guys."

Tegan chuckled. "I never thought I'd hear you say that."

"Yeah, me either."

"I'll try to contact Manatu. He needs to know what's happened. Cal and I will be off the air for a while, but someone will answer the phone and contact us."

"Keep your heads down," Knolls said.

Bimini Station — 0815 hours

Tegan told Cal and Sara the latest news and left them to await Edward's return. She dove to the portal with only a mask and fins. When she entered the Outpost, she walked down the ramp to the second level control room and sat down in the recliner. Tegan looked at the sphere above her. Tentacles of white and blue lights swirled within it. She adjusted her body to the newer-model recliner, which was more accommodating to her size than the one at Guana Cay. It was slightly shorter and not nearly as restrictive. The holographic display lit up in front of her as her arms locked onto the armrests. Symbols scrolled, some familiar, others foreign. Suddenly, the sphere brightened. Manatu's face appeared.

Tegan said, "Good timing. I was trying to figure out how to reach you. We need to talk."

"The Idimmu are on the move," Manatu said.

"That's what I wanted to tell you. They've also found a way around our communication blackout."

"We are aware of that as well. Why are you in the Bimini outpost?"

"We thought it would be a better location for us," Tegan said. "More secure, easier to get in and out of. If the president is awake and communicating with the Idimmu, then they probably know the general area where the outpost is located. Do you think the city is compromised?"

"No."

"Knolls returned to Washington," Tegan said. "He's aware of the situation. He said the Awakened are under guard and unable to interfere. He's provided the location of the outposts and the city to our military commanders." She paused, then added, "He also told them about you."

Manatu's eyes narrowed. "That was inevitable. He couldn't very well explain all that has happened and the information about the outposts without disclosing our involvement. He's protecting you, isn't he?'

"Yes, and he won't tell them about Arklight."

Manatu nodded. "The safety of you and your child is our primary concern. We want to send a ship to bring you here where you can be better protected."

"That isn't going to happen. Besides, you said the city was safe."

"That is true, I will send a ship to Bimini and keep it on-site so we can evacuate you within minutes if you are threatened."

"Won't that compromise our location?"

"We will find a way to prevent that. When there is a window of opportunity, we will come." He looked away from her.

Tegan heard several rapid bursts of chirps, not understanding anything he was saying. "Is everything alright?"

Manatu faced her again. "There are several smaller ships breaking away from the fleet with a trajectory to the Abacos."

"I'm sure President Collingsworth told them about the marker and about his men finding the portal."

"It seems much of their advancing fleet will land near us and in the Arctic. The ships coming to the Abacos can have but one purpose—to find and destroy the outpost and us. I'm certain that they believe we are involved and helping you."

Tegan bit her lower lip, then said, "When will their ships arrive?"

Manatu checked another monitor. "There will be eight ships over the Abacos in thirty minutes."

"I need to warn the people in the city. They're using the digital system for messages, but I can't talk to them. Is there a way to make a general announcement?"

"There is. I will make the notification. I must go," Manatu said.

After Manatu's image disappeared, Tegan sat for a moment, watching the light dance within the sphere. She stood and walked up the ramp. Garth, Maggie, and Jessica, stood by the portal, talking. She told them what Manatu had told her.

"We need to warn the people that are still on the islands," Garth said.

"You'll need to phone as many as you can and have them contact everyone they can," Tegan said. "They need to hide."

"There aren't many places to hide on the islands," Garth said.

"Then tell them to go to sea."

"They'd be sitting ducks on the open water."

"I think that's their best option," Tegan said.

"You mean a moving target is harder to hit."

"Let's get topside and start making calls," Tegan said.

"I'll stay here in the outpost with Cal's parents," Maggie said.

"I appreciate that. Let them know what's going on."

Tranquility — 0830 hours

Tegan, Garth, and Jessica surfaced behind *Tranquility*. Cal and Sara stood above them.

"I don't know where Edward is!" Sara cried. "He said he was coming straight back. He should be here by now, and he's not answering his phone."

Tegan could tell she was in a panic. "Sara, I'm sure he'll be along shortly. I need to use that phone to call Knolls. It's important."

Sara handed her the phone.

Tegan dialed Knolls and put it on speaker.

"Hello," answered Knolls.

Tegan said, "Manatu told me that eight Idimmu ships are headed for the Abacos."

"I kind of figured they'd target that area," Knolls said. "I'll warn the general now that I have confirmation. We have some new toys we want to try, but we want to hold them in reserve for a coordinated strike."

"Any chance we can get some help?" Tegan asked.

"I'm not sure. I'll check. You think the Idimmu discovered your use of Arklight when you created the communications shield?"

"Not likely," Tegan replied. "The shield didn't energize until it was positioned in the troposphere. Manatu thinks they believe the Igigi are involved."

Cal said, "I know resources are limited, but do you think the Navy has anything they can scramble from Boca Chica NAS?"

"I'll check. Thanks for the update. Let me give this info to General McLaughlin, and I'll get back with you."

"Okay, Rob," Tegan replied. After Tegan disconnected she looked at Cal and said, "I need to tell you what Manatu told me."

When she was finished, Cal said, "Manatu may be coming around to our way of thinking after all."

"He can't take an active role to intervene, but he does seem committed to protecting us and providing intelligence. That has to be rubbing some of his people the wrong way."

"I'm sure," Cal said. "Maybe you should take Manatu up on his offer to relocate you someplace safer."

"Not a chance. I'm not leaving you and our friends behind. I won't go until there's no other possible way to keep our baby safe."

"It might make things easier for me."

"No!"

"I still can't reach Edward," Sara said, sounding more concerned.

"Garth, do you want to take the *Deep Current* over and check on him?" Cal asked.

Tegan saw a boat approaching and pointed. "Hey! Is that Edward?"

Garth grabbed the binoculars and stared at the vessel. "That's him, but why is he coming from that direction? That's the long way around. I don't see anyone following him."

A few minutes later, Edward was tied alongside the *Deep Current*.

"You scared us to death," Sara said. "Why didn't you answer the phone?"

"Because I lost it over the side," Edward replied. "I had it in my hand when I was loading up, and I dropped it. I got fuel and as many supplies as I could carry. No one would take any payment. They told me to take whatever I needed."

"How were the food supplies at the store?" Cal asked.

"They were nearly cleaned out. I was able to find some canned goods. I hope you really like baked beans. I also got the extra scuba tanks and gear you wanted. The air station will be available for scuba tank refills until they lose power."

"That's good news," Cal said.

"I'm sorry I had you all worried."

"At least you're safe," Garth said. "Why did you take the long way around?"

"I'm not sure," Edward replied. "Just paranoid, I guess. I didn't want anyone following me out here. Going the other way gave me a chance to see if anyone was behind me. I can tell something has happened. What is it?"

Tegan filled him in, then said, "Why don't you all get below. I'll stay topside and keep watch for a few hours. Knolls should be calling back soon."

"I'll help them get the supplies below and then come back and stay with you," Cal said. "If we need to evacuate the boats, it's better to have everything we need below."

"Sounds good," replied Garth.

Five minutes later, Tegan was alone. The only sound was the wind blowing through the rigging and the gentle splash of the waves periodically striking the hulls. She looked out over the water and wondered when Manatu would send the ship. If they had to leave Earth, she knew that wherever they went, she'd never see the beauty of the ocean again.

Tranquility — 0855 hours

Cal surfaced and boarded *Tranquility*, then said, "Everything is stowed and secure."

"Now for the hardest part, and the part I hate the most—waiting," Tegan said.

Seconds later, eight F-18 Hornets screamed over them, headed east toward the Abacos.

"Wow, they're nearly on the deck and almost supersonic," Cal said.

"Is that unusual?" Tegan asked.

"Definitely," Cal said, grabbing the binoculars. "I think Knolls got us some help."

Tegan took the binoculars and looked to the east. Heavy black smoke billowed in the distance. Tegan froze. Streaks of fire etched the sky as dark objects dropped like meteors. "Cal, what are those?"

Cal took the binoculars from her and looked. "I don't know. There's too many of them to be the ships Manatu told you were headed for the Abacos."

"They're also too close. Could those be dropping over Freeport?"

Tegan found another pair of binoculars and looked again. The fiery streaks turned darker and became more numerous. She could just make out black podlike objects as they slowed. Suddenly, there were trails of horizontal streaks and flashes.

"The fighters are hitting them," Cal said. His voice had a hard edge to it. "It has to be Freeport. Those things aren't ships. They looked like pods to me."

"That's what I thought, too."

More streaks of fire lit up the morning sky. Larger ships were hurtling into the atmosphere.

"The angle of entry is further south," Cal said. "Those are the ships, and they're headed eastward."

"Cal, call Rob and give him an update. I need to get below and contact Manatu." Tegan grabbed her mask and dove over the side.

Deep Secure Command Center — 0900 hours

"Incoming!" came the announcement just as Knolls ran through the doorway.

General McLaughlin said, "Sound the alarm. Secure the facility."

Knolls asked, "General, did we engage over the Bahamas?"

"Yes, we were able to shoot down at least fourteen of the small pods that were ejected from some of their ships and one of their smaller spacecraft. Our aircraft came under fire by some kind of pulse weapon from the larger ships that arrived after the pods. We lost half of the squadron."

"Did they go after the outpost?" Knolls asked.

"We're not sure," General McLaughlin answered. "The area is a bit chaotic right now. We know they're landing pods on Grand Bahama. There are ships nearing the outer islands in the Abacos. Did your friend tell you about the pulse weapon?"

"No," Knolls replied.

"They pack a punch. The good news is that they're short-range weapons, so the pilots we lost learning their range were not lost in vain. Now, if you don't mind, I have other things to attend to unless you have new intel."

"No, sir." The large blast door banged shut. He was stuck here for a while. Knolls looked at the monitors. Many of the monitors that had heads of state on them earlier now displayed tactical imagery. There were so many targets. If this was only the tip of the iceberg, he thought they were in deep shit. He turned away just as General McLaughlin slammed his hand on the table.

"Guess that answers that question," McLaughlin said.

"What's happened?" Knolls asked.

McLaughlin didn't answer him. He walked to where McFarland was sitting and said, "Several ships have landed in and around the Washington metro area. One of them is at the medical center where the president is being held. It appears the Idimmu are accompanied by animals that are killing everyone they encounter."

"What?" McFarland said. "Is there a way I can see these things?"

"Yes, sir," McLaughlin replied, then shouted, "Put the medical center feed up on monitor eight."

Knolls looked at the monitor. He couldn't believe what he was seeing. A pack of Xunta ripped a small group of people to shreds. Blood, arms, and other assorted body parts flew into the air as the Xunta waded through them.

"Commander Knolls, do you know what those things are?" McFarland asked.

"No, sir. I wonder if those are the Xunta the VP said were going to be released if we didn't put them back in power? They weren't in any database I saw while in the Igigi outpost or anything ever reported to me. They look prehistoric. Their teeth resemble a saber-toothed tiger's, only bigger."

"Well, that's what's landing in those pods."

As Knolls watched the monitor, a large Idimmu ship landed in the field where the attack had just occurred. The Xunta gathered around the base of the ship. A hatch under the ship opened, and a staircase dropped to the ground. Two gray-skinned aliens walked down it and stood in the field. It looked to Knolls as if they were posing for pictures with the creatures.

"Can someone zoom in on those?" Knolls asked. The picture grew larger until he could see them clearly. "The gray aliens are Etu Inu Idimmu. I've seen their images before."

"Are they what the president calls Antediluvians?" McFarland asked.

"Yes," Knolls replied. "As I told everyone earlier, the Igigi call them Etu Inu Idimmu. We shortened it to Idimmu. It means demons in Sumerian. Note the texture of their skin. It matches the sample we have in storage."

The Idimmu had dark, almond-shaped eyes. "See the eyes?" Knolls said,

"Dark-Eyed Demons," McLaughlin muttered. "That description fits."

The camera zoomed in on one of the Xunta just as it turned. Knolls sucked in a deep breath. "Holy shit! Will you look at that thing?" Its red eyes glared at the camera as if the creature knew it was being observed. It opened its maw, displaying massive, razor-sharp teeth. The saber-tooth-sized canines still dripped blood. Then it snapped its jaws closed and continued to stare at the camera.

"Is that fur or hide?" General McLaughlin asked.

"I can't tell. If it's fur, it's densely matted. They have to be seven feet tall."

"Judging by what they did to the people standing near the building, I'd say they were designed for only one purpose." McFarland said. A small group of Capitol Police officers ran toward the alien ship. "Can we talk to those officers? You've got to warn them off."

Just then, one of the Xunta broke from the pack and ran at the officers. "I think we're too late," McLaughlin said.

Knolls couldn't believe what he saw. The four officers momentarily froze in place. They looked petrified. One of the officers managed to pull his firearm from the holster just as the Xunta tore into him. Knolls thought the officer next to him was moving in slow motion. Then he saw the muzzle flashes. At point-blank range the officer fired into the creature. No sound came from the monitor, but he saw the creature turn and roar. Several of the rounds had hit the creature in the head. Yet it wasn't fazed. A second later, the other two officers opened fire. The officers were all acting as if they were so frightened that they couldn't function normally. They reloaded as they backed away and fired again.

The creature moved quickly, attacking and killing the other three officers, then almost casually loped back to the ship as if nothing had happened.

"All those rounds at point-blank range and I don't even see a mark on that thing," Knolls said. "What caliber do they carry?"

"I'm pretty sure it's a forty-five. Send out a warning that small arms fire is ineffective," McLaughlin yelled across the room.

Another officer appeared on the screen armed with an M-4 rifle. The officer knelt and fired on the group of aliens by the ship. Two of the Xunta moved to shield the Idimmu. Knolls could see that the .223 caliber rounds hit their targets. Suddenly, the same Xunta that had attacked the other officers broke from the group and charged straight at the officer holding the rifle. The officer ejected a magazine from the weapon and reloaded, then resumed firing at the approaching threat. As the creature closed, the officer backpedaled, then froze like the other officers had done. The creature pounced on him.

When it was finished, it turned and loped back to the group again. Knolls could see that some of the rounds had penetrated its thick hide. Small streams of black liquid oozed from the beast's chest and neck, but it didn't seem to notice. "The rifle rounds penetrated the hide, but it didn't stop the thing," Knolls said.

"Pass the word on what we're facing," McLaughlin ordered. A second later, a small group of people came out of the front door of a medical building. "Is that the president, the vice president, and General Stewart?"

Two of the creatures hauled the three of them toward the alien ship. Another creature hobbled behind, dragging an injured leg.

The camera zoomed in on the trio.

"That's them," McFarland said. "They have the president. What are they going to do with them?"

A moment later, automatic weapons fire came from the entrance of the medical building. Knolls counted at least six Marines as they spread out around the doorway. The injured creature turned and started back as quickly as it could, its jaw snapping over and over again.

General Stewart fell to the ground. Knolls guessed that one of the bullets had hit him. An Idimmu motioned with its hand, and one of the Xunta ran to General Stewart, knelt, and tore his head off. Then the Xunta stood erect and snapped its jaws repeatedly, as if it had enjoyed killing the general.

The Marines at the doorway backed into the building as they continued firing at the advancing Xunta. The creature finally stopped, staggered, and then roared as it fell forward.

"I think they got one," Knolls said.

The Xunta that had killed General Stewart ran toward the Xunta lying on the ground. When it reached it, it knelt, checked it, then turned and ran back toward the ship, leaving it behind.

Two creatures dragged the president and vice president into the ship. The Idimmu and the remaining Xunta followed them up into the ship. The staircase retracted, and then the black, sleek-looking ship rose into the sky and rapidly disappeared.

"I want that creature in the lab, like yesterday!" McLaughlin bellowed. "We need to know what its physiology is and what can pierce that armored hide."

Knolls bolted for the sealed door, but the stone-faced sentry stopped him. He hurried to the nearest secure, unused landline phone. He sat at a desk and looked at the tracking display of the eastern United States and the Bahamas. There were too many targets to count. He noticed two large circles over Grand Bahama Island and another over Marsh Harbor. He knew that each circle represented multiple targets that had landed. He dialed Cal's number.

Tranquility — 0925 hours

Cal's phone rang.

"That's a new number," Cal said, looking at the caller ID. He pushed the answer button and put it on speaker. "Yes."

"Cal, it's me," Knolls said.

"We've been trying to get a hold of you."

"I've been locked in a secure facility under the White House. Listen, I don't know how much time I have, but you need to know what's happened here." He told Cal about the president, vice president, and General Stewart, confirmed there were ships over the Abacos and Grand Bahama, and described the strange beasts to him.

"I guess the Idimmu came better prepared than we expected," Cal said. "We saw dark objects falling from high in the atmosphere to the east of us. We also saw a squadron of F-18s fly over us headed that way. They looked like they were engaging them."

"They were, and we lost a few aircraft to their energy pulse weapon. We were able to shoot down one of their smaller ships and some of the pods, and we damaged a few others. The pods are easier to splash than the ships, and they're carrying the creatures. By the way, small arms won't kill them. Tell Tegan that we know what a Xunta is now, but see if she can still find anything on them. Their craft are much faster than anything we have in the air. Even if we have enough planes, it's going to take a shitload of missiles to bring them down. Their ships are tough."

"Did anything land on Man-O-War?" Cal asked.

"Pilot reports indicate the smaller pods have landed all over the area. I can't say for certain if they're on MOW. Isn't there someone left that you can call?"

"I'm not sure. Sara's parents are still on Elbow Cay."

"They need to leave," Knolls said.

"I know. Sara's tried to get them to." Cal sighed. "I guess the pods are their version of an armored personnel carrier."

"They don't need an armored personnel carrier. The Xunta hide is like armor. Like I said, small arms won't bring them down. It takes an unbelievable number of rifle rounds to stop one of them. I don't think they feel pain."

"All I have is my Glock and spears for my spear gun," Cal replied. "How about fire? Maybe we could make some makeshift flamethrowers."

"Or your wife can build something that will knock them down. You know what I mean."

"Yes, I do. What do you think the Idimmu are going to do with the president and VP?"

"Probably assess them to determine if they still have propaganda value or can send out disinformation. I heard the SecDef was eviscerated by the Xunta in his room before they snatched the others. It won't be long until the footage of one of those creatures tearing someone apart gets out on social media. It'll scare the hell out of everyone."

"At least Stewart's death was a fitting end."

"I thought it was, too. Cal, I need to go. Just stay out of sight and don't engage one of those beasts if you come across one."

"Based on what you said, staying hidden is our only option."

"You won't be able to call me, so I'll try and call you every chance I get."

"Sounds good."

Cal put the phone down and looked to the northeast, where plumes of dark smoke rose over Freeport. Tegan broke the surface behind him. "Welcome back. Did Manatu shed any light on what's happening?"

Tegan climbed into the sailboat and said, "Yes. He said there are Idimmu ships landing in the Arctic and Antarctica. There are far more of the smaller ships than he predicted."

"Did he happen to mention anything about a seven-foot creature with red eyes and saber-tooth canines that kills people?"

"No," Tegan replied. She looked concerned. "Is that a Xunta?"

"Yup. We need to tell him the Idimmu have them killing people." He told her what Knolls had said.

"I'll advise Manatu. What do we do now?"

"We wait, learn what we can, and hopefully get a miracle."

Tegan nodded. "I'll go back down and see what Manatu can tell us. He seems different since the Idimmu arrived."

"How do you mean?"

"He's sounding… more agitated, maybe even aggressive. I think he wants to get more involved in helping us."

"That could turn the tide for us," Cal said.

"Do you want me to send someone up to relieve you?"

"No thanks."

Tegan kissed him, and her belly glowed.

"Is there nothing we can do without her knowing about it?" Cal asked.

"Not anymore. She and I are bound. What I know, she knows or is learning."

Cal smiled. "That could put a crimp in our sex life. You'd better get going."

Tegan put her mask on and dove over the side.

Monan Command Ship

The Monan stretched. She was pleased with the progress of the first wave. Not even half had arrived, and already they were digging in at the South Pole. She had lost far fewer ships than anticipated. She was more certain now that the humans would not be able to stop their larger ships without using their most powerful weapons, and she still didn't think they would use those. Many of the Awakened had been liberated and were aboard their ships. She would soon put them to work and call for the second wave of ships. She conveyed her feelings of appreciation for their success to the others.

She acknowledged a message from Dractor. All was proceeding as planned. The humans encountering the Xunta were behaving as expected.

Good, she thought. Perhaps President Collingsworth could get them to lay down their weapons by telling the world the killing would stop.

London, England — 1430 hours BST

"This is Ian James reporting from outside of Buckingham Palace. Just minutes ago, creatures fell from the sky in podlike ships and began landing all around the city. Tall, frightening beasts with brown hides and red eyes are emerging from the pods. I was close to where one landed and barely made it away before it started killing everyone it encountered."

He struggled to keep his composure. "I can hardly describe what I witnessed. The killing was horrible and the sounds they made as they ripped people apart was ghastly. Anyone outside should seek shelter immediately. They appear to be hunting in packs, like hounds."

Ian took a breath. "I witnessed a group of people near Piccadilly that seemed frozen in place. They didn't even try to run as the beasts attacked them and tore them apart."

He took another breath and looked around. The camera operator panned to the crowds of people running toward them.

"I can only think that the people who've seen these creatures are doing what I did—I ran. Everyone that is listening needs to—Oh, God!"

The camera operator caught the slaughter, which was sure to be broadcast around the world. Three Xunta tore through the group that had been running toward him. It reminded Ian of dolphins herding fish into a small shoal, then darting through them to feast. Torn bodies, and parts of bodies, flew into the air as the Xunta ripped through the group repeatedly.

"Let's get the hell outta here!" Ian shouted to his cameraman. "We need to find shelter." He paused, tapped his ear, and then said, "I know we're live, but those things are killing everyone. We have to find a place to hide." Another pause, then Ian screamed, "I don't care, they can terminate my employment if they want to, but we're leaving."

"I'm ditching the camera," the cameraman said. The camera hit the ground, then several of the beasts could be seen running past.

Ian screamed, "I can't move!" His mike was still transmitting. "No!" Then the mike went dead.

Monan Command Ship

A pink glow bathed the multitier command deck. Technicians toiled at their stations, absorbed in their tasks. *The Xunta will indeed be our key to victory*, the Monan thought. Images being sent from her ships hovering over the cities filled the viewer screens. The Xunta were killing humans in droves and meeting light resistance. They were creating pandemonium, just as she'd planned.

The Monan walked to a console, placed her hand on a technician's shoulder, and conveyed her message. The technician was coordinating the activity in the Bahamas, and he reported that the Xunta had slaughtered much of the population that had been out in the open on the islands. The viewer showed empty streets. No doubt that some people were in hiding. Others had taken to the water. Boats filled with people crowded the harbors, while others gathered along the coastlines. She would deal with them in due time. She issued an order to withdraw some of the Xunta from the islands, leaving a few in each island town. For now, containment was good enough. She'd conveyed the message she wanted sent to the world and to the Igigi.

They had not encountered any Igigi or found the underground cavern the president had told Trakar about, but they would not stop until they did. Trakar hadn't been given an exact location, only the general area. An oversight, but something she would remedy now that she had the Awakened back. She watched the viewers as the Xunta prowled through Marsh Harbor, Treasure Cay, and Hope Town, looking for people. It would take time, but they would clear the islands. She felt great pride at knowing that this time they were prepared to meet their enemy.

The Monan knew the Igigi were watching. She wanted them to witness the human carnage she'd unleashed. She remembered the stories of what had happened so long ago in the desert. If she could draw the Igigi out of hiding, she would do the same to them. But first, it was time for the Awakened to tell their people to stop resisting and that if they complied, the killing would stop.

New York, New York — July 31 — 1000 hours

The ship landed on a nearly empty street. Xunta poured from beneath it and established a perimeter. President Collingsworth and Vice President Preston were ushered off the craft. They stood in front of the doors of a tall building, an orb hung in the air in front of them, and an Etu Inu Idimmu stood beside them. The building was the home of a national news station.

"I'm President Collingsworth," TC yelled. "I need a camera crew to broadcast what I have to say. It's vital to saving our planet and our people."

It took several minutes and several more requests before someone ventured to peer out of a window above them. The president looked up at the woman and shouted, "Thank you for being so brave. You have nothing to fear. I need to broadcast an announcement. Please open the door."

The woman disappeared from the window. Several minutes later, she appeared at the main entrance, unlocked the doors, and stepped back. TC could see the fear in her eyes. He recognized her as an anchor at the station.

"My name is Dora Stein, Mr. President."

"Yes. I know who you are. Thank you, Ms. Stein. I need to broadcast a message to the world. Will you help me do that?"

Stein looked past him at the Etu Inu Idimmu and then at the vice president. Several Xunta stood across the street.

TC could tell the encounter was being recorded or possibly being broadcast by the man holding a camera. Another man dressed in a suit stepped up beside her.

"I'm Jerry Zarnowski. I'm the managing producer of the early morning show, Mr. President. What message do you wish to send?"

"Are you broadcasting now?" TC asked.

"No," Zarnowski replied.

The president walked slowly forward and stopped a few feet from him.

"I need to get on the air in order to stop what's happening. Speaker McFarland and the others are acting out of fear. They attacked the Antediluvians without provocation, and now they're having to defend themselves. Mr. Zarnowski, Ms. Stein, I need to tell the world to stop fighting. The Antediluvians mean us no harm."

"What about the beasts?" Stein asked, pointing at them.

"The Xunta are only protecting the Antediluvians. I need to go live so we can stop the carnage. The Antediluvians will recall the Xunta if the military stops their attacks."

"I'm not sure we can do this without approval," Zarnowski said. "Martial law has been declared, and all of our broadcasts have to be approved by the White House."

"I'm still the president, and I'm authorizing it," TC said with an edge in his tone. "You will broadcast my message." He saw the hesitation on their faces, but knew they would do what he asked.

"Yes, Mr. President. Follow us."

A little while later, Thomas Baines Collingsworth's message was broadcast to the world.

Deep Secure Command Center — 1020 hours

"The president is on TV," General McLaughlin announced. "We need to shut him down. Now!"

Knolls nearly choked on the muffin he was eating. This was what he'd suspected would happen, but not this soon. He'd seen the BBC broadcast earlier. Apparently, there were some kinks in Global Freedom. The media was supposed to be under their control.

Someone rushed over to the TV and turned up the volume.

"We must stop this slaughter," the president said. "They will not attack if we stop our hostilities. Speaker McFarland is a treasonous and cowardly man. He has convinced the military to take over the White House and wage war on these peaceful beings."

A camera panned to an Idimmu standing a few feet away. It did look pretty harmless.

The president continued, "They launched an attack on the Antediluvians first without my authority. The Antediluvians are only defending themselves. Speaker McFarland has imposed martial law to silence the media, but these courageous people have stepped forward to save millions of lives. This is my only hope of reaching you and stopping what's happening. Do not resist, do not shoot at them, and you will not be harmed. You must convince others around you to comply."

Stacy Preston moved up next to the president. "Please, we are telling you the truth. They mean us no harm."

"Shut that broadcast down!" McLaughlin commanded.

"We're working it," someone yelled.

Other monitors with other Awakened world leaders began broadcasting the same plea.

"Well, at least their spiel is consistent," Knolls muttered.

A moment later the image of the president was replaced by a test screen pattern.

"General McLaughlin, that's going to scare the hell out of people," McFarland said.

"That's why we're going to have you on camera in less than five minutes. You need to let the world know this is propaganda and that the president and his people are still under Idimmu control. You need to impress upon the people that we have engaged the enemy, that we're destroying their ships, that the Idimmu want to create sympathizers to disrupt our efforts, and that the Xunta are their weapons. The people will want to believe the president. The people need to be reassured that we will stop them and who the real enemy is. Sir, we have to stop their propaganda machine in its tracks."

Knolls knew what the general was trying to do, but he wondered if it would be of much value. The vast majority of Americans still loved President Collingsworth. McFarland's announcement might create more sympathy for him and start a civil war, giving the Idimmu even more power. It wasn't his call to make, and he couldn't stop it even if he wanted to, so he'd just watch like the rest of them.

A few minutes later, Speaker McFarland addressed the world. He told everyone that the Supreme Court Chief Justice had sworn him in as President of the United States and that both the president and vice president were under Etu Inu Idimmu control. He explained what had transpired, including much of the information Knolls had provided and the fact this was not the first war humanity had fought against the Idimmu. He omitted the fact that the Igigi had helped save the day the last time and that they wouldn't be helping this time. Knolls thought it was a smart move to keep the speech positive.

McFarland explained that the Antediluvians were not "ancients" to be trusted as their name implied. They were Dark-Eyed Demons, so named during the last war. His speech came from the heart and it was compelling.

What surprised Knolls the most about the speech was McFarland's honesty about the threat the Xunta posed and the amount of firepower it took to kill them. Knolls hoped the people would believe the new president, because if they didn't, this war was going to be even more difficult to survive.

CHAPTER TWENTY-ONE

Cal sat with Garth at the stern of the *Tranquility*. His parents were below watching the news on television with Sara and Edward. After hearing about President McFarland's and Collingsworth's speeches, Tegan and Maggie had taken the tram to Sanctuary to tell everyone what was happening in person. Cal had stayed behind to await the latest update from Knolls.

Manatu hadn't been able to provide any information on the Xunta. They had never encountered them before. Cal knew that Knolls would want to learn whatever he could about them when he called. A second later, Cal's phone rang. He answered and put the phone on speaker. "Give us some good news, Rob."

"I do have some. The Idimmu haven't taken out our satellites yet. I believe it's because they think they'll need them to spread propaganda or disinformation, and to scare us into submission."

"As if the Xunta weren't scary enough."

"I was able to get a current aerial recon of the Abacos."

Garth moved closer to the phone.

Knolls said, "It appears they've pulled some of the Xunta off of Great Abaco and Elbow Cay. There were quite a few deaths there, mostly because so many people were out in the open when they landed. Treasure, Marsh, and Hope Town were the hardest hit population centers. We have only spotted a few Xunta in Marsh Harbour in the last few minutes. Treasure and the north part of Abaco appear clear. It seems like they've made their point and are content to patrol the streets. Did Sara reach her parents?"

"She did, finally," Garth replied. "They're planning to leave the island by boat and head this way as soon as they can. Any activity on MOW and Scotland?"

"Nothing reported, although Great Guana is crawling with Xunta. They're in search-and-destroy mode there. I'm betting Collingsworth told them the outpost is there."

Garth clenched his jaw.

"Going to sea is a good decision," Knolls said. "The Idimmu don't seem interested in hitting any of the boats that are offshore."

"Small miracle," Garth said. "Can you get the word out to everyone still on the islands?"

"We're working with the Bahamian government to do just that. They're sending some of their Coast Guard ships north to the Abacos. They're talking about using the cruise ships that are in Nassau to evacuate some of the residents. We've encouraged them to organize civilian flotillas and put as many people on the boats as possible."

"That's smart," Cal said.

"Another interesting fact is that the Xunta don't seem to like the water," Knolls said.

"How do you know that?" Cal asked.

"Surveillance camera footage caught a Xunta run to the water's edge on Seven Mile Beach next to the marina. It was chasing a potential victim. The person jumped in and swam into deep water. The Xunta waded in as far as its waist, then returned to shore."

"So they can't swim," Cal said.

"Not sure if it's that or they can't kill while in the water. Our preliminary necropsy of the Xunta we killed indicates the muscle tissue is incredibly dense. The hide is like Kevlar. Internal organs are unique, as is its brain. The creature has four hearts in the chest cavity that circulate an oxygen-enriched, black blood. The doctors here think that if you shoot through one of the hearts the other three will take up the slack and the damaged one seals itself off. The real scary part is that it appears the damaged heart will repair itself so long as blood is pumping through the body."

"How can they determine that?" Cal asked.

"The doctors saw that two of the hearts were almost completely healed. They probably would have been functional in a few more minutes if the other two hearts hadn't stopped. It was only the damage caused by hundreds of rounds that prevented that from happening."

"So we need really big guns."

"And we need to hit all the hearts at the same time."

"What about its brain?" Garth asked.

"Smaller than expected for such a large skull. The bone structure is five times as thick as ours, and the brain is about a third the size. Most of the brain appears to be used for motor function. The olfactory senses appear to be even better than a shark's. They could probably smell us from quite a distance. The communication center is in a frontal lobe and is quite unique."

"How do they communicate?"

"Good question. We think telepathically and by excreting a powerful pheromone. The doctors found glands along the jaw line. When one doctor sliced into it, he was paralyzed with fear. The pheromones apparently stimulate the human fear center. Consensus is that these things were engineered for one purpose, to hunt and kill human beings."

"What does it eat besides us?" Cal asked.

"The digestive system looks like it can process just about anything organic. I don't think these things are particular," Knolls said.

"Anything else?"

"Those are the highlights. Did Manatu provide any insight on these things?"

"No," Cal replied. "They've never seen them before. The media is reporting that the Xunta are loose in a number of cities."

"They're creating havoc from Rio to New York, from London to Beijing to Tokyo. All of the highest-populated areas. The military strategists think their activity is designed to draw our forces away from their primary landing sites."

"According to Manatu, most of their ships are landing in Antarctica and the Arctic."

"He's correct. There's some discussion about nuking everything if it looks like we can't stop them."

"Are you talking about a Masada scenario?" Cal asked.

"Yup. If we can't have the planet, then neither can they."

"How about the second group of ships Manatu told us about. Have you seen them yet?" Cal asked.

"No. We're still waiting for the rest of the first group to clear. They've only moved a little over two thousand ships within the outer marker. That's about thirty thousand miles out. Long-range optics have spotted the last of the first group further out, but they're stealthy, so we can't get an exact count, not that it matters. We don't expect to see any of the second group until they're nearing the outer marker. There's a steady stream of ships headed for the polar regions. Satellite imagery of Antarctica shows they're burrowing deep into the ice. Tell Tegan we need Deep Sky to be cold-resistant."

"Any luck jamming the microwave signal?" Cal asked.

"It's complicated. Jamming them gums up our ability as well."

"Have you started moving people toward the outposts?" Garth asked.

"Yes. They've established a logistics and selection process, but as with all things, there's some issues, so let's say it's in its infancy. As expected, all the power players want first dibs for their families."

"You'd think people would find a way to get along under the circumstances," Garth said.

"Not a chance. The pressure is only bringing out the rotten character of some people," Knolls said. "I think the military will have priority. It's a diverse group. Many governments are working to open additional shelters left over from the Cold War era. We're even looking at the unused nuclear waste sites we built out west that are only being used for records storage. It will take some time to get everything sorted out."

"What about using mines and caves?" Cal asked.

"They're looking at everything that can house people underground to save as many as possible. Other countries are doing the same. They're also sending troops, missiles, and a new laser weapon to guard Spitsbergen."

"Are you talking about the Svalbard Seed Vault?" Cal asked.

"Yes. I think you know why."

"In case we nuke ourselves and we need to start over."

"Exactly. It's going to be an Ark of a different type."

"Isn't the vault pretty close to where the Idimmu are going to be operating?" Cal asked.

"We discussed that, but the Norwegians claim they can get people, troops, and equipment onto the island without drawing attention and keep them hidden. We've left that to them. There's simply too much to deal with all at the same time."

"What about this new laser weapon?" Garth asked.

"It could be our best hope for attacking their bigger ships. It's too soon to tell how effective it will be on ground forces. The Russians and Chinese have a version of the laser, too."

"I know you're busy so I'll let you get back to it," Cal said. "Thanks for the update. Try to call again at 1300 hours if you can."

"I'll do my best. In the meantime, stay where you are, and if pursued, get in the water."

"That won't be difficult to do."

The line went dead.

Cal looked at Garth. "At least MOW has been spared."

"For now. I wish I'd stayed and fought those things."

"It wouldn't have helped. You heard what Rob said. You'd need a very big gun to do any damage. You can help more people by doing what we're doing. I think the Idimmu are using the Xunta to force us into hiding. They attack in mass, create havoc, people run and hide, and then they move the bulk of the Xunta to a new location and repeat the process."

"Why?"

"So they can do what they need to do without interference and with limited resource exposure. I think they want to settle in before they start eradicating us in earnest. That makes the most sense, especially if they have a limited number of Xunta to unleash."

"Why don't you head down and find your wife?" Garth said. "Let her know what's happening and see if you can get an update from Manatu."

"Alright." Cal stood and walked to the hatch. "Mom, Dad, I'm heading down for a while. Do you want to join me?"

"No. We like the view from here better," Jule replied.

"Suit yourself. I'll be back in a few hours. Garth, come and get me if they become a pain or something happens."

Garth chuckled. "Will do."

Cal went over the side and started down. He felt more comfortable knowing the Xunta didn't like the water.

Monan Command Ship

Everything is working in our favor, even without the full support of the Awakened, the Monan thought. Their losses were still minimal, the Protectorate foundation was being laid, and the damage they'd inflicted against the human enemy, thus far, had been worth the losses. They had met no resistance in Antarctica, not even a single air assault. The small bases that the humans had around the continent were not a factor. Xunta were already advancing on those. Soon the icy continent would be theirs.

The Arctic landing sites were proving more troublesome. They were meeting heavy aerial resistance over Russia and Alaska. They were losing pods and some smaller ships to missiles, but nothing that would impede their landings.

She issued an order for more Xunta landings in cities along the east coast of North America. As an afterthought, she ordered additional pods dropped on Andros and New Providence, then dispatched additional scout ships to reconnoiter the smaller islands in the Abacos and the surrounding area.

The intelligence the Awakened had provided had been invaluable. The president claimed the Igigi stronghold was under Great Guana Cay. The entrance was underwater. She felt frustrated by that bit of information. The Xunta were too heavy to swim, and developing equipment to allow them to breath and function underwater would take too much time. For now, they would have to dig through the island to get to them.

They still hadn't discovered how the Igigi had blocked their ability to communicate within the Earth's atmosphere. The energy necessary to create and sustain the barrier required a power they hadn't encountered before, and she wanted to know how it was done. They needed to find the source and shut it down.

The Monan moved gracefully back to the viewer, then regarded the tactical displays and the technical data. It was time. She gave the order to the second wave commander. Two-thirds of their transports would advance ahead of schedule. She could feel the yearning of her kind wanting to lay claim to the world, and she didn't want them to have to wait any longer.

Turning to face the others behind her, she made a deep-throated grunt. It was a sound rarely heard, and the others on the bridge turned in surprise. They seldom used audible noises to communicate. This was a special occasion. It was the sound of her aggression and commitment to the rest of them. It was a war cry of solidarity. The others on the bridge bowed and followed her lead. Soon the passageways, cabins, and flight decks of the other ships echoed her call to action. They were united with a common goal, and they would prevail.

Dahlgren, Virginia — 1240 hours

The Trench was a mess. Empty styrofoam coffee cups littered the tops of consoles. Food wrappers and discarded pieces of paper dotted the floor, which was normally kept pristine. Jacob Miller had called his wife and told her to go to her parents' house in the rural and sparsely populated area east of Chattanooga, Tennessee. He'd told her to stay there until he came for her. It had taken some time to persuade her to leave without him, but she finally acquiesced.

T3OA Miller hadn't left his post since yesterday morning. He was tired, his eyes were bloodshot from staring at the monitors and lack of sleep, and he desperately needed a shower.

Neela Anderson was asleep, her head cradled in her arms on top of the desk next to him.

Then the alarm sounded. It was almost an hourly event. He scanned the data at his terminal, then switched to the scope. When he saw the image, he couldn't believe it. The size of the new targets dwarfed the other motherships. "Neela, wake up!"

Neela opened her eyes and looked at Jacob's screen. "That's not good," she said.

"No shit. Confirm this for me. I'll call Spriggs and Vandenberg."

Minutes later, he had confirmation. Based on what he knew about the enemy ships, these had to be the first of the transports he'd been told about. He knew they carried well over a billion of the enemy. As Miller watched, the ships just kept coming.

"I think we're screwed," Neela said. "There are thousands of those massive things."

"Nearly twelve thousand if the intelligence is right. I'd say they're advancing their bulk transports, which means a lot more of them will be landing soon. We can hardly handle what they've already sent." Jacob shook his head in disbelief. "I think every living human on this planet is going to have to fight if we want to survive."

"I'm not really religious, but I'm going start to praying," Neela said.

Deep Secure Command Center — 1248 hours

Knolls was getting ready to leave the bunker to call Cal when the new information came in about the transports. Operation Global Freedom was in full swing. Logistics, targeting, and communications centers were operational. He had to admire what they'd accomplished in such a short time. They hadn't completely secured the cities where the Xunta were first released, but they knew how to kill them now, and they were having better success.

Many of the Xunta bodies had been airlifted to labs where they could be examined in hopes of finding a weakness. All of them were identical, so much so that the experts believed the Xunta were being manufactured. With the samples they had obtained, he wondered if Tegan could program Deep Sky to infect the creatures and kill them. He wanted to get her started on exploring that possibility, which was to be the focus of his next call. A fast-acting virus could bring them down, or at least reduce their numbers. If Tegan could begin working with the samples they'd acquired, she might just turn the tide. He knew the lab in Little Abaco was operational.

Knolls looked over at General McLaughlin. No one was around him, so he decided now was a good time to approach him. His call to Tegan would have to wait a few minutes.

"General McLaughlin, one of my medical researchers needs something to prep Deep Sky for battle against the Xunta."

General McLaughlin looked at him and said, "You're talking about the woman who created it. What was her name again?"

"Tegan Locke."

"Isn't she already working on Deep Sky?"

"She is." Knolls knew this was going to be a hard sell. "I want her to create another strain of Deep Sky that will target the Xunta. She's the only one who can make this happen. I also need to take a specimen to her."

"Then do it."

Knolls could tell that the general didn't understand the logistical problems associated with getting the job done. "Sir, I'll need support and transportation."

McLaughlin stared at him. "You want to go back to the Bahamas?"

"Yes, sir. North Bimini to be exact. Where you found me."

"With all that's going on, do you really think that's wise?"

"Probably not, but I need to be on-site. Can you get me to Alice Town? I'll arrange transportation back to the outpost. And I need an intact Xunta, one we haven't completely autopsied or maybe even one that's near death."

"You're kidding, right?"

"No, sir. Tegan is going to need a complete specimen in order to determine if Deep Sky will be effective. Alive would be better."

"Seriously?"

"Do we have one?"

"Kiss my ass, Commander. We aren't going to capture one of those things alive for you. We can't even get close to those damn things without self-contained breathing equipment."

"A dead one will be fine," Knolls said.

"I'll have a jet at Andrews ready in fifteen minutes and a Coast Guard Jayhawk waiting for you in Miami when you land." The general picked up the phone.

"What about my specimen?"

"I'll see what I can do."

"The fresher the better, but I'll take whatever you can provide."

General McLaughlin took a deep breath and said, "Commander, you've done well. I need you to stay in one piece and to check in every two hours after you land. I want updates on your progress with the bioweapon. Is that clear?"

"Yes, sir," Knolls answered. He noticed that the general was thinking about something. "Is there something else?"

"Just a second," McLaughlin replied. He brought up an electronic communique on his pad. "Here's something interesting. A Dr. Mike Peters was doing work for us at AUTEC. He had to land on South Bimini when the shit hit the fan. The TH-57 he was on developed engine trouble. The Jayhawk I send you back on can pick him up."

"Who is he?" Knolls asked. The name sounded familiar to him.

"He's an acoustical research scientist. I think he could help us if these things start operating underwater. Maybe he could assist us in building an acoustical weapon."

"I thought I recognized the name. I'm familiar with the Navy's USO work."

"I figured as much. Just see that he gets aboard your helo and heads for Cape Canaveral."

"Yes, sir," Knolls said.

"Good luck."

Tranquility — 1315 hours

Knolls's call was late. Cal was surprised to hear that he was coming back to Bimini.

"When do you think you'll arrive?" Cal asked.

"I can be there in a little over two hours. First stop will be Miami. I may have to wait for a specimen to arrive. I'll try and reach you from there when I leave. I need to fly to the airport on South Bimini in order to find a doctor that command wants flown to Canaveral. I'll need you to pick me up."

"We'll be there. Do you really think you can get a specimen?"

"I won't know until I get there. See you soon," Knolls said, and disconnected.

Cal heard someone at the stern. Tegan was just coming up the ladder.

"Did I hear you say he was bringing a specimen here?" she asked, putting her mask and fins on the bench seat.

"That's what he said. The question is, will Deep Sky be ready in time?" Cal asked.

"The lab is fully functional. We have the Idimmu specimen from the 1947 Tonopah crash. I can begin testing multiple infectious variants anytime. I still need to program a kill switch."

"Good."

"Cal, I think if Knolls can get us a Xunta, that will be the priority. If they're susceptible to infection, we should kill them first. From what we've heard, they're free to roam, so they'd be easily targeted with an aerial dispersal."

"I agree," Cal said. "Let's hope they weren't engineered to resist viruses. Perhaps your work will save humanity after all. Just not the way you planned."

"We won't know for sure until I examine one of them and test it with Deep Sky. Cal, what's that out there to the east? I only caught a glimpse of something dark."

Cal scanned the area with the binoculars. He didn't see anything. "Maybe it was an aircraft. Knolls said the military was doing surveillance over the islands, and they'd be at a high altitude."

"This was lower and closer."

"How long do you think you'll need to create a weaponized version that can attack the Xunta?" Cal asked as he continued to scan the horizon.

"I don't think it will take long once I have their DNA mapped. With the new equipment that the medical, biological research, and genome team brought with them, a week, maybe less. I hope Rob will have more information by the time he arrives. Where is he landing?"

"At the airport on South Bimini."

"Is there anything else we need to retrieve when we pick up Rob from the airport?" Tegan asked.

"It's not *we*. I'm going alone in the *Blue Angel*. It's fast and maneuverable. You're going back into the outpost."

"You're not going alone. Take Edward or Garth with you."

Cal sighed. "Alright. I could use an extra hand. I'll ask Garth."

Tegan pointed. "There. I just saw the dark shape again."

Cal focused the binoculars on that area and slowly scanned the horizon. "I still don't see anything out there," Cal said. "I think I'll go down with you. Just to be safe, I'll have my dad keep an eye out for anything flying over there."

"I'll keep watch," Jeffrey said, walking out on deck from the cabin.

"I need you to watch the area to the east and northeast." Cal handed him the binoculars. "Tegan and I need to go down for a few minutes. If the phone rings, answer it. We're expecting a call from Rob."

Jeffrey nodded and sat down. "I heard your conversation. And if I see something?"

"Send Jessica down if it's an emergency."

"Will do."

Tegan and Cal put their masks and fins on and slipped over the side.

Bimini Outpost – 1330 hours

"I'm going to go brief the MBRG team," Tegan said. "I need to get them ready to go to work as soon as we receive the specimen. They may have some ideas. There are some new people I've never worked with before."

"What about checking in with Manatu?"

"I'll do that, too," Tegan said as she walked down the ramp to catch the tram.

Cal needed some quiet time to think. He went to the control room and sat down in a recliner. *Had they missed anything?* All of the supplies were stored. They had provisions enough for several months, not counting what the Igigi could provide. There was no shortage of water, unless the ocean dried up. The desalination system ran off Arklight power, as did everything else. Now all they needed were bigger guns. He should have thought to ask Knolls to bring some. He'd ask him to bring them when he called from Miami.

Cal stared at the sphere and wondered what more he could do. A few minutes later, he heard the sound of running feet coming down the ramp. He sat up just as Jessica appeared, breathing hard.

"We got trouble," Jessica said. "You need to get topside. An Idimmu ship just overflew North Bimini and dropped a pod. Your mother won't leave without your father, and my mother won't leave without them."

"Stay here," Cal said. He ran to the lift, rode it up, and went through the portal and into the water without a mask.

When he reached the stern of the *Tranquility*, an odd noise was coming from the island. Cal climbed aboard and saw that his parents were already in diving gear. Maggie stood by the railing, also ready to go.

"Where is it?" Cal asked. Jeffrey pointed toward Bailey Town on North Bimini. An Idimmu ship hovered about a hundred feet above the island. "Shit! You guys get below, now!"

"Where else do you think we'd be going dressed like this?" Jule quipped. "We'd have gone down sooner if your father wasn't so stubborn. He said he had to wait to be relieved."

"Well, Cal said to stay here until he returned. Now he has returned. You and Maggie could have gone down with Jessica, like I told you to."

"Can you all finish the argument below?" Cal asked. "Ease yourself over the stern and try not to attract any attention."

"Let's go!" Maggie hissed. "Cal's right, we don't have time for this."

They disappeared quietly over the stern.

Cal looked at the Idimmu ship through the binoculars. It was smaller than the Igigi ship, but just as dark. The delta-winged configuration made it look fast and sleek. It would be hard to see at a distance unless it was banking. It was moving slowly back and forth between Alice Town and Bailey Town. The strange noise it made was intermittent and it was probably coming from its propulsion system.

As he continued to watch, two boats sped out of the gap between North and South Bimini. The ship continued its slow movement and didn't pursue them. The two small craft altered course and headed straight for him.

"Isn't that just great," Cal said. "Just lead them right at me."

More boats left the harbor, running at high speed. Most of them turned northwest once they were clear of the breakers. It was too late to wave off the first pair of boats. One of them approached and slowed as the other sped past.

"Don't go back to Bimini," a man at the helm yelled. "They've landed on the island. One of those monsters is killing everyone in sight." Before Cal could reply, the boat roared away.

He called Knolls's cell phone. It went straight to voicemail. He left a message warning him about Bimini and asked him to bring rifles. When he hung up, he saw several more boats exit the harbor and head south. The last one to appear was a large motor yacht. It began meandering back and forth in the channel, each time getting closer to the beach, as if no one had the helm.

The Idimmu ship shadowed the yacht, keeping its distance. Suddenly, a blinding blue pulse of light shot from the front of the Idimmu craft, and the yacht exploded. The stern of the vessel, engulfed in flames, streamed black smoke into the air.

The Idimmu ship that fired the blast of energy reminded Cal of the folklore story Alex had told them about in what seemed like a lifetime ago. It fit the Lakota Sioux and Iroquois legends of the Wakinyan Tanka and the Hino perfectly. As the ship banked gently, floating closer to him, he realized it could be seen as a giant winged "Thunderbird" that shot lightning from its eyes, affirming the Native American legends.

Other boats steered away from the burning hulk that lay dead in the water. The Idimmu ship stopped and hovered over the burning yacht. Then a dark form rose into the air as it was lifted from the bow of the boat. It was smoldering, but moving. He could tell by the size and shape that it was a Xunta, and it had survived the explosion and the fire. *Knolls wasn't kidding, they really are one tough animal to kill*, he thought. Once the Xunta was back on-board the Idimmu ship, the craft turned back toward North Bimini.

Cal relaxed a little and watched as more boats fled the island. A large sailboat cleared the breakers and went unchallenged as it hoisted its sails. *Why isn't the Idimmu ship destroying the other boats leaving the harbor?* Cal wondered. They have the ability, yet they don't attack the boats.

Two hours later, his cell rang. It was Knolls. "You in Miami?" Cal asked.

"No, I'm on a Jayhawk headed to South Bimini. I couldn't get a Xunta specimen. I got your message. I brought two M-4's and five hundred rounds of ammunition with me. Any change there?"

"An Idimmu ship is still patrolling North Bimini and it blew up a yacht. Then they rescued a Xunta from the burning boat. As best I could tell, it was still alive, but a little barbequed. They didn't attack any of the other boats. I guess they blew up the yacht in order to recover the Xunta. They used a pulse laser of some type. It didn't seem as powerful as I would have imagined, but it did the job. Any idea why they didn't blow up the other yachts fleeing the harbor?"

"They haven't attacked any vessels at sea. The military thinks it's because they have no value to their long-game. Where's the Idimmu ship now? Never mind, we see it."

"You're that close?"

"I made better time coming back than I thought I would."

"The Idimmu ship hasn't shown an interest in us yet," Cal said. "One of the people making a run for it stopped and said a Xunta was killing everyone on the island. I don't know if it was the same one I saw being rescued or not. There could be more of them roaming around the islands."

"We'll watch for them."

Cal said, "A Jayhawk is no match for one of those ships. Are you still planning to land at the airport?"

"If we can."

"Good luck. The Idimmu ship may not care about boats, but it may be a different story with anything that flies."

"We've dropped close to the deck, maybe fifteen feet above the water. We're hoping it thinks we're a boat. It's too late to get air support in here. Just so you know, the latest report I received while in Miami says Xunta are running amok on Grand Bahama, Andros, and now Nassau. Can you still come and pick me up, or do I need to commandeer a boat and make my way to you?"

"I'll pick you up at the marina at the southern tip of Port Royal. I'll be leaving in just a minute on the *Blue Angel*. Just call me when you land so I know you're there."

"Will do, Knolls out."

Cal watched the Idimmu ship cruising north, which was a good thing if Knolls was close. He scanned the southern horizon for the Coast Guard Jayhawk. He didn't see it, and hopefully the Idimmu wouldn't either. Then he heard the sound of someone exhaling and saw Edward swimming toward the *Tranquility*. "Edward, why didn't you stay put with the others?"

"I thought you may need some help."

Garth also surfaced and headed for the *Tranquility*. Cal saw that Garth had sealed his Glock in a plastic bag. That was good thinking.

When they were aboard, Cal said, "Knolls is landing at the airport. He's on a Jayhawk. We need to start that way."

"I'll get the *Blue Angel*'s engines started," Edward said.

"I thought we might need this," Garth said, handing Cal the Glock.

"You might be right. Thanks."

Cal's blood raced when he looked back and saw that the Idimmu ship was gone. He scanned south and saw an orange and red glow blossom above the southern tip of the island. A few seconds later, the sound of an explosion reached him. Then he saw the Idimmu ship again as it banked to the north. Cal dialed Rob's cell, but he didn't answer.

As the *Blue Angel*'s engines fired up, Cal couldn't take his eyes off the billows of black smoke. "I think the Idimmu just shot down Knolls's Jayhawk," Cal said. "Let's get going."

Garth and Cal jumped into the *Blue Angel* and cast off. Just as they were pulling away, Cal's cell rang. It was Knolls.

"What's your status?" Cal shouted. "It looked like they shot you down."

"They did. We'd just started hovering to land when it hit us. I was by the door and was blown clear. The fuel didn't go off right away so the crew escaped the worst of it. Three of the crew are in need of medical attention. One is dead."

"Are you able to get to shelter? It looks like the Idimmu ship is going back north."

"How long before you reach us?"

"Maybe fifteen minutes. If we can't make the marina, we'll run in as close to the beach as we can. The *Blue Angel* has a shallow draft. Just let me know where you want extraction."

"Roger. I'll leave the crew near the beach by the marina. I still need to find someone, so the timing should be perfect for your arrival. I'll call you back in a bit."

Cal said, "Edward, turn the boat around."

Edward pulled the throttles back to idle as he spun the wheel. "Why?"

"We're going to be pick up three wounded. Edward, I need you to go down and have Tegan set up triage on level one before Garth and I get back."

"No way, I'm going with you," Edward replied. "I can handle this boat in shallow water better than either of you."

Cal looked at Garth and said, "He's as obstinate as you are."

"That's my son," Garth said. "Get going, we'll have everything ready by the time you get back." Garth dove over the side just as they reached the *Tranquility*.

Cal said, "Your father is one very good human being. You remind me of him more every day."

"I hope you mean only his good qualities," Edward replied as he shoved the throttles forward.

Port Royal, South Bimini — 1605 hours

Once he'd hidden the injured crew at the edge of the beach adjacent to the marina, Knolls took off at a run. A cut across his forehead was still bleeding, but he could tell it was superficial. It probably looked bad. Head wounds always did. He saw a golf cart in front of one of the buildings. The keys were in it. He jumped in, turned the key, and then floored it. Five minutes later, he was at the airport. He saw the TH-57 helicopter sitting on the tarmac and steered toward it. It had landed adjacent to a small building at the west end of the five-thousand-foot runway. As he approached, he called out and two men stepped out of the office and walked toward him. One was a tall, young man in a Navy flight suit, and the other was a middle-aged man in khaki slacks and a polo shirt.

"Dr. Peters, I presume," Knolls said.

"Yes. You're bleeding."

"I know, and you will be too if we don't get going."

"Were you near the explosion we heard?" Peters asked.

"Yes. We need to go."

"I can't leave my bird," the young aviator said.

Knolls looked at the lieutenant. "What's your name?"

"Bushman. Lt. Kelly Bushman."

"That explosion you heard while you were hiding was my Jayhawk being shot down by an Idimmu ship. See these?" He pointed to the commander rank insignia on his uniform.

"Yes, sir."

"Leave the chopper and get in the cart. That's an order."

Bushman looked at the helo, then back to Knolls. "I signed for that. I'm responsible for it. My co-pilot is in the office."

"Listen up. I've got three wounded, two seriously, and one dead back on the beach. I've got a rescue boat that's inbound for an extraction. The Idimmu ship that shot me down is still hovering over these islands and there's a Xunta running around killing everyone. I'm not in the mood for a debate. Leave the bird, retrieve your co-pilot, and get in the golf cart."

A second later, Knolls heard the sound, and then the shadow of the Idimmu ship passed over them. He and the other two men looked up and froze in place. The ship descended toward the center of the runway, and a hatch opened under the craft. A Xunta stood in the hatchway, looking down at them. The sound of its snapping maw carried across the tarmac.

"I think I'll go get my co-pilot and leave the bird," Lieutenant Bushman said.

"A wise decision," Knolls replied. "Make it fast."

The Xunta sprang from the hatch when the craft was still thirty feet in the air. Bushman's co-pilot had just walked around the corner of the building. He didn't have a chance to run. The Xunta was on him before Bushman could even warn him.

"Let's go!" Knolls shouted. The Idimmu ship departed, heading east.

Bushman turned and ran for the golf cart as the Xunta tore into the other pilot. Knolls glanced back as he drove away. The Xunta eyed them and then crashed through the doors of the building in search of closer prey.

Five minutes later, they were back at the marina. Knolls called Cal while he ran to where he'd left the Jayhawk crew.

"Almost there," Cal answered.

"That's good because we got company right behind us."

"I saw the ship. We'll be there in one minute. Head for the beach, I'm not wasting time coming around into the marina."

Knolls ran to the water's edge and saw the partially submerged rocks along the shoreline. He could also see more submerged rocks farther out, and knew they'd have to swim to the boat. No way could Cal beach the boat without risking putting a hole in the bottom. Then he saw the *Blue Angel*. It slowed as it approached. He ran back to the others.

"Let's move!" Knolls commanded. He helped one of the injured get to his feet.

"We can't leave Commander Dawson's body behind," Lt. Jackie Nelson said.

"We don't have a choice," Knolls replied. "Now get moving."

They moved as fast as they could toward the shoreline. Knolls could see Cal on the bow. It looked like he was aiming his Glock toward them.

"Get your asses in the water!" Cal yelled.

Knolls negotiated the rocks along the shoreline and waded into the deeper water, carrying the most seriously injured crew member over his shoulder. Mike Peters followed, supporting another member of the crew. Lt. Bushman helped Lt. Nelson get into the water, his arm around her. Nelson's dark, short-hair was matted with blood. She was more seriously injured than he'd known.

He heard the scuffle of feet before he could smell the rank odor of the Xunta. He looked back to where they'd left Commander Dawson's body. The Xunta eyed them briefly, then strode over to the pilot's body. It looked at them again, as if it wanted to make sure they were watching, then picked up the body and tore it apart. It took a step toward them and roared.

Watching such an attack on a monitor and seeing it in person were two different things. Knolls thought the creature was deliberately trying to terrify them. It roared again and charged them, snapping its jaws, bloody saliva flying from its mouth.

"Hurry up!" Knolls yelled as he waded deeper into the water, his panic spiking as the Xunta got closer. He knew what was causing his visceral fear response. He pushed his panic down and yelled, "The Xunta excrete a pheromone that causes fear. Try to ignore it."

He looked over his shoulder at the Xunta as it grew closer. The right side of its body and face were badly burned. Stripes of its flesh dangled from its shoulder, exposing dark muscle tissue. Some of the Xunta's skull bone was visible. *This had to be the one Cal saw rescued from the yacht*, he thought.

Edward nudged the *Blue Angel* a few more feet forward. The wooden bow thudded against a rock, but not hard enough to do any damage. Knolls knew this was as close as Edward could get to them. The sound of Cal firing at the creature boomed across the water. He knew the bullets would just bounce off its armored hide without slowing the animal's progress.

Knolls finally reached the boarding ladder. Edward yanked the injured crewman from his shoulder and dragged him onto the boat. He followed them into the boat, his legs trembling with fear and exhaustion. The others soon reached the ladder and got on-board. Knolls ran to the bow and stood beside Cal.

Panting, Knolls said, "Do you feel the sense of fear?"

"I don't need any damn pheromones to make me feel any more fear than I already do," Cal said. "Look at that thing."

The Xunta stopped and stood waist deep in the water where the *Blue Angel* had been moments before. It roared and slapped the water.

"Good thing it doesn't care for water," Cal said. He took aim at the Xunta.

"Try hitting it in the head," Knolls said.

Cal emptied his magazine into the creature. The Xunta wobbled, then fell backward and sank beneath the surface.

"Christ, what kind of ammo are you using?" Knolls asked, not believing that the forty-five had brought the creature down.

"Nothing special," Cal answered. "Hollow points, and I aimed where you told me to."

Knolls looked around. "Where's the Idimmu ship?"

"I don't know," Cal replied. "It was headed east a few minutes before you arrived on the beach. Maybe it figured the Xunta would create havoc by killing people on this island while it patrolled."

Knolls smiled as the *Blue Angel* backed away from the beach, then said, "Wait. Now we have the specimen Tegan needs, and it's as fresh as a daisy. Edward, stop the boat."

"Are you out of your mind?" Cal asked.

"Cal, you killed a Xunta with a small caliber firearm. That's never been done before. We need to know why, and Tegan needs a Xunta to test Deep Sky against."

Cal looked toward the north again. "I saw what that ship did to the yacht when that thing was aboard. If it comes back, we're toast."

"Then let's not bring it aboard. I'll tie a line around its legs, and we can tow it back. If the ship returns, we'll cut it loose and run like hell."

"I have a better idea," Cal said. "Secure it where it is, stand off and see what the Idimmu do. If they leave it alone, then we can come back for it later. I don't want that thing in the outpost, at least not until we're sure they can't find it."

"That does sound better," Knolls said. "Edward, take us back to shore, drop us off, then back away and wait for our signal to return."

"You want to go back there?" Edward asked.

"Yes, and right now, before that ship returns."

The *Blue Angel* motored back to shore.

Knolls grabbed a line, and he and Cal jumped back into the water. They cautiously waded up to the Xunta that was just beneath the surface. Black blood oozed from its skull. The right backside of its head was missing.

"The injury from the fire must have weakened it," Knolls said. "I haven't seen one up close before, but I know from the ones they've dissected that the skull is incredibly dense. It's tough to penetrate even with an armor-piercing round."

"Guess I got lucky. Let's get this thing secured and get out of here."

They dragged the Xunta to shore and tied its legs to a large boulder on the beach. It was too heavy to drag completely out of the water, but it would be easy for the Idimmu to see when they came back.

Knolls said, "What we've seen so far is that once a Xunta is dead, they usually leave it."

"Let's hope they stick with that pattern. Any chance we can recover the rifles you brought?"

"I doubt it. The chopper is toast."

Ten minutes later, the *Blue Angel* was a mile offshore and headed for the outpost. They watched the Idimmu ship make a low pass over where they'd left the Xunta. It circled for a few minutes, then hovered. Several minutes later, the ship shot skyward.

CHAPTER TWENTY-TWO

"You did what?" Tegan cried as she tended to the most seriously injured crewman lying on the aft deck of the *Blue Angel*. She'd decided not to wait for the injured to be taken down to the outpost.

"I killed a Xunta," Cal repeated. "It took all the rounds I had, but it finally went down."

She looked up at Knolls. "How close did it get to you?"

"Closer than we wanted, but we didn't have a choice. The specimen is waiting for us to retrieve it." Knolls moved away to make a call.

She looked back at Cal. "Seriously?"

"I thought it best to leave it on the beach," Cal replied. "We waited offshore until the Idimmu ship returned. They circled the carcass and then flew off. Knolls said they aren't interested in their dead."

Tegan shook her head and wrapped a bandage around the leg of the crewman she was tending, then said to the crewman, "It missed the artery, but it's a deep wound. I'll need to stitch it when we get you below. The tibia on your other leg is fractured, and I'll have to set it. You'll be good as new in no time. I'm sorry to say that the only pain killer we have is Tylenol, and we don't have much of that. Cal, hand me the plastic wrap."

"What's the plastic wrap for?" the crewman asked.

"To keep it watertight for the trip down to the outpost." He looked puzzled. She looked at Cal. "You didn't tell them?"

"No. We had other things to deal with at the time."

"Tell us what?" Lt. Nelson asked.

Tegan stood up and didn't answer her. She checked the injured arm on the other crew member. "Shoulder is badly bruised, but not dislocated." She pushed on the crewman's ribs, and he winced. "I think they're only bruised. I'll wrap them later. They'll hurt for a while. Good news is I don't think there's any internal injuries. We can get you put back together as soon as I get you to Sanctuary."

"Where?" Lt. Nelson said.

"Cal, please explain to them where they're going while I check the lieutenant's head wound."

Cal gave them an overview of the situation.

"Sir, with all due respect, what you just told us sounds a bit out there," Lt. Nelson said. "We have to get back to Miami."

"You aren't going anywhere," Knolls said. "I briefed General McLaughlin about what's happened. He says all of you are to stay here until otherwise notified. He told us to retrieve the dead Xunta, and he was complimentary about how we killed it. It's ours to do with however we please."

"General McLaughlin," Bushman said. "You mean the commander of USNORTHCOM?"

"That's the one. I work directly for him and President McFarland."

"What's happened?" Tegan asked, knowing by Knolls's tone that some other calamity had occurred.

"There are more Idimmu ships than we can stop. Tegan, we need Deep Sky, and we need it fast."

Tegan turned away from Knolls and looked at the cut on Lt. Nelson's head. The bleeding had stopped on its own. "That may need a few stitches. You were limping. Let me see the leg." Tegan knelt and checked it. "The ankle is swollen, but not broken. I'll wrap it for now."

"Did you hear what I just said?" Knolls asked.

"Yes, Rob, I heard you."

She looked at Peters and Bushman. "Are you two injured?"

"I'm fine," Bushman replied.

"Me, too," Peters said.

"Okay then, let's get everyone below. Cal, when I'm done patching them up I want to go with you to Port Royal." Tegan looked up at Knolls. "Rob, I need to bandage your scratch, and just so you know, MBRG has been testing a new Deep Sky variant on the Idimmu specimen they brought with them from New Mexico. It will take a while to determine its effectiveness. I think I have the kill switch program figured out, but I'll need some serious radio transmitters to send out the signal. After I patch up the wounded, I want you to take them to Sanctuary. Take Jessica with you. She can show Dr. Peters and the others around."

Tegan stood after wrapping Lt. Nelson's ankle. "Lt. Bushman, you'll be going with us back to get the Xunta. I don't want the specimen getting contaminated by marine life. If this thing is as heavy as Knolls says, it may take several of us to get it aboard."

"I don't think anything would eat that thing," Cal said.

"I need to preserve what I can of the tissue and organs, if it has any."

"It does," Knolls said. "I brought copies of the reports of the necropsies on my pad."

"Where's your pad?" Tegan asked.

"It's on what's left of the Jayhawk."

"We can check the wreckage and see if your pad survived," Cal said.

"Or I can get them forwarded to my phone."

"Which is where?" Cal asked.

He reached to his beltline. "Shit. It must have fallen in the water."

"Call your friend in Washington and have them downloaded to one of our phones," Tegan said.

"Anything else?" Knolls asked.

"Yes," Tegan said. "Send one of the MBRG technicians over. I want another set of trained medical eyes on this thing."

"Who are you people?" Lt. Nelson asked.

Knolls smiled. "We'll tell you all later."

Lt. Bushman said, "Commander Knolls, you may work directly for the president, but it looks like out here you answer to her."

"It would seem that way," Knolls replied.

$$\infty$$

Getting everyone down to the outpost wasn't as difficult as Tegan had imagined. They had plenty of dive gear topside for everyone to use. The group was, as expected, in awe of their new surroundings. She knew they would be even more impressed when they saw Sanctuary and Little Abaco.

An hour later, Knolls returned with Dr. Misa Takahatshi. She'd been Tegan's replacement after Tegan was thought to have been killed. Like Tegan, she'd been recruited under false pretenses.

After inspecting the instruments and supplies Misa had packed in watertight cases, Tegan said, "We better get started. It'll be dark soon. Cal's already topside with Edward, Garth, and Lt. Bushman."

When they reached the lift, Misa and Knolls put the cases on the platform.

"I heard a rumor you once threatened to skin Commander Knolls alive," Misa said. "Is that true?"

"It is. I almost killed him."

Knolls nodded. "I had it coming. Can we just move on?"

Tegan smiled at Misa, then said, "He really did have it coming, but I'm glad I didn't kill him."

After they surfaced, Cal took the cases, helped them all aboard, and they set off for Port Royal.

Port Royal, South Bimini — 1830 hours

Edward guided the boat to where it had been earlier. Cal, Tegan, Misa, Knolls, and Bushman jumped into the water and waded ashore. Garth had insisted on coming along. He stayed on the boat with Edward. They kept the engines running.

The Xunta was still lying on the beach. It looked untouched.

"It's a bit odiferous," Tegan said as she approached the body. "I wish we'd brought gas masks."

"I think they smell that way all the time," Knolls said. "From the reports I've seen, they don't carry any infectious pathogens. They're actually quite sterile."

"The Idimmu must not have a sense of smell," Cal said.

"Or the Idimmu have grown used to it," Tegan said. "It's like living with a smelly dog. After a while, you don't notice it anymore. I'm not worried about catching anything from the animal. The decontamination light at the portal will take care of anything we might be exposed to, but I'm afraid that odor will linger with us like skunk spray for a while."

"Can't we just get this done?" Cal asked.

Tegan and Misa pulled on their surgical gloves and went to work taking samples. Cutting through the hide was nearly impossible. They found it easier to enter the body cavity through its side, where the hide had been burned away. Tegan removed the four hearts from the chest cavity, while Misa removed whatever the other organs were from the lower torso. They found no reproductive organs. The soles of the Xunta's feet were as tough as car tires, and its muscle tissue felt like steel.

Tegan lifted the remains of the small brain from the massive skull, then said, "It looks like Cal's rounds did a number on it. Not very impressive, is it?"

"Nope," Knolls answered. "The doctor that dissected the first one of these things found the olfactory portion of the brain to be abnormally large."

"I see that," Tegan said.

Knolls said, "Maybe the Xunta communicate with the Idimmu this way. The communication shield you put in place wouldn't stop them from communicating in close proximity, would it?"

"Probably not. I'd say that long-range communications are sent by another means. Look at these glands along its neck." Tegan used a scalpel to slice open one of them. Instantly, she froze in terror. A few seconds later, she could move again. She looked at the others. They'd also been paralyzed by the concentrated vapor.

Tegan felt the warmth and touched her belly. "We need to extract these glands without releasing any more of the chemical."

"I think we'd all appreciate that," Cal said.

"That's going to be tricky," Misa said.

"You're the trained surgeon, not me."

Misa smiled at her. "Human surgeon, not Xunta. I'll see what I can do. You might want to stand upwind of me."

"I should have warned you about the glands," Knolls said.

"That would have been nice," Tegan replied.

They moved away. Misa held her breath and quickly cut one of the glands out of the Xunta's neck without rupturing it, then secured it in an airtight container. "Done," Misa said.

"That thing is almost unrecognizable now," Cal said, looking at the Xunta carcass.

"It still stinks, though," Knolls said.

Tegan and Misa double-checked the vacuum-sealed bags and containers where the pieces extracted from every part of the creature were stowed. All of them were secure.

"Misa, I want you to open the gland samples in a positive vacuum chamber," Tegan said. "We can't afford any of those pheromones becoming airborne and getting into the city."

"I believe the air is constantly being purified, but I'll follow biohazard protocols," Misa replied.

Cal and Knolls checked the wreckage of the Jayhawk. They recovered one M-4 along with the ammunition, but they couldn't find Knolls's pad. They walked back to the water's edge.

Knolls said, "Tegan, do you want the carcass?"

"I don't think we'll need it. I have plenty of tissue samples and organs."

Cal said, "I want to do one last thing." He walked over to where the scattered remains of Commander Dawson lay in the sand. He picked something up, then covered the remains as best he could, stood, and saluted.

"What'd you find?" Tegan asked when he returned.

"Dog tags," Cal replied. "They need to find their way back to his family and he'll need a proper burial."

"When things settle down, I'll see to it," Knolls said. "I should have thought of retrieving his tags."

"Easy to forget under the circumstances," Cal said.

The sun was low in the sky when they boarded the *Blue Angel* and started back to the outpost.

Monan Command Ship

The Monan strolled across the mess deck to her private dining room. She felt the success of their mission within her grasp. The Protectorate would be completed within days, well ahead of schedule. Dractor had done well. There still hadn't been any significant resistance, and the Xunta were performing well. Thousands upon thousands of humans had been slaughtered and many aircraft had been destroyed. Many of the major cities were still inundated with the Xunta. Their losses had escalated, but not enough to be a major concern. She'd decided to recall all of the ships in the Bahamas except one. It would stay above the Abacos for the time being and monitor the Xunta that remained on the islands. They had not discovered the underground Igigi facility yet, and the Igigi had not shown themselves. She wondered if they had already left the planet after realizing they couldn't win this war. The second wave was prepared to land and was awaiting her order. She knew nothing could stop them.

She decided that the majority of the Awakened were of no further value to her. They had gleaned as much intelligence as they could from them. The president and vice president might still be useful. She issued a command to terminate communications with the others. She ordered her first full meal in several days and contemplated her next move.

Deep Secure Command Center— 1930 hours

President McFarland couldn't believe the reports. Operation Global Freedom was a spectacular success. Logistics, communication, and intelligence coordination between all the countries involved were going better than expected. They were learning more about the Etu Inu Idimmus' tactics and the Xunta by the hour. Unfortunately, they weren't stopping them from landing. Military aircraft were being shot down at an alarming rate. The loss of satellites was increasing, and the International Space Station had been destroyed less than an hour ago. The advanced laser cannons were effective against the Idimmu ships, but there were far too many ships and not enough lasers to stop the onslaught. The loss of human life was staggering compared to the number of Idimmu and Xunta they'd killed.

In some of cities the ground forces were routing the Xunta. They knew how to kill them, but the Xunta weren't fighting to hold terrain. They just roamed the streets and killed targets of opportunity. It seemed that the Xuntas' true mission was to create panic and chaos in order to draw the military forces away from the polar regions where most of the Idimmu were still landing. McFarland knew that their strategy was working.

"Mr. President," McLaughlin said, "we have several groups ready for transport to the outposts."

"How many people?"

"Forty thousand of our citizens have been vetted, mostly military family members. The next group will be larger. Transports are prepping now to move the first group to staging areas along the Florida coast."

"What about the other countries?"

"Many countries are still processing their people. For now, each country will use the outposts nearest them. If we have time and the ability to do it, the city in the Bahamas will house people from all the nations."

"How will they get into the outposts?"

"According to Commander Knolls, the Igigi will provide access when they arrive. Power, food, and water are already in place. We also received word that the Svalbard seed vault is full and sealed."

"That's good news." McFarland said. He stood and looked through the operation's window at the men and women working, then up at the tactical monitors. "General McLaughlin."

"Yes, sir."

"Tell me we can defeat these things."

"Mr. President, we will beat them. I'm counting on Commander Knolls and his Dark Moon team to come through for us. We have the resolve, sir. Now all we need is a better weapon."

"We've lost so many satellites."

"We anticipated this. Global Freedom provides a means to communicate and execute the war. Our progress in processing the number of people for relocation, finding and stocking underground shelters in such a short amount of time, has been remarkable."

"It's amazing how much we can accomplish when we come together as a species. Let's get our people hidden—ASAP."

Bimini Outpost — July 31 — 1950 hours

Tegan and the others had unloaded the samples, and everything was secure in the outpost.

"Take the samples to the lab and have the biotech start mapping the Xunta DNA, then compare it against the necropsy reports that Commander Knolls will give you when he gets them," Tegan instructed Misa. "I'll be over in a little while."

"Certainly, Dr. Locke."

Tegan looked at Knolls. "Rob, I have everything I need to put Deep Sky into operation. You can let your command know that I will do my best, but we need those reports."

"I know," Knolls replied. "I'll head up and check in. I'm sure they're ready to start transporting people to the outposts."

"I need to contact Manatu to tell him we have Xunta samples," Tegan said. "He may want to inspect them himself and look at the photos we took of the carcass."

"The Igigi could expedite running our tests, if they're willing to help," Knolls said.

"If only they would," Tegan replied.

"Why don't you and Cal go topside," Knolls said. "It may be the last sunset you see for a while."

"Cal, why don't you go up with Rob? I'll be up shortly."

"I just realized we didn't leave anyone topside," Cal said. "I'll see you in a bit."

The two men left her alone.

Tegan walked to a recliner and connected. The sphere came to life. Manatu stood looking at her.

"Yes?" Manatu said.

"We have something you'll want to see," Tegan said.

"A Xunta?"

"Good guess. We took tissue samples. The carcass is still on the island."

"How did you obtain it?"

"It attacked the people on Bimini. When Cal went to rescue Knolls and the crew of a crashed Coast Guard helicopter, it attacked him, and he was able to kill it."

"I see," Manatu replied.

"The thing is a savage animal. From what we can tell, it's designed for only one purpose—to kill anyone that's not Idimmu. I don't consider it intelligent, and I hope you will agree once you examine the samples we took."

"And if I agree with you?"

"I hope you will assist me in modifying Deep Sky so that I can kill them. I know you won't help us fight the Idimmu, but I don't think you would be violating doctrine if you helped me kill the Xunta."

"If the creature is deemed an animal, I will see what I can do."

His response wasn't what she expected. She felt a sense of hope. "The Idimmu are using a ship-based energy pulse weapon that has already killed many people. I saw nothing in the UEE about them having any weapons with that power."

"We registered their use of the weapon."

Tegan waited for him to say something else, but he remained silent. "Manatu, can I neutralize their energy weapons or build a shield to protect people, aircraft, ships, and structures?"

"I believe you and your child can do almost anything."

"I'll take that as a yes. Can you provide me with the analysis you've done on the weapon so that I might get started?"

"Yes. It is stored where you can access it."

Tegan's stomach glowed brightly for a moment. Even her child understood that Manatu was going to help them. "My daughter understands your deeper meaning."

"That is good. We will come to you and examine the specimen samples. We will use the docking hangar at the Bimini Station. I must complete my work here before we leave. I have to make sure the other outposts are functioning properly, so I can't tell you when we will arrive."

"We look forward to seeing you and Makita."

"Tegan, we will be bringing others with us. They want to speak with you and learn about how you and your child accessed the Arklight field."

"I'm not sure I will be of much help, but I look forward to meeting them."

"Until then," Manatu said, and the sphere became opaque again.

This should be an interesting meeting, Tegan thought. She got off of the recliner and walked up the ramp to the portal. Jessica stood there. "Jessica, are you waiting for me?"

"Yes," Jessica replied. "I overheard your conversation with Manatu. I know I shouldn't ask, but do you know what you'll name your baby? Every time I've heard you talk about her, it's either 'my child' or 'my daughter.' Don't you think you and Cal should give her a name? I mean, she's aware of what's going on. I just think she should have a name."

Tegan's belly glowed. "You may be right. We haven't given it much thought." Her belly glowed again. "I guess it's time we gave her a name."

"Good. I was thinking about it, and I think *Kyla* would be pretty."

"That *is* a pretty name. I'll see if Cal likes it." Tegan felt a slight nudge in her belly as it glowed again. "It appears she likes it, too."

"Can I go up with you?" Jessica asked.

"Of course."

Tranquility — 2015 hours

Tegan and Jessica sat next to Cal at the stern of the Tranquility. The sun cast a warm glow as it touched the horizon.

Tegan took Cal's hand, then said. "It's beautiful."

"Yes, it is," Cal replied.

Knolls walked to the railing on the *Deep Current*, where he'd just finished a phone conversation. He had a big smile on his face.

"You look happy," Tegan said.

"I am. I have great news. Alex and Nate are alive."

"What?" Tegan and Cal shouted in unison, and Jessica clapped her hands.

"How can that be?" Tegan asked. "Makita said they never surfaced."

"Where have they been, and why haven't they called us?" Cal asked.

"One question at a time," Knolls replied, still smiling. "They were found on the beach at the north end of Great Guana around noon yesterday."

"So why didn't they call us?"

"That's the bad news. They were both badly injured by the blast. When they were found, Alex and Nate were unconscious. They were rushed by boat to the medical center on Treasure Cay, and then they were airlifted to Miami."

"Why Miami?" Cal asked.

"Because of the severity of their injuries. Alex was shot and had lost a lot of blood. Nate had a head injury and didn't wake up until this morning. Alex is still out."

"How did you find out?" Tegan asked.

"When Nate learned about the invasion, he tried calling your cell."

"Which went down with the *Whispering Winds*," Cal muttered.

"Nate told his doctor he had vital information about the Idimmu, and he was eventually connected to someone that routed his information to the Pentagon. In his message he mentioned my name, and someone there knew I was at the DSCC. The information was sent there, and when General McLaughlin heard that Nate claimed he was aboard the *Whispering Winds*, he made the connection."

"Did he say how they got off of the boat?"

"He did. When the SWAM rocket hit starboard hull of the *Whispering Winds*, it fractured the port side hull just behind their cabin by the engine. They were able to swim through an opening after the compartment flooded but not before the special ops team opened fire. Alex was hit in the abdomen. As luck would have it, a scuba tank with a regulator had lodged in the wreckage just above them. They managed retrieve it and swim away, staying underwater until they ran out of air."

"That's why Makita didn't see them," Tegan said.

"I have the number for the hospital," Knolls said.

"Fantastic," Cal said.

"What else did you learn, Rob?" Tegan asked.

"The Idimmu have been destroying our communications satellites. It's a wonder I got through to the general. He says they'll have a hundred thousand people vetted and ready to go to Sanctuary in a few days. They're staging the first forty thousand along the east coast of Florida and will shuttle them over to us by boat."

"A boat parade will give up our location," Cal said.

"He said he has a plan."

Tegan asked, "How will we know when they're coming if we lose cell service?"

"We'll have to rely on the good ole' radio. What did Manatu say?"

"They'll be headed our way in a few hours. He and some other Igigi are coming to inspect the samples we took from the Xunta. They also want to examine me. The good news is that if the Xunta are deemed nonintelligent, they may help us stop them. In the meantime, my daughter and I will try and develop a shield against their ships' energy weapon."

Jessica said, "See how odd that sounds. She needs a name."

"Okay. Cal, Jessica thinks we should name our daughter, Kyla. What do you think?"

As Tegan's belly glowed, Cal said, "I like it."

"Me, too," Tegan said. Somehow, the name felt right for the baby. "Kyla Strong Locke is a good name."

"Jessica, how did you come up with that name?" Cal asked.

"I looked at baby names online after I heard Tegan was pregnant. I thought the baby should have a name that would mean something to us all. It's an old Hebrew name. It means victorious."

"It's fitting," Cal said.

"Rob, what do you think?" Tegan asked.

"It sounds like the name of a future leader," Knolls said.

Tegan put her hand over her stomach and felt the warmth. "She agrees."

"Great!" Jessica shouted.

"We have a lot of work to do, but we will prevail," Cal said.

Tegan took Cal's hand and pulled him close, then said softly, "I know. I know."

"For now, we hide and hit them where and when we can," Knolls said.

"I need to call Nate and check on Alex and then see if we can get them here as soon as possible," Cal said.

Antarctica – Igigi Base

Manatu was engrossed in verifying that all of the outposts were operational. He knew that questions would continue to arise about the power source. So far, the people seemed to believe the explanation that it was being generated by the conversion of thermal heat.

The rustle of Makita's robe made him turn. "Is there a problem?" he chirped.

"Analysis of where the Etu Inu Idimmu structures are being built indicates we are in no danger of discovery. May I assist you?"

Manatu nodded and chirped his appreciation, then said, "Tegan and her child are safe for now. They have killed one of the creatures and are analyzing it. We will depart within the hour to examine the samples they collected."

"I am aware."

"From what I've seen and from what Tegan has said, the Xunta appear designed for the sole purpose of killing humans. Tegan does not believe them to be intelligent. They have no reproductive organs, and as best as I can tell, they are bioengineered. She has requested our assistance in stopping them."

Makita raised an eyebrow. "Then we must help her."

Manatu stopped working and looked at her.

Makita added, "I agree with Tegan's assessment of the creatures. The others consulted also agree. If the examination of the samples does not contradict our beliefs, we will assist them."

Manatu continued to stare at her, then said, "This was discussed without me?"

"Yes. I knew what you intended to do, so I reviewed and forwarded the information you had stored on the Xunta. Takatu has examined how the Xunta attack. They are predatory, animalistic, and have predominately only one drive. They appear to only take instruction and perform as directed. They don't appear to have a sense of self. I can find no violation of doctrine if we intervene to stop them."

Manatu didn't know how to respond. He was stunned.

"When we are done here, I will prepare our ship," Makita said.

Manatu found his voice and said, "We do not have time to notify the Council of our findings and wait for their authorization if we wish to stop the human slaughter. If we act, we will be acting alone and without their approval."

"We will do what is right."

Manatu almost smiled. "Yes, we will." He resumed working, with Makita standing next to him. They were walking an uncertain path, but he desperately wanted to follow it to the end. They would do more than watch this time. He felt a sense of pride and purpose for his clan, as he knew Ninurtu had surely felt so long ago. He only hoped their destiny would be different.

CHAPTER TWENTY-THREE

Bimini Outpost — August 01 — 0100 hours

Tegan stood in the control room facing a semicircle of five Igigi. All of them were dressed in forest-green robes. Manatu introduced the new Igigi, then Makita bowed and walked to one of the recliners. Takatu had been introduced as the human biotechnical engineer. Tegan wasn't sure what that meant, but she figured he was the Igigi that would be showing the most interest in Kyla. The other two Igigi, Baktu and Powta, were more interested in examining the Xunta specimens. From what Manatu had just explained, if they concurred with her findings, they would help destroy the Xunta.

"That's wonderful news!" Tegan said.

"It's incredible news," Cal said as he and Knolls walked up to the group.

"We will not use Arklight against them," Manatu said. "We will help Tegan design Deep Sky to be more effective against the Xunta and help with the aerial dispersal of the infectious agent. We may also be able to offer advice on building a handheld conventional weapon that your military can use against the Xunta. However, these weapons will not be designed for use against the Etu Inu Idimmu."

"I understand," Knolls said. "Our preliminary analysis of the Idimmu attacks indicates the Xunta are their primary weapon. If we can neutralize them, then we'll be on a more equal footing. Any help you can give us for stopping them will be greatly appreciated."

"May we see the Xunta samples?" Powta asked, speaking slowly. She was shorter than the other Igigi and appeared younger than the others.

"Take us to them," Baktu said. His delivery sounded mechanical.

"Certainly," Tegan said. "Rob can you escort them to the lab on Little Abaco?"

"No problem," Knolls replied. "Who's going?"

Manatu said, "Takatu will stay here. The rest of us will accompany you. Makita, will you join us?"

"Yes, I am nearly done here. I am sending the latest update to the other outposts."

A minute later, Makita joined the group and they walked down the ramp to take the tram.

Takatu said bluntly, "I wish to examine you and your child."

"I know," Tegan said. "Where would you like us?"

"The recliner will be fine," Takatu replied, then pulled a small instrument from a satchel hanging from his shoulder. The instrument was the size of a cell phone and had a small, strobing, white light on it.

Tegan sat down, and Cal stood next to her.

"What's that?" Cal asked, pointing at the instrument.

"It is a scanner." When Takatu went to raise Tegan's shirt, she grabbed his wrist. Takatu pulled his hand back.

"I want to know exactly what you're planning to do before you begin. Understand?"

"I understand. This device will map the progress of the child's development since the time Manatu last scanned you. It will not cause pain. It will not harm your child."

"Our child's name is Kyla," Cal said.

"You may proceed," Tegan said.

Takatu spent a few minutes scanning Tegan, then walked to a workstation without saying a word.

"He doesn't have the best bedside manner, does he?" Cal asked.

"No, he doesn't."

A few minutes later, Takatu came back, wearing the same bland expression. "Kyla is healthy and is growing at twice the normal rate."

Tegan said, "Do you mean that she will be born in just a few months?"

"Yes."

Tegan knew that Kyla was developing faster than normal, but she never imagined she would be born that soon. "When exactly?" she asked.

"I cannot say. It will depend on her, but I think it will be in November."

"Wow. How is that possible?" Cal asked.

Takatu said, "I do not know. Her essence is something we have never encountered before."

Tegan said, "Can you tell how she's able to interact with the Arklight field?"

"I believe so. Her brain is different. Both hemispheres of her brain are joined by a new feature that encapsulates the corpus callosum and is nestled behind the frontal lobe of the cerebral cortex. In addition, she has a genetic trait that has never been cataloged, as do you, but hers is slightly different."

"What's the corpus callosum?" Cal asked.

"It joins the two cerebral hemispheres and allows information to pass between them," Tegan answered. "Manatu told me that I was more Igigi than any other human since Trudor, Ninurtu's first twin daughter. How is our DNA different?"

"You carry a strand of DNA base pairings that is unique. Your daughter carries them as well, but they are enhanced by additional base pairings of an element I do not recognize. I have detected an extension of her nucleotides, which could account for the new section of her brain, which you do not possess. At first review, I would say that these additional pairings are somehow directly linked to the Arklight field."

Takatu turned to Cal. "Calvin Locke, may I scan you?"

"Why?"

Tegan said, "Basic genetics. If he maps your DNA, then compares it to mine, he can work out the sequencing. Although DNA is a funny thing when it comes to base pairings."

"This is true," Takatu said. "Especially when there is a new component."

"Go ahead," Cal said, and he laid down on a recliner. "I'm starting to feel like a freak."

"Welcome to our world," Tegan replied.

Takatu scanned him and then went back to the workstation. After several minutes, he returned. He looked puzzled.

"Well?" Cal asked.

"Calvin Locke, you are unique, but in a different way than Tegan. My results are inconclusive. I must run further analysis on the chromosomal variants. If you will excuse me."

"Wait a second," Tegan said. "What do you mean by unique?"

"Is this a bad or a good unique?" Cal asked.

"It is not bad, but it still does not explain Kyla's genetic sequence. Cal, you carry a trait that is also from an ancient Igigi and human pairing, but it is consistent with what we would find lying dormant after so many generations. I need to study this further and consult with the others. Please excuse me."

"Wait," Tegan said. "May I see the results?"

"Yes. They are already in the system. You may access them." Takatu walked down the ramp.

"I guess you're not the only one that's special," Cal said with a smile.

"I guess not." Tegan leaned back in the recliner and accessed the UEE.

Little Abaco City — 0200 hours

"There is no question, the Xunta are genetically engineered," Baktu said.

"I agree," Powta said.

"As do I," Makita added.

"Then we are in agreement that they are not intelligent beings and are, therefore, not protected by doctrine," Manatu said.

They all nodded as Takatu walked into the room.

"I heard," Takatu chirped. "I will review your results while you give me your thoughts on the genetic analysis of Tegan, Cal, and their child, Kyla. I wished to be present for your review."

"Very well. Is there something new to report?" Manatu asked.

"As suspected, Kyla is growing at an accelerated rate. Of greatest interest is her brain." Takatu explained his findings.

"The new portion of her brain has grown substantially since our last scan just a few days ago," Manatu said.

"Yes, and I believe it is still developing," Takatu said. "That is what I believe she is using to access the Arklight field. Even without the new component of her brain, she is incredible."

"Yes. I could tell that from Tegan's first scan," Manatu said. "Cal's genetic review is most interesting, but I do not see how Kyla could have inherited this new element from either parent. It seems as if it was spontaneously created."

"That is my belief, as well. Cal's DNA could have been a catalyst for the new pairings, but it does not explain everything. She is linked to the Arklight field by something I do not understand. Tegan is as well, but to a lesser degree. Together they are a power of unknown ability."

Powta said, "They are indeed. They must be protected. I believe Kyla is a new intelligent life form that could change the face of the universe. If she reproduces and her kind survives, they will be the first species to control Arklight from within themselves."

Baktu faced them. "To protect them, we should remove them from this world."

"I agree," Takatu said.

"I believe it would be best if we waited until Kyla is born," Manatu said. "We must first destroy the Xunta. If the Council disagrees with our decision to intervene, perhaps having Tegan and Kyla with us will convince them our actions were necessary for their protection."

"I believe that is wise," Makita said.

"Do you all agree?" Manatu asked. They were all chirped in agreement. "Good. We need to expedite the creation of the weapon Tegan seeks."

"What happens once Kyla is born?" Powta asked, "What if Tegan does not wish to leave this world?"

"Then we will take the child," Baktu replied quickly. "She must be studied."

Manatu shook his head. "That is not an option. It will be necessary to keep the family together."

Manatu caught Takatu's questioning glance. "You wish to say something, Takatu?"

"I agree with Baktu. We must protect her. I suspect Kyla is somehow modifying her DNA as she grows stronger through the use of Arklight."

"Or is it possible that Arklight is modifying her?" Manatu said. "Perhaps that is the source of the new element."

Powta said, "Takatu, once Kyla is born, will she need Tegan to continue to have the ability to control Arklight?"

"I cannot say. They have a very strong bond. Kyla is learning, feeling, and understanding all that Tegan experiences. She will know what Tegan knows at birth. I'm not sure what will happen if we separate them."

Manatu looked at Makita. "Let us find a way to keep them all together."

Makita bowed her head slightly, then said, "I understand. I will begin work to create a weapon the humans can carry that will stop the Xunta. Powta and Baktu will assist Tegan with Deep Sky."

"How will you keep the humans from using your weapon against the Idimmu?" Takatu asked.

"The weapon will discharge an electromagnetic field that severs the neurological impulses only within the Xunta's brain."

"Could that be used on a global scale?" Manatu asked.

"Not without using Arklight," Makita replied. "The weapon will be constructed from those materials that only a human can access. If an Idimmu should recover one, they will assume it was designed by a human. Once I provide the specifications, humans will be responsible for constructing the weapons."

"What is the Idimmu status?" Manatu asked.

"The Idimmu are continuing to land, and they bring more Xunta with them," Makita said. "Reconnaissance shows many of the Xunta are roaming the ice around the outside of their city in Antarctica. We need to learn where these creatures are being produced. Perhaps that will assist in their destruction."

"I agree. Let us begin," Manatu said.

EPILOGUE

Tranquility — August 01 — 0630 hours

Tegan looked at the water. A gust of wind caught her hair, moving it across her shoulders. She'd had little sleep last night after she'd learned what she could from the UEE. Takatu's revelation had disturbed her, and the review of the scans and genetic signatures confirmed what he'd said.

Kyla was more than a special girl, Tegan thought. There was an element in Kyla's genetic sequence that was new to both human and Igigi physiology. Tegan couldn't understand how her daughter could have evolved or how the element could have been introduced. She knew there were dynamics at work that were being guided by an intelligence far outside of anything she could fathom. She couldn't even begin to know how to research or grasp what she felt. It wasn't quantifiable.

She felt Kyla nudge her. Kyla wanted her to rest. Tegan pushed her windblown hair away from her face, then walked forward to the bow of the *Tranquility* and sat down. The sun was rising, and the sapphire blue water would soon be as inviting as ever. If only it would stay that way.

Tegan felt the connection with Kyla as she relaxed. An image flashed in her mind—the red sky of the alien world she'd seen before. Kyla was there. She was fully grown, standing on the rocky shore, gazing at her. A smile bloomed on her beautiful face.

A sudden influx of knowledge surged into her mind. Tegan knew that Kyla had passed the information to her, but she wasn't the source. Kyla had only been the conduit. The new information carried a message. Tegan didn't know it's origin, but the message was clear.

Tegan touched her belly as tears of joy ran down her cheeks. Now she fully realized the enormity of the gift she'd been given.

"I understand," she whispered.

ACKNOWLEDGEMENTS

First, thank you for reading the second novel in the ARKLIGHT series. I hope you enjoyed it.

To my wife, Terry, thank you again for everything you've done. Your support means so much. The honest analysis, suggestions, developmental ideas, and your patience in the countless rereads and the work you've done on this novel can't be measured. I could not have done this without you.

I am indebted to my beta readers, Jeff Weber, Abby High, Ellen Picardi, and Darlene and Richard Kingas. Your enthusiastic comments have been a source of encouragement and motivation.

My sincere appreciation to professional illustrator Laurie Allen Klein for her original artwork. Your renditions of ancient petroglyphs for the cover and chapter headings were inspired. I was fortunate to have your keen artistic eye on the design.

To my editor, Mr. Paul Thayer of Thayer Literary Services. Once again, your editing skills, suggestions, and mini-lessons have been invaluable.

Finally, I want to thank Kimberly Martin and her team, Jason Orr, and Stephanie Anderson at Jera Publishing for all of their work preparing the second novel in the ARKLIGHT series.

A NOTE ABOUT THE AUTHOR

G. B. Holley is the author of the ARKLIGHT Ancient Alien Adventure series. He is a native Floridian and a retired law enforcement commander who spent more than three decades serving with a Florida Sheriff's Office. He's a former leadership and high liability trainer and was an adjunct instructor at St. Petersburg College for many years. He earned his MPA and BA degrees from the University of South Florida, Tampa, Florida. He's a pilot and loves reading science fiction and adventure novels. He enjoys flying when he's not writing.

Connect with Gary:

www.gbholley.com
facebook.com/gbholley1
twitter.com/gbholley1

AUTHOR'S NOTE

I hope you enjoyed the second book in the ARKLIGHT series. Please leave a review on Amazon and let me know what you thought of the story.

**Read on for an excerpt from the third book:
ARKLIGHT Regulus, coming soon!**

Do you want to be notified when the next book is released? Subscribe to my email list at www.gbholley.com.

ARKLIGHT
Regulus

Tegan Locke jumped as if she'd been shot. Her belly glowed brightly. She put her hand over the light and rubbed softly until the glow tapered away. *It was just a dream,* she thought. She rolled out of the bed, stretched, took in a deep breath, then exhaled slowly. She missed the days when her morning routine consisted of meditation and watching the sunrise.

Tegan felt the boat rock, then saw Cal looking down the companionway at her.

"I was just coming to get you up," Cal said.

"I'm up. I felt something."

"Like what?"

"I don't know. It was an odd sensation, and then there was a flash, like a warning. Kyla felt it, too."

"Everything's quiet," Cal said. "I do have some news though."

"Good news?"

"Sort of." Cal walked into the cabin and sat at the dinette.

Tegan sat down across from him.

Cal said, "Manatu told me about my family ancestral tree and how it relates to Kyla."

Tegan leaned toward him, her curiosity peeked. "And?"

"Cal! Tegan!" Jessica shouted.

From the urgency in Jessica's voice, Tegan knew there was something seriously wrong. Perhaps that was what she'd felt. "Coming," Tegan shouted back as she bolted past Cal.

As soon as Tegan got on deck, she saw the dark outline of the Idimmu ship approaching from the east.

"Well, their timing sucks," Cal said as he walked up behind her. "You guys get below."

Tegan didn't bother to reply. She felt a strong need to protect her child and dove off the stern without mask or fins. She heard a splash behind her as Jessica hit the water. A minute later, she was inside the outpost. Tegan's belly glowed brightly. "I know. We're safe here."

It wasn't unusual for the Idimmu to make passes over the islands, but it had been nearly a week since the last one, and they almost always came out of the northeast. Cal picked up the binoculars. The hair on his neck stood on end. He'd learned to trust his instincts long ago. There were two strike ships, one trailing the other, and they were at low altitude. Lower than usual. *A new tactic*, he wondered. The ships were heading right for him.

The first ship banked away just as it reached the western shoreline of the island. The second ship suddenly turned south and headed for South Bimini. Cal watched as numerous Xunta leapt from the ship hovering over North Bimini. It wasn't the first time he'd seen them drop Xunta, but the last time they'd only dropped one of the beasts on the island. He shook his head remembering what it took to kill that one. This time, they were landing in force. It didn't make any sense. Bimini wasn't of any strategic importance to them. Something had changed.

A laser blast from the strike ship over North Bimini caught him by surprise. He saw debris fly into the air, most of which was ablaze. Another explosion came from South Bimini. Cal could see the second ship was hovering over the airport and it was repeatedly firing at the ground. Cal figured they were cratering the runway. *But why?* Sometimes supplies and people were dropped there. He wondered if the Idimmu had taken notice of all the people landing around Bimini and had decided to investigate.

Several more laser strikes followed over North Bimini. More buildings exploded. The laser strikes continued for several minutes, then stopped abruptly.

Cal scanned the beach and saw a man and a woman, each carrying a child, running toward the water's edge. *Why were they still on the island and not below?* He felt a sense of relief as they swam to a small boat that was just offshore. He noticed a Xunta watching them.

The Idimmu ship over North Bimini swooped in low over the beach, hovered for a moment, then landed. A ramp lowered and two Idimmu walked onto the beach and a Xunta ran over to them. The Xunta was fast, faster than any other one he'd seen. Then he realized the Xunta was also smaller and lighter colored than the one he'd killed. A second later, the Xunta dashed across the beach, splashed into the water at a run, and swam toward the small boat.

"That's not good," Cal said aloud.